# Blackwattle Road

# Blackwattle Road

## Ann Charlton

HODDER

A Mark Macleod Book

Published in Australia and New Zealand in 2003
by Hodder Headline Australia Pty Limited
(A Member of the Hodder Headline Group)
Level 22, 201 Kent Street, Sydney NSW 2000
Website: www.hha.com.au

**National Library of Australia
Cataloguing-in-Publication data**

Charlton, Ann.
  Blackwattle Road.

  ISBN 0 7336 1734 4 (pbk.).

  1. Problem families – Fiction.  2. Deception – Fiction.  I. Title.

  A823.4


Designed by Mary Egan
Typeset by Egan-Reid Ltd, Auckland, New Zealand
Print in Australia by Griffin Press, Adelaide.

*For all my family, close and extended.*

**Acknowledgments**

I would like to thank Selwa Anthony for finding the right publishers for this book, Mark Macleod and the people at Hodder Headline for being those publishers, and Carol George for her help and support

# *Family Trees:*
# *Who's Who in Blackwattle Road*

The question mark denotes that the male parentage is uncertain.

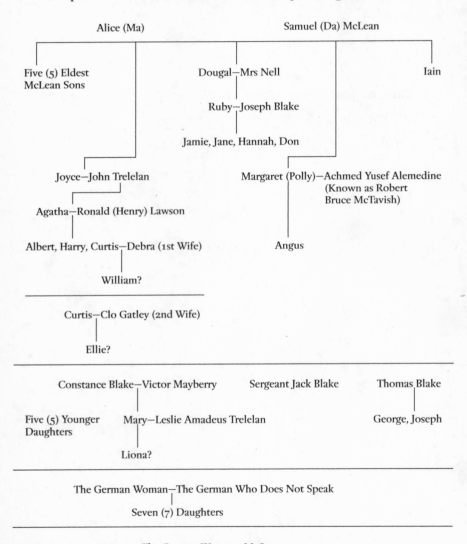

Alice (Ma) — Samuel (Da) McLean

Five (5) Eldest McLean Sons

Dougal—Mrs Nell

Iain

Ruby—Joseph Blake

Jamie, Jane, Hannah, Don

Joyce—John Trelelan

Margaret (Polly)—Achmed Yusef Alemedine
(Known as Robert Bruce McTavish)

Agatha—Ronald (Henry) Lawson

Albert, Harry, Curtis—Debra (1st Wife)

Angus

William?

Curtis—Clo Gatley (2nd Wife)

Ellie?

Constance Blake—Victor Mayberry

Sergeant Jack Blake

Thomas Blake

Five (5) Younger Daughters

Mary—Leslie Amadeus Trelelan

George, Joseph

Liona?

The German Woman—The German Who Does Not Speak

Seven (7) Daughters

The German Woman—Mr Lawson

Ronald (Henry)?

***Landscape***: *a prospect of scenery, more or less extensive, such as is comprehended within the scope or range of vision from a single point of view.*

At times I trace back over the past, though rarely with spite. Old age has taken away any malice. It has healed my grief. Yet I must admit that sadness sometimes touches me as I look through the leaves of a eucalypt bonsai (one of a kind) and out over William Lawson Park. Beyond the park are the housing estates. Beyond the estates are the rich men's homes. Their backdrop is the range of mountains that curve around us to the north, west and south like a comforting arm. In my younger days I thought of it as a barrier protecting Angus, Curtis and me from the vagaries of the outside world. I know better now.

I also know that crazy old one-legged man still wanders those mountains. He searches for Curtis, who would be stretched along the branch of a eucalypt, head to trunk, almost a part of the tree. I do not know if he hears Angus calling his name. Perhaps one day he'll reach out and the two will be together, as I always believed they were meant to be. Some of us have never been able to let go.

In this story, the first in a line of those unable to relinquish a belief is Angus's father, who sought a new life in Australia during the winter of 1907. It was then that the *Eastern Star* berthed at Newcastle after months at sea. The engines had barely cooled when the local derelicts began prowling the dock, hoping to find something that could be scavenged and sold. There was nothing unusual in odds and ends falling off the back of a ship, as they now fall off the back of a truck. Yet all that fell from this ship was rust and garbage, and a slight, dark-haired youth who had been called 'boy' for so long that he'd almost forgotten his name.

Of course he did not actually fall off the ship, but he was an exaggerator, a fantasist. Being precise was never important to him. He told his life in a way that would appeal to his listeners. These were always and only his son Angus and me, Liona, the girl next door. No one else displayed an interest in hearing about those early years. Yet if Achmed Yusef Alemedine had left the ship at any other time, Curtis and I would have experienced very different landscapes. There would be no Angus. There would be no story to tell.

# Part One

# Preparation and Groundwork

# Chapter One

He stopped at the gateway to the docks and looked back at the *Eastern Star*. He saw nothing else. The grey sky and water, the vagrants, the wharf and all the paraphernalia that rested there, none of it registered. All he saw was the ship. And while he looked, he tried to erase every deck and cabin from his mind. No matter what happened to him now, he would never return. This he vowed, swearing an oath on the bundle of papers he called his journal which lay against his heart, tucked down inside his shirt to keep it from the rain. The facts and thoughts recorded there had become his dogma. They were the only truth he had known since his god deserted him twelve years earlier to the day: Saturday, August 10. He regarded his arrival at a safe harbour on this same date as a powerful sign. It had to mean that his life was on the verge of a great change.

He was supposed to have stayed below decks whenever the *Eastern Star* arrived at a port, but the master had gone ashore to arrange for fresh food and water. That created a chance to fulfil the promise of the omen by escaping. Helped along by a push from his one friend, a little English bosun, he'd taken that chance; glancing behind him with every second step, expecting a hand to slam down on his shoulder at any moment. But the call of 'Boy, get back here' had not eventuated.

Everyone on the ship called him Boy, although to him, being a boy meant carefree and loving things he'd only ever seen; never felt or enacted since he was four, when he first experienced the bird that would haunt him for all the years of his life.

Tying an old hemp blanket around his shoulders — he'd stolen it in an effort to keep dry on a wet and windy day — he walked into a cobbled street lined with a hodgepodge of buildings. Despite the fact that he hadn't given it more than a cursory glance, he recognised one of them as an inn by its discharge of light and sound. He did not know what the other buildings were and he did not care. His eyes were fixed on the muddy road before him. It headed west, away from the ocean, and he strode out along that road as if he owned it. He could feel goose pimples popping up all over his body. Not from the cold. He'd grown used to the cold. And a stabbing thought that his tingling skin could be the beginning of an allergic reaction was instantly dismissed. He'd been dreaming of this walk for most of his life and here he was, taking it at last. Head up, chest out, swaggering a little. He knew how to tread the path to freedom, and he thought he had made it. He thought he was free to choose the direction his life would take from this moment on. And so he might have been, had the two thugs decided to thump the tall thin man ten minutes earlier, or later.

Achmed Yusef Alemedine was not a brave man. His next action could be chalked up to that sudden impulse which some people think of as valour, and others call stupidity. Many years later he told his son and the girl next door that in the poor light, with their long brown coats flapping in the wind, the thugs reminded him of carrion birds.

'Picture me as a child,' he said, 'in a hole scooped from sand, covered by my father's body. Behind me are the burning tents. Surrounding me are the dead and dying of my parents' faith. Birds circle overhead. They are huge and brown and exactly alike, except for the one with a third eye staring out from its chest. It lands on my father's back and rips at his burnous. I scream and my father lifts his head. "Run," he whispers. "Run while I keep the bird here." I run, and the bird does not follow because my father has kept it there.'

He told this shortened version of his father's death many times. It was always a precursor to what he termed his Australian story. He rarely mentioned the years in between. Yet the sight of those men in their birdlike coats brought back the memory of both the death and the between years, evoking enough anger to blind him to their size. The smallest was a good head and shoulders taller than him. The other, the one whose red beard glowed like an alarm even in rain gloom, had the build of a wrestler. But Achmed gave no thought to size or warning beards, or to the thugs' motives for attacking the tall thin man. The fear of a few minutes ago had turned to the kind of rage that kicks in with a charge of adrenaline. It was a rare feeling for him, and he liked it. He liked the way it sent his blood pulsating throughout his body. Pumped up into a frenzy, he wrenched a paling off a nearby fence and ran to avenge a long-dead father.

His first good whack caught the largest assailant squarely on the temple. As that man fell, Achmed screamed his triumph and hoisted the paling for a swing at the other. The scream was his undoing. Turning in time to avoid the blow, the thug snatched the length of wood and swung it in an upwards arc, which might have finalised Achmed's choices forever, if his reflexes hadn't been honed by years of abuse. He automatically protected his face. His left forearm was broken, but so was the nerve of his attacker when a shouted 'Coppers!' warned of approaching police. The thug bolted, dragging his mate behind him through the mud.

The tall thin man climbed unsteadily to his feet and shook his head in the way a shaggy dog shakes water from its coat. His cheeks flapped with the effort, and if this action was meant to revive him, it almost worked. Sending a stream of curses after the disappearing thugs, he staggered over to Achmed.

'Good of yer to join in, though I coulda handled them meself once I got me second wind,' he said, blowing bubbles through the blood oozing from his nose as he spoke.

Achmed tried to roll away from the spray of blood and a gust of beer-tainted breath. The effort sent pain spearing up his arm and into his head.

'Busted yer arm, ay?' the tall man asked, adding a *tsk tsk* to his sympathetic frown when Achmed cried out. 'You shouldn't have let that bastard grab the chunk of wood off yer. Bad mistake, that.'

Bending, he grabbed Achmed by the collar and tried to haul him erect. The effort was too much for a drunk who had just been on the wrong end of a beating. He toppled forward, finally succumbing to the alcohol and the blows by subsiding into semi-consciousness. He and Achmed were lying head to head on the roadside when the cause of the 'Coppers' warning strolled into the light of the tavern doorway.

Sergeant Jack Blake had watched the fight from its beginning. His normal procedure was to allow a street brawl to find its own conclusion. He would then let the beaten go, believing them to have been punished enough, and wrestle the victors off to jail. Yet he knew all about the tall thin man: the Scotsman, Dougal McLean. He'd hauled him off to the cells a half-dozen times already. And perhaps he was awed by the depth of foolishness in such a little bloke making someone else's fight his own.

'What's going on 'ere?' he demanded. 'And who might you be, ay?'

Achmed looked up at a short wide man whose stubby nose and ears barely disturbed the outline of an almost perfectly rounded head — which was closely shaven and completely bald. His thin lips were only noticeable when he spoke. He had the shoulders and back of an ox, and a pot belly bulging below a barrel chest matched the jut of his backside. Yet to Achmed, of more interest than any of this was the gleam of kindness in pale blue eyes.

Still, this man represented authority. He was an officer of the law. If given the wrong answer, he might recognise a deserter. Deserters were thrown in jail. Or sent back to their ship.

'Well, come on, I'm waiting,' the sergeant said.

Achmed's instincts told him to run. Then he remembered the counsel of his friendly bosun. 'If anyone asks, say y'name fast then tell 'em you're twenty-one and an immigrant from bleedin England.'

He repeated the bosun's instruction haltingly, for while he had learned the value of obscuring the truth, he knew the danger of telling outright lies. The only reaction was a blank look. He reiterated the statement, this time adding an apologetic shrug and his most engaging smile.

Sergeant Blake's expression conveyed the fact that he hadn't understood a word and the smile was wasted on him.

'I could march you orf to the station,' he said. 'But that won't help yer English and I'll get nothing I can believe out of that Scotsman.'

After a few moments of beating a two-finger tattoo on his chin while studying Achmed's face, he pointed the fingers like a pistol and added, 'I'll let you orf this time, but mark me words, I'll be keeping me eye on the two of ya.'

Giving them both a long hard stare, he strolled off to continue his routine patrol.

Dougal McLean looked at smooth cheeks, honey-tinted skin and a resigned expression. Eyes the colour of ale reminded him of a better place to be than a dimly lit street in drizzling rain. Rolling to his feet, he staggered off in the opposite direction.

'If yer wanna come with me, I'll fix that arm,' he offered, making the invitation plain with a beckoning thrust of his hand.

Achmed glanced up at the sky, then along the street, searching for an omen. Not being prone to decisiveness, he needed something to help make up his mind. The only sign he could see was a few men crouched in nearby doorways. He had no way of telling whether or not they were homeless. Perhaps they were waiting for the rain to ease before moving on to the welcome of their families, although not one light waited at any window. The only waiting he could see was in the posture of these people. They stirred, as uneasy as he, when a shouted curse cut short the howl of a dog. A horse neighed. A baby cried. The darkened windows of houses rattled a protest at a sudden gust of wind. The tavern door burst open and three men stumbled out, singing loudly. The Scotsman was almost out of sight.

Achmed pulled the blanket into a cowl, protecting his eyes and dreams from the look of that place. Running after the long lean man, he fixed his stare on the roadway again. Only after having climbed a staircase and entered a second doorway did he note his surroundings: a board floor, a bed with iron posts and a sagging mattress, a scarred wardrobe, a small table, a fancy stool and a stout wooden chair. Faint with pain and the beginning of a new fear, he held onto the back of the chair and waited for whatever this moment might bring.

Muttering something that sounded as if it were meant to be soothing, Dougal McLean nudged him towards the bed. When Achmed hesitated, glancing back at the door, he growled something not so soothing. Looking more glassy-eyed with every passing moment, he tore a couple of strips off the bed sheet, then peeled off Achmed's shirt. Enveloped in a fog of alcoholic breath, Achmed gritted his teeth as, with the careful concentration peculiar to a drunk trying to be sober, the Scotsman bound the broken arm between two legs snapped from the fancy stool. They both passed out as Dougal tried to tuck him under a heavy woollen rug.

Twelve hours later, a short plump woman uncurled from the foot of the bed and regarded him with an unblinking stare. He had entered the conscious world disoriented after a dreamless sleep. When she stretched, yawned, then shifted to a more comfortable position, she reminded him of a cat. His heartbeat slowed to normal when he looked beyond her. The tall thin man lay sprawled along the tipped-back wooden chair. His lanky legs were draped over the table like a rucked cloth.

Spread out like that, he looked to be a loosely connected series of lines and angles. There wasn't a scrap of extra flesh or fat. His nose and chin jutted out from an oblong face set on a long neck. A thatch of sandy-coloured hair all of one length reached to just below his collar, and his pale eyebrows drew a straight line above short thick lashes. Sunspots and freckles made his fair skin appear much darker.

His facial muscles twitched every few moments, implying that his sleep was far from peaceful. Those like the plump woman who knew Dougal McLean's body knew it lacked the quality of stillness. Even when he was drunk to the point of senselessness, his toes wriggled. At first the woman had believed this to be a defence — a warning for people to keep away when he lacked the awareness to distinguish friend from enemy. She later recognised it as a plea for attention. He was a middle son in a large family. In his younger years his busy mother would stop whatever she was doing when she saw those twitches. She'd soothe him with hugs or stroking hands. This the plump woman did now. Reaching out, she lay a reassuring hand on his knee. His eyes opened. They were an amazing shade of blue, almost violet. The tenderness in his smile showed that he and the woman were on intimate terms.

Achmed sighed relief. They were married, or lovers at least. That meant he would not be expected to compensate either one for his overnight stay. At least, not in a manner he refused to specify when he later told the story.

'Hey, Dougal, y'little mate's awake,' the woman said when she heard the sigh.

Her voice had the throaty purr of a feline, and although the thought of being within reach of any animal would normally cause Achmed's pulse to thump, this sound caused another awakening. Realising that he had kicked his covering aside during the night, he blushed and cupped his hands over his groin. Her mouth widened in a knowing grin.

'Not so little,' Dougal acknowledged, 'and by the way he waded into them blokes last night, he coulda been ten feet tall. But all that's down the road and round the corner. What's yer name and game, mate, and where did yer come from before I saw yer near the docks?'

The English Achmed had learned to understand was the kind spoken by the little bosun. The Scotsman's burr-edged accent sounded vastly different. Achmed could only interpret half the words, and they didn't make much sense to him. Holding out his hands palms upward, he twisted his face into apology and shrugged.

'Don't y'know what we're saying, lovey?' the woman asked.

He smiled and nodded. She had the same cut and folded vocabulary as the English bosun. Yet he directed his answer at the tall thin man.

'Sir whose name is Dougal, the gift of a good night's sleep is a gift beyond my ability to repay,' he said, speaking two thirds Arabic and one third London cockney.

Dougal McLean looked at the woman and shook his head.

'Glad y'can understand me, lovey, 'cause we don't know a bleedin word y'saying,' she answered for him.

Achmed jumped to his feet, unashamed of his nakedness when the woman's smile showed she wasn't offended by it. Clumsily at first, and hampered by a broken arm that ached with every movement, he bowed, touched her lips, then grinned expectantly. The woman understood that she had to ask the questions. She repeated Dougal's query.

Achmed's first mime was that of a small boy being rescued by a camel caravan. He tried to sketch the beatings and the chains, and the fact that he had worked for an apothecary, an embalmer, then an importer–exporter of exotic artefacts (often stolen) before that latest master sold him to the ship's captain. He understood by Dougal's frown and the woman's bewildered expression that his mime had failed dismally. So he concentrated on his life aboard the *Eastern Star*.

The woman appeared puzzled, then disturbed. Troubled by her growing agitation, he stroked her arm and tried to explain that it was all behind him now. She grabbed him in a hug and squeezed so hard that he had difficulty breathing. He relaxed against the softness of her curves. In this way he comforted her by allowing himself to be soothed. And he was soothed. He would have stayed tucked away in those enfolding arms until the woman grew tired of it, if Dougal hadn't tossed the old hemp blanket at him.

'Okay, laddie. Don't push yer luck,' the Scotsman stated gruffly.

Not wanting to get this man offside, Achmed extricated himself and tied the blanket around his waist.

The woman turned, hands on hips. 'Don't be such an arse, Dougal. Y'must be able to see that the boy's been through enough already without you starting in on 'im.'

Dougal's expression showed that he hadn't seen much of anything that made sense. The mime had been inventive and energetic enough, but too far beyond his experience. All he could make out, he said, was the fact that the little bloke had jumped ship after working as a cook's helper for three ocean crossings. A name and birthplace had been repeated a half-dozen times, but both titles were gibberish to him.

Signalling for the woman to interpret, he said, 'I know all I need to know anyhow, so sit yerself down and stay still for a change. Yer like a sparrer dreaming of cats with all that twittering about. Yer can stick with me for a while, though I can't make head nor tail of who you are. But I have to call yer something.' Grinning widely, he added, 'And I suppose Sparrer is as good a name as any.'

So Achmed Yusef Alemedine, whose antics reminded Dougal McLean of a nervous bird, was retitled Sparrow. His actual name and origins became lost in time and misplaced embarrassment. During the next few years he added a Scottish accent to his broken English, which was also burdened with the flowery embellishments he liked to add to his tales. For the rest of his life very few people understood much of what he said. As in everything I have written, the story is not exactly as it was told, but as it was interpreted, or envisioned, by me.

Sometime during that same morning a banging on the downstairs wall brought everyone to their feet. The plump woman dragged a Gladstone bag out of the wardrobe, and while she packed his few possessions, Dougal pulled on his clothes. He stood fully dressed by the door in one minute flat. Sparrow admired their efficiency, not realising that the ease of it came from experience.

'I won't be going with ya this time, Dougal. Best y'find a place of y'own. And y'better take the lad or they'll belt him instead,' the woman said.

Dougal straightened his back and clenched his fists as though he'd decided to make a stand. The volume of the downstairs thumping soon drove that thought out of his head. Being often foolish but rarely foolhardy, he snatched up his bag and ran.

'Come on, lad, I'll look after yer,' he called back from the stairwell.

'Is it the vulture men again?' Sparrow asked fearfully.

Understanding meaning by tone, the woman nodded. 'Them or others like 'em. Workmates wanting their money. If y'ever get any, lad, don't lend it to him. Dougal likes to gamble.'

Smiling at this simplification of her lover's addiction, she shoved Sparrow's journal down his shirt, wrapped him in the old hemp blanket and pushed him into the hallway. The Scotsman had fled through the back door as his workmates crashed through the front.

# Chapter Two

For the next few months Dougal kept his promise. He included Sparrow in the hastily packed baggage during moves between grimy hotels. By the end of October they were in a charity home for the poor and needy; and while the Scotsman supposedly spent most of his time searching for work, Sparrow stayed in bed. Fear of the strangeness of this new country and its inhabitants was his reason, or his excuse, for doing nothing. Yet on that last day of October, his greatest fear was the notion that Dougal would desert him, forcing him to make a decision without the flicker of an omen in sight. For the twentieth time that day, he sat up and looked around the room; hoping he had missed, until now, the one small glow about to become a blinding light.

To his left was the door. He had trouble sleeping unless he was close to a means of escape. To his right a double row of narrow beds stretched back to the far wall. These basic wooden frames covered with slats and thin, straw-filled mattresses were made up with blue and cream striped sheets. A neatly folded blanket at the foot of each one matched the greyish shade of the walls and floor. The whole was dimly lit by a half-dozen grimy windows. The air surrounding him, polluted enough to be almost visible, held the essence of unwashed bodies, urine and a disinfecting lye soap.

Pinching his nose against these smells, he pulled the old hemp blanket up around his chest and plucked the material into creases, soothing himself by sliding the between-skin of his fingers along the folds. The threadbare covering was his comforter now, like a rubber teat to a small child.

As Sparrow continued to stare around the room, a man in the next bunk drew in a wheezing breath and glared at him, as though Sparrow, and not countless cigarettes smoked over fifty years, could be blamed for tar-strangled lungs. Opposite him, a youth watched the door for salvation, which usually appeared in the form of an innkeeper or farmer seeking cheap labour. A few sailors waiting for ships swapped stories of wild storms and exotic ports, and two brothers in addiction sat side by side, passing a bottle back and forth and finger-counting each other's swallows. Beyond them, a scarecrow of a man had begun the chant that stifled the voices in his head and kept at bay the horrors that haunted his nights. The rest of the beds were filled with transient old men who lay motionless, staring up at the ceiling.

Sparrow kept his eyes averted from the two boys who slept under their beds. He understood their need, and at least they still cared enough to hide from nightmares that weren't always confined in sleep. The old men's patient wait for an end to it all horrified him, as did their willingness to go when death finally decided to take them. He knew of others whose lives had been far harder than theirs, yet those others continued to fight.

Pulling the blanket over his head, he hunched down, blending into the mattress. Night was just an hour away. Dougal should have been back by now. Perhaps the lateness of his return meant success in finding a job, although his growing reputation had turned out to be a problem. Dougal missed days of work without a reasonable excuse, and he was often the centre of outbreaks of violence when his workmates bashed him for no reason. At least none they would give to an employer. What man would admit to being conned out of his hard-earned wages by a shabby Scotsman, especially one whose only claim to fame was persistent bad luck?

The scarecrow's incantation interrupted these thoughts of Dougal.

The words were foreign to Sparrow, yet he echoed the chant to discourage the unseen spectres from shifting their attention to him. Without loved ones or places he wished to be, Sparrow had no names he could list to ward off the things he feared most, so he borrowed the list he heard now. It made no sense to him, but the scarecrow obviously believed it to have power, and Sparrow was too wise to the habits of ill-fortune to leave anything to chance. Besides, the words had become familiar enough to be soothing and this night he needed comfort. This night he placed the words in a song the English bosun had sung on the nights he pined for home.

When that one became boring by repetition, a boy crawled out of his safe place and sang a song learned on his mother's knee. After just one hearing, Sparrow repeated the lyrics as if he'd known them forever. He had discovered that if one harmonised words with music they were much easier to repeat. He'd already known that melody combined with emotion made words inconsequential.

It was the boy's song that lured Jack Blake into the charity home. He approached Sparrow's bunk, weeping in the same quiet way his grandmother had wept as she bade him goodbye thirty years ago. The tune had taken him back to the incredible softness of callused hands, of bony arms around him. He remembered a feeble voice singing of blue skies and lush fields in a place of greyness and hunger.

'So it's you again, is it?' he asked when the lament had ended. 'Where did you learn that song?'

The boy dived for cover when Sparrow pointed in his direction.

'Well maybe now you can sing me one of yer own.'

A shrug conveyed the fact that Sparrow knew no others. At least, none with words the sergeant would understand.

'Then we'll have to teach you some more. And what are you doing in a place like this anyhow? Why aren't you out there working like a respectable man?'

Sparrow displayed the reason: an arm not long out of splints and wrapping, a pale thing lying thin and weak against the blanket like something just crawled in from the garden.

'I hear yer still with the Scotsman?'

Having become more practised at body language in this English-speaking country, Sparrow used that to explain. Dougal McLean was like the old blanket: thin and thready and with no particular warmth, but one of the few familiar things in a sometimes hostile land.

Jack Blake stared at him for so long that, although the sergeant's eyes were open, Sparrow began to think he'd dozed off. His face was expressionless, his body relaxed. His pot belly and jutting backside drooped a little, matching the sag of his jaw. He had even adjusted his stance to spread his weight evenly.

Sparrow had seen this sort of thing on the ship, on crew standing watch after being awake for long periods because of the threat of an attack from pirates. Lack of sleep combined with stress would send them into a trance-like state. If startled into sudden awareness, they'd fly into a rage and Boy — who had been sent to remind them of their duty — would be soundly beaten. So now he remained still, afraid that any move would cause a similar reaction.

He was to learn that the apparent shutdown was merely a component of Jack Blake's thought process. But that knowledge came later. Now he almost wept with relief when the sergeant blinked, nodded, and spoke.

'I see loyalty there in yer eyes and I think you a fool for it,' he said slowly. 'But I suppose it's rare enough to be rewarded. Tell you what, any time you gets into trouble, come over and see me at the lockup. Bring yer bludging mate if you have to.'

Understanding the gist of this, Sparrow tried to voice his thanks. Sergeant Blake cut him off by walking away. At the door, he stopped and added, 'Meanwhile you gotta build up that arm. Clean this filthy hole yer living in for a start. When yer ready, I'll see about getting you some work.'

These kind words created a new resolve in Sparrow. After two months of doing nothing but wish and dream, he finally climbed out of bed. For the next few weeks he killed bedbugs and cockroaches, and dragged urine-soaked mattresses into the sun. He peeled vegetables in the charity kitchen. When his arm had regained its strength, the sergeant found him a job washing dishes and occasionally cooking at a local inn. The owners paid him with a small wage and the use of a room on the back veranda. Meals weren't part of the bargain, so he and Dougal usually dined on leftovers rescued from the hotel's bins.

And while Sparrow worked for their keep, the Scotsman stayed in bed all day, preparing for the nightly assaults. As the sun went down, he rose and headed for a dockside hotel. There he joined the poker or blackjack games, using his body for credit. A reputation for being untrustworthy seemed to earn him the trust of loan sharks and gamblers. He couldn't fool them, they said, yet they continued to lend him money he couldn't repay. Satisfaction was usually obtained in the darkest shadows of a doorway — which might have been the real reason for their apparent generosity. Dougal's black eyes and some-times broken bones were a convincing warning to others who might consider reneging.

If his body became too bruised to be an asset, Dougal used it to solicit sympathy and free drinks. On the nights he wasn't playing cards, he drank himself into a stupor. Then his little mate dragged him around the corner to the local lockup.

It never occurred to Sparrow to ask permission each time this happened. The sergeant had made the offer that day in the charity home and Sparrow had taken him up on it. It was as simple as that. Offers should never be questioned. If asked to be repeated, they would most likely be retracted. Besides, the hotel owner wouldn't allow Dougal to stay in that little back room if he was drunk and there was nowhere else. No one else would offer a bed to the Scotsman. And the sergeant rarely objected. In fact he'd stated more than once that Dougal's rightful place was behind bars. The few times he did protest was when he noticed Sparrow tending Dougal's wounds or cleaning up his vomit.

'Next thing you'll be wiping his bum fer him,' he said on the day he caught Sparrow spoon-feeding the Scotsman. For the third time that week, the two had spent the night in a cell.

Dougal held up his hands to display swollen fingers. 'There were three of 'em. Big buggers,' he mumbled through split lips.

'Everyone knows you go down with the first hit,' Jack Blake sneered.

'If yer want me out, just say so,' Dougal said wearily. 'I'm in no fit state to have a go at yer, not with these bloody hands. And I know if I did, you'd be slamming the door and throwing away the key. Which is what yer hoping for, I reckon. And you sit back down,' he added when Sparrow jumped up and stood between him and the sergeant. 'You'll be all right. He'll be kicking me out, not you.'

'Best thing for the little bloke is for you to piss orf to parts unknown,' was Jack Blake's parting shot.

Sparrow still found English almost impossible to imitate, mainly because the many different pronunciations confused him. But he could now comprehend most people no matter what their accent. He trailed the sergeant into the office, trying to think of ways to make peace between his two friends.

'Yer wasting yer time and yer heart with that one,' Jack Blake said as he slumped into a chair. 'I see you working yer guts all day for bed and board, then singing round the taverns at night just to get that bludger his betting money. What sort of a bloke lets a youngster do that? I know you think he's yer mate, but he'll dump you like a ton of bricks if you stop being of use to 'im. Know what I reckon?'

He glanced up to make sure his words were being understood. One look at Sparrow's face changed the reckoning.

'I reckon I'll keep me trap shut,' he finished quietly.

Understanding that nothing more would be said or done, Sparrow tried to show his gratitude. Moving around the chair, he began to knead the tension from Jack Blake's neck and shoulders.

The sergeant pushed him aside. 'Enough now. It's not my way. Never will be,' he said gruffly.

'You are wrong, this thing you think of me,' Sparrow said.

At Jack Blake's, 'Sorry mate, didn't understand a word of that,' Sparrow drew the shape of a woman in the air, clutched his genitals with one hand, and leered. He then tried to cap off the act with a squirting sideways spit. He'd seen this done during an argument, and he understood it to be a sign of one man out-toughing another, like squinting glares or bumping chests. But as he fixed his mouth into what he hoped was the right position and began the squirt, he couldn't bring himself to defile the sergeant's floor.

Jack Blake grinned when a glob of saliva slid down Sparrow's chin.

'Don't feel bad about it,' he said soothingly. 'Spitting don't come natural to everyone. And I got the message all right. I'm supposing that looking after him is all you have to give, though I can't see why you think you owe that mongrel anything anyway. I got no thought of throwing you out, if that's what's worrying you. Said you'd be welcome here in the lockup if you wanted a safe place. Told you it was all right to bring yer mate, and I meant it. If you wanna thank me, you can sling a mop around the cell floors every now and then. And maybe knock me up a meal when I'm too busy to go out. If you've got a mind to it, that is.'

From that day on Sparrow repaid the sergeant's kindness with walls that gleamed and toilets that shone, by scrubbing floors until they almost regained their tree smell. Searching the local shops and gardens for the freshest ingredients, he cooked meals that would bring tears of joy to any gourmet's eyes, and Jack Blake's taste for fine food was commonly known, as was his love of music. The sound of a tuneful voice delighted the sergeant even more than an exotic recipe. Whenever he heard one of the sad Irish songs, he couldn't resist handing over a few pennies.

Sparrow gave this occasional payment to the boys at the charity home. It was a small compensation, he said, for the fact that they always seemed pleased to see him. He knew charity could be better served by showing them how to bring out the mother in a woman, or the mate in a man, by using gap-toothed grins and pleading eyes. He would rather have taught these wily ways, and he might have done so had he been able speak their language. He could not, so he donated the coins which would otherwise have been thrown into a poker pot or dice game.

At this point it could be said that Sparrow worked and sang for nothing. Yet to his way of thinking, he earned something more precious than money. I can only guess it was the right to come and go as he pleased, although this was a right he lacked the courage to act upon. Striking out on his own was too much of a responsibility. Besides, for one of the few times in his life he was well fed and almost free of fear. He could see no good reason to relinquish those things. He might have continued working at that inn by day and cleaning the jail by night forever, if Jack Blake hadn't decided that it was time for him to have a proper home.

'What you want is a decent job,' he told Sparrow midway through the following year. 'I reckon I can set you up with Mrs Nell. That woman knows everybody who's anybody in the whole of the state. Nobody will go fooling around her joint. A course I can't stop them blokes from waiting round a corner if you takes the bludger along, but I can see yer not the sort to leave him. Clean him up and maybe she'll find something for him to do around the yard.'

Cleaning up Dougal was not a simple matter. He donned fresh underwear twice a week, but a bath and a change of outer clothes only happened twice a month. He laid the blame for this squarely upon his mother. Her persistent scouring throughout his childhood had worn his skin to parchment, he said. The dark blemishes had been caused by the closeness of his blood to the atmosphere. He could only be coaxed to wash by taking him for a swim, which was the Scotsman's favourite pastime but a nightmare for Sparrow, who had never learned the art.

He spoke to us just once of his only attempt at mastering the art of surfing. The subject had been raised as a means to describe Dougal's neck-to-knee woollen swimming costume, the rash it caused on his inner thighs, and the soothing power of bicarbonate of soda. When pressed for more information, he muttered something about a frenzy of birds led by — of all the unimaginable things to be on a sandy beach — a three-eyed bird. And though he could describe in detail Dougal's heroic action in pulling him out of the waves, he could never remember how he came to be among them in the first place.

# Chapter Three

Mrs Nell's 'joint', as Sergeant Blake called it, was a wooden two-storey building which could have been classed as a mansion. Twenty rooms in all, it should have looked out of place in a street of working-men's cottages. Instead, it had the air of being the reason for their gathering. Its white walls reflected the promise of a bright spring day onto the surroundings, like a queen distributing largesse. Its arrogance often caused a twitching of the local women's shoulders.

A row of poplars screened the front yard. Beyond the trees lay a rose garden, and a well-clipped lawn neatly divided by a gravel path. This led to an imposing sandstone and white-pillared porch. Mrs Nell's guests liked to promenade on this veranda. On a hot day they would lean against a column and pretend to be waiting. For what or whom did not matter. It was the feeling of kingliness or queenliness that they desired. And if they did happen to be waiting for a particular person, they could be sure that person would see them as someone of a high social standing. Sandstone and white pillars did that for one, even if one had to pay dearly for the privilege of one's surroundings.

A back entrance could be gained through a high wooden gate embedded in a fence of thick hedging. A pathway wound through a large vegetable garden, bypassed a hen house, woodpile and duck yard, and ended at a narrow wooden veranda. One of the two doors on the veranda led to the servants' quarters, the other into a large kitchen. It was, of course, to the back entrance that Sparrow and Dougal went.

They were a sorry-looking pair on the day they arrived at Mrs Nell's house for men and women of refinement. Dougal was ocean-washed but stiff with salt, and walking with the splay-legged gait of a man suffering from sunburn. Sparrow, pale enough to look powdered, still trembled from his ordeal. He shuffled down the path, glancing back with every step as though he might take flight at any moment.

In fact he did take flight — shinning onto the roof of a nearby shed when he saw the three dogs that guarded Mrs Nell's vegetable plots. He howled in terror as they flung themselves against their chains until they were almost strangled senseless. Sparrow was still afraid of dogs, cats, cows, horses; of dark spaces and unknown places; of most men and some women. Of the three-eyed bird still haunting his dreams every second night.

Chaos reigned until Dougal roared the dogs back into their kennels then hauled his little mate down from the roof. The only thing Dougal feared was having no money or place to gamble.

Mrs Nell frowned to show her displeasure at their nonsense, although it didn't surprise her. Sergeant Blake had told her about these men.

'The Scotsman likes to fight,' he had said, 'though he couldn't punch his way out of a wet paper bag. He likes to gamble, but he couldn't win a smile from a ruddy saint. He likes to drown his sorrows when he loses. He hardly ever gets on nodding terms with a washcloth, and he tries to race off every woman he meets. With some success with those who ain't too fussy, it has to be admitted. And I have to tell you that the little feller's scared of his own shadow most of the time, but he can wash and iron anything from yer undies out, and he don't mind doing a bit of mending and cleaning. Best of all, he's happy to go down to the Chinee's place for little bits of this and that, herbs and smelly potions, to whip up a feed the likes of which has to be tasted to be believed.'

One of Mrs Nell's two weaknesses happened to be spicy food, so she agreed to offer the little bloke a job. She'd made no promises concerning the Scotsman. Yet anyone could see that these two came as a mismatched pair.

'Two weeks trial,' she said to Dougal. 'The little feller can help out in the kitchen and do a spot of cooking on the chef's day off. You can clean out the fires, look after the hens and garden and do a bit of painting. I'll let you share Mad Basha's old room. It's the one beside the stairwell. She died last week and your first job will be to clear out her belongings.'

Dougal regarded Mrs Nell thoughtfully. A big woman with thick arms and callused hands, her dark brown dress swept the ground at her feet and revealed no more than a centimetre of skin at her neck. Its severe style was lightened with a ruffle of pink lace around her wrists. Her hair, thick and mud-coloured, was pulled back in a plaited roll. Tendrils had escaped and lay in tight little curls at the side of her face, echoing the capricious nature of the pink lace. As if to deny the fact that this frivolousness could be deliberate, her eyes had the colour and glint of metal filings. She also had a straight-back walk, as if her spine went all the way down to her heels. But he knew a hungry woman when he saw one.

'Yer on,' he said without bothering to consult with Sparrow.

The length of his study caused Mrs Nell's cheeks to pink a little, but if she was flustered, she covered the fact reasonably well.

'And do you also speak for your friend?' she asked haughtily.

Dougal nodded. 'Seeing as how he can't speak for hisself.'

Her expression wavered between consternation and sympathy as she asked, 'Is the lad a mute then? Can he be trusted not to go berserk on us?'

'I can speak, but I have trouble with the English, you see,' Sparrow said to reassure her.

'Gibberish!' Mrs Nell stepped back from him, though the step was small to show she wouldn't be cowered by any man, mad or not. 'I had enough of that with Madam Basha.' She glanced sideways at Dougal. 'I won't allow another loony in my house. It upsets the guests.'

'Loony? What is the meaning of this loony?' Sparrow asked.

'Cuckoo,' Dougal explained, grinning. 'You know, bonkers. Two bricks short of a wall.'

Believing this to be a description, Mrs Nell glanced behind her as if measuring the distance to the back door, then she swung back to Sparrow and stared him in the eye. Her shoulders straightened and she thrust out her chest. She would not take another backwards step, though she had half turned from him and pulled her chin in close to her throat.

'You must take him away,' she said. 'I can't think what possessed Sergeant Blake to send him to me in the first place.'

Sparrow's body jerked about, as if he needed the toilet, as he turned from her to Dougal then back again. His mouth opened and closed without uttering a word, and he waved his arms around while he tried to think of a way to prove his sanity. This made him appear dangerous to Mrs Nell. Drawing back her arm, she swung it in a full force roundhouse right that sent him flying off the path. He bounced as he hit the ground, buried his face in the grass then curled into a ball.

'That's a bit much,' Dougal drawled. 'It's not the lad's fault if he can't get his tongue around the English language.'

Mrs Nell was already bending over Sparrow. 'He just doesn't speak English?' she exclaimed, and made a *tsk tsk*ing sound when he cringed away from her. 'Well how was I to know? You should have made it plain from the start, you stupid Scots ignoramus.' She shot a glare at Dougal, whose grin had widened. 'Come on, lad, get up now.' With one tug on his arm she hauled Sparrow erect. 'It's your mate I should have given a good thump to, that's what I should have done. I didn't hurt you too much, did I?' She brushed off his shirt, but gently, trying not to frighten him.

Her arm was cosy around his shoulders, and he felt sure her bosom would be just as soft and warm. He would have liked to lay his head against that heaving curve, but after a glance at Dougal, he knew better than to push his luck. Reaching up a tentative hand, he laid it against her cheek.

'You dear lad,' she said, and reciprocated the gesture.

Sparrow knew she would have pulled him into a hug if Dougal hadn't spoken at that exact wrong moment.

'If yer thinking of kissing him, yer could save one for me.'

'You!' She turned to Dougal, squaring her shoulders again. When she saw the look in his eyes, a dark flush crept upwards from her throat.

'You,' she repeated, quickly regaining her dignity, 'can follow me, the two of you, and I'll show you what you'll be doing.'

She led them on a brief tour while detailing their duties. She also explained Madam Basha — the previous owner of the mansion — whose private room had been a condition of purchase.

'Mad as a cut snake she was. Never let anyone into that room of hers, and I, for one, haven't been in there yet. No doubt it's crowded with junk and filthy into the bargain. That's your problem now. You can clean it out and burn the contents. Take it or leave it, I don't want to hear any whining.'

Dougal decided to take it, and Mrs Nell set him to work chopping wood for the kitchen fires. The job of cleaning just naturally fell to Sparrow.

Creeping along the hall to Madam Basha's old room, he paused at the doorway, gathering kindly thoughts to send before him like a white flag. He felt sure that insanity was a communicable disease. Why else would Mrs Nell cross herself each time she spoke the former occupant's name? Perhaps madness could flake off in little pieces and lie in wait between floorboards or underneath a mattress. And Madam Basha had died in this room, so her essence might have remained after they took her body away. Yet when he finally dredged up enough courage to enter, he saw a huge bed turned into a tent by a draping of green canvas. He knew then that if her spirit did remain, it was surely kindred to his own.

The floor had been painted the colour of sand. The walls were a sun-scoured blue. The only furniture was the tent-like bed and a large, ornately carved wooden casket. The latter contained one white burnous (soft and warm), three cotton caftans (one cream, two brown), two pairs of sandals, odds and ends of bead jewellery, and a false bottom. In that compartment he found a pouch constructed of soft black leather. It held a dozen diamond rings, two diamond-studded gold necklaces, two black pearl brooches, and thirty-seven precious stones: diamonds, emeralds and a half-dozen large and stunning rubies.

The robes fitted perfectly, as did the footwear. Tying a thong around his waist, he made the leather pouch comfortable against his crotch. Donning one of the caftans, he strapped on a pair of sandals and went in search of Mrs Nell.

For as long as he lived in that twenty-room house, he continued to wear the caftans (the burnous in winter) and the sandals. Mrs Nell had instructed him to throw out whatever the room contained, or keep whatever he fancied. (Not knowing about the jewels, of course, and the rest was rubbish to her.)

'An inheritance,' she insisted.

The occupants of the house were accustomed to seeing those clothes on Madam Basha, so he also inherited the name.

# Chapter Four

As months added up to years with no uncommon events to mark their passing, Basha's time at Mrs Nell's guesthouse could be called the contented part of his life. The established routine of his days, and the certainty that they would continue in much the same way, enabled him to reinvent himself. That new self was vastly different from the timid, frightened Achmed Yusef Alemedine who had run from the *Eastern Star*. There he'd forgotten that generosity and affection had ever existed. As Basha, he rediscovered these things.

The desert room brought back memories of an early childhood when he was loved, freeing him of the nightmares concerning cramped spaces, hunger and blows. He lost his dread of women, for the maids not only allowed him entry into their circle, they welcomed him in. Their friendship gave him a kind of protection he'd never known. He treasured this newfound camaraderie, not realising that in their eyes, the caftans neutralised his masculinity.

His fear of men was tempered by the residents, who treated him in a polite way, as a gentleman to a servant. Many regarded him as a friend, if not an equal. None were ever harsh or even rude. Mrs Nell's obvious fondness for him made sure of that. Outside the guesthouse, his soaring tenor voice and cheery manner made him popular with most of the working class, whose ancestry was mainly English, Scots or Irish. They always seemed pleased to see him, and were even more pleased when he consented to sing for them. Yet he did have a problem with, as Dougal described it, 'Some blokes' weird sense of humour'.

'They're just having a lend of yer. You know, pulling yer leg. Don't let it worry yer,' Dougal would say.

But it did worry him: the jokes about his slim stature, the way they called him 'pretty boy' and laughed at what they termed the 'bum fluff' on his chin. These were all grievous insults to him and shredded what self-esteem he had built up at Mrs Nell's guesthouse. Of course these men laughed while they offered the insults. They were quick to pat him on the shoulder or tell him, 'No offence intended, mate,' if they saw he was offended. And they did ridicule each other in much the same way. But it was not Achmed Yusef Alemedine's way. It was not part of his culture. He was mortified by it, despite Dougal's comforting words.

At other times he ran afoul of bigots who made him the target of their racism and small-mindedness, yet though he hated the sneers directed at his mode of dress, his way of earning a living and his manner of being different, he could not change these things. The caftans set him apart but they gave him a security of self, helping him to feel confident and liked. And so he was. Everyone in Mrs Nell's house liked Basha. In the clothes Jack Blake had given him, he was just the funny little feller who hung around the Scotsman, or What'shisname who could sing a bit.

Dougal insisted that housekeeping was women's work. The maids hated it and wished to be doing something else, but they could only agree. Basha had been hired as a kitchen hand and casual cook. He was foolish enough to spend most of his spare time cleaning. Not one of them could understand his pleasure at the sight of clear windows, gleaming furniture and shiny floors. Without the necessary words, he had no way of explaining that the rubbing and scrubbing made him feel closer to home, and to Achmed Yusef Alemedine, 'home' had always been a mysterious, otherworld place, belonging to everyone else but him.

As for the matter of his being different, he only knew that others were not like him. So he avoided derision by staying in the guesthouse throughout the day and, during the rare times he accompanied Dougal at night, by adding a swagger to his walk and learning to spit like a man.

He also learned how to prepare meals that stuck to a man's ribs: mashed potatoes, thick red meat swimming in gravy, vegetables stewed to a mash, dumplings and puddings likely to go through the floor if dropped, with plenty of salt, tomato sauce or sweet vanilla custard to disguise the lack of texture and flavour. His own style of cooking, learned long ago in another land, was restricted to Mrs Nell and Jack Blake. The gift of this maker of splendid food had earned the sergeant a dinner invitation at least three times a week. A fact that stirred Dougal's resentment.

'Look at him, sitting up like a toff in her private rooms. Scoffing hisself while we have to eat in the kitchen,' he'd say to anyone who'd care to listen.

'It is not the kind of food you enjoy.' And, 'Did you not tell me that chilli combined with garlic makes your visit to the toilet a misery?' were Basha's usual comments.

Understanding most of this, mainly because of the repetition, the Scotsman would snarl something about, 'The fat slob treating me like I'm lower than a snake's belly.'

'Yer know she's the real reason why he set yer up here,' he pointed out one night when Jack Blake had been even more caustic with him than usual. 'Nothing to do with being yer mate. He's just getting into her good books.'

Basha smiled and nodded. He did not feel resentful. He loved the sergeant as he loved the Scotsman, and he liked the fact that they were now on equal footing.

'Trying to get in her pants, too,' Dougal said. 'But he left his run a bit late, didn't he?'

This was said a little too loudly while Mrs Nell escorted Jack Blake to the door. She turned and glared. The sergeant's back stiffened, but he chose to ignore the words when she took his arm and smiled into his face. Basha gave the Scotsman's ankle a hefty kick.

'Meaning that she probably still feels a loyalty to her late husband,' Dougal added quickly.

His face had been twisted into a caricature of humility when Mrs Nell turned. It slid into a look of hopeless yearning when Jack Blake swung around and glared at him. The sergeant seemed comforted. He hugged Mrs Nell's arm closer to his side and strolled onto the veranda. Basha kicked Dougal's ankle again.

'Not to worry, mate,' the Scotsman said softly. 'I know what that bloke can do. There'll be no more protection around here if he gets wise to what's going on, and I know she'll toss me out on me ear if me mouth gets too smart.'

Basha nodded again. As long as Dougal knew those things, and as long as he wished to stay at the guesthouse, he'd be careful. What more could be asked of him?

By now he knew that Dougal had been right about Mrs Nell. She was a hungry woman. Yet even with a husband dead these past seven years, she had a position to uphold. She would not appease that hunger willy-nilly. A lover must first take her fancy, and she had never been fanciful. He must know how to keep his mouth shut and his body clean. Above all, he must have the strength and constitution of a stallion. Dougal had boasted on day one that he could satisfy most of those requirements; being sparse of words and robust of body and, even if he said so himself, possessed of the right equipment that knew which way was up.

Mrs Nell coaxed him to cleanliness by personally washing his clothes and body. She built him up with good solid food (mashed potatoes, thick red meat, etc) until his walk gained a waddle. When he was clean and layered with fat, she took him into her bed.

Around midnight she'd fall into a dreamless sleep, giving Dougal the opportunity to fulfil his other needs. He made a deal with a bank clerk (at ten percent commission) to place his and Basha's wages into the care of Hailstorm Hec, owner of the Big Fist Inn. This unpretentious establishment held the best poker games in town, and a nightly dice game in the alley beyond its kitchen.

# Chapter Five

Having rarely received pay for his labour before, Basha had no objection to the Scotsman commandeering his wages. In fact he considered the money to be well spent if it made Dougal happy. He could find no fault with his job, his male mates or his women friends. Yet fate or foolishness persuaded him to set out in a search for kinship and love, even while he had no recent experience of what those things could be.

During the post-midnight hour on the day of his third anniversary in Australia, he was caught following Dougal through a window and given a beating in lieu of his friend. Dougal owed money again, and the irate lender had sent a few bruisers to teach the Scotsman to pay on time. He'd been too quick to catch so they asked his little mate to pass on the message. A broken nose, and the knowledge that it would happen again, helped Basha to make his decision. It was time to go his own way, to seek his own fortune, he said; which would hopefully include a wife.

'And children to bless me with immortality,' he managed to convey to the sergeant and Mrs Nell, using actions and a few understandable words as they applied ice packs to his face.

'You taking the bludger along?' was Jack Blake's only question, and it was asked with too much eagerness for Basha's liking. He had thought the sergeant would hate losing him. Yet he understood the reason. Sergeant Blake would sacrifice just about anything to be rid of Dougal McLean. He was at first angry, then showed a comforting amount of concern when Basha said he intended to travel alone.

It was up to Mrs Nell to persuade him to stay, and she did try, coaxing him with offers of advancement to head cook or butler. When that didn't work, she stamped her feet and shouted. She even tried tears. He cried with her, but he wouldn't change his mind.

Dougal had become restless during the past few weeks. The Scotsman had dropped hints that he was thinking of moving them both to Sydney. Basha didn't want to live in a city where unfriendly policemen might demand to see his papers. He did not want to sing for his and Dougal's supper. The thought of living in charity homes or cheap hotels again made him shudder. He tried to explain this to Mrs Nell, but all she comprehended was his determination to go. She found no comfort in the fact that he was leaving Dougal behind.

'How long will he stay, do you think?' she asked, although her tone suggested she already knew the answer.

'As long as he wants and no longer,' Basha sighed. He placed his hands across the bowl of her stomach, turning away from the set of her face and the clench of her fists. 'There's always the sergeant,' he whispered, adding another sigh at the futility of saying more. Mrs Nell couldn't understand much of what he said. She wouldn't have listened if she could.

'She wants marrying, and that ain't my way of doing things. Told her so right from the start,' Dougal said halfway through his lunch a few hours later.

'Man's words are made of excuses,' the parlourmaid sniffed as she snatched his plate of curried sausages away.

Basha's expression showed agreement and disapproval.

'And that look is a bloody good reason,' Dougal said, 'for you to get out of this place. It's time for us to be moving on.'

He paused to study Sparrow's face (he'd never stopped calling his little mate by that name). His measuring glance took in the dark honey complexion, the high forehead, the black hair and brown eyes. 'Egyptian looks, like Madam Basha's,' Mrs Nell called them. If Dougal had to describe that face, he would have used the word pretty, despite the swollen nose. He knew it was a word Sparrow detested when applied to his looks. In fact it seemed to frighten him. Dougal had no idea why, and he'd never tried to find out. 'If yer can't do something about a thing, then yer best leave it alone,' was one of his favourite sayings. But most of all, when he looked into that face, those eyes, he would have seen admiration and trust; and the Scotsman knew full well that he, Dougal McLean, should never be admired or trusted. Although he thought of Sparrow's voice as good as an open wallet, for one of the few times in his life he chose in someone else's favour.

'I s'pose I could take yer along with me, but I reckon you'd hold me back,' he said. 'I can't go on looking out for you forever, yer know. Me ma is already taking care of me da, me six brothers and two sisters, but I know she'll make yer welcome at Mount Tumblebee. That's where yer ought to go for the sort of life yer after.'

And so, eager to find what others claimed to be a normal existence (home, wife, children, etc), Basha made ready for his journey. He folded his belongings into a blanket roll — a comb, an extra flannel shirt and a pair of boots that rubbed blisters on his heels if he wore them for more than an hour. Dougal had told him that country folk would never accept the caftans or the sandals.

He also packed the journal he'd begun while owned by the master of a desert caravan. That leader of men and camels had allowed another slave to teach Achmed how to inscribe the language of their homeland.

'So my ancestors will never be forgotten, and all because of that first good man,' he would say with a beaming smile, omitting the fact that the good leader had sold him to a child trader. But that is another story. One he never mentioned. As far as I can see, it is of no importance to this one.

# Chapter Six

Early the following morning, after his usual breakfast of strong black coffee sweetened with golden syrup (or cocky's joy, as the locals called it), he said goodbye to those friends whose work forced them into a pre-dawn rising. The maids and handymen who could sleep a little longer had farewelled him at a party the night before. Mrs Nell had announced his leave-taking at dinner, and every guest (and Sergeant Blake, of course) had wished him well, clapped his back or kissed him (depending on gender) and sworn that their lives would never be the same once he was gone. Dougal had shaken his hand, then shambled off to the pub.

'If I hang around I'll just talk yer into staying,' he'd said, 'and you and I both know it's time for a change.'

Basha did know, and he managed to stay stoically dry-eyed until he reached the privacy of his bedroom. There he cried like the child he had never been, and finally fell into a dreamless sleep after Mrs Nell tiptoed in and swore the position of butler would always be waiting.

Buoyed by the knowledge that he could return whenever he wanted, and by a surety that many people hoped he would, he left his misgivings at the gate when he closed it behind him. As he marched along the dusty streets, a late autumn sun urged him on with the promise of another fine hot day. Yet that sun's warmth was a mere struck match when compared to Basha's enthusiasm. He hummed a jig while passing cleaning ladies rubbing sleep from store windows. He waved to men sluicing stale beer and urine onto the footpath, which was their way of making their taverns a haven from the stinking streets. He smiled at unseen women watching him through fluttering curtains, and he laughed at three boys aping his walk. Those boys threw stones when he wouldn't chase them. As he quit the town's borders, he sang Italian arias learned from a homesick wine merchant.

Two hours later, alone on the road, he was overtaken by a recollection of tales about Australia told by former shipmates. He remembered stories of striped tigers, feral yellow dogs, and snakes by the millions. The little English bosun had whispered of wild black men filling their bellies with unwary travellers, of eagles carrying a fully grown sheep in one claw and predatory wingless birds standing taller than a man.

These stories had no credibility to one whose land memories were of teeming cities and vast expanses of sand. Not even his vivid imagination had foreseen the vegetation surrounding him now. The dark, unfamiliar trees were twisted into nightmare shapes. The ones with dead grey branches reminded him of gallows trees waiting to blossom with thieves. He'd seen these things while accompanying his third master in a search for stolen artefacts. Yet those trees had stood in lifeless paddocks. These were decorated with birds that screeched at him, that took flight in dazzling white clouds, still showing outrage at his presence. On occasion they were joined by pink and grey screeching birds, and others, brown, who laughed at his fear.

He kept to the middle of the road to avoid the hanging vines that coiled back upon themselves, like snakes trying to swallow their own tails. When he found the courage to look beyond those vines, he saw sharp-edged bushes bowing to a wind that had long since died, and undergrowth mysteriously moving. Even worse was the combination of odours. They had no recognisable source, no matter how hard he tried to find them among the various smells stored within his memory.

Terror formed an icy ball in his chest and slowly froze outwards. He pounded down the road with the sound of his own slapping feet urging him on. When he could run no more, he fainted.

He later swore that the three-eyed bird would have come for him there and then, if the gods hadn't sent one of their stranger angels to save him.

'Bloody queer place to be taking a nap, mate.'

The voice snapped him out of a dream crowded with all the horrors he'd been trying to escape. He looked up at sunburned skin, finely drawn eyebrows, high cheekbones and eyes the colour of a spring-water pool.

'I thought I saw something in the bushes,' he mumbled.

'Yair, all right,' the stranger said. 'Whatever ya reckon. Me name's Carl Rusher, by the way.'

The friendly tone helped Basha to stagger to his feet. 'I am Achmed Yusef Alemedine,' he replied when the world stopped spinning around him. 'Once called Sparrow but recently known as Basha.'

Carl Rusher understood just one word.

'Basher, ay? Ya don't look it. Still and all, I used to get Masher until me frigging mates decided I was better suited to plain old Carl. Just piss an' wind after all, is what they reckoned. But then, they never did see me in action.' He grinned suddenly. ''Bout the same bloody size, ain't we? And better looking than most wimmin as well. Two things we got in common that we'd be better off without, what d'ya say? Climb aboard me wagon and I'll give ya a ride to wherever it is yer going. Or as close as I can get. That suit ya all right?'

Considering the circumstances and his frame of mind, Basha answered as best he could. The words were as unintelligible as the circumstances, but the frame of mind was not. The angel of rough speech and a pretty face calmed him with a mug of warm ale and an encouraging thump on the back. Basha couldn't understand much of what he said, no more than Carl could make sense of Basha's reason for sleeping in the middle of the road. Yet each listened politely to the other while the road passed slowly beneath them.

A half hour before sunset, Carl set up a camp consisting of two log seats and a smokeless fire. Ignoring a new lot of birds that were loudly protesting this invasion of their territory, he brewed a billy of tea to a tar colour. While two rabbits roasted on green-twig spits, he made a dough of flour and water, wrapped it in bark stripped from a melaleuca tree and buried it under the glowing coals.

Once he had tasted Carl's cooking, Basha had to agree that, 'Ya can't beat bunny and damper for a bloody good feed, ay?'

After a few more mugs of ale, he stopped watching for wild men, snakes and wingless birds. By then the screeching clouds had grown tired of their constant scolding.

'Going off to the creek for a drink before they roost,' was Carl's explanation. 'Shows they got more sense than looks, ay? They are a bit bloody noisy, but ya get used to them after a while. Haveta, dontcha?'

A few minutes passed while Basha sat with his head bowed, shifting words around in his brain until he understood them. Finally he looked up, smiled and nodded, and accepted another mug of ale. Sipping it slowly, for he was beginning to feel the effects of what Carl called 'me own home brew', he listened while his new friend identified the odours of eucalyptus, sunbaked earth and the acid stink of ants crushed beneath his boots. Now Basha had time to study the trees, their darkness became blue-grey, red, umber, gold and uncountable shades of green; all intermingling as the sun melted over faraway mountains. He felt the wind that argued with the treetops. Seeing grasses part and undergrowth quiver, he merely wondered at the creatures going about their everyday business.

More at peace than he'd been for some time, he listened to a few of Carl's songs and pleased the man with a few of his own. They taught each other words and tunes over another ale or two. Gathering armfuls of leaves, they made beds beside the fire.

Basha lay back, filling his lungs with the smell of slow-burning wood, rabbit grease, and the stench of his own ale-tinged breath.

Emptying his mind of cities and deserts, he restocked his memories with the landscape he had travelled through in the wagon. When this was done, he turned to Carl and said, 'I wish to be an Australian'.

Carl repeated the sentence twice, copying Basha's method of rolling the words around his mouth and into his brain for understanding.

'Yair. All right. Whatever ya reckon,' he said at last.

The answer sent tremors through Basha's body.

'Does that to ya,' Carl agreed.

Minutes later he was sound asleep and snoring.

Not wanting to miss a second of this momentous night, Basha decided to stay awake and guard the fire. He fed it slowly, an inch at a time as the ash fell away, and revisited his life as far back as he could remember. After studying each year for a few seconds, he banished it to the darkest recesses of his memory. The only ones kept in the light were those beginning on August 10, 1907. In this way, he reasoned, his new nationality would not be tainted by the past.

Being young at the time, barely twenty if he'd counted right, he had no way of knowing that some doors are not so easily closed.

At dawn he organised a breakfast of leftover damper and hot black tea while his fellow Australian tidied up the camp site. Although resolve was still strong in Basha's mind, he could not bring himself to help hitch the horses to the wagon. But to give him his due, he did refuse the loan of a rifle to shoot a few of the birds. Arriving at first light, they made his senses reel with their perpetual screeching.

'Just galahs and corellas and a few cockatoos,' Carl said. 'Maybe they'll leave us in peace if ya knock off a few. Though they'll go anyway once they've told us off for being here.'

Basha was sorely tempted to use the rifle. Especially when a raven flew to a nearby branch and stared down at him with its evil eye. But Carl was right. After one last ear-splitting chorus, the birds went about their business.

Many hours later, after countless stops to empty out the ale he drank continuously, Carl pulled up by a track angling away from the road. Basha was told with many gestures that, 'If ya follows that track you'll

47

find the name printed on ya letter. Everybody and his brother knows the frigging McLeans.'

He found, with the help of a spare bottle of ale and the kindness of a crude man, that he was no longer afraid to travel alone. Half an hour later, he also found the McLean clan living in a hut on a hill they called Mount Tumblebee.

# Chapter Seven

Dougal's mother could scarcely believe that such a skimpy young man had the courage of a lion. Yet how else could you describe someone who had rushed right in, with no thought for himself, and joined Dougal in a fight against six roughnecks trying to steal his hard-earned wages?

'It's no good doubting,' she told the others. 'It's here, written in Dougal's hand. I've always said good things come in small parcels. Though I can't understand why such a man should be given the name of Sparrow.'

He did try to explain that Sparrow wasn't his rightful name. She clasped her hands around his neck and pulled his head down, smothering his protests against her shoulder. (This neck-pulling head-hug was essential, she being slightly shorter.) So Basha linked arms with Achmed Yusef Alemedine and was never seen again. They both knew better than to argue with a mother.

This mother, known to everyone as Ma McLean, had been considered the beauty of the mount before thirteen children (two buried in Scotland, two on the hill) and life in an unfamiliar land had changed her shape and outlook. Her body had been thickened by childbearing, her breasts pulled down to her waist by a series of sucking mouths. Years of hard work had callused her hands and formed muscles in her arms and legs that most men would envy. They had also given a slight stoop to her back, which she usually hid under an ill-fitting, ground-sweeping brown dress covered by pinafores made from burlap. Topping all that was what Dougal had called a sprig of mountain heather — thick curls the colour of snow, eyes blue enough to be mistaken for violet, skin as delicate as petals. Ma never left the shelter of her home without a hat. She would not set her feet on the floor until they were encased in brogues thicker than her accent.

She ruled her family with a wit more incisive than the six-inch, pearl-topped pin decorating her Sunday hat. If wit failed, and it was never blunted by the hardness of her voice, she emphasised the wickedness of her sons' ways with prods of the pin. In Dougal's words, the McLean boys often resembled newly pricked sausages lined up before her frying pan.

The eldest McLean, known as Da, was the mould from which most of those boys had been cast. Except for his green eyes, he was an older and even more blotched version of Dougal. For the past twenty years the skin on his face, arms and shoulders had been exposed to a hot southern sun, like bread fixed to a fork and held over a roaring fire. The result was a growing spread of sun spots and recurring peeling. That hot southern sun might have taken his life, if coal dust hadn't won the race against melanoma.

He was a moody man, often quiet to the point of rudeness, yet sometimes loud enough to be considered a nuisance. On weekends, when fertilised with beer, his sentences were tangled and angled skywards like paspalum after the spring rains. On weekdays his words became tussock grass: short and sparse with gaps between the clumps.

The day of Sparrow's arrival being a Saturday, Da welcomed his son's little mate with a long-winded speech and a mangling of the hand held out to him. He then introduced his family one by one, beginning with seven-year-old Iain and ending with the youngest daughter, christened Margaret but commonly known as Polly.

The eldest daughter had fled to a job as silk spinner at a hosiery mill in Sydney. There she had married the first man to ask, which prevented

Da from sending her brothers to drag her back home. Considering her to be a deserter and a turncoat, the clan never mentioned her name again. This properly raised Presbyterian lass had committed the sin of adopting the ring-kissers' faith. Anything, she said at the time, to be free of a houseful of men, the mine, and this mountain of dirt with the pretty misnomer of Tumblebee.

Yet these conditions delighted Sparrow. He was now an Australian, and communities like the one at Mount Tumblebee were as endemic to his country as the eucalypts. The McLean dwelling enchanted him. It was exactly as Dougal described.

A sprinkling of sawdust covered the trodden-earth floor, and the smell of eucalyptus was all pervasive. Cracks in the slab walls had been packed with the papery bark from melaleuca trees and sealed with tar. Chaff bags hanging from strands of wire divided the area into four even-sized rooms. Ten stools — made by stretching bagging over branches halved then crossed — one solid wooden table, and two cupboards made from packing cases crowded into one of these rooms. The others held one brass bed, a pile of folded stretcher bunks, a gleaming cedar wardrobe and a number of closets consisting of tarred paper nailed across wooden struts. The only doorway was an oblong hole blocked at night by the upended table.

A copper cauldron encased in mud bricks was fired up every Sunday to give the family linen its weekly scalding and the McLeans their weekly bath. A nearby creek provided the means for 'a splash and a promise to do better next time', as Ma called their daily wash.

The kitchen was a corrugated-iron addition joined to the hut by a v-shaped arch of timber. It held a kerosene stove and a round tin bath. A square box covered in wire — and a coating of flies drunk on the smell of slowly rotting mutton — hung in the darkest corner of the kitchen. The walls were almost hidden behind boxes holding flour, salt, sugar, cheeses, tea and a variety of fruit and vegetables, fresh and dried.

Surrounding this home was a dozen huts identical to the one Da had built, and a few which were little more than humpies erected from corrugated iron and bagging. Yet the people were washed. Their clothing was well worn but clean. More importantly, their welcome of Dougal's little mate was as robust as the McLeans'.

Although these neighbours had mostly immigrated from Scotland, there were a few Irish, Welsh, Italians, a German, one woman of English descent and her partner whose ancestors had been convicts. The Irish were of the Catholic faith, yet still the McLeans' closest friends and borrowing partners: a cup of sugar, a hat on going to town day, the price of a billy of beer the day before payday. A mate's religion was his own business.

The Italian family, headed by Antonio known as Tony, spoke with an Italian-Scottish accent. The Irish and Welsh were, to a small degree, easier to understand. (Which refers to the adults of course. The children's dialect was now classified as Australian.) The lone German hadn't spoken a word since his wife ran away with a farmer who lived out on the western plains. She had taken their eight daughters with her.

Mary Mayberry Trelelan, who occupied a hut opposite the German's humpy, spoke carefully enunciated English. She had fallen in love out of her class and eloped with a labourer hired to make her parents' large house even larger. Having fled Melbourne more than six years earlier, they were still hiding out — though Mary's mother would have been delighted to be relieved of her eldest daughter. Or so Mary decided during one of the many times she repeated her story.

She would always begin with, 'You must remember, Liona, that your grandmother, Constance Mayberry nee Blake, was of poor Irish descent. Leaving Newcastle to take up a position as governess in Melbourne, she worked hard to better herself and marry well. This she did, and she was determined her six daughters would continue that tradition.'

Then, with a sly sideways glance at my father, she'd usually add, 'I must admit that I was a grave disappointment to her.'

*As you are to me,* her expression said as she looked at me again, though she never spoke those words aloud.

'It was an era of romance and magic. Not like these modern times when every i must be dotted and every t crossed,' she said if I complained about the lack of details. 'You must allow your imagination to bloom,' she chided me. 'Do not become an empiricist like Leslie Amadeus. That is much too restrictive, and it can sometimes be quite painful.'

I must admit that she amazed me with this instruction. In all things except the telling of her story, my mother was the soul of pragmatism.

'Who am I to argue? She tells a charming tale,' were my father's dryly spoken words when I asked for his version of their meeting.

# Chapter Eight

It was the visitation that altered Mary Mayberry's life. To her, the appearance of the jaguar man was an announcement that she was meant for something other than the expected. Until then there hadn't been much difference between her and other daughters of the 'upper class' in Melbourne. A role model to her younger sisters, she was always well groomed and her manners were exemplary, although she did have a tendency to read stories of fantasy and romance. Still, she had a sweet singing voice, a talent for playing the violin and a quiet but firm way of dealing with servants. Everyone who knew her agreed that when she reached the age of seventeen, she would choose a husband of equal social standing and become a perfect wife. Mary also deemed this to be her future, until a few days after her fourteenth birthday.

On the evening her menstrual flow began, Mary saw the one she knew she was fated to marry. 'A revelation,' she told her mother, who placed the blame directly onto Mary's father.

Victor Mayberry, dressed for a night out in a black dinner jacket, had presented his daughter with a painting of a jaguar crouched in a jungle. 'Because she's always been fond of cats,' he said.

When his wife pointed out that something soft and fluffy on a kitchen hearth might have been more appropriate, he shrugged.

'It's the spirit of the thing that counts,' he argued, and hung the painting on the wall opposite Mary's bed. To counteract the effect this pagan art might have on her eldest daughter, Constance Blake Mayberry hung a painting of Christ in the wilderness.

Mary stared at these images for more than an hour before the vision appeared. It wasn't a dream, as her mother insisted. Mary wasn't asleep. She saw what she saw. She heard what she heard.

She heard the distant beat of drums, soft and lazy at first, build to an angry thump that shook the house. She saw the cat leap out of the jungle and race across the desert. As each of its paws hit the ground, grains of sand were caught by a wind and whirled across the sky, like a bow across taut strings, until she was encased in a sound sweet enough to bring rain to an arid wasteland.

Dressed in a man's black jacket, Mary flew above the rain, following the jaguar as it ran to a distant ravine. She cried out as the animal leapt into the abyss and she followed it down. The jacket was torn in two as claws reached out and caught her. A mouth on her mouth swallowed her screams as they plunged deeper into darkness. Minutes or hours might have passed before they drifted upwards. Bathed in sunlight again, she turned to look at the cat. Beside her stood a man with flowing golden hair.

Seventeen years later, after having long since passed what was then thought of as her prime, Mary was still unmarried, and the once irreproachable daughter had become an embarrassment to her parents. Intelligent without being obviously so, she was attractive without being beautiful. The music she played on her violin was said to make the angels weep. But she had just passed the age of thirty without finding a husband. Mary Mayberry was classed as a failure.

No one thought to praise her for her patience.

For all of those seventeen years she waited for her jaguar man, by day working as a volunteer at the hospital or visiting the homes of those less fortunate than her to nurse their sick. Her spare hours were spent playing the violin and reading, and assisting her younger sisters to set up their houses as they married. She would not go so far as to help with their children. There were always better things for her to do: growing vegetables for those in need, teaching music to those who wanted to learn and working for any charity who asked for her help.

In other words, for those seventeen years she did much the same as she continued to do for all the days of her life.

The nights were different. She dreaded the nights. She'd been moved from the west wing, which was the main part of her home, to a room at the back of the house. She hated that room. It was small. Pokey. A punishment room. Her mood was at its lowest the moment she opened her eyes each morning and saw the walls surrounding her, so close she could scarcely breathe. That same feeling came upon her as she entered her room at night. She would cry herself to sleep. She would cry when she woke.

'But,' she said, 'I never gave in to despair.'

Yet she was close to it until the day of her thirty-first birthday, when she woke to an absence of a morning mood which was usually darker than the blackest raven. Through her window she could see a sky bluer than normal. She could hear birdsong that was mellow and warbling instead of the usual squabble of sparrows. No doubt the sparrows had fled because of the song, for she knew it as that of a butcher bird; but still, she recognised the notes as being part of something more momentous than a simple birdsong. Especially with the sound of a hammer on wood providing the background tempo, so much like a drumbeat, and growing louder as she listened. Sure that it had to mean something, she leapt out of bed, scrabbled her violin out of its case and played the sweet sad music heard so long ago.

Leslie Amadeus Trelelan resisted for as long as he could. This was the first time he had worked for weeks. He did not want to lose the job, although he deemed it to be beneath him. Leslie was a poet and a preacher by inclination. He was also an exceptional pianist. But being an inborn talent, he couldn't claim credit for that, and as good as he was, he would never be able to copy the music swirling around and through him at that moment. He had no choice but to follow the sound. It led him to a small room at back of the Mayberry mansion.

Mary did not notice the moleskin trousers and grey flannel shirt, or the hammer in his hand. She saw the cat as it left the jungle and raced across the desert. She cried out as it leapt into the abyss, then she followed it down, mouth to mouth as claws tore the jacket from her body. She felt again that terror as they plunged into darkness; until a sweet piercing thing carried her upwards into light. When she opened her eyes and saw a tall, finely-featured man with long hair (almost golden), the jacket torn in two and the spread of her blood on the sheets, Mary knew she had found her jaguar man.

She also knew that her father would never consent to her marrying a mere labourer. He would decree a convent for her, and for Leslie Amadeus a whipping followed by a month or two in jail. They had to elope.

'Immediately, before we're discovered,' he told her.

Tying her jewellery and all the money she could find into a bundle, Mary tossed it and the torn black jacket into a bag, which she pushed through the window along with an umbrella, Leslie Amadeus and her violin. Donning two outfits of clothing, from inner wear out, she followed him up the path and onto a train to the New South Wales border, always keeping a few steps behind him as befitted a seemly woman.

For the next few months they walked all day and visited the desert most nights, pausing when needed to sleep and eat or to chop wood for a meal. Now and then they stayed at a low priced tavern, or they accepted a bed offered by a friendly family. Between towns they erected rough bark and branch shelters under a tree. At times they passed through tiny villages where nobody saw them except koala, wombat or possum, and an occasional Aborigine who slunk away as if they carried the plague.

Mary never did come to understand why the Aborigines avoided her and Leslie in this manner. Her guesses, and there were quite a few of them, were much too fanciful to be correct. In truth it was probably the fact that these Aborigines were blamed for a stolen loaf of bread or a freshly baked pie, a handful of flour or sugar and even underwear and shirts — some of the many things that went missing while the villagers were away from home, doing whatever it was the inhabitants of tiny villages did. No doubt those occasional Aborigines soon learned that to be in the same vicinity as the runaways brought white anger down upon their innocent heads.

About sixty miles south of Sydney and needing a rest, they paused for a month while Leslie slopped pigs. Mary gave music lessons to a farmer's daughter. They might have stayed longer if Leslie hadn't considered the labour to be beneath him.

They walked on, always heading in a northerly direction, and another month and Sydney passed without Leslie finding work that suited his talents. Their visits to the desert slowed to twice a week and gradually became briefer. Mary's will hadn't weakened. Her body hadn't lost its litheness. It was Leslie who grew paler and thinner, who developed blisters on his feet and constipation through irregular meals. His almost blond hair lost its sheen. His chest lost flesh. By the end of the year he no longer had the power to lift Mary out of the ravine.

She mended the jacket and wore it every night in an effort to make him soar towards the sun. Leslie sunk deeper into darkness. He had no piano. He was too tired to preach or create poetry. The continuous walking was far harder than anything he'd ever done. Only Mary's pleas, and perhaps fear of Victor Mayberry's anger, kept him from stealing aboard however many trains it would take to shunt him back to Melbourne.

As summer approached they left the cooler weather behind and continued on into relentless sunshine, finally reaching Mount Tumblebee during the longest drought that district had experienced in years. They missed Newcastle by accident, having wandered onto a side track to find shelter under the trees. One track then another brought them onto a dirt road heading west, where they hitched a ride on a log carrier drawn by a team of bullocks.

Mary lost that day in a weary, heat haze dream. For most of it she sat in a half-stupor, pretending to listen to geography and botany lessons from the garrulous teamster. And, after he had slept for three or more hours, Leslie's constant complaining. Although admitting that riding was much kinder on his feet than walking, the smell of farting bullocks and the driver's halitosis was more than Leslie could bear. He moaned about the heat and dust. He grumbled about the lack of overhang from the drought-bared trees, demanding that Mary hand over her umbrella. Which, having a complexion to protect, of course she refused to do. He continued to groan and sweat and fidget until the driver dropped them off by the side of the track, wished them a good day and pointed the way to the village.

Another hour or so passed before they reached Tumblebee Creek. By then Leslie's voice had worn to a croak, yet he continued to reproach and berate, even as he peeled off his sweat-soaked jacket and collapsed in the shallow water.

He was hot and hungry and tired, and wishing he'd stayed to face Victor Mayberry's anger. Better to be whipped than carry the cross of Mary for the rest of his life, he said.

Taking up her violin, she stumbled away from the creek. A faint trail led her to the tiny settlement on the hill known as Tumblebee, and to the McLean hut where the village women were performing the rites of rain.

It was Ma who threw the ancient bones, covering the scatter with a mixture of shattered creek stones, winter flower and spring water. She sang the songs in a language only she understood. She made a slit in the third finger of her left hand to squeeze a drop of blood onto a storm seed, but a chatter of voices broke her concentration. Lifting her head to listen, she did not realise until too late that four extra drops had fallen.

The settlement women regarded her with questioning eyes.

'Tend to your kin,' she told them. 'There's nothing can be done about it at this particular time.'

They joined the settlement men, who were watching Mary walk slowly up the track, moving in time to the sweet sad sound pouring out of her violin. Ma led her to the shelter of a tree then sat at her feet, listening to music that could make an angel weep. It was only after

Mary had grown colder and sadder as dark clouds shielded her from the sun's warmth, as a soft mist reminded her of seventeen years of crying nights, that Ma stood and placed a hand on her shoulder.

'Enough now,' she said, and though Mary wasn't sure if it was enough music or enough tears, she lowered her arms. 'This way,' Ma added, leading her into the McLean hut. Behind them a myriad of rivulets began to gather on the parched ground — a prelude to the wettest summer on record.

Filling a tablecloth with slabs of bread and cheese, one of the women knotted it onto a stick and settled it over Mary's shoulder. Ma dried the violin with a soft white towel and placed it in a hut deserted by an English family.

'Go and feed your man and bring him here,' she said. 'We'll stock your cupboards and put clean sheets on your bed. You can pay us back when he gets a job in the mine.'

'How do you know I have a man?' Mary asked.

'Why else would you be crying?' Ma said, and gave her a nudge to start her through the doorway.

Mary ran down the track berating herself for leaving a morbidly depressed man alone by a creek. Perhaps he had drowned himself, she thought as she ran. Or he might have returned to Melbourne to face her father's anger.

Much to her relief, she found Leslie sitting on the root of an ancient fig and staring at Polly McLean, who lay sprawled out, naked, by the edge of the slow-moving water. He did not look away as Mary joined him.

Yet who could blame him for that, Mary later asked her only daughter. Polly was young at the time, not yet fourteen, but she had the figure of a fully matured woman. And although her eyes were then reddened and swollen, their particular shade of blue was amazing. Her long hair gleamed with golden lights, which made a change from Mary's reddish brown colouring; and just as the rich cream tint to her skin was so different from the pale milk tone of Mary's complexion, so they had opposite natures. Mary had passed beyond her era of sadness and yearning. She felt herself to be blessed with a tranquil nature. By the way Polly thumped the ground and uttered a series of ear-piercing shrieks, it was obvious that she was inclined to frustration.

Mary smiled at Leslie's erection and took off her clothes. 'Eat,' she instructed, and while he made a sandwich of slab bread and cheese, she joined Polly in the water. A few softly spoken words soon cut to the heart of the young woman's discontent.

'I'll never get away from this place,' Polly said. 'I'll marry a miner and be stuck on this mountain forever.'

Mary plaited the long blonde hair into a coil around Polly's head and told a tale of deserts and ravines.

'Will he be able to find me here, this jaguar man?' Polly asked.

'Not a jaguar,' Mary said. She'd never been a fool. 'For you I see a different animal. Young and strong and handsome. Perhaps a bear is more your style.'

'Will he have music?' Polly asked.

'Of course. That's how you'll know him,' was Mary's prediction.

Further predictions were cut off by Iain McLean's young face staring at them through the dripping branches.

The Trelelans moved into the hut deserted by an English family. Just until the rains have gone, they said at first; until Da found Leslie a job at the nearby coalmine. The months drifted into years while Leslie left each morning for the deep darkness of the pit and returned each evening to Mary and the sun. She taught reading and writing to the settlement children by day, played her violin to the adults at night. Her music was usually fast and frantic — songs to dance a jig by. But sometimes during the long hot summers, she played the sad sweet tunes that caused the angels to weep.

# Chapter Nine

'A man without work is a man without respect. And respect is something you need to earn, being stuck with a name like yours,' Da told Sparrow at 5 a.m. a few days after his arrival. Frowning his sons' laughter into silence, he added, 'Get up now and eat. We've got you a job with us.'

Sparrow jumped out of bed and dressed in a hurry. Too excited to eat, he refused the oatmeal porridge laced with butter and brown sugar that Ma had cooked. Gulping a glass of milk instead, he grinned at the catlike sounds the McLean brothers made. He knew they were fooling when they made fun of him. They were his mates. He was one of them now, another Mount Tumblebee worker; and though he had no idea what that work could be, he thought it had to be something fulfilling. Da carried a canary in a lattice cage. Men led by song could only be happy in their labour.

As he followed the McLeans into the narrow, rutted track laughingly called Main Street, he noticed how the kerosene lamps lit up the windows of every hut in the village. Their brightness and warmth were echoed in snatches of laughter and the voices of children. There were no harsh words. No petulant slamming noises or whining cries. He could hear, though faintly, the sound of two voices humming in tune. Staring slowly about him, he filled his lungs with the fresh, cool air and breathed out a sigh of contentment. Expanding his dream of being an Australian, he decided that this village and its inhabitants were where and who he was meant to be. Once they saw how hard he could work, the McLean family would accept him as one of their own. He'd be as close to them as he'd been to Dougal. Ma would become the mother he couldn't remember.

He smiled broadly as she joined them in the street, promising to send Polly with their lunches when the fresh bread had been baked, when the ox tongues — which she'd boiled, curled in tins then pressed down with bricks last night — were ready to be turned out and sliced.

After she'd finished fussing, making sure they were all wearing scarves to keep out the cold, Da and each of her sons kissed her in order, the eldest to the youngest. Seeing Sparrow watching, she pointed to him, curved the pointing finger to a beckon and tapped her cheek.

Conscious of Da's eyes on him, and wary of what Dougal had called pushing his luck, he approached cautiously and gave her a hasty peck on the temple.

'Call that a buss?' she laughed.

One bear hug and a smacking kiss on his forehead later, she whispered, 'You look after my boys now,' as she pushed him away.

Those words, even more than the glory of a kiss that he knew to be genuine in its affection, made his heart sing.

Returning the jocular greetings as most of the village men joined them, the McLean clan and Sparrow set out along a trail through woods lit only by a sickle moon. The canary trilled continuously, and at times the shrillness of its song seemed to reach a pitch that sounded like desperation.

Perhaps it could see or hear something he couldn't, Sparrow thought as he glanced over his shoulder, but he dismissed that idea as nothing more than a whim. So many people were afraid of night, of darkness, of the things that might be searching for them in particular, or for the things that might bump into them by mischance. Things that could come upon you suddenly out of dark and lonely woods. Yet he knew that of all the uncountable kinds of misfortunes, only a small percentage were supernatural. Most calamities were caused by humans. And now, when he listened intently, he could hear the sound of bootsteps coming towards him from his left. More to his right and others behind him.

At the point of yelling a warning to the McLeans, he realised that they had reached a convergence of trails. Here they were joined by groups of miners, thirty or more, all of whom shook his hand or clapped his back. Despite the canary's song becoming louder and shriller, he couldn't stop smiling. Being mate to the McLeans meant entry into this circle.

Yet his smile began to fade as dawn brightened the sky, allowing him to see the fine black dust under his feet and cloying the air he breathed. He had never seen such a phenomenon as these flying motes of darkness, and he wondered at the McLeans' disregard of it. He could only assume that it was nothing new to them; but still he hung back, waiting for some kind of reaction as they approached a series of towering black mounds.

Rounding these hillocks, he watched his newfound friends enter a hole cut into the side of a hill. The pit of his stomach rumbled a warning when the canary fell silent, fluffed its feathers and shat. The rumble slid down to his bowels as a group of blindfolded ponies were led into a downwards sloping tunnel. It was then he recognised the mounds as coal, and he knew that coal had to be fetched up from the darkest, innermost reaches of the earth where men were never meant to be.

Finally understanding the McLean expectations, he fell back against a tree, slid down in a squat and shat. The last Da saw of Sparrow that day was a not too clean pair of heels heading for Tumblebee Creek.

Heading for the same location, though from the opposite direction, Polly McLean's bare feet dragged furrows through the dirt as she scuffed towards the water. Having just finished flogging thin rugs in an attempt to rid them of the burrs her brothers carried in on their boots, she felt in need of a bath. The day being warm and all the men at the mines, she had decided that the creek would be better than the old tin tub. It would be easier to wash her hair.

While she walked she glanced at caves staring back from a neighbouring hill, remembering a childhood ambition to investigate their secrets. She'd never found the courage, and besides, Polly had her own dark places. They hid crevices in which she could disappear forever. Her only identity was that of daughter and sister to the McLeans. To find another she must follow the precedence set by a sister and one of her brothers. Yet the sister had vanished into a crevice known as Sydney. Dougal had exchanged the black hole of a mine for the darkness of an addiction. There was no escape from Mount Tumblebee or the McLeans. She would marry a miner and be part of them forever.

Until Polly's fourteenth birthday, dreams were nothing more than flickering images which dissolved the following morning. She had never read a book, or listened to the myths and legends Ma had recounted to the unnameable sister. Polly's knowledge of the intangible was as limited as her vocabulary. There were no words to label the yearning which tormented her nights and troubled her waking hours. If she tried to explain, Ma accused her of being too big for her boots and too fond of looking in a mirror. Yet she knew there had to be something more than life on the mount, even if she hadn't the ability to imagine what that something more might be.

Then Mary Trelelan plaited Polly's hair into a halo and told a tale of deserts and ravines. 'Someone young and strong and handsome. A bear-like man,' she'd said. 'You will know him by the music.'

Mary had been so sure. She'd spoken such perfect English that Polly was forced to believe her. Yet years later, all she could see at Mount Tumblebee were miners and McLeans. What was the point of washing her hair if all she had to look forward to were years of drudgery?

Frustrated with her life and the world in general, Polly turned to make her way back to the settlement. It was then Sparrow's plaintive mumble lifted to a scream. In the only way he knew, he cried out against the unfairness of life, and she recognised the feeling. Listening to a voice containing the essence of grief, she felt only joy. The words were of a speech she'd never heard before, yet their difference served to heighten her elation.

Pushing through scrub to the creek, she saw a smooth-skinned youth with a honey tint to his skin, so unlike the blotched paleness of the McLeans. He no longer wore the oversized moleskin trousers, or the grey flannel shirt that lent bloat to a lean, well-muscled body. She allowed herself to be dazzled by his youth and good looks — and by the jewels spilling out of the pouch that lay forgotten near his hand. Clothed in nothing but the sun's warmth, this man she had thought of as alien and comical became the realisation of a dream.

Shrugging out of her dress, she entered the water and led him to a grassy slope beneath the ancient fig. He followed meekly enough, but when she tried to kiss his lips, he held her away. To Achmed Yusef Alemedine, sex was something to be tolerated without complaint or the consequences could be painful. Any thought that it might be a pleasurable experience had long since vanished, and he saw no reason to gratify what he thought of as a whim. After all, what could this female do to punish him?

'I am a free man now. An Australian,' he told her.

Not understanding a word he said, she looked into his eyes and smiled agreement while her hands inspected his body.

'There's no need to be afraid of Da or my brothers. I won't tell them a thing,' she promised while she rubbed and stroked. These actions seemed to arouse her more than him, but she persisted. 'And I won't tell them about your fortune. They'd be sure to make you pay too much for your keep. Scotsmen are known to be misers.'

Sparrow heard what he deemed to be a threat and was instantly on the defensive. 'I have told Ma about my jewels. She showed no interest,' he answered quickly.

Polly understood just one word. 'Ma is my mother. Of course I won't tell her that we made love,' she whispered.

Love was another thing altogether. Love was something he could barely remember. That word, and the hand squeezing his genitals, produced the effect she was after.

Some time later his lament began again when she noticed his wet clothes hanging on a branch, and his boots covered with a film of black grit. Although Polly had never been particularly sensitive to other people's problems, it could not have been difficult for her to see what troubled him. It must have pleased her to realise that she'd finally found a man who would never be a miner.

'Not to worry,' she said. 'Ma promised Dougal to look after you. She'll find something that you can just naturally do.'

And so Sparrow became odd job man to the community on the mount. He cleaned shoes, ran messages, jogged to the hotel for a billy of beer then back without spilling a drop. He bathed and played with the children. He tended fires, washed clothes and cooked meals, yet nobody laughed at the little bloke performing tasks that were meant for women. Through Dougal, Sparrow was Ma's responsibility. That made him a friend of the McLeans, and everyone knew their reputation. Those who treated a friend of theirs with disrespect had to leave town in a hurry, if they didn't want to be thumped by five hearty Scotsmen.

It was these same Scotsmen who decided to change Achmed's name once more, insisting that Dougal's mate should have a worthy title.

'No respectable man wants to be likened to a handful of feathers', and 'You canna be a proper man without a fitting name', they said.

Even suspecting that they'd choose something mischievous didn't prevent Achmed from agreeing. These men had been miners all their lives. His refusal to join them must have been seen as an insult. Even if he had possessed the ability to explain his horror at the mere thought of descending into those tunnels of darkness, they wouldn't have had the ability to understand. Besides, he'd grown accustomed to being given nonsensical titles by those too inattentive to listen to his real one. And he truly believed that anything would be better than Basha or Sparrow. A basher he wasn't and never would be, and what could more ridiculous than giving someone with an aversion to birds the title of Sparrow? He had no knowledge then of how warped their sense of humour could be.

The surname was offered by the Irish family — a reward for his constant care of their eleven children, they said; and there was no way he could refuse it without hurting their feelings. But he was foolish enough to say he would have liked something to show his connection to Dougal.

'Something Scottish,' Da agreed. 'Something to celebrate the way you helped my son.'

'A hero's name,' the brothers added, looking sideways at each other. None of them had ever believed Dougal's letter.

And so, much to the glee of the Mount Tumblebee miners, Achmed Yusef Alemedine, with his honey-coloured skin, black curly hair and the darkest of brown eyes (Egyptian looks, Mrs Nell had called them,) was awarded the proud Scottish name of Robert Bruce, and the Irish title of McTavish.

'A name fit for a king,' Da told him; though from that day on, everyone called him Mack.

Polly resolved to ward off their laughter with marriage, although none of the miners who had sought her hand could see a reason for her decision. The newcomer was too fine-featured to be considered good looking, they said. His physique would never be called impressive. He had no conversation. He couldn't hold down a proper job. The work he did was usually left to women. He was more to be pitied than laughed at, and Polly had never been moved by pity before. Nor was she likely to be hypnotised by liquid brown eyes, as some of her friends insisted. Polly rarely looked into anyone's face, except her own in the bedroom mirror.

The Welshman believed a soaring tenor voice must be the fascination. Tony suggested the little man's way with children. The more practical Ma asserted that his sizable bag of precious stones was certainly in his favour. The McLeans were too polite to ask how he had come by the treasure, or how Polly might know of its existence.

'He knelt at my side and held out a diamond ring,' she confessed to Mary. 'I saw love in his eyes, and a way out of Mount Tumblebee. I'm tired of waiting for a bear-like man, and I will not marry a miner.'

'Perhaps he merely sought information as to where he could sell the ring,' Mary suggested quietly.

Her comment was not intended to offend. It was just a simple point of view. Mary concerned for Polly's welfare.

The two women had been friends since one rescued the other from drowning on Polly's fourteenth birthday. Who had saved whom had never been clear, nor did anyone believe that one or both had been naked at the time. Polly's brothers would have thumped anyone who accused her of improper conduct, and Mary's mother was sister to *the* Jack Blake, sergeant of police at Newcastle who was known far and wide as an honest cop, so how could his niece be anything but a superior person? She played the violin like an angel, and everyone knew that violinists would never show an ankle beyond their bedrooms. Besides, Mary was married to Leslie Amadeus Trelelan, who was, so he said, an exceptional pianist and poet. Granted he was poor, but he was also a lay preacher. Lay preachers were supposed to be poor. It would be presumptuous of them to consider being otherwise. Those who insinuated a less than spiritual relationship between Mary and her Scottish friend were laughed to scorn. Or thumped by five hearty Scotsmen.

This, Mary felt, could be the reason for Polly's decision to marry Robert Bruce McTavish. A woman's role in life was cooking, sewing, scrubbing and caring for her menfolk. Making herself meek so they could be strong. Emphasising their power by cringing under an upraised hand. Bolstering their egos with fluttering eyes and a swooning body. With six men in the house, Polly's life was filled to overflowing with household tasks and the endless chores of cringing, bolstering, fluttering and swooning (though her greatest delight was admiring herself in a mirror).

Whatever her reasons, Polly agreed to marry the man with the soaring voice, the bag of precious jewels and the incongruous name. The wedding took place a few days later.

# Chapter Ten

Somewhere around this time Ma woke in the middle of the night to the sound of strange music. Wrapping herself in Da's old winter coat, she tracked the noise to the banks of Tumblebee Creek. There she found Mary attempting to create a tune on her violin. The sound was harsh and atonal.

'I'm trying to make a child,' was the explanation.

'Then you've got a lot to learn,' Ma told her. 'The best way to do that is at home in bed with your man.'

The eldest of twelve, and the first of her brood born nine months after marriage, Ma had no memory of a time without children. It seemed she had always known tiny fingers tugging at her clothes. Her nose clogged with baby smells, her ears ringing with their demands, her eyes reflecting smooth skin and downy hair — these were the underpinnings of her life. She could barely remember a time when her hands weren't naturally curved to fit those tiny bodies. Even now, with Iain long gone from her womb, she still had the feel and shape of childbearing. The village children would cling to her skirts whenever she allowed it.

She searched Mary's eyes, trying to imagine a world without those things. The first images were of quiet, of peace, of time to be herself. Yet when she tried to imagine that self, she could not give it form or substance.

Mary looked inside Ma, breathing her smells, seeing and hearing the older woman's nature. She was pleased for her. She liked her shape and makeup. But she didn't wish it for herself.

'Are you happy?' Ma asked, curious now.

'I was,' Mary said, 'until Leslie said a man is not a man without a son, and a woman can't be truly his until she gives him one.'

Mary had recognised the ridiculous saying as belonging to Da, but she knew it pierced Leslie's ego. She did not believe that he wanted a child, yet when her monthly cycle remained uninterrupted, he grew listless and depressed. He began to hint that they should go back to Melbourne. 'To write poems that people will want to listen to,' he'd said. 'It seems we can't be creative here.'

He then left to spend a week in Newcastle to inquire about train fares and, perhaps, send a message to her mother. She recognised this as his way of teaching her a lesson.

'Do you think I've left it too late?' Mary asked Ma. 'Do you think I could be barren?'

'Sit before me,' Ma instructed. 'Squat on your haunches, like so. Don't take your eyes off the moon.'

Mary stared up at the moon and breathed deeply, filling herself with its light. The older woman crouched on the ground and placed an ear to her navel, listening intently.

'You're fertile all right,' she said at last.

As she turned to leave, her top lip lifted slightly.

'It's that Leslie Amadeus,' she called back over a shoulder.

Mary continued to play the harsh, atonal music until she was joined by the man who lived in a humpy under a tree — the German who never spoke at all. A big man with a thick body and an oblong face, she considered him to be more handsome than her husband, even if he did not have Leslie's mane of almost golden hair. His was mouse-coloured and cropped very short. His hands were small and neat, his skin smooth and white. The mouth organ he held to his lips accented their width and fullness.

He played a tune she had never heard before — soft and timid and shyly inviting. Mary couldn't help but join in. She copied his gentle breaths with soft fingertip touches, alternating follow and lead until their minds attuned. Their creativeness became as one. The music grew stronger, the breaths longer and deeper. His touches became thrusts, with broad sweeps of sound: provocative one moment, demanding the next. She matched the play of his mouth and those delicate hands, and made a child on her violin. The appearance of one, the intelligence of the other — in this way she combined the characteristics of the German and her jaguar man.

Yet despite Leslie's desire for a male child, Mary did not care to compare penile peculiarities, so she did not try build one. It was, I believe, an unfortunate omission. Leslie might have been more concerned for the wellbeing of a son.

# Chapter Eleven

On the day of her return home from a week's honeymoon in the mining village of Weston, Polly insisted that the time had come to leave Mount Tumblebee. Having no idea where she wanted to live, or even where there was to go, she stuck a pin in the map of New South Wales, hoping it would find a place where the swell of her stomach wouldn't be ticked off on counting fingers. Perhaps too far for a suspicious mother to visit. She jabbed three times, yet each jab kept her within a one hundred and eighty mile radius. It was as if the steel of Newcastle attracted the pin like a magnet.

Finally settling on a dairy and fishing community fifty miles south of Sydney, she conjured up a romantic picture of herself as a milkmaid. Or perhaps she'd just bask in the sun while her new husband milked or fished.

Upon making further inquiries, she discovered that the town she selected also contained brick and coke industries, besides the longer established enterprises of timber cutting and coalmining. There were telephones, an ambulance service, schools and technical education, a hospital, horseracing, and electricity lighting the main street at night.

'A perfect place to begin a new life,' she said, for with her would go a foetus later christened Angus.

Polly chose Augustus, but she was foolish enough to send Mack to register the birth. Angus was the misinterpretation of an impatient clerk. Yet Mack liked his son's name. Although it wasn't as popular as Scotty or Jock, he thought it had a cheerful cadence. And even better, at least to him, was the fact that Da had given it his seal of approval. When Polly complained of the name being almost as unsuitable as Mack, he smiled and nodded. Living with a houseful of men and a forceful mother meant that anything Polly said was ignored or shouted down. Her voice had been defeated to a mumble. Her new husband couldn't understand more than a few words she spoke. She couldn't pick out more than a smatter of his conversation. Yet they talked to each other for hours on end, airing their grievances and detailing any problems that cropped up. It was the saying, not the hearing, that mattered.

At this point Mack congratulated himself for marrying a McLean, thus endowing his son with a ready-made family tree: a host of aunts, uncles and cousins to give him roots, and branches for him to lean on. Yet Da died of coal-dusted lungs a few years after the wedding. His eldest son followed less than three years later. Four more died in a mining disaster that same year. Dougal and Iain were the only sons who managed to live beyond their forties. You will hear more of these two later.

After moving into a large hotel in the growing township, Polly roamed the area in a smart little sulky pulled by a small bay mare. Aiming to find a suitable position for their home, she soon discovered an ideal location not far from a lake which was twin to the Sea of Galilee. At least, it was much like the pictures in her Bible — or so she later insisted when asked why she hadn't chosen a more socially acceptable site closer to town. After all, claiming religion as a reason was less humbling than admitting to being swayed by superstition, as had happened on the first day she'd allowed Mack to accompany her on the search.

'A sign! A sign!' he'd shouted, pointing to a large stand of native black wattle.

To him, the masses of yellow flowers appeared as the pot of gold at the end of a rainbow. He hadn't the ability to convey this thought, but his excitement and the decisiveness of his tone convinced her. Of course the stand would have to be cut down in order to build a house, but this fact didn't disturb him too much. Surely living on top of the spot where the pot had appeared would bring nothing but good luck; and naming the track running past his front gate Blackwattle Road was an epitaph that would make sure those trees would never be forgotten.

Whatever the reason — superstition or religion — it was here Polly decided to settle down, and of course she wanted her best friend to settle with her. She insisted that Mack buy ten half-acre blocks. Two for them to build on, seven for an investment and one for the Trelelans.

Leslie did not need to be persuaded. The coal mine was just another job keeping him away from poetry and preaching, he said. The Mount Tumblebee families had found his sermons boring.

'Miners could never possess enough intelligence to comprehend the art of preaching,' he insisted. 'If these people had any brains at all, they'd be living closer to ocean breezes. We'll take God and music to the dairy farmers and fishermen.'

As it happened, he found his god already there in the form of a dozen churches, but the townspeople were happy to pay for their children to learn piano and violin.

These tuition fees helped Leslie to borrow the amount of money he needed to build the home he had always wanted. It was much smaller than the Mayberry mansion, but erected on more classical lines than the McTavish house. Due more to Mayberry taste than a bid to outdo their neighbours, of course.

Mary did have money of her own, though she had to wait for her mother to die before a bequest from a forgiving Constance Mayberry came into her hands. When the sad event occurred a half-year after the move, Leslie and Mary added another two rooms to the side of their home, another four rooms above. The extra space allowed them to display antique furnishings, wall drapes, crystal, fine china, paintings, a priceless silver service and three trunks of books. They built a nursery at back of the house, for Mary also brought a foetus with her. This one was christened Liona Mayberry at birth. Trelelan was somehow omitted at the time. Perhaps forgotten in all the excitement.

The oversight was corrected in November of 1917, at the same time my parents attended a wedding service which Mary said was held to renew their vows. She planned it after receiving a letter from Ma McLean, which happened to bear information about the German who did not speak at all. Led by a soldier at home on leave, the local Mount Tumblebee men had chased him into the woodlands. Ma waited for them to sober up before sending her sons to bring the German back. They searched for a week without any luck. He was never seen again. She distributed his belongings among the settlement families — except for the mouth organ. Ma thought Mary would like to have that, what with her being so musically minded.

# Chapter Twelve

I was born next door to Angus McTavish at 7 Blackwattle Road in April of 1913. At 6 p.m. precisely, when the hands of the clock were aligned but as far apart as they could be, we burst forth. No slaps were needed. We screamed the moment our heads were free. Our mothers claimed this to be due to premature births, and perhaps that was true. Perhaps we were not yet ready to begin our lives, although I'm inclined to believe we had a premonition of how those lives would be. Whatever our reasons, all similarity ended a few minutes later. Only one midwife lived in the vicinity of those two houses. She naturally attended my mother. After the cutting of the cord, I was whisked away to my room. The midwife cleaned and swaddled me while Father consoled my mother for her terrible ordeal. Polly McTavish had only her husband in attendance. He, not knowing any better, kissed his squirming son then stopped the screams with a mother's nipple.

A few days after my birth, Leslie Amadeus declared that he couldn't bear the sight of my mother breastfeeding me. A heathen practice, he called it, and probably unhygienic.

From that moment on I was fed cow's milk from a bottle that could be propped up on a pillow. This saved my mother the bother of remaining with me while I drank, and it began the custom of my eating alone. For the rest of the days that I lived with my parents, my mother served their meals and mine at separate times. The reason for this (my father said) was because they liked to eat late, which wasn't appropriate for a child. I think it became a habit; though later, from about my tenth year on, I usually had my evening meal next door with Angus.

In our early years, he and I did the usual baby things at around the same time. Apart from the normal squabbles of self-willed children, we played together happily enough. It was on our fourth birthday that he began pulling my hair if I entered his yard, and pelting me with whatever came to hand when I learned to keep my distance. He had realised that Loby, as he called me, was his father's version of my correct title. That was around the time his mother began pointing out the unsuitability of his name while praising the prettiness of mine.

'Liona Mayberry does have a certain lilt to it,' my mother had agreed. 'I think it will suit my daughter well. I'm sure she'll be a musical person.'

Yet I never did learn to perform or create. My voice was tuneless, my hands all thumbs when I tried to play the piano or violin. I grew to love all forms of music, but I was more of a scholar than anything else.

Angus was a list maker, but only of those things (mostly people) that really got up his nose. He spent hours counting the things that exasperated him, and the list always began with his name. In later years he lost his loathing of the title and drew it around him like a cactus skin. That time came too late to unwarp him.

His attitude changed again on the day we entered kindergarten. He glared when I introduced myself as Liona and threw punches at anyone who asked for his name. I stepped into the breach and launched him into school life as Fred. From that moment on we were inseparable — before and after classes of course. It wasn't the done thing for girls and boys to mix at school, which is probably the main reason why I later became known as an intellectual. When I couldn't be with Angus, I studied.

But I'm getting ahead of my story.

# Chapter Thirteen

The Trelelans made a good living teaching music. They made a better one when a local realtor offered Leslie employment. He found, to his pleasure and financial advancement, that selling real estate was something else in which he excelled.

Mack, on the other hand, couldn't find the kind of work that Polly had envisioned. When he visited a dairy farm in his quest for a job, the smell of his fear of animals drifted across the paddocks, heralding his arrival. The beckoning odour brought the working dogs out from under the homestead verandas. They followed the scent to its owner, bellies low to the ground and white foam gathering around their grins. Mack saw them coming and ran, but they were masters of the hunting and sorting game. His only talent lay in the sweetness and strength of his voice, which he used to good purpose as he screamed his way back to the gate. He then limped home to Polly with the backside missing from his trousers and his pride more tattered than his shirt.

He decided to try the fishing fleet, not realising until too late that memories would return to haunt him. Amazed by the way he could retch for hours without seeming to pause for breath, the fishermen welcomed him onto their boats. He gave them something to gossip about when the weather was bad and fish were scarce. But the only wage he received was smiles and claps on the back, until he was bruised by their blows and the pity in their eyes.

Yet a man without work was a man without respect. People would laugh and point and nudge — even more so than when they heard his mismatched name. Mack had to gain his neighbours' esteem and retain Polly's pride in her choice of husband. A dairy hand, a fisherman, neither of those would do it. What he needed was employment a little more elite. Everyone admired a successful businessman, that he knew, and he also knew how to look the part. Within a week he had acquired a dapper brown suit, a hat with a jaunty yellow feather, a sober brown umbrella and highly polished shoes to match an imported leather briefcase.

At first a clerk, then an accountant, within two years he became known as the manager of an old and prestigious firm. He was respected by the village people, adored by his son and envied by Leslie (or so Mary said, though her husband never admitted to that emotion).

Polly took him to the railway station in her smart little sulky. Evenings, she trotted him home from the five-thirteen. He tipped his hat to Mary, raised the umbrella to Leslie, greeted his loving son with a hug, then marched inside to cook dinner. On weekends he relaxed by working in the vegetable rows which stretched across the lower half of the McTavish yard. The front garden was massed with native shrubs.

The hours after dinner, far into the night, he filled with the chores of cleaning, sewing and caring for his family. Mack had made this promise when he married Polly. Or so she said, and he would never argue. If he did not cook, clean, sew and care, his house would resemble a pigsty. His family would starve and go about naked. His son and the girl next door would never know adult attention. The Trelelans were too occupied with each other and music to bother with children. Polly was far too busy working for charities with the other ladies in town, and watching others watching her.

This cooking, sewing, etc was no great sacrifice for Angus's father. Cleaning was the greatest joy of his life, next to his wife and son and gardens. He found pleasure in seeing Polly and Angus a dozen times in one room, staring back at him from furniture polished to a reflective shine. His soaring tenor voice echoed through the house while he sewed gowns and shirts; and sometimes a dress for the girl next door, who was more at home in his house than she'd ever be in her own. Yet even with all the chores he was bound to do, he still found time for the telling of his stories. Having listened to Mack's mangled English since the day we were born, we had no trouble understanding him. In fact what others regarded as garble became our second language. It was perfect for sharing secrets.

When we were small, there was much pushing and shoving as Angus and I fought for a place on his lap. The loser's howls would then have us all on the lawn or the floor where everyone could be equal. This was a set tradition, a game we played (and how he loved it!) to show how much we adored him. Later, about age five and upwards, we'd sit at his feet with bowls of toffee or popcorn propped on our knees. His hands would stroke our hair or rest quietly on our heads while he dreamed aloud of days gone by. These were always tales of his two male mates, his circle of female friends; of happy times at Mrs Nell's residence for men and women of refinement.

Not that he ever regretted leaving, or would consider going back, he'd say. Not without Angus and darling Polly.

'And Loby too,' he'd always add, planting a gentle kiss on my forehead. 'We wouldn't be a family without our Loby.'

He cherished his son and me, and he received unquestioning love in return. He placed his wife on a pedestal and worshipped at her feet.

'She is fragile and beautiful, like priceless china,' he said when Angus asked why his mother differed from other mothers. 'We can but love her and keep her as she is. As we would preserve a painting by Rembrandt, or a Mozart symphony.'

Polly did not understand his words, but she heard the tone of praise. Neither Angus nor Mack realised her frustration. She had no desire to spend her nights alone on a pedestal, or be preserved like a jar of peaches. She wanted to play rough-house with her son, as she had with her brothers. She wanted to be stroked and touched by her husband. Her body craved heat and thrust and multiple orgasms.

She began to dream of those caves in the hills back home. She began to wish she had explored a little before settling down with Mack. After all, she'd only married him out of pity because her family altered his name. If not for them, she wouldn't be feeling this way. If it wasn't for him, her body wouldn't be filled with cravings. At least, these were the things she told herself, and her friend next door, when she began to watch the ripple of muscles on the hairy, bear-like back of our sanitary man.

For those ignorant of that particular expression and employment, I refer to the pre-sewerage days, more commonly known as the time of the backyard dunny. Twice weekly the truck would arrive to remove what my mother termed nightsoil containers, but what most people referred to as shit cans. The men manning these trucks were normally young and strong, and probably had no great sense of smell. An easygoing attitude would be needed to shrug off the constant insults — usually phrased in badly poetic terms — aimed at their way of earning a living. No doubt it was honest work, but the cruelty of children is a time-honoured cliché. Those like Angus, with nothing better to do, would follow the men chanting unprintable rhymes until the truck was out of sight. Or, as in Angus's case, until his mother ordered him into the house then lingered to apologise for his behaviour.

Polly had always liked to be looked at. She took a special delight in the way this man's eyes undressed her, as did, eventually, his hands. An event which came to pass during the winter of 1928, when Madam Basha's last jewel had been turned to cash, when most of Mack's land had been sold to the Trelelans.

Mrs Anthony Rees had visited a Sydney store to buy linen for her second daughter. Pausing on the way home to admire a soaring tenor voice, she was horrified to recognise its owner. Mr Robert Bruce McTavish, who had supposedly become head of the accountancy firm of McTavish Incorporated, was in reality an invention of the man who sang for a few pennies tossed into a hat with a jaunty feather.

A day later Mrs Anthony Rees suggested that Polly resign from two charity committees and hand over the moneys collected for a third. Former lady friends sent children to turn her away from their doors. Invitations to various luncheons were withdrawn. At the end of the week she discovered a box of groceries on the doorstep. An accompanying note from Mrs Rees asked to be put on Polly's list if she decided to take up cleaning houses.

The mere thought of becoming a drudge again was all the excuse Polly needed. Not having enough courage to say goodbye, she waited until Mack was away from the house, then she packed a bag and ran to the bear-like man. His parents owned a cafe in Dubbo and he'd promised to wait for her there.

# Chapter Fourteen

To most people, mention of the Great Depression brings back images of rich-men-turned-poor jumping out of windows, of families thrown out of their houses for nonpayment of rent and of politicians promising a quick end to it all. They think of villages of tar-paper shacks springing up around the outskirts of town. They remember people wrapped in newspapers sleeping on beaches, women waiting patiently in handout queues, and an endless parade of men roaming the land in search of work. The lucky ones, those whose memories retain only the brighter side of life, talk of bonds forged by troubles shared. They remember the helping hands of families no better off than themselves, and the wry jokes of a vast working class who had become accustomed to hope being their only salvation.

To me, any mention of that time brings back the memory of what Polly McTavish nee McLean did to her son and husband.

Angus followed her to the railway station, begging her to stay, talking, shouting, screaming at her until his voice faded to a whisper. He danced around her, clutched at her skirt, even tried to trip her up when she wouldn't slow down. As she boarded the train, still refusing to listen or even look at him, he sank to his knees, dropped his head back and uttered one loud howl that seemed to go on forever.

I had tagged along behind them, but I stayed back, afraid to go close. I believed his pain would turn to anger at any moment, and when angry, Angus was liable to lash out at anything or anyone. It wasn't until he fell forward, on hands and knees, and retched again and again until it seemed as if his ribs would crack, that I tried to comfort him. I'm not sure what I said — probably just a string of senseless soothing noises. But whatever it was, it seemed to help. He allowed me to drag him to his feet, and he leaned on me for most of the way as we staggered home. There by his gate, to my amazement, he hugged me so tight I could scarcely breathe. Until that moment, Angus had never been one for touching.

'You won't tell anyone. About me back there,' he whispered.

'As if I would,' I whispered back.

'I hate her,' he said.

I nodded.

'Just you and me. We'll be his family now,' Angus said fiercely.

Apart from school, I'd always spent most of my time at the McTavish house. My parents' time was filled with working, teaching music and each other. They rarely had any left over for me. Angus knew that. He turned away, not bothering to wait for a promise, and we went inside to break the news to Mack.

At first he worked all day in the garden and stood by the gate at night, watching for Polly's return. Despite my optimism and Angus's coaxing, by the end of the month hope had disappeared with her. Mack's horror of ridicule became a bird of prey swooping over his head like a giant nesting magpie.

'But there are no vultures in Australia, and no eagles have been sighted anywhere near our lake for years,' Angus told him.

'Open your eyes,' Mack said as he tiptoed around the house, locking every door and window. 'It is here. It has found me. Watch. Wait.'

Angus followed him from room to room, opening the doors and windows. Watching and waiting was never in Angus's nature. At the front veranda he pointed to the working birds going about their everyday business.

'Sparrows, willy-wagtails, finches,' he said. 'Cuckoo-shrikes, rosellas, starlings and honeyeaters. Nothing bigger than a seagull.'

Mack saw women gossiping at their gates, the smirks of men, the pointing fingers of children. He retreated to his bedroom and pulled down the blinds.

'If there was a bird, even one as big as you say, it couldn't open doors,' Angus shouted as his father shoved a chair underneath the handle.

That night, when Mack woke to find the bird clawing at the covers of his bed, he remembered his father's words.

'Run!' he screamed at Angus. 'Go for your life while I keep it here.'

Angus refused to run, and Mack decided that the only way to keep his family safe was to never open his eyes again. If he would not see the bird, then surely it could not see him. Yet the very next day he swore it hovered overhead as his son led him along the street to beg for credit at Murphy's store. He might be blind but he wasn't deaf, he said. Couldn't they hear its shrieks of triumph? He'd always known it would never forget the boy locked within its eyes.

Angus stayed to beat up the Murphy twins while Mack ran for home, holding a hand against the picket fences so he wouldn't need to see the way. He blamed the bird for his torn and bleeding fingers. He swore it had eaten the food when he found the pantry empty. That night he screamed in pain as its talons clawed at his chest, but he grew sullen and quiet when my parents arrived with a doctor.

'We're here to help,' my mother told him. 'You have no money, so you need your health to find work to support your son.'

Mack opened his eyes and squinted at her. 'And you need to leave me alone,' he mumbled.

Mother looked at me and shrugged to show she had no idea what he was saying.

'Tell her to go and take that strange man with her,' he said to Angus.

The doctor, an abrupt man, a man accustomed to being treated like a royal visitor by his patients, slammed his black doctor's bag down on the kitchen table.

'Enough nonsense,' he said, waving his stethoscope in Mack's face. 'I've been told there are chest pains. I need to listen.'

'Then listen to this,' Mack said, showing his agitation by jerking up and down in his chair as if he needed the toilet. 'I will take that thing and shove it up your nostrils if you do not leave my house.'

Angus snorted laughter. But to give him his due, he didn't interpret his father's words. However, Mack's tone was enough to cause umbrage. The doctor snatched up his bag and left without another word.

'My dear friend, you really should see a doctor about those pains in your chest,' my mother began.

Mack cut her off by turning his back and moving his chair to face a corner.

'The man's lost his senses, that's obvious. What he needs is a psychiatrist,' Leslie said bluntly. 'I will arrange it.'

'You will arrange nothing,' Mack told the walls, speaking slowly and pronouncing each word as clearly as he could. 'I will not be ordered around by the offspring of convicts. I am a free man. An Australian.'

'You are an illegal immigrant and can be deported at any time,' my father snarled.

These words had an effect that none of us would have envisioned. Mack stood, turned, lifted his chair and, uttering a cry of rage, flung it with all his might, aiming for Leslie's head. A connection would have meant murder, but luckily for them both, my father had taken a step forward as he spoke. His ankle turned and he staggered sideways. The chair missed him by centimetres. Before Mack could grab it up for another try, Angus grappled his father around the waist and swung him to the floor.

While all this was happening, my mother and I stood and stared, unable to believe what we were seeing. There was no time to utter a protest, at either the cruelty of the words or the viciousness of the action. Mack had never shown signs of a temper before. He'd never even raised his voice. Now he stared at Leslie Amadeus — who was also spread-eagled on the floor — with an expression that showed he meant further violence the moment Angus allowed him to stand. And that he was enjoying every second.

'Come, Leslie,' my mother finally said, dragging him to his feet. 'We will not stay where we have no welcome. And,' she added while helping him to the doorway, 'it's just as well that my friend Polly escaped before he did violence to her.'

'Him do violence to her?' I asked.

Surely my mother knew she had that the wrong way around.

'As he has just done violence here,' she stated coldly.

'My father shouldn't have said the things he did,' I answered defiantly.

The look she shafted at me was pure ice. I shivered at its intensity. She opened her mouth and I shivered again. I knew that whatever she was about to say would destroy me. But before she had a chance to speak, Leslie Amadeus cut in.

'Go home, Liona,' he said.

I stood there staring from him to her for what seemed like minutes, but was probably seconds. His words had paralysed me. What precisely was home? Where was home? These people, my parents, were almost strangers to me. At that exact moment I wanted them to love me above all else, as I never wanted anything so much in the whole of my lifetime. But my mother's attention was on my father, and her face held an expression that I would have given my life to have directed at me. He had glanced at me as he spoke, but they were joined again now. I was excluded, as I always had been, and right then I had the strangest feeling of something spilling inside of me. Perhaps it was the death of expectation.

'You heard your father,' Mother said, still looking at him. 'Go home. Now.'

'I am home,' I told her with all the haughtiness I could muster. Which wasn't much. I was barely fifteen at the time, and fifteen-year-old girls have little chance to practise haughtiness. Submission perhaps. But not this time. I turned away from her and squatted beside Mack, meaning to help Angus keep him under control. But the look of contempt she darted back at him as she left defeated Mack as no action could. He began to cry, harsh, deep sobs that I thought, or hoped, might be a catharsis and the start of his resurgence to the Mack of old. But the sobs became wails, then a drizzle of tears lasting, on and off, for days.

I did try to apologise for my parents. Neither he nor Angus would listen. They wanted nothing more to do with those so-called friends. Mack even accused them of helping Polly to leave him.

'Leslie Amadeus was always jealous of my accountancy firm,' he said.

I did not point out that his firm had never existed — I was far too busy constantly repeating that same phrase concerning his bird.

His next step into malnutrition and madness was the neglect of his once precious gardens. Stubbornly refusing to leave the house for any reason, he stood by the kitchen window day after day, watching his yard turn into a jungle of onion weed and prickly lantana. During this time, Angus delivered bread, milk and newspapers before and after school. Any spare time was spent thumping all those under the age of twenty who dared to laugh at his father.

By then Mack had forgiven my parents. At least, I think he'd forgotten what had happened. And being good Christians, they were bound to return the favour, though my mother's Christian duty didn't extend to me. I had sided with Mack against Leslie Amadeus, and although he showed his usual indifference towards anything pertaining to me, she would not pardon my sin. Reproachful looks and 'Honour thy father and thy mother,' was her only communication to me for many months. I retaliated by spending more of my time next door. She didn't seem to notice.

After a year or so had passed, Angus and I cleaned up the garden. And while he grew and harvested vegetables which he sold from a barrow beside the highway, Mack huddled in a chair and talked to the walls. His words were mostly incomprehensible. If asked to repeat or explain, he claimed he was inventing a new language. It would, he said, earn him a fortune one of these days. Then he'd return to his homeland a rich man. But just for a visit of course. Just to show his son that being different was only a matter of opinion.

Perhaps it was this mention of his homeland that started him reading the journal he'd begun as a ten-year-old slave of a camel driver. He read it and reread it, and with each reading his nightmares grew longer and darker. Only by pacing the floor for most of the night could he keep them and his ever-present bird at bay. He had stopped cooking, cleaning and sewing some time ago. Now he had to be forced to eat and bathe. He vowed that his food was drugged, and he would only enter the shower if fully clothed. For a reason neither Angus nor I could fathom, he seemed to delight in his body odour and gauntness. Even more mystifying was his satisfaction on the morning his once glorious voice couldn't be forced to rise above a whisper. To me, that was the hour Mack actually died.

Three years from the day she left, Polly returned. Her skin was leathered brown. Her hands were callused and hard. Her fingernails had been bitten to the quick. Her dress had split at the seams and her shoes were paper-thin at the heels. The once carefully coiled blonde hair was tied back with a piece of string. Her face rested on three chins.

Mary said that Polly's beauty was ruined along with her life. Leslie insisted that her punishment was well deserved. I was too young to be asked for an opinion, yet being naturally inquisitive, I'd formed a habit of looking beyond the surface. Even then, as young as I was, I saw a glow in Polly's eyes that had never been there before. I heard the smile in a voice that had once held a perpetual whine.

'I'm not back for good, so don't worry about that,' Polly said cheerfully, turning her face from the drowning in Mack's eyes. She wanted no money. She knew there was none. Nor the rest of her clothes. 'They wouldn't fit anyway,' she said with that chuckle in her tone.

She desired nothing for herself, but Nick wished for a child and his parents would never accept a baby born out of wedlock. Nick, being the only son, would inherit the cafe in Dubbo one of these days. He naturally wanted his bloodline to continue. Polly wanted many sons.

'Like Ma', she explained. 'Ma had her last baby at the age of forty-five, so it's not too late to begin.'

'You have a son,' Mack pointed out in a painfully husky voice.

Polly tousled Angus's curls. 'This one was always yours,' she said.

Angus did not duck his head or turn away. If he quivered, nobody knew it but him.

'So what do you think? Can I have a divorce?' she asked.

'Go, before the bird sees you here,' Mack whispered. 'Go and I'll keep it with me.'

Polly had, of course, heard of Mack's bird. She'd always believed it to be some kind of mental delusion — a fear, a phobia like all the others he had. Yet now she could plainly see it reflected in his eyes. She felt its presence. Its smell was all around him. No doubt she sensed his death was near and that would make any form of legal separation unnecessary. Not once did she try to banish the apparition with true facts and analysis, or even attempt to comfort him. Which, perhaps, was only sensible — her instinct for self-preservation. Watching his every move as she backed through the door, she kicked off her sole-thin shoes and fled to the safety of our dark and lonely railway station. Angus saw her leave, but this time he did not follow.

That night Mack wrote a will leaving the McTavish house to his only child. He designated Leslie Amadeus as the trustee of his estate until Angus came of age. He woke Pastor Greentree in the middle of the night to witness his signature, then he knocked on the door of lawyer Rees until that gentleman confirmed the will's legality. Returning home during the early hours of the morning, he kissed the sleeping Angus and placed the will by his bed.

Some time later, after drinking two bottles of home brew he'd made from a recipe given to him by Carl Rusher all those years ago, Achmed Yusef Alemedine, known progressively as Sparrow, Basha and Robert Bruce McTavish, gave himself to the bird. In so doing, he performed a sacrifice that would guarantee its withdrawal and the safety of his son. Or so he wrote in a scribbled note to his next-door friends, Mary and Leslie Trelelan.

# Chapter Fifteen

I expected Angus's grief to be loud and inconsolable when we discovered Mack dead the following morning. I thought he'd cry and scream and thump his chest when he found the will and he called to me and we ran to that room. Instead, he stopped at the doorway and stared down at the floor. He would not look at his father. He did not flinch when I screamed, or utter a sound as I knelt by the bed and stroked that pale, smooth forehead. I know my pain showed in my face. How could it not show when I felt as though someone had thrust their hands into my chest, breaking every rib bone one by one.

Angus's expression didn't alter. He didn't utter a sound when I pushed open a window and shrieked for my parents. He did not move when they came, when the doctor arrived, when the ambulance took his father's body away. Only when I grabbed his shoulders and shook as hard as I could did he finally speak.

'Why did he have to look so bloody peaceful?' was all he said.

The next day he made a bonfire of all his father's belongings, omitting nothing. He burned clothes, furniture, bed and bedding, even the window curtains. He was determined to get rid of everything that might remind him of their life together. When I pointed out that punching holes in the walls wouldn't drive Mack's image out of his head and heart, he cursed me with every vile word in his vocabulary.

Throwing a few of those words back at him, I left him to his mission.

It was me who rescued the pile of papers, tied with twine, that Achmed Yusef Alemedine had called his journal. I offer no excuse, or even a knowledge of my intentions. I saw the book at the edge of the fire and I snatched it up. A journal is a perfect memento for one with a love of reading. And I knew Angus would regret those hours of fury. He did the following day.

By then I'd become too angry to offer him any sort of comfort, not even senseless soothing noises. I remembered the tales Mack had told of his arrival in Australia. I remembered him telling us of the old men at the charity home. Their patient wait for an end to it all had horrified him. There were others whose lives were far harder than theirs, yet those others continued to fight, he had said. Was he such a hypocrite, then? Did he not know how much he was loved and needed? Did he have no understanding of the hole he would leave in our lives? Or didn't he care? I couldn't find it in my heart to forgive him. Nor could I understand Angus's need to find excuses, for after the funeral he hoed his vegetable rows, then wrapped a change of clothing in a blanket. He wanted to talk to friends of his father, he said, and I supposed he meant Dougal McLean or Sergeant Jack Blake. They were, after all, the only friends his father ever had.

'And then,' he said with that flick-eyed look of guilt bequeathed to most loved ones by a suicide, 'I might go on to see Polly.'

I close my eyes and see him standing there, looking so much like his father. The same slight build and honeyed skin, the same ale-coloured eyes and wavy brown hair. Yet Polly is in the shape of his face and eyes. His lips are hers, usually thinned in stubborn determination. He had also, I decided then, inherited his parents' selfish natures. Who else but Mack and Polly's son would suddenly get up and go, not caring about the ones he left behind? After all, both parents had left him voluntarily. One for a cafe in Dubbo, the other for a gossip-free grave.

Yet I was smart enough to keep those thoughts to myself. I did not beg him to stay. With all the wisdom of an eighteen-year-old, I knew I couldn't live without him, and therefore, he could not live without me.

Though never beautiful, I was comely enough, as big as I was, and with a wit and intelligence Angus had always admired. We were best friends on the brink of being lovers. I knew he'd be back, and soon.

# Chapter Sixteen

He hitched a ride in a truck carrying tinned pineapples to Queensland. This, for those not in the know, is equal to carrying coals to Newcastle, or troubles to those already burdened.

'I didn't have the guts to go round the back like I was family or friend,' he confessed later. 'So I thumped on the wall like I was a bloody paying guest locked out after midnight. The old woman opened the door, took one look at me, sat right down and burst out howling.'

The once large and vigorous woman had gone to seed. 'Like a lettuce left in the ground too long,' were Angus's exact words. Her muscles had softened and folded. Flab hung from her arms and chin. Her skin and hair had faded to a matching drab colour.

Angus stood and stared at her, not knowing what else to do.

A huge man with wide shoulders and watery blue eyes loomed in the doorway. An extended navel pushed out from his great whale of a gut and burst through his shirt closure. His legs were bowed and his feet splayed to take the weight of his body. The rounded head and flat-featured face appeared as a pimple on a pumpkin. An equally flat stare flicked Angus then darted beyond him to take in the empty yard.

'It's Basha come to help me,' Mrs Nell sobbed.

'He's too young to be Basha,' the old man said.

His tone was a statement, as flat as his eyes and face. Yet Angus caught the hint of an inflection which did not match the overall lacklustre impression.

'I'm Angus McTavish,' he said.

'That's your problem, mate. I got enough of me own,' the old ex-sergeant sniggered.

Angus's fists clenched. Anyone else who laughed at his name would have felt their strength by now, but the old man's face had no protuberances. Knuckles would slide off into the air. A dead centre hit on that balloon of a gut would cause an explosion, or he'd sink right in and never be seen again.

Jack Blake read his thoughts with a measuring glance. 'You can have a go,' he dared, 'but you better make it a good un. I'd hammer a little bloke like you with one good clout. But then,' he sniggered again, louder this time, 'you make it too good and I hit the floor, this place will come down on us all.'

Angus thought the old geezer was probably right. He relaxed and turned back to the woman. Before he could speak, a hand around his throat held him suspended in midair.

'I used to make a living taking care of blokes like you,' the big man said.

The words exploded in a garlic-tinged gale as Angus buried a boot in that huge stomach. He landed on his feet and assumed a fighting stance when the strangling hand automatically opened.

Mrs Nell shaded her eyes and peered upwards. Her sigh was a deflation. She collapsed, hitting the back of her head on the floor. Jack Blake, bent double by the kick, dragged her upright as he stood. His face remained blank, although his gentleness could have been interpreted as expression.

'He's got more spunk than Basha ever had, I'll give him that,' he said.

'People here used to call my father Basha,' Angus offered.

Jack Blake held out a hand, taking the offer as it was intended.

'I knew you were something to do with him,' Mrs Nell said.

'He with you?' the old sergeant asked, and that odd inflection was even more pronounced.

'My father is dead,' Angus mumbled, misreading the question. 'Doctors said he'd taken something to make his heart stop beating. He knew about things like that. Things from plants.'

'It was the bird.' Mrs Nell's tone dismissed the subject. Another flow of tears was not for Angus or his father.

'What about the other one, is he with you?' the old man persisted.

'What other one?' Angus asked.

'You'd better come in then. I'm Jack Blake, as I suppose you know. And I guess you know me wife. Leastways, who she was.'

Holding Angus's arm in a vice-like grip, as if afraid he might disappear from under their noses, Mrs Nell, now Mrs Blake, led the way to her private rooms. She slumped into a chair the moment they entered.

'I still have Basha's caftans and burnous if you want them,' she said. 'And if you can cook like him, you can start working for me tomorrow.'

Angus murmured a kind refusal, afraid she'd cry again. His kindness was wasted when she did.

'Do you know where Ruby's taken my little boy?' she asked. 'Basha would have known. There wasn't much he didn't know, although it was hard to understand the telling. He's such a dear sweet thing, my little boy. I always wanted a son.'

Jack Blake sat on the only piece of furniture likely to hold his weight. The double-sprung chair lowered to the floor as his great backside expanded across the seat.

'Ruby's the daughter,' he explained to Angus. 'She had a kid a few years back, but the no-good bloke what did the job run off and left her. Then me wife decided that she wanted to do the raising.'

'It was you who had him run out of town,' Mrs Blake wept.

'You told me to. Like you always told me to,' the old ex-sergeant protested.

Her body swelled with indignation, lending at least the outline of the woman Angus had expected to see.

'What sort of man always does what a woman says? Now she's gone after him and taken my little boy.'

'Her little boy. Her frigging boy,' the old man insisted.

'I want him back. You promised you'd get him back for me.'

'Haven't I got all me mates on the job? What more do you want me to do? They'll find 'em sooner or later, but I say you're better off without her.'

'Ruby's my daughter. My own dear girl. You know nothing at all. It was me who had her, not you.'

'You had a vacant-brained tart. Being stupid and spineless is in her bloodline,' Jack Blake shot back.

Angus listened as the whale of a man and the puffer fish of a woman began to throw insults at each other; though before long he realised that it was building up to something else, and it was more a roundabout way of airing past grievances than anything like true rancour. The old man's eyes brightened with a great fondness for his wife as her voice grew louder. Her tears continued to flow, but in spurts now, accompanied by the stab of an accusing finger and an occasional smile of approbation when he let loose a particularly inventive insult, which was always directed at the missing daughter and the 'no-good bloke what done the deed' (another Blake, it seemed, but this one from the 'black sheep side of the family'). When Angus wandered away to the stairwell at the back of the house, they did not look away from each other or deviate the line of their attack.

Except for a large wardrobe in one corner, the desert room was exactly as Mack had described it. Angus did not enter. Old stories had led him to anticipate a feeling of warmth and sunbaked air. The atmosphere in there was humid. The wetness of tears had permeated every crevice.

He left the house without saying goodbye and strode towards the gate, in a hurry to be out of that place. The twenty-room mansion, viewed from this same spot an hour ago, seemed to have shrunk. Paint moulted from cracked and shabby weatherboards. The once white pillars were a gritty shade of grey, and the sandstone floor of the veranda had sunk in patches. Windows were sealed with whitewashed boards, which lent an appearance of cataracts over aging eyes. The entire building had a forward lean, as if it was about to fall flat on its face at any moment.

This was not the imposing guesthouse his father had described. That pitiful old hag bore no resemblance to a woman sometimes nicknamed Old Rambum. And how could that ailing elephant be the scourge of criminals, a sergeant known for his toughness and kindly nature? Reality was a tumbledown eyesore, and a foolish old couple happily ending their days keeping boredom at bay by throwing word darts at each other.

Yet at least they had not invented a mythical winged creature to provide an excuse for surrender. They cared enough about something or someone to live.

Angus turned and strode away.

He heard the ocean before he saw it, heard the slap of surf on sand. The sound carried him onto the beach in a flood of homesickness. Peeling off his clothes on the run, he plunged into the saltwater purity of the Pacific. He allowed its waves to pummel and roll him, to wash the sweat from his skin and the vision of contented suffering from his eyes. He swam against the swell until his muscles ached. When he could swim no more, he floated to shore and lay flat out in the backwash.

Some time later the crash of surf had flattened to a gentle lap of waves then retreated, leaving him high and dry. Perhaps he'd slept. He couldn't be sure. His head ached with a slow dull thump. His skin felt as if an army of ants had invited themselves for a feast. Groaning, he opened his eyes one after the other and looked directly at a flock of seagulls flying upwards in a column. The last was still on the beach while the leaders aimed for a sun that was a red glare, hunched between two dark clouds surrounding it like outspread wings.

A prodding in his chest deepened to pain. His heart began to deviate in its beat. Terror fought gladness for a place in his mind when he recognised the shape over his head.

His father's bird might have come for him then, if another shadow hadn't loomed, if something cold and wet hadn't been draped across his nakedness. If the derision in a drawling voice hadn't made him feel rather foolish.

'I saved yer pants but the rest of yer gear went for a swim.'

The voice belonged to a tall, sandy-haired skeleton of a man aged somewhere between fifty and sixty. He had a pointed chin, a long thin nose, and sunspots fighting the freckles for space on his skin. His grin was vaguely familiar, although Angus couldn't place it then.

'Thanks,' he said, and hurriedly pulled on his trousers.

The man had already walked away, his stare fixed on a moving white mound at the base of a dune. Angus refocused his eyes to the mound and finally recognised the shape: two shapes intertwined as a white backside pumped between outspread legs. Eyes averted, he cursed the man as a bloody old pervert. The curse had expanded to a diatribe against human nature in general when the man turned back to the ocean and took off at a gallop.

The words 'Weeping Jesus!' pierced the sound of slapping waves and a small child's cry. Another cry, thin and shrieking, froze Angus where he stood. A naked woman, breasts bouncing, blonde hair flying, raced across the sand.

Darkness grew larger and nearer, speeding forward in a direct course from the sun. Angus dropped to his knees and cowered there, feeling the cool air of the ocean's breath on one side, the terrible heat of a desert wind on the other. The shadow of a giant bird loomed directly overhead. He felt his heart suspend its beating as claws reached out.

'Help me!' the tall man called. He stumbled out of the waves and thrust a small boy into Angus's arms.

The claws withdrew. The wings returned to cloud and drifted away as Angus laid the small body over a shoulder and pummelled his back. The child convulsed then jetted a stream of water.

'You're all right now,' Angus whispered thankfully. 'You'll be all right.'

Even he wasn't sure if he meant the boy or himself.

'You shoulda been watching him, Ruby,' the man accused.

The boy, pale and thin with ginger-coloured hair, grabbed for the woman and pressed his face into the soft hollow of her throat. She did not try to cover her nakedness. She would not look at Angus or the tall thin man.

'You've been following me,' she said into the sand, and stepped back, ready to walk away.

The man reached out and laid a hand on her shoulder. It was a gentle touch, more a plea than a command for her to wait and listen to the words that were building up inside him. Angus could see this process taking place. The man's chest swelled. His throat arched. He swallowed to lubricate his vocal chords.

'I just wanted to tell yer. To talk to the boy,' he began.

The woman cut him off with, 'I told you before, Dougal McLean, you're years too late. He's nothing to do with you.'

Shrugging off the hand, she hurried towards another man, younger and also naked, standing below the dune.

The tall man turned to Angus, but Angus didn't want to hear those words either. He was too caught up in the joy of discovery to listen to what would probably be a list of excuses. He walked away from the tall thin man, the woman and the little boy, all alike enough to be family. He arrived home the next day with a sunburn that kept him standing for over a week. The haunted, flick-eyed look had gone.

Somehow, the gods alone know how, Angus had taken the misery of his father's friends and his mother's relatives, wrapped these ingredients in a cloud cooked by a late afternoon sun, and created a recipe for confirming the reality of a three-eyed bird. Turning rejection to sacrifice, he made a larger-than-life hero out of the meekest and most humble man I have ever known.

# Chapter Seventeen

Abandoned by her best friend, Mary Mayberry Trelelan turned to the church for comfort. Leslie Amadeus turned back with her. He sold his stocks and bonds long before the crash of 1929 and placed half his money in real estate. The remainder was cached in a hole in the wall behind a cupboard in an upstairs bedroom.

During the Depression they ladled out soup and packed boxes of food and clothing. They nursed the sick and wept at the funerals. At night they gave free concerts in the park for the unemployed. Confident of their daughter's strength and intelligence, they left her alone to shape her own nature, to form her own ideals and friendships.

Perhaps they missed the fact that I had never been a friendly person. Loner was the twist to my name and the evaluation made of me in my younger years, usually by those whose company I regarded as boring. The so-called 'upper class' of my town, those with the surnames of Rees and Falls who knew of the Mayberry connection, constantly pursued my parents with dinner and luncheon invitations. Their offspring were ordered to curry my favour, but I refused any association with the likes of them. They were definitely not my kind of people. Especially after Polly ran off with the dunny man and her son and husband were declared persona non grata. Angus and Mack, and to a lesser degree my mother and father, were the only company I ever needed. They were the only ones I held in esteem. Except for Curtis, who came along later, they were the only ones I ever loved.

At school I preferred to study and read rather than play my classmates' silly games. Boys were not impressed by the fact that I was bigger and more intelligent than most of them. Girls, with their preening and primping and conversation to match, were extremely irritating. I learned Arabic and Chinese and spoke to my peers in those languages. I wore trousers at a time when they weren't considered 'nice' on a girl. Proud of my height and thickness, I wore tight clothing, changing to loose and baggy when a snug fit became more fashionable.

By the time I reached womanhood, I had formed a habit of ignoring those who spoke to me, whether or not they teased. My time was taken up with a number of correspondence courses, all of which I passed with ease. My spare hours were spent with Angus.

The odd couple, people called us, and I played to that in every conceivable way. It was my reason, my excuse, for keeping to myself. Besides, I quite liked the classification. Angus was my friend and foe, my confidant and my accomplice. After my parents died, he was the only family I had.

My father faded quietly into a short illness then death during the year of my twenty-first birthday. My mother followed him closely, as had been her lifelong habit. They bequeathed the hole-in-the -wall money and all their belongings, including eight homes along Blackwattle Road, to me, their beloved only child. After placing several thousand pounds into Angus's empty bank account (assuring him that it was money owed to his father, which was a lie he never questioned), I settled into a life without material need. Or any other kind for that matter, for by then Angus had become my lover.

Although he threatened to sell his home and emigrate to New Zealand each time the inhabitants of our town annoyed him, which averaged out at twice a week, Angus remained in his shabby old house. He lived without esteem for anyone or anything except his gardens. Suspicious of all persons who would seek his friendship, he had no friends. He did not work, for he regarded all employers as blood-suckers, all employees as toadies. In his own words, he didn't give a rat's hiccup about nobody or nothing. He chose to become a professional eccentric and horticulturalist.

'The local gardeners can get their vegetable plants while taking a gecko at a Steeltown weirdo,' he said.

Everybody loves to laugh at an oddball.

Angus's rudeness usually drove prospective customers away, so I was the one who dealt directly with the public. Yet the products of my yard were never sold. Once my parents had passed on, Angus wasted no time in returning my acre of land to what it had been before we arrived in Steeltown. No one wanted to buy shrubs habitually pulled from their own gardens as weeds, or plants that grew in abundance with no help from herbicides, pesticides and synthetic fertilisers. These were the native plants Angus loved most. Probably because they were despised by the townspeople.

So we continued for the next few years: lovers one day, enemies the next, and fighting continuously over the fact that Angus refused to change my name by marrying me. We were both too proud, or bloody pigheaded as he would say, to change our names to Smith, as Curtis suggested when he was old enough to consider the matter.

# Chapter Eighteen

Curtis was born on the 6th July, 1939. I was recovering from a bout of influenza at the time.

Everyone who has ever had the flu knows that with it comes a certainty of death, if not the actual wish. This sudden realisation of mortality is usually accompanied by the rebirth of a childhood conviction. I had been conceived by music, and as the sickness settled in my chest, I attempted to invoke immortality by playing a tune remembered from that conception.

I did try to replace the tune with one of my own but I hadn't inherited my mother's talent. I could not originate. I could only borrow. My playing had become a screech of frustration when Agatha Lawson called on me.

Agatha was still rotund from nine months of layering fat along her body to cushion the womb. Her face was apple-contoured and coloured with content, her brassiere was further distended by sopping pads. Her hands were curved to fit the shape of a tiny head and backside. Her eyes had the slightly bulbous shape of a night animal — a transformation common enough in the mothers of newborn infants. She gave the impression of a handful of balloons tied with varying lengths of string, although perhaps this image would only be perceived by an oblong and childless woman like myself.

Being the only one in Agatha's life even remotely resembling kin, I was revered by her. My 'oddities' were excused as the result of losing my parents when I had barely reached voting age. Loss of family excused everything in Agatha's eyes.

With the utmost care and caution, as if this child was a firstborn and not the last of three, she placed Curtis across the width of my stomach.

'I want you to be his godmother,' she said to me. 'You're my only family outside my sons.'

'Who is godmother to your other children?' I asked.

'Relatives of their father. But that's not important. Curtis is important. I've waited seven years for him,' she said.

I looked down at the mound of Curtis in my lap. I breathed in his smell and stroked the sweet curves of him. I unfolded the rug and counted each finger and toe before moving my study upwards. The shape of his face was a reminder of Angus. He had the same frowning stare. His lips were wide and full, like mine.

'I want you to be his godmother,' Agatha Lawson said to me. And so Curtis became my godson.

Angus later accused me of deliberately misinterpreting the word as godsend, yet I had been convinced that semen-and-egg was not the only method of conception. My mother told me so, and I had no reason or wish to disbelieve her. She was not in the habit of lying. Angus, on the other hand, could intertwine fantasy with reality whenever it suited his purpose. I once thought of this ability as a conjuror's trick peculiar only to him. Hindsight now enables me to recognise it as the sap in his family tree.

'The first seven years are the most important,' I told Agatha as she bent over Curtis and me.

She snatched him from my shuddering legs.

'I shouldn't have come while you're sick, but I have to get it settled before Henry picks one of his sisters again,' she said.

Henry being Agatha's husband.

'You won't have to do much, being godmother,' she continued. 'Just remembering his birthday and giving him words. Stories, you know? The Lawsons already have my other two. This one's a Trelelan.'

I agreed so Agatha would leave, and because influenza had temporarily revived a forgotten belief. Yet I made a condition that neither she nor Henry would ever set foot through my gate again. Agatha was a compulsive tidier. After her visits I spent hours restoring my belongings to the parts of the floor where I felt they were better suited. Henry was a space cramper, the type of man who stands close to a woman in order to look down on her. As he and I were both the same height, and I refused to take part in the promotion of his ego by remaining seated when he approached, he would lift his shoulders and chest-swell like a frog. This seeded within me a craving to plant an elbow in his diaphragm. I had succumbed to the urge on three separate occasions. We were not on good terms.

Perhaps that was another reason why I accepted.

Determined to take my position as godmother seriously, every morning bright and early — the moment Henry left for work — I walked to the Lawson house six blocks away. Not wanting to wear out my welcome, I seldom stayed longer than necessary to check my godson's progress.

To smell his hair, his skin, his breath. To touch the sweet curves of him and feel his texture. To watch gassy smiles turn his gnome-like face into that of an angel. To make sure he knew me.

When filled to overflowing with the sight and sound of my Curtis, I would return home and present Angus with a word picture. Perhaps a little too enthusiastically at times, for after five days had passed Angus refused to listen.

'Enough is enough,' he said. 'You stopped them from coming here, now you're always over there. Stay away, Loby. Give that poor bloody woman a break.'

I remembered something my mother said when Leslie Amadeus ignored me even more than usual. 'Some men are often jealous of the time a child takes from them,' she had told me on numerous occasions.

The smile underlying her words was understandable. I would have been ecstatic had he ignored her in preference to me.

I copied that smile while repeating her words to Angus. He disappeared for a week. I was forced to believe his vow that he hadn't left the house, though I called through his keyhole every hour on the hour. Yet he had very few friends and nowhere else to go. Or so I believed at the time.

# Chapter Nineteen

Angus and I experienced our first lengthy separation two years after the official declaration of world war two. I do not capitalise the name because Angus said that war has been capitalised upon too much already. We listened to the announcement together, and for me it began another bout of influenza, this one induced by contemplation of horror. He nursed me back to health with shared rum toddies while adding to the catalogue of people he hated. It had grown many pages longer by the time I recovered. I had a relapse on the day he enlisted.

Angus believed humankind to be a type of bacteria. We climbed out of a bog and changed into upright creatures without ever truly evolving, he said. We were still bacteria and would eventually kill our host unless some great miracle of metamorphosis occurred. He insisted that Hitler aimed to drag us back to where we started, and that just served us bloody well right.

Because of his convictions, I couldn't believe that Angus had been swept away by patriotism on the day he enlisted. Having no one else to blame at the time, I blamed Henry Lawson — who was a relative of sorts, with the rightful given name of Ronald. In his days of rugby league football, the team had nicknamed him Henry because of his habit of quoting poetry to anyone who'd listen. The poetry was usually that written by Banjo Paterson, but who can understand a football team's rationale?

Henry was the only boy in a family of nine children. When the long-awaited son finally appeared to this western plains farming family, Mr Lawson Senior had reached the age of sixty. He died a few years later.

Probably of asphyxiation brought on by a houseful of females, Angus said.

Perhaps in order to avoid the same fate, Henry left home at the age of sixteen for an apprenticeship as a boilermaker at the Newcastle steelworks. He arrived at my town in time to help produce the first load of iron in a steelworks by the sea. He met Agatha at a church social a week after she buried the last of her maiden aunts.

No doubt Henry married Agatha because of the contrast between her and the nine females in his family. They were all loud of voice and extremely assertive. Especially the mother, who disgraced her German accent with a tendency to spit her esses. She had left her first husband to live with a farmer about nine months before Henry's birth. Although most people say he resembles his sisters too closely to have a different set of genes, I believe that a mother knows the father of her son. Mrs Lawson claims the western plains farmer, so who are we to doubt her word? Whatever the truth, and it has no importance except perhaps to Henry, this large tribe of females were very loud, very vocal and disgustingly demonstrative. They were also exceedingly proud of his brief football career, his large size and his overbearing manner. The only title they ever bestowed on him was that of Our Man of the Family.

Our Man of the Family is the best front row forward ever to play a game of football. Our Man of the Family has to have steak twice a day. We never do anything without first asking Our Man of the Family.

Angus believed this to be the real reason why Henry left home at an early age. Being Man to nine women in one household is beyond anyone's capabilities, Angus said.

Except for his small, neat hands, Henry appeared to be the ultimate macho male. He was large-chested, square of head and broad-shouldered. His hair was mouse-coloured, his legs resembled tree trunks. Handsome when he smiled, he was little-boy sulky when he did not. Yet a ripening pod of a gut, a backside beginning to sag and a slight blurring of the once sharp lines of his face became evident on a second look. His wide, full lips were perpetually thinned until alcohol slackened his mouth. When sober, he had the same kind of movement as a man wading through waist-deep water. He had a permanently s-shaped spine and what he termed 'a dicky hip' — the result of old football injuries.

In November of 1940, while gathering manure along the roadside, Angus met old schoolmates, and Henry Lawson, on the road to signing the next few years of their lives away. He accompanied them to the local hotel, trying to convince at least a few to stay with their wives and children. Although amazed by their loudly spoken belief that they were heading for some kind of freedom, he somehow ended up drunk and an infantryman. He'd been stabbed in the back by men calling themselves friends, he said; and by his own hand holding the pen.

'By that bloody Henry Lawson,' he growled as he added more names to his list.

# Chapter Twenty

An old railway hall had been commandeered by the army, the purpose being to shunt volunteers to the front line as fast as possible. Bare walls and a board floor, topped by a corrugated-iron roof, served to emphasise the sun's heat on a scorching afternoon. Rows of chairs lining two walls were filled with men in various stages of undress. Hot, still air accented the smell of sweat, cigarettes, Californian Poppy hair oil and beer breath. Every few minutes the men on the end of the chair lines were summoned by medics to have their names ticked off. They were then poked and prodded, the beat of their hearts measured, the state of their blood pressure monitored, and their testicles grabbed while they coughed, moaned and cursed.

As the game of musical chairs continued — each man sliding one seat along to the call of 'Next please' — Henry and his mob of volunteers shuffled through the doorway. At least, those like Angus who were bleary-eyed and weak-kneed shuffled. Henry's walk was cocky, chest out and head up. A picture of proud expectancy.

'Here. We're here,' he stated, as though everyone in the room would have been waiting for his entrance.

All eyes did turn to him, and he grinned.

'We're here,' he said again, this time in a voice choked with emotion.

'For moment I thought he'd bust out bawling,' Angus told me later.

113

'I know I almost did. So did some of the other blokes. But not for the same reason. We were wondering what the bloody hell we thought we were doing. Over there's something a man knows he can handle when he's with his mates, but he's not so bloody sure about when he's standing in a room full of half-naked strangers. Most of them looked like they'd rather be somewhere else. Anywhere else. But not that bloody Henry.'

Henry stripped to his undershorts and pushed to the fore, his manner a clarion call to all who would fight and die for their country. He jumped the queue, marching past the row of chairs. His eyes dared anyone to deny his right of passage.

Not waiting to be called, he strode up to a weary looking medic, saluted smartly and snapped, 'Ronald Lawson. Sir!'

In one glance the medic noted the s-shaped spine and the lean to one side to protect a dicky hip. The corner of his mouth twisted in a grin of derision. Yet he said, 'Forget it, mate,' kindly enough as he jerked a thumb in the direction of the door.

'Bugger that,' Henry whispered, giving quick sideways glances around the room.

'Come on, on your bike. And think yourself lucky,' the medic answered.

'Can't do that to a man. I come to sign up. To volunteer. Do me bit,' Henry said, his voice growing louder with each shake of the medic's head.

An outburst of catcalls greeted his shout, along with a few mumbles of 'Lucky bugger' and a couple of half-hearted cheers. Also several calls of, 'Never mind, mate. There's things to be done at home.'

Henry didn't acknowledge the jeers or the applause, or the sympathetic smiles or the knowing smirks. All he heard was the silence of a victory parade that should have been welcoming a Lawson hero home. He saw himself on the sidelines again. A bench warmer. A bum. A bloody girl, his mates at the pub would say.

The medic gave him a shove and yelled, 'Next!'

Henry threw a punch. It started at his knees and ended over a shoulder when the medic swayed aside. Henry crashed to the floor, along with his dreams of purple crosses and free beers forever.

A general unintelligible mutter died at the moment of inception, killed by the curled upper lips of two burly orderlies. Angus shattered the routine apathy by yelling, 'Silly bastard!' as he started forward in the direction of Henry's prostrate body.

Even Angus couldn't be sure if he meant Henry or the medic, or if he intended picking the one up or pushing the other aside. Yet before he had travelled more than a few steps, he sensed a punch travelling towards the back of his head. He ducked and swung a punch of his own, giving a 'Yahoo!' for the sheer joy of it when his knuckles crunched against a chin.

Conflict erupted like a summer storm: five minutes of furious sound and action. Unlike the average movie fight scene, this was not goodies against baddies where everyone joins in and all have superhuman powers of recovery. This was a real donnybrook where some men ducked under a table or fled through a door. Where those hit hard enough stayed hit and crawled into corners to moan about a broken nose or a loosened tooth. It was an all-in free-for-all of boots and elbows and fists; anyone dishonourable enough to use any kind of weapon was set upon by a group.

Before long, just a hard core of glory brawlers remained — those like Angus who exulted in crunch and thud, who had a craving to feel arm weary and sick, to take the pain from inside and put it on the outside where it belonged. As if by democratic vote, this bunch grouped together in the centre of the hall. There they stood back to back, staring at a dozen military policemen who jogged through the doorway grinning their delight, as if someone had posted an early Christmas.

Henry yelled a warning. No one was sure to whom. Between the beer and the bad back, he couldn't get up to join in. He lay with his face on the floor, howling like a child forgotten by Santa Claus while batons and boots softened the core of brawlers.

Angus and old schoolmates: Col Burnett, Barry Dickson, David Watling, a brown lump of a man nicknamed Toady — and a few others

I've forgotten now — were thumped and stomped into submission. The police hauled them off to the lockup. They were thrown into the drunk tank, where they spent a sleepless night after the constabulary threatened them with another hiding if they even so much as snored.

They did not see the medic again. Anyone fit enough to fight the military police was deemed fit enough to fight for his country. The army gave the new recruits five days to settle their affairs then sent them off to Dubbo for six weeks of intensive training.

Henry continued to bewail the stupidity of a government who couldn't recognise a fighting machine when they saw one, until the day it accepted him into the Volunteer Defence Corp. He had a uniform at last. One he wore with a pride which would have tested the seams of less stout clothing. Given the honour of defending a nearby bridge, he performed this duty with gusto and a pick handle over one shoulder, challenging everyone who dared set foot in his domain.

No one was spared his attention. That included men on their way to or from work, women visiting ailing relatives, and Civil Defence Corps volunteers on their way to installing barbed wire along the beaches. He wouldn't allow one child to drop a fishing line, not even from those places handed down from the days of hand-hewn wooden trestles.

Men jostled and cursed. Women screamed abuse. The children pelted him with old prawns ripened in the sun. Time and again he found himself sprawled out in the water, but Henry could not be swayed from his duty.

Yet he could be relieved of that duty. And so he was after just three weeks, when the authorities wearied of the endless protests. Fighting and swearing, he was stripped of his uniform and pick handle then given double shifts at the steelworks to dissipate his excess energy.

Within six months, thanks to a word from a kindly foreman, Henry became convinced that the mill couldn't spare his boilermaking expertise. Certainly not for such an insignificant structure as a local bridge.

# Chapter Twenty-one

The following few years were a blur of sock-knitting, food parcel packing and reading every newspaper I could get my hands on. And waiting for a postman who seemed to take a fiendish delight in trudging past my gate, leaving nothing more than the shadow of his smile. Not one letter arrived that wasn't a bill or a circular.

Angus told me later that a war is nothing to write home about. Details of his position in it would have been censored, and anything else that might have crossed his mind was already known by me, or should have been guessed.

'You've known me all me life,' he said. 'You know what I'm thinking before I even think it.'

I pointed out that it would have been nice to know whether he still walked the earth or if he'd found a new home beneath it. He explained that a bird of prey had begun visiting the trenches at night. He didn't write for fear it would discover our relationship and turn its attack on me.

He returned in December of 1943 with a bonsai'd tree under one arm and part of his left leg missing. His skin was the colour of dark smoke and his hair hung at least a good deal longer than the current trend. The end of his beard met with the few scrappy curls on his chest. He was significantly lighter.

He stayed for two days and nights then disappeared again for another seven months. His second homecoming coincided with Curtis's fifth birthday.

He'd decided to come back, he said, because he couldn't find a place or people different from our steel town — or steel city, as Steeltown had become. Many years passed before I learned of his trip to Perth. Not that I was worried at any time. I had complete confidence that my Angus would never desert me.

The wooden leg was a nuisance, he told me later, but kids loved it. They called him Captain Hook or Long John Silver. If he confessed to an ache in ankle joints no longer there, they thought he was pulling their legs. Sometimes he could actually see the long-gone thing, the fuzzy black hairs and toenails needing clipping. It haunted his nights, hopping around muddy trenches looking for the rest of him. Or it lay rotting in a cave with a homeless dog munching out its marrow.

Often in those dreams it became an arm waving up at him through a mound of bodies. He would wake screaming, rubbing his eyes to erase the picture of men, some no older than eighteen, strewn around a field. Their blue-mottled faces stared sightlessly up at the sky. Somebody's kid. Somebody's son who'd never have a kid of his own. Maybe the last of the line in a grandmother's much loved family.

It was after one of those dreams that he decided to get to know some of his own family. The people he most wanted to meet were his mother's kin, the clan McLean.

That pegleg might have been a nuisance, but it won him a lift every time he raised his thumb.


Mount Tumblebee was nothing more than a few tumbledown shacks. The coal dust lining their lungs had killed off most of those early miners. Their sons and daughters, those not gone to war, had moved to a nearby town. After many door knocks, and many cups of tea served with hot buttered scones, Angus finally learned that Da and all the McLean boys bar two had been killed by the mines, and that Ma had taken Iain to Western Australia.

Two months later he reached Fremantle via cars and trucks and boats. Having no interest in scenery, none stayed in his mind longer than the time it took to leave it behind. He met many people not worth talking about. Others liked to do all the talking, which suited him fine. Angus had never been much of a talker. Thinking about the journey later, he couldn't remember one person standing out from the rest. Most were no different from the average Steeltowner. The truck driver who offered him a lift into Perth was full of gossip about people Angus had never known.

It was a friendly place, Perth, even to a man dressed in a sailor's dungarees cut off at the knees and displaying a battered wooden leg. Which was, by then, decorated with the names of the crew from two fishing trawlers. Men tipped their hats to him. Women smiled and nodded. The waitress at the cafe where he had his first decent meal in weeks was happy to sit down and chat. The man at the post office was eager to give out information.

'Everyone knows the McLeans,' he said. 'Just as they know that Ma died of the sugar two weeks ago. You'll most likely find Iain at home, but you're not likely to find a welcome. The bloke's gone a bit queer since he laid the old girl to rest.'

He made Angus sit down, gave him a glass of water and would not allow him to leave until the colour came back to his face. When finally satisfied that Angus was well enough to walk, he helped him out to the footpath, hailed a taxi and gave the driver Iain's address. He then watched and waved until the taxi was out of sight.

'I thought for a while there that he was gunner insist on coming with me,' Angus said.

The McLean home was a white weatherboard cottage almost hidden under a tangle of native roses. It stood at the end of a dead-end street. A vegetable garden — a delight to Angus's eyes — covered the length and breadth of the yard. Neat rows of beans, carrots and cabbages, all well hoed and weeded, stretched from fence to fence, east to west, broken here and there by squares of newly turned soil. A narrow pathway of stepping stones joined the gate to the front porch. The perfume of Sweet Alice growing between the stones wafted in the breeze. Huge wooden tubs, which held more of these sweetly scented plants, outlined the shape of the house.

Dazed by the sight and the smell of this place, Angus hop-stepped onto the veranda and banged on the door.

'Nobody home,' a voice called. 'Go away or I'll set me dog onto you.'

'Is that you, Iain McLean?'

'Dogs don't talk so it must be.'

'I want to pay me respects.'

'Consider them paid and go.'

'I'd like to hear about Ma.'

'She's dead, what else is there to say? Who are you anyway?'

'The name's Angus McTavish.'

A slight pause then, 'Polly's boy?'

'The same.'

'I heard the bird finally got your dad.'

'Thirteen odd years ago now.'

'An unlucky number that. You'd better come in.'

'What about your dog?'

'Give me a minute and I'll lock him away.' Another pause, then, 'Okay, the door's unlatched.'

The house inside showed evidence of a caring hand. The furniture and linoleum shone. The walls had been whitened with Kalsomine paint. The curtains were a bright yellow. Jugs of Sweet Alice sat on every cupboard, and the air felt thick enough to make every breath seem like a slug of whisky. By the time Angus reached the kitchen, he had the stagger in his hopping walk of someone not quite drunk enough to fall.

Iain was the one McLean male not made in the image of his father. Square-shouldered and stout, his face had a moon shape and his cheeks and forehead were always pink, as if he had just come in from the sun. Except for a thin white scar beginning at his right ear and disappearing into his collar, his skin was blemish free. His hair had become a showy shade of silver, although he couldn't have been much older than forty. His eyes were blue enough to be mistaken for purple.

He lay full length along a sofa near the window, wrapped in a crocheted woollen blanket. When Angus staggered in, Iain looked into his face and nodded. He looked down at the pegleg and nodded again.

'How long ago?' he asked.

'Ten months or more now.'

'Still feel it?'

'Mostly just nights. See it then too at times.'

'Itch?'

Angus nodded. 'Drives me mad.'

'Know where you left it?'

'In a paddock over the other side of the world. Well rotted now I'd say, though sometimes I see a dog chewing out the marrow.'

'I see mine dancing along a railway track.' Iain tossed the blanket aside. 'We make a good pair, eh? One leg between the two of us.'

Angus looked down at two legs ending just above the knees.

'That where you left 'em, on a railway track?' he asked.

'Thirteen years ago now. Told you it was an unlucky number. Doing a jig on the sleepers, remembering Da on his birthday, how he could dance when he had a mind to it. One of the brothers playing the bagpipes while Da went hell for leather over a couple of crossed sticks. Though Ma could always dance better and go longer. Ma could do anything better and longer. She's gone you know, Angus. Jesus, Angus. She's gone.'

Angus allowed tears to slide down his face as his uncle sobbed into the blanket. He had a feeling that this was the first time Iain had allowed himself cry, and he was proud to join his uncle's sorrow. He had never known Ma, but from what he'd heard she deserved all the tears anyone could manage.

'Drunk as a skunk I was,' Iain went on fifteen minutes later, as if he hadn't been interrupted. 'Too drunk to hear the train whistle. Don't remember much more than that. Just a shuddering going through to me bones, then a thump and somebody screaming. Haven't touched a drop since. Learned that much sense from Dougal.'

'You're not telling me he's lost a leg or two as well?'

'Worse. His daughter. She came looking to meet him when he was drunk and in the middle of a card game, winning for one of the few times in his life. He went looking for her when he sobered up, but she had him run out of town.'

'Where is he now?'

'Last I heard, wandering the country up north somewhere. I wrote him about Ma care of a mate of his, but I don't know if he got the letter. Hang on, I'll make us a pot of tea.'

Iain swung off the sofa and propelled himself across the floor, mostly using his knuckles. Angus had noticed benches lower than normal. He'd guessed the reason to be compensation for Ma's lack of height. While watching Iain make a mound of sandwiches with the efficiency of long practice, he recognised the true worker in this house.

'Why don't you use that?' he asked, pointing to a chair on wheels parked just inside a bedroom door. It was a heavy, cumbersome thing. Homemade, Angus thought.

'Don't like people supposing there's something amiss with me,' Iain said with a grin. 'And I can move a hell of a lot faster without that thing. Use it when I visit town, though. Have to then or I'd be minced by the pebbles and layered in dogs' dung. Busts me arms shoving those wheels along, or someone else's arms if they volunteer a push. If I could find something lighter and faster, I'd give it a go. In that thing, all I get is pity. Something I don't need or bloody well deserve. I'm as spry as any bloke I know. A bloody sight spryer than some. And like Ma used to say, anyone who gets drunk and dances on railway tracks can't expect the gods to smile on them for long.'

'Ma was blind for over a year,' Iain continued as he poured the tea. 'She couldn't walk for two or more. When the gangrene set in, she wouldn't let the doctors use a knife. Said she'd go out of this world the same way she came in. Got so she couldn't bathe or take care of herself, and she wouldn't let me do it for her. Not right for a boy to see his mum naked, she'd say. She got to smelling something awful. That's the reason for the flowers. Ma's given name was Alice, did you know that? Not many did. Everyone called her Ma because that was her nature. People get named for their personalities sooner or later. A lot around here call me Gasbag.'

'I've got a friend who used to call me Fred,' Angus said.

'Good old plain old Fred? Don't think so, mate.'

'Your family named my father,' Angus said.

Iain heard the accusation and shrugged.

'Da always said the name suited him better than the others he had.'

'He never liked it,' Angus objected.

'Polly didn't like it, you mean. And if you're going to tell me you prefer Fred to Angus, then a Fred you ought to be. Ma always said that an Angus was exactly the kind of kid Mack was sure to have.'

'Was my mother here for the funeral?'

'No kin here when Ma got sick. No kin here when she died, and there was a long hard pull of years between the two. Her heart was too strong to let her go in a hurry. But she's gone now and glad of it, and I'm glad for her. I got sick of people knocking on the door and telling me sorry.'

'That why you got the dog?'

His uncle's smile hit Angus hard by reminding him of Polly.

'No dog, mate,' Iain said. 'That was me. You know, you're the spitting image of your dad, but sometimes when you stare like that, I can see more than a bit of Polly in you. You've got her eyes you know. Except for the colour. That shade of brown belongs to Mack. Polly writes once a month and she's doing well enough, though her in-laws like to keep her on the outside. Tell me about yourself, then we'll talk about Ma, and Da and Polly and my oldest sister Joyce, along with all the brothers. It's been a long time since I talked about kin with kin.'

From that moment on, Angus and Iain worked side by side in the garden during the day and talked half the night. More content than he ever had been, Angus might have stayed for a year or two, if not for Polly and her three daughters. They arrived seven weeks after him.

Polly had lost most of the weight she had gained the last time Angus

123

saw her. Her face had grown a few wrinkles and thinned a little too much, and her eyes were reddened from days of weeping. Yet apart from these minor details, she still seemed to be the same young Polly. Her skin was still the colour of rich cream, and she still had a tangle of glossy hair. She still liked to watch others watching her.

She gave Angus a quick peck on the cheek before crying on Iain's shoulder. 'Nicky's heart just stopped beating,' she sobbed, 'then his parents threw me out. For not giving them the gift of immortality with a grandson, they said.'

'Does that mean my father's still alive?' Angus asked.

Polly noticed the sideways glance he flicked at his three half-sisters.

'Women bond the blood and bear the children, so it stands to reason that women are responsible for the bloodline. Men only continue a name,' she said.

Perhaps Iain saw the rejection and was moved to alleviate Angus's hurt. Or perhaps it was simply a case of men colluding to put a woman in her place. Whatever the reason, he said, 'The ancients believed that the essence of a person is in their name. As long as that name is being spoken, the person is alive.'

'A man's reasoning to deny women their rightful place in the scheme of things,' Polly snapped.

She did not bother with further argument. She knew Iain's words held hidden barbs that only she and Angus understood. Mack's real name, which Angus had heard only once and then as a child, had long been forgotten. As far as he knew, it had never been recorded.

'He lives through the bird,' Angus muttered, but more to soothe his own wounds than a forlorn hope of making Polly feel uneasy.

She retaliated by cuddling her daughters, by brushing back their fringes and planting mother-soft kisses across their eyes. Something she had never done with him.

Those girls were sweet and pretty enough but sadly lacking in spirit, or so Angus said. They cried for the sake of it, and trembled at any sudden noise. They cowered away from him whenever he tried to make conversation, staring above his head as if he should have been taller.

When Iain tried to cheer them with his mimicry, they hid behind Polly's skirts.

'They've lost their father, and they've been kicked out of the only home they've ever known. Give them time and they'll settle down,' she begged, avoiding Angus's eyes as she had avoided his touch since that first cold peck on the day of her arrival.

Being the youngest of nine children, Iain had learned patience as a means of survival. And he possessed his sister's smile. By the end of a week he'd won the children over. They crawled into his lap whenever he sat still long enough to allow it. They followed him around the garden like a set of triplet shadows. He told them stories of Mount Tumblebee and the McLeans. They talked of Dubbo and their dad, a cafe in Main Street, and friends they seemed to miss more than the family who had turned them away. When Iain suggested that they enrol at a nearby school, they settled down to a new life and were almost content.

'Seems I'm the only fly in their ointment,' Angus said when they continued to run every time he entered the same room.

'It's your father's bird,' Polly explained as she stared up at the ceiling.

'It has nothing to do with them,' he answered, reaching for her hand.

She moved out of his way and stared down at the floor. 'How do you know it won't follow you here?'

'Because my father kept it with him.'

Polly frowned. 'So his father said.'

Angus felt the beat of its wings, chilling the air until he shivered. He could almost feel the claws at his chest. Its shadow clogged his nose until the effort of trying to breathe brought tears to his eyes.

'I'll go,' he said. 'I'll take it with me so they'll be safe.'

'Watch out for it, Angus, and watch over the ones you love. If the bird can't find you, it might go after them. One day they'll be needing your protection.'

She hugged him now. A warm, soft hug. But as he kissed her cheek, she glanced through the window at her daughters.

'Where will you go?' Iain asked when Angus went to shake his hand.

'Back to Steeltown, I guess.'

'Don't let Polly chase you out. The only reason she wants you gone is to save facing her own guilt every day.'

'If I stay she might take the girls and go.'

Iain looked at his newfound nieces weeding a patch of beans. The fear in his eyes was not for Angus's bird. Iain had watched his family dwindle until only a few remained. He had held Da's head and watched him die. He had nursed his mother until the day of her death. All his life had been surrounded by age and death and dying. Now youth and living were here in his yard, he couldn't choose to let them go.

'Where do you think this bird is now?' he asked, looking at the girls.

'It knows about my people back home,' Angus said, 'and Liona will be waiting.'

# Chapter Twenty-two

For all of the years after his father died, Angus had faith in the importance of a title. That's why, although he hated his own, he refused have it changed, or to change mine.

'The ancients believed that the essence of a person is in their name. As long as that name is being spoken, the person is alive,' Iain had said, and Angus chose to believe him.

'With a different name you'd be a different person,' he told me. 'And when you die, all they'd keep alive would be old Liona McTavish. The Trelelan and Mayberry names and all your young days would be forgotten.'

'Perhaps my essence is in the name Loby,' I told him. 'You've called me that ever since I can remember.'

'I can't do to you what they did to my father,' he said. 'I've tried ever since I talked to Iain, but I'm blowed if I can remember Mack's proper name.'

I did not tell him that I had translated his father's journal. It was an act of curiosity I have never regretted. That journal held the only correct and proper spelling, in fact the only memory of Achmed Yusef Alemedine.

It was on the tip of my tongue, but I decided to wait a little longer. The power of resurrection is a heady thing, not to be used lightly. And

I believed that this business of names was a lot of nonsense anyway.

'Surely the people themselves and how they connect to each other are much more important than a name is,' I said, and we continued to argue that point for the rest of the year.

During that time Angus refused to speak of the war or his experiences in it, except to swear that his leg had been removed by friendly fire. By the same kind of men who inveigled him into the army, by the likes of that 'bloody Henry Lawson'.

Henry rose to the top of a list which had grown to novella length, with Agatha a close and crowding second. Angus said she epitomised the type of woman who drove the average Australian male away to war.

Until the age of six Agatha had lived in a suburb of Sydney, in a narrow house that faced a biscuit factory wall. If asked about her childhood, she'd retire to a corner of the room, press her lips together and stare at her feet. I could never be sure if this was because of unhappy memories or a foot fetish. She wore socks to bed in the middle of summer. Henry vowed she wore them in the bath. Her shoes always gleamed with a mirror-like shine, and she never wore sandals, or flip-flop thongs when that mode of footwear became popular. Agatha insisted that the display of naked toes was equal to the fanning out of a lyrebird's tail as it tried to tempt a mate.

Her father was John Trelelan, a distant cousin of Leslie Amadeus. He died in the 'great' war not long before her fourth birthday. Her only memory of him was a large white smile almost hidden under a thick black moustache. The pain she felt at recollecting his death was mostly induced by thoughts of her mother.

# Chapter Twenty-three

On the morning the yellow telegram arrived, Joyce Trelelan fainted for the first time in her life. Though to set the record straight, she remained unconscious for no more than a couple of seconds and she didn't actually fall to the floor. She later told her friend Abigail Gatley that this temporary blackout was not caused by grief or shock, as one might expect, but by a mind trying to escape all-out panic. After all, who had she ever been but her mother's daughter, her brothers' sister and John Trelelan's wife?

Staggering into the kitchen, she fortified herself with a glass of cooking sherry. Then, as alcohol always made her feel either lustful or miserable, she wandered into the lounge room and opened her photograph album, intent on ensuring the latter reaction. Joyce had promised herself on the day her family disowned her that she would never cry again. Yet surely being made a widow was a good enough reason for breaking that vow. The first half-dozen pages were filled with pictures of her and John, and as she touched them one by one and remembered the time they'd been taken, each memory encouraged a fresh onrush of tears.

Her favourite had always been the professional photograph posed on their wedding day. It showed John seated with his hat on his lap to cover his erection, and her face lowered as if in shyness. Reality was an attempt to hide wet-lipped anticipation. Her hooded eyes seemed to be staring at something beyond the border. Perhaps at the snap of John in uniform. There he was, going off with a smile on his face, promising to be back as soon as the war had been won.

'It'll be like a holiday,' he'd said, adding that lewd grin he did so well. 'As soon as the buggers are on the run, I'll be home. Back in our bed before you realise I'm gone.'

But the buggers hadn't run. The buggers had killed him instead.

Turning to the centre page, she studied a picture of her workmates lined up in front of the hosiery mill — tier upon tier of spinners and packers, mostly female. They all looked prettily posed and self-conscious, except for Blue O'Neil. He stood directly behind her, brushing against her as he did whenever he had the chance. Touching, smiling, winking. Twice as brazen after winning the promotion to foreman. Since John had left with that stupid smile on his face, there were times when the heat of her body almost overpowered the coolness of her head. Yet Blue O'Neil's little power plays were equal to a bucket of cold water.

She knew he'd be worse now, with John Trelelan gone forever.

Slamming the album shut, she stumbled around the room, touching various knick-knacks John had given her throughout their marriage: a large blue vase for their first anniversary, a cute china animal every birthday, and the kewpie doll for bringing Agatha into the world. Joyce had never allowed him to spend money on expensive presents. Any extra over the budget went towards pulling back the mortgage.

How could she live without him? How could he do this to her? Who would know the secret places of her body and touch her there? Who would make her feel loved and wanted and good, and not just a slut for running off with the first man who asked? Who would protect her from Blue O'Neil? And from herself, she asked Abigail many months later.

The crying continued for days as Joyce slept fitfully, usually for just minutes at a time. Sometimes she hugged Agatha and cried into her pinafore, but more often than not she ignored the child, except to scold her for being a girl and not having any brothers.

'The women in our family always have boys,' she would say, then she'd send Agatha around the corner to stay with the babysitter, Mrs Ade. 'Until you stop upsetting Mummy.'

After eight days of crying, Joyce returned to fifty hours a week at the hosiery mill on the other side of the city. At home she cleaned house and tended the flower garden. Agatha stayed with Mrs Ade, which she'd always done while her parents worked, so nothing had really changed. John Trelelan had been a travelling salesman, away from home for days at a time. Joyce had always been fidgety on those weekdays.

As the months went by, the old routine underwent a reversal. Work days became her contented days. Tears were confined to weekends after the Saturday nights Blue O'Neil sidled through the door. Joyce's sobs, louder and harsher now, were accompanied by the shattering of little china animals the moment he quit the house.

After his sixteenth nocturnal visit, she smashed the blue vase and threw the pieces onto her bed. The following night's attempt to glue the remnants together was interrupted by Abigail Gatley.

Abigail had been fought over by every young male in the area, until she married Bill Hind to keep the peace — or so the neighbours said. They considered her somewhat of a misfit. Mostly because she rarely wore shoes and always dressed in red. She had also committed the sin of remaining childless after three years of marriage. Yet the local women forgave her for that when she lost her husband to war.

'Maybe Abigail is something of a soothsayer. Like her aunt Rachel, the only Gatley to marry a man of gypsy blood,' they said.

Joyce and Abigail had never said more than good day to each other before, although their husbands were mates until John married out of the mob. That home-grown mob had tried to make Joyce feel welcome, but she'd felt left out, and showed it, when they talked of the good old days. So they left her there, out of it, barely touching the fringe of their friendship. She retaliated by arranging parties and picnics with couples from the hosiery mill. John continued to have a beer with young Bill Hind on Fridays, but wives were never included in that tradition. Joyce hadn't seen Abigail for over a year. She confessed to surprise at seeing her now.

'I'm here because of the telegram. It came a week ago, though it seems more like yesterday,' Abigail said as she climbed the steps to the front veranda. 'When I think about it, it feels more like last year,' she admitted over a cup of tea in the kitchen. 'What I'd like to know is what you do when you're neither single nor married but stuck somewhere between the two. When Bill was alive but over there, I could still go to parties and picnics. Now he's dead, the women treat me like a leper.'

'Join the club,' Joyce said as she tossed blue glass into the garbage. 'Would you like another cup of tea? I'd offer something stronger but all I've got is cooking sherry.'

Abigail draped her legs over the table and leaned back to admire her painted toenails. 'Then trot it out,' she said.

From that day forward, Agatha seemed to have gained another mother. Two mothers, actually, for her own stopped sending her around the corner to Mrs Ade. Instead of being ignored, she was fussed over and admired. On Mondays she became a kewpie doll with painted lips and cheeks, and layers of petticoats holding her skirt out around her like a fallen halo. Tuesdays, they pinned scarves to her singlet — filmy squares of material that hovered like a multicoloured aura as she walked. Wednesday was flower day. For the rest of the week her clothes depended on a book being read.

Blue O'Neil's visits became less frequent. At times he begged through the keyhole for an hour before Joyce finally let him in.

'But only to stop the neighbours from gossiping,' she'd tell him.

If Abigail was at the house, the two women would smother their laughter in each other's breasts while Blue O'Neil's pleas turned to groans, the moans faded to silence, then a creaking gate signified the visitor gone.

On Saturdays Abigail and Joyce went shopping with their arms around each other while Agatha clutched at their skirts. On Sundays they rode trams to the beach and walked most of the way home. They whispered secrets and swapped herstories while they strolled the city streets. On week nights Agatha learned to cuddle up with whispered confessions to soothe her to sleep at any hour. They ate when hungry, wore what they liked regardless of fashion or age, and ignored any man who turned to stare or whistle.

The local matrons smiled upon this friendship, although a habit of drinking claret on each other's porch met with stern disapproval. A glass of beer or a nip of something stronger might be common enough, but wine was a posher suburb's drink. That sort of thing belonged in the privacy of their kitchens. Somewhere out of sight of the local men.

It was on Agatha's fifth birthday that Joyce invited Abigail to move into the Trelelan house. Joyce's home was almost her own. The Hinds had always rented. And Joyce earned a reasonably good wage at the hosiery mill while Abigail barely earned a living sketching children's portraits.

Their female neighbours, those in the closely knit community of inner-city streets, greeted the arrangement as not only necessary but sensible.

'If women can't look after each other when there's no men around to do the job, what's this world coming to?' was the general consensus of opinion.

True, Joyce was Catholic and Abigail a Callithumpian (the local term for one who had never been baptised), but they were friends, not partners in marriage.

The gossip settled down to speculation about Blue O'Neil. He visited the house on the second Saturday of every month to join the poetry sessions. They read Yeats, Keats, Byron, Shakespeare and, as the months wore on, sonnets of their own creation. At times they permitted him to read, and he seemed to enjoy that, even while being constantly interrupted to correct mispronunciations.

During this time Joyce adopted the mode of going barefoot and dressing in red. She clad Agatha in pinafores of yellow or orange. The little girl's feet were always properly shod. As they wandered the streets or strolled the pocket parks, the women began to leave her sitting on a park bench, staring at her shoes until they returned. Or they deposited her with Mrs Ade, like a small amount of money that could only grow if it was tucked away and left alone.

A year to the day that Abigail came to live with them, Agatha left the classroom and sat on a low brick wall, waiting for a mother who never arrived. There was no sense in crying or yelling. Experience had taught her that. She could walk home by herself, yet she was supposed to wait. 'Unless there's a very good reason not to,' Joyce had always said.

There were no clouds promising rain, no menacing men or tormenting children. All Agatha could see were women gossiping over fences, a half-dozen kids playing tag in the street and a shattered bottle scattered across the footpath. A stump-tailed mongrel cringed from fence to fence, its snuffling quest for anything edible screened by patches of shadow.

Half an hour passed before Agatha decided that something had to be done. The women were frowning in her direction. She hated being stared at.

The dog had found something to eat in somebody's garbage. He brought it to the shade of her wall seat, perhaps mistaking her in her stillness for another outcrop of brick. Leaving no time for her mind to form pictures of gouged flesh, she slithered down and slid a hand between the dog and a chop bone he'd found. The animal showed his teeth in a warning snarl and glared from his one good eye. The snarl became an anxious whine when he recognised his tormentor as being human.

Agatha's high-pitched giggle chased the cur as he scurried away from a kick aimed at his ribs. While the women and children turned to watch him run, she grabbed a triangle of broken bottle and made an incision across her palm. The cut was deep enough to draw blood, but not hard enough to hurt too much. The pain was somewhere else, but she didn't know what to do about that. There was a routine for a cut or a bite. Sliding the captured bone into her pocket, she ran down the street crying for Mrs Ade.

That night she slept on Mrs Ade's sofa. The next day Mr Ade broke down the Trelelan door. The open house revealed empty wardrobes and dirty dishes. Agatha's clothes were piled in a heap on the kitchen table. When Mr Ade telephoned the hosiery mill, the secretary said that Joyce had been fired after a dispute with the foreman, Blue O'Neil. She had picked up her severance pay yesterday morning and, after being met at the gate by a woman dressed in red, left in a taxi heading for town.

A marriage certificate fossicked out of the wastepaper basket showed that Joyce's maiden name was McLean. No McLeans or Trelelans lived in the immediate area, so Mrs Ade was asked to look after Agatha until someone more willing could be found. Yet Abigail Gatley had never been popular with women. This fact cast suspicion on the femininity of Joyce Trelelan. The local women had always suspected her of being somehow different, and Agatha was of the same bloodline. Mrs Ade had the welfare of six daughters to consider. Besides, the little girl was definitely strange. No normal six-year-old would cry because an ageing chop bone had been taken out of her apron pocket. That same week Mrs Ade placed advertisements in several Sydney newspapers before hustling Agatha off to an orphanage.

Nearly two years passed before a Miss Jane Trelelan — Catholic, stiff-backed, grey-haired and sharp of tongue — arrived at the Church of England home to take charge of the deserted child.

'I know my duty and would have been here sooner,' she said, 'but I did not see the advertisement until yesterday morning.'

Aunt Jane was in the habit of purchasing every newspaper published each day. As she persisted in reading every single word to ensure she received her money's worth, her stack of material had grown to mammoth proportions. She was nineteen months behind and slipping further back every week.

Except for a small cameo of Joyce Trelelan, Agatha left her few belongings behind when she went to live with her aunt. Her hair was cropped in search of lice, her body was scoured to remove the contamination of 'that heathen home for Godless children'. She was clothed in sensible dresses and leather shoes and given a weekly allowance to spend on any magazine she chose. Fiction, being nothing more than a gathering of lies, was strictly forbidden. She was never hugged or kissed, never beaten or ignored.

After school and every Saturday, she learned how to cook and clean. At night she learned how to read a newspaper from front to back, column to column, except for the sporting pages. To teach social consciousness, Aunt Jane read aloud the items concerning adultery, abandonment and divorce. She would point out the probable reasons and obvious cures, then ask for suggestions. In this way Agatha learned to solve all kinds of family disasters. Inside her mind, of course.

'And best to keep it there,' Aunt Jane said. 'Nobody will listen if you speak, and it's only what our minds contain that matters, after all.'

As it happened, Aunt Jane never caught up with her reading. She died two years after taking Agatha into her home. The child was sent to Aunt Bea of Armidale — no particular religion, stoop-backed, white-haired and softly spoken. This aunt read nothing but an occasional romantic novel, but she had no objection to Agatha reading whatever she pleased.

It was in a London paper, one of Aunt Jane's carried to Armidale in three boxes of similar material, that Agatha found news of her mother.

*HIND, ABIGAIL. nee Gatley. May 14, 1924, at a private hospital, of Lebe Lane, London, formerly of Sydney, Australia. Loved sister of Joyce Trelelan. Aged thirty-one years. Rest in peace.*

Aunt Bea died three years later, leaving Agatha to be raised by a procession of maiden aunts in a succession of small towns. Most of the Trelelan women were not the marrying kind, and those that were turned out to be extremely fertile. The result was an unlimited number of spinster aunts waiting to pass Agatha along the line.

# Chapter Twenty-four

I could never understand why Agatha married a man ten years her senior when she had such a morbid fear of being alone. Angus said it proved his assertion that the woman had excrement for brains. He said this judgement was verified when she gave birth to Albert, then two years later to Harry, and four and a half years later to Curtis. Angus said everyone knew that daughters returned after marriage, while sons were lost for life.

Agatha set about disproving this adage by lavishing all her love on Curtis. For the first few months of his life they seemed to be permanently fixed to each other. Agatha managed to complete most household tasks while he slept, even preparing the evening meal in the early hours of the morning. The moment he woke, she bathed him then retired to her bedroom. They spent more hours hidden away in that room than anywhere else. I would arrive to find her lying next to Curtis, cooing, whispering, watching him sleep. On the few occasions she allowed me to hold him, she snatched him back after a minute or two.

I rarely objected. I fully intended to teach him the things I wanted him taught, but I could wait until he understood more than milk from a teat and slop from a spoon. Agatha could impart the elementary arts of dressing himself, walking without falling, and the beginnings of speech. I knew my time would come when Curtis had mastered these basics, though he had to learn them with no help from his older siblings.

During the early months of Curtis's life, Albert and Harry were kept at a distance. Agatha said their rough and rowdy ways disturbed their little brother. They were forced to play outside. By the time he reached his first birthday, they'd begun to pretend he didn't exist. If he tried to follow them into the yard, they shoved him back inside and closed the door on his screams. When Henry insisted that Curtis join their games, they soon had him howling with frustration.

This fact horrified Henry. No boy of his would be a namby-pamby, he said. He cuffed and cursed the child, trying to make a man of him.

'It's for your own sake,' he'd say as softly as he could manage, which wasn't much softer than a dull roar. Having to compete with his eight sisters all his young life, Ronald (Henry) Lawson had learned to be a loudmouth. 'You gotta live up to your brothers and me. I wouldn't do it if I wasn't fond of ya, and when ya get older you'll thank me for it. You know that, dontcha, boy?'

Curtis would stare at him wide-eyed then nod, but by the age of three he'd developed a habit of crying each time his father entered the room.

People began to talk. Henry's cronies at the local hotel made snide remarks. No boy, they said, would show such an aversion to his real father. Babies swapped at birth became the general verdict, and that was enough to place doubt in the mind of a man who accepted pub opinion as learned philosophy. Henry paid a visit to the local midwife, demanding she admit to the exchange. She upheld her reputation by placing a list of babies born around the same time as Curtis in newspapers and shop windows. The twenty-four hours either side of him were birth-free.

Not one of those cronies at the local hotel even considered the idea of Agatha being unfaithful. That kind of thing never went unnoticed. To make doubly sure, Henry harassed her every day for a week, trying to force a confession. Agatha believed he wanted to drive her away because he'd found another woman. She too began to cry each time Henry entered the room.

To atone for his mistakes, he beat up a couple of well-known womanisers, placing the blame on them for casting doubt on his wife's morality, and spent the next six months exclusively with Curtis. He taught his youngest son rough words and rude songs to combat Agatha's influence, and he took him to the park, to football games, to the beach. He allowed him an occasional sip of his beer and gave him an occasional hug.

These acts of preferential treatment caused the gap between Curtis and his older brothers to widen; especially with Harry, whose nose was already out of joint when he was deposed as the youngest son. If their parents weren't nearby, Harry would tease, hassle and bully until Curtis learned to stay as far from him as he could in a three-bedroom house.

Although little more than a toddler, Curtis soon realised that his father's displays of affection were the cause of his brothers' spite. He began to avoid him as he avoided them — mostly by running to his mother for protection. The trouble was, because of all that extra time Henry spent with his youngest son, he did grow to favour him above the other two. How could he help it? At that young age Curtis was an exceptionally endearing child. He had a way of smiling at you, a way of reaching out and cuddling up as if no one else existed but you and him. A way of melting even the hardest heart. Except, of course, for his brothers — who were far too boisterous and rough to ever be called lovable.

I suppose, when I think about it now, they were just typical preteen boys.

Somewhere around this time I had an altercation with my next-door neighbour, who happened to be the midwife, Rosie Yates. She accused me of spreading gossip detrimental to her profession. I was naturally hurt and annoyed. Nobody wants a neighbour intent on making mischief.

By then I had put my inheritance to good use by purchasing a block of flats near the beach, two shops in the main street, and another in a northern suburb. Being a thrifty person, I had little use for cash. My mother had left more than enough furniture and linen to last me for two lifetimes, and I was a vegetarian. Angus's garden provided the bulk of my meals. Clothing was inexpensive, as I hated the rawness of new materials and I was never a stylish person. I much preferred my workday clothes to be already broken in. I usually wore overalls during the day, these being found in abundance at the local charity stores. At night I copied my mother's habit of dressing for dinner. Her penchant for loose gowns and soft woollen shawls had been passed on to me, although no one saw me dressed that way except for Angus. And, much later, Curtis. Nor did anyone guess, for I made those gowns myself. I washed them, along with my other clothes, once a week and hung them in the garden shed. I had never relinquished my wood stove and water heater, and I lit candles at night, so my bills were naturally small, my assets continually growing. I now owned three times as much property as my parents ever had, including the real estate agency where my father had worked so many years ago.

Through that agency, I made Rosie Yates a very attractive offer for her house. Anonymously, as always. No one but I and my solicitor knew the extent of my assets.

Mrs Yates moved within the week, and that settled the problem of my being a half-hour walk from my godson. Agatha soon heard of the cheap rent on offer for the cosy home next to mine. The Lawsons moved in to 5 Blackwattle Road as Mrs Yates moved out, and so they became my neighbours.

# Chapter Twenty-five

I did not entice Curtis into my home. Agatha sent him to me when I was being tormented by Albert and Harry. They persisted in jumping my fence to escape having to play with their younger brother. I tried installing a large and savage dog, but they befriended the animal and caused it to snarl at me.

'I need to visit the doctor. You know, women's things,' Agatha told me from the footpath. (She and Henry had kept to their bargain. Neither had set a foot through my gate after the christening.) 'I don't want to take Curtis with me and you're the only one I can trust. Will you watch him for an hour? I know he'll stay with you. He'd love that jungle you call a yard.'

In the days of my parents' youth, it was customary, provided the purse allowed, to acquire the land surrounding one's home to house one's genetic produce. Or, as in the case of my parents and the McTavishes, to allow for vegetable gardens and a henhouse. My home sat on one corner of a block that would normally have held four houses.

My vegetable garden had been reclaimed by native shrubs and trees: banksia, grevillea, various ground covers and climbers, a dozen towering eucalypts, a couple of wattles, a flame tree and two ancient she-oaks. It was the perfect place for a child to gain a love of nature. After all, a godmother's duty is not to feed, bathe, pick up after, wash dirty nappies, or discipline. I aimed to shape his mind and make my godson a better person. Angus was the best person I knew. If I could make Curtis more like him, I'd be doing the child a favour. A love of plants was an ideal beginning.

'Curtis is my godson,' I told Agatha, 'so of course he can visit me whenever he wishes. He can stay now, and at any other time, but on the condition that you keep Albert and Harry away from my surrounds.'

The decision was not hard to make, or to enforce. Even a smother-love mother needs free time, and the older children were content to remain in their own yard if Curtis was in mine. And so my untamed bush became a special gift to my godson, as I knew it would be. He appreciated it more than any other. Except for the seeds from Angus's bonsai.

That bonsai came into Curtis's life, along with Angus, on the weekend before the child began school. Someone (probably Agatha, who liked to keep him to herself) had filled his head with stories of teacher atrocities and peer cruelties. He had reached the point of throwing up whenever he contemplated his initiation into education. I turned him over to Angus with complete confidence that he would banish the boy's fears. I must admit that he surprised me by agreeing, although I once heard him telling the door of his backyard toilet that Curtis reminded him of himself. (Until the advent of sewerage, and unknown to the local council, Angus emptied his own toilet in the dark of night once a week. Where, I did not dare contemplate.)

I returned from a shopping trip to find Curtis chatting with the bonsai. From this one-way conversation, I discovered that the minia-ture eucalypt housed a spirit which had been robbed of its rightful home after its own tree had been sacrificed. Probably by some bloody godforsaken ratbags who had nothing better to do with their time than to sit around scribbling on murdered trees. The spirit chose the bonsai for an obvious reason. It wouldn't even make a cigarette paper. So it was safe from the idiots who ran round chopping down trees because they had nothing better to do with their time, except to get drunk and procreate snot-nosed kids who'd grow up to run round chopping down trees. I learned that anything now made from wood should be made from other materials; especially the boxes and packets filled with processed food and sold to dim-witted housewives too lazy to cook the real thing.

I learned a number of things of this nature, but I recognised the source as Angus's general perverseness. The only useful information I gleaned was the fact that people are what they are. You can't change 'em, so leave 'em be and get on with your own life. Bugger the lot of 'em anyway.

At first I thought Angus had given the bonsai to Curtis and the child had decided to hide it away at my house. Agatha considered gifts as bribes for his affection. I should have known better. Angus never gave anything away. If he did, he would not have given the bonsai. I had no idea then how it came into his possession. The story of its acquisition changed as frequently as his moods. He vowed it had brought him solace throughout his years at war.

Pictures of Angus running from bullets with a stunted tree tucked under one arm were too ridiculous to consider, so I slid those images behind the sight of him hopping around his yard with that same plant. Everyone has negatives shoved into the back of their album where they will never be studied in the light of commonsense.

Since his return, the bonsai had stood by his bedside at night, on his table while he dined, on a stump in his garden while he worked outside. He spoke to the spirit and swore it always gave him good counsel. When I argued that the advice came from within his own psyche, he smiled.

I did once try to establish a rapport with the spirit, but I made the mistake of attempting the liaison beside my bedroom mirror. A tall robust woman with a too-large mouth, a too-soft chin and hair with a mind of its own, appears ludicrous when seen in earnest conversation with a few bent twigs. Angus heard my snorts of laughter and snatched the plant away. He refused to speak to me until I apologised to the tree. That particular silence lasted for many weeks.

I still do not understand what the bonsai did for Curtis, for surely a five-year-old has no inner voice to give him counsel. Yet a few hours conversation with Angus's miniature tree definitely changed the child. He no longer threw up at the thought of school. He stopped following his brothers around like an unwanted smell. He began to spend most of his time with Angus or me, defying his mother when she tried to keep him at home. Even she had to admit that he was more content in our houses than he was in his own, especially when his father and brothers were present.

'I suppose that's because you're so much more like us than you are like them,' I told him constantly.

As expected, Curtis became imbued with a love of plants and planting. He listened, watched and learned by shadowing Angus around the yard.

'Remember your preparation,' Angus told him. 'What goes into the soil germinates the seed and forms the plant.'

Curtis pestered his father with questions about his own preparation. Perhaps Henry didn't understand, or perhaps he didn't want to speak of his family tree. After meeting his mother and eight sisters, I, for one, can't blame him for that. Whatever the reason, his answer was always a football story. This being unsatisfying to Curtis, he turned to me for information. Knowing next to nothing about the Lawsons, I gave him the clan McTavish. He dug them into his soil and was content.

Curtis did try Angus as a confidant. He was told to quit his bloody whining. So the child began to tell me, via the bonsai, of his problems and dreams, of all the nitty-gritties troubling a child, a youth, an adult. I listened attentively, for Curtis had access to the juiciest Steeltown gossip. Agatha cleaned houses to supplement her family's income. She knew everything about everyone, and this youngest son was the sole recipient of that information. She did not spend enough time with the older children to pass rumours on to them.

When Curtis tried to turn Agatha's mind from strangers by asking about her ancestry, she refused to be turned. Instead, she led him through the private lives of half the families in town, making him privy to every last grinding, shameful, cruel and dirty detail. These stories troubled the child and gave him nightmares. He would come to me, trying to fit the jigsaw pieces of inhumanity together. I repaid him by relating what he wanted to hear. I gave him the Trelelans. Not Agatha's parents. I knew nothing of them. At least, nothing I had a particular wish to impart. I gave him Mary Mayberry and Leslie Amadeus, telling their story a dozen times or more, despite a protest from Angus.

'Why are you talking about them?' he asked on the day he caught me in the act. 'Your mother and father are nothing to do with him.'

'I've always been interested in people and how they connect to each other, you know that,' I said. 'And it's to do with the Trelelan bloodline, which, to me at least, is very apparent in Curtis.'

'Because his mother carries the line from her father,' Angus stated.

'What would you know?' I asked dismissively, turning away.

'I saw it in your journal,' he said, looking from me to Curtis.

'Spying is nothing to boast about,' I answered loftily, privately vowing to keep my facts and figures, my birth, deaths and marriages certificates, and my many notes of personal opinion hidden from that day on. 'But all things considered, he's more a McLean than anything else. He reminds me of your mother. Especially around his eyes and chin. As you pointed out to me just the other day.'

Angus couldn't think of an answer for that. I had spoken the truth. Neither he nor Curtis knew at the time that Joyce Trelelan had been born a McLean.

# Chapter Twenty-six

Although Curtis never learned to like school, he was usually the centre of a group of children. He encouraged their admiration with strange and daring deeds, like jumping from the school toilet roof onto a pile of newspapers. Paper was made of trees and trees were his friends, he said. He cried for days when a broken leg proved him wrong.

Angus explained how the ratbags had adulterated the paper until it forgot what it used to be. He then proffered a dozen seeds as a leg-break present. They were, Angus said, offspring of the bonsai.

'That's nonsense,' I said, being sensible. 'The bonsai has never seeded.'

'Not that you saw. Which only proves that you don't see everything,' Angus growled.

Curtis knew that Angus never thought twice about stretching the truth to tell a better story, while I made a point of never actually telling a lie. Yet the child wanted to believe. With parents like Agatha and Henry, there was little enough fantasy in his life.

I halved one of the seeds while he watched, appalled by my sacrilegious act. 'There's no way of telling,' I said after a few moments of study. 'These could have come from any of the trees around here. You'll know when they sprout, but by then it won't matter. It's what you want to believe that counts.'

'Don't go twisting this into something that suits your own purpose. I just wanted to make the kid feel better,' Angus told me. 'Can't make a wattle into a eucalypt, no matter what you believe.'

'A cuckoo lays her egg in a currawong's nest, and the currawong rears it as one of her own. But that doesn't change the nature of the cuckoo chick,' I pointed out, smiling at Curtis, who looked even more bewildered. 'You'll see what I mean one day,' I told him.

'Very clever, Loby,' Angus said.

He looked at me with an odd, sad expression. I waited for him to say more, but he turned to stomp away.

'Will I plant them in your yard?' Curtis asked.

'They'd just be strangled by what's already here. They need someone to take care of them properly. I think you should plant them next door,' I said, nodding towards the Lawson yard.

Angus swung around. 'Just chuck 'em,' he snarled. 'They'll grow if and where they're meant to grow. Where they bloody well belong.'

'Are you telling the boy that it doesn't matter where his seed is planted?' I asked in the most dulcet of tones. 'Then how will he know which is his?'

'He'll know. Then he can tend which is his and mind his own bloody business with the rest. But what would you know about that — ay, Liona?'

Angus and I went into our respective houses and banged our respective doors. It was a typical ending to one of our everyday arguments. Curtis jumped the fence and planted the seeds in his own yard. He was disappointed when the eucalypts grew taller than their parent within a few months, but he lavished on them an affection close to brotherhood.

His flesh and blood brothers did not uproot the seedlings, as I feared they might. Being ten years old at the time, Curtis had learned to wield Agatha's love like a club over the heads of his siblings. And no doubt the brothers realised that those trees would put an end to the football lessons.

To Henry's mortification, even Albert and Harry, as big and as willing as they had grown to be, were not natural rugby league forwards. When they reached mid school age, he decided that experience could bestow what his genes had not. Every second afternoon he marched them into the yard to tackle, pound and train them until they reeled with exhaustion. By the time Agatha prepared the evening meal, they were bruised, bloodied and punch-drunk. All to no avail. The junior league selectors continued to prefer youths who did not stumble, drop balls, miss tackles, then try to make up for a lack of talent with bombast and blows.

A yard crowded with eucalypts was a perfect excuse to avoid those training sessions.

Henry soon realised that he was doomed to disappointment. He contented himself with gathering the boys and a carton of beer onto the front porch, usually after their evening meal. They listened with the required bright eyes while he relived his days of glory. Agatha dragged Curtis into the kitchen to listen to her.

So he continued throughout his school years: a sensible, likable boy dubbed strange by the adults of Steeltown, which made him popular with their children. He had no interest in girls until Debra Watling happened into his life.

# Chapter Twenty-seven

I first met Debra when she arrived at my house one Saturday morning looking for a donation of household items. Things like vases, spare linen or towels to be sold at the Salvation Army flea market, which was held on the second Saturday of each month.

'Or plants in pots. My mother said they sell very quickly,' she said in a small voice, and her expression showed how much she disliked the idea of being sent out to cadge for contributions.

Debra was then a twelve-year-old decorated in bows, frills and laces. Her hair was dulled from too frequent washing, her skin was scrubbed raw, her nails were bitten to the quick. She was also big-eyed and peach-skinned — the epitome of cute, as her mother had been at that age.

I remember that Maidy Watling.

Standing next to cumbersome lumbersome Loby by the bus stop near my house, the peachy-cute Maidy Greentree. I remember that artful toss of her long blonde hair and the way she always walked with a forward thrust of her pubis. I remember how she half turned away from Angus, showing her body to its best advantage.

Annoyed by the silly, cow-like look on his face, I returned to my gate, expecting him to follow. He boarded the bus and sat next to her, not seeing me on the outside looking in. He then disappeared for almost a week. Not that I missed him. I was ill with the flu at the time, and busy knitting booties for my little Curtis.

When I pried into Maidy's background to find an equaliser, I discovered that her parents lived by the adage that if nobody can be found who will speak ill of you, then you must be exceptionally good or maliciously evil. I found no hint of evil in the Greentree parents. True, they were exceedingly moralistic, but in the days of my youth so were many of Steeltown's inhabitants. I could never decide if that was a penance or a compensation for being poor. The wealthy minority were as capitalists everywhere. They attended orgies every night, drinking, carousing, parading nude. Or so it was said around the shabbier parts of town.

Through Agatha via Curtis I knew of Maidy's disposition. I could easily imagine the kind of life she forced her daughter to live. My parents had been wise enough to ignore their only child, allowing me to rear myself and form my own nature. Debra was being mentally bashed and moulded, physically scrubbed and pared down. I felt sorry for her, although the way she kept a wide space between us proved her wariness of me.

Even as a child, she did not fear Angus. Yet most people, especially children, were apprehensive of this man. He had become a rather daunting figure, never having followed the mode of camouflaging the loss of a leg by wearing trousers. Instead he chose to accent the wooden replacement with a twining of ivy. He refused to wear a modern prosthesis, which was more aesthetically pleasing, 'Because,' he said, 'they make the bloody thing out of metal.' His clothes never matched in colour, and his body gave off an odour of mulch and manure. In fact he made himself as repulsive as possible in order to enjoy contempt for those showing their revulsion.

On the day of that visit by Debra, he was unusually reticent. Yet she became fascinated by him, despite his appearing even more derelict than usual. He scowled. She smiled. He made rude noises. She laughed. He muttered curses to warn her away and she followed him into his yard.

I waited for him to become threatening when she admired the bonsai. Her grandmother had possessed one very much like it, she said. Angus had always maintained that his bonsai was one of a kind. I didn't expect him to take kindly to a chit of a girl denying its individuality.

'I never saw hers,' Debra said, 'but it's in my mother's wedding photos. I suppose she threw it away when Grandma died. My mother doesn't like plants in the house. She says they make germs and take away the good air.'

I supposed Maidy had no idea that Debra would enter Angus's premises. Most women, certainly ones like Maidy, were in the habit of keeping their children as far from him as possible. Yet everyone knew of my relationship with Angus. Our neighbours thought of us as a couple of crazies who maintained a friendship because of our bond of abnormality. The friendship was necessarily platonic because of his appearance and my background and intellect, or so they said. They had no conception of how his hands could work independently of each other, one soothing and stroking while the other explored the most personal crevices of my body.

But enough! I kept my sexuality private, like my dinner gowns.

As for Curtis, his interest in Debra began a few weeks before Christmas of 1954. He had turned fifteen, gained his Intermediate Certificate and begun to ponder on what to do with the rest of his life.

Through lack of application, his marks were not good. That limited his choices. Horticulture was his vocation, but Steeltown had long ago chosen industry above the land. Angus suggested he head for farming country on the other side of the mountains, yet I felt sure the boy would be miserable away from his home town. I pestered everyone I knew, and those I did not, to give him a job turning their untidy yards into gardens. More than a few were willing after I promised to pay his wages. I felt sure that a local landscape gardener would recognise his talent and give him permanent work. Meanwhile he had time to consider anything else that might happen along. Perhaps an apprenticeship when he turned sixteen. Where, or doing what, I had no idea.

He was happy enough marking time this way. It kept him away from his father's ill temper, his brothers' spite and his mother's meddling. Although she did insist that he help with her charity work. It was Agatha who sent him to the Watling house with knick-knacks for the flea market. Richard Rees helped him to carry the boxes. Richard was Curtis's best friend.

# Chapter Twenty-eight

Richard glanced at the upstairs window and quickly looked away.

'Don't look now,' he said to Curtis. 'They're up there watching us.'

Curtis looked immediately, as Richard knew he would.

'Who is? Where?' he asked.

Richard switched his box to the other shoulder. 'Hang on, slow down a minute. Give me your box. I'll carry them both.'

Curtis answered in a falsetto voice, 'Oh, Richie, you're my hero'.

'What d'you care? You're not interested. Okay okay, you have first choice. No, wait a bit. Just hang on to that box. I know what you're like. You'll take both and make me out to be the weakling. Which one do you want, Debra or Amanda?'

'Tell you what, you can have them both.'

'There's something wrong with you, Curtis.'

'Yeah. I want you for myself.'

Richard snorted and staggered, and Curtis couldn't help noticing how his mate managed to look graceful. Even at this age of acne and awkwardness, Richard always reminded Curtis of a tree swaying in the breeze.

Dumping his box onto the footpath, Curtis glanced at the two girls framed in an upstairs window. If he had to choose one, which he had no intention of doing, it would probably be Debra. For some reason, probably her pale hair and skin, she reminded him of a flannel flower.

Debra Watling stared down, comparing the boys and wondering if she had made the right choice after all. Not long after entering high school, Amanda had decided to marry Richard Rees. She had, she said, been in love with him since kindergarten. In the spirit of competitiveness that existed between the girls, Debra declared her own purpose. They shook hands and vowed to remain friends no matter who became the victor. Now Debra couldn't be sure if she really wanted whatever Amanda wanted. Richard had good looks, a good family, money and a position in Steeltown. Yet she sometimes thought of him as rather bland. Curtis was a fascination. The boys were of the same general appearance, although Curtis was slimmer and not so obviously muscled. And Richard had an open expression which beguiled most people, while Curtis had a habit of staring until she was flustered by his attention. Yet when she sought his eyes, they looked beyond her to something she couldn't see. She imagined filling them with herself instead of the horizon. A shiver of excitement at this prospect was disquieting.

Amanda Falls leaned against Debra's shoulder and stared back at the boys, waiting to see who would look away first. Her olive skin and wavy brown hair was a perfect foil to Debra's white-blonde fairness. Both girls had become aware of this fact on the day they first sat next to each other at school. Maidy had commented on the advantages gained by such a contrast, and because they looked so good together, Amanda's mother had allowed the friendship to prosper. Marianne Falls led the committees not headed by Richard's mother. Along with Elizabeth Rees, she was Steeltown society. She could afford to be generous for the sake of her daughter's appearance.

'I love them both,' Richard whispered to Curtis.

'Amanda's mother would never let me in the same house as her,' Curtis whispered back, 'and I've always thought she was a bit on the sly side. Reminds me of a wisteria vine. All sweet-smelling and clingy, but tough as nails and hard to get rid of once it's got itself established.'

'What about Debra?' Richard asked.

'Her skirts are too short and she's always swishing her hair around. But soon as anyone gets close, she runs. I'd say she's a tease.'

The words were no sooner out of his mouth when Maidy's voice smacked across his ears.

'Debra, get away from that window at once. How many times must I tell you? Who are those boys and what are they doing out there? I'm going to call the police.'

Although Debra made her answer deliberately indistinct, her tone was a vocabulary. Amanda stayed at the window, ignoring it all as Debra trailed Maidy around the house.

'Go to the door,' Curtis hissed at Richard. 'Tell the old hag why we're here.'

'Why don't you go?'

'Because she'll know who I am and that'll make it worse. She knows you're Elizabeth Rees's little boy.'

Knowing his mother's name always worked like a charm on the matrons of Steeltown, Richard hefted his box and strode to the porch.

'Mrs Watling,' he called through the open door. 'It's me, Richard Rees. I've got things for the charity drive. Mother asked me to deliver them here.'

Maidy appeared at the door. Richard held his breath. He had never noticed Mrs Watling before, except as another Steeltown matron. But as this Steeltown matron stood behind the security screen, her nylon housecoat was made almost sheer by the hall light just behind her head. She reminded him of Rita Hayworth's Sadie Thompson — all juts and curves and hidden crevices marked by highlights and shadows. The haloed blondeness of her long hair promised the pot of gold at the end of a rainbow. He lowered the box of knick-knacks to hide the evidence of his lust.

Maidy tried not to smile. Passing forty had not spoiled it for her. She hadn't lost it after all. It had merely gone to sleep while circumstances forced her into exclusively female company.

'It' was Maidy's name for the aura of sensuality she had possessed since puberty, despite the pressure of strictly religious parents. When she was twelve, boys had turned to stare at her, perplexed by the then new feelings she created just by smiling in their direction. Older men recognised her and tried to lure her, not realising that she was the seducer. By the age of sixteen Maidy knew she could take everything they owned and leave them thinking the reverse was true. Yet she saw the labels pasted on less perceptive girls by yesterday's lovers. She learned to pretend affront at any hint of a proposition, although it cost her many a sleepless night. At the age of twenty, when hunger could no longer be appeased by her own hand, she spent two weeks in Melbourne with a man who was married and therefore safe. On returning to Steeltown, she had a number of brief but passionate flings. But only with men who, for reasons of their own, could be relied upon to remain discreet.

Debra was born in June of 1940, eight months after Maidy married David Watling. Maidy aimed to climb the social ladder in Steeltown, so fear of discovery meant she had to remain a faithful wife even after her husband's wartime death; yet the aura remained, reaching out across a crowded dinner table, on the tennis court, on a bus or a train. It spread from her in an enveloping cloud that shortened a man's breath or zapped him like a lightning bolt. But the men who attracted her were always the husbands of the society women she wanted to impress. Her only consolation was in knowing she could look at those men and 'it' would stroke them.

Sometimes a perceptive wife sensed the danger. She'd hurry her man home and to bed, seeking reassurance in grunts and thrusts and the swiftness of his orgasm. Maidy guessed this would happen. It was a vicarious pleasure, but better than nothing. She delighted in knowing the husband would visualise her face while he fornicated with his condescending wife.

Now she could cause her pretty little daughter's boyfriends to sit up and take notice. This knowledge made her appear even more sensual than usual.

'Richard, how sweet of you to come,' she breathed, and Richard almost groaned. 'Tell me,' she said, 'who's out there at the gate?'

'Um, ar, a friend,' Richard croaked. 'He's got more. Other stuff. Things.'

'Debra, go and help the boy,' Maidy said. 'I'll get us all a nice cold glass of lemonade.'

Amanda paused on the stairs to tilt her head in the Lana Turner way. Widening her eyes à la Doris Day, she stumbled on the last step so Richard could catch her as she fell. This trick, old even then, had succeeded twice before with Richard, though he'd probably seen it in the movies at least a dozen times. Richard Rees was an ardent movie fan, a fact made obvious by his Clark Gable grin and Humphrey Bogart stare. Yet now he wouldn't release the box of knick-knacks covering his embarrassment and Amanda merely succeeded in knocking him to the floor.

She looked into eyes filled with the vision of Maidy's haloed body. Although old enough to recognise lust, she was still young enough to fear it. She turned slightly, trying to hide the shock of surprise at the sudden clenching of her vulva. Folding her arms to cover hardened nipples, she jumped up and chased Maidy into the kitchen. Richard gasped a few deep breaths while trying to imagine water spiking down from an icy shower.

Debra walked onto the porch and beckoned to Curtis. He put down his carton and straightened up slowly. As he walked to her, the sympathy in his eyes sent the same tremors through her body as Amanda had experienced with Richard. He held her by the shoulders for a few moments then slid his hands to her forearms. His fingers tightened before letting go. She smiled and nodded.

'I'll leave you to drink your lemonade. But just fifteen minutes, then you must be on your way. Don't want the neighbours gossiping,' Maidy said, and hurried up the stairs, having noticed Amanda's raised eyebrows at her state of undress.

Richard watched the ceiling while he gulped the lemonade. He insisted on leaving the moment he emptied his glass. Debra and Amanda later agreed that his unusual reserve was probably caused by bashfulness at Maidy's presence. When told the truth, Curtis collapsed across the fence in a fit of laughter.

Richard was trying to push him the rest of the way over when Clo Gatley ran up the street, followed by a few of the local Lotharios. Clo slowed to a walk and smiled into Curtis's eyes. The smile turned to a laugh when his chin dropped. She shook her unfashionably long hair in his face, and strode on. Her loyal followers shoved him back into the Watling yard then continued the chase, yelling insults over their shoulders.

# Chapter Twenty-nine

Now that Clo Gatley has wandered onto the scene, I should introduce her properly. Preparation and groundwork, Angus would say. What type of soil formed her twists and gnarls?

To me, Clo was a column of stone. If I looked into her face, I saw only the blank stare of the marble angels who guard our local cemetery. When I tried to see through her eyes, everything I looked at became indistinguishable. I could not see into her, or out of her. She blocked me at every turn. I do not know if that was deliberate, or the shade of an enmity we brought from a former life.

Jamie Blake, whom I will discuss in more detail later, knew her better than anyone. As children they lived in the same inner-city suburb of Sydney. Although five years her senior, Jamie knew Clo well enough to be called a friend. This friendship was re-established when, at the age of eighteen, Clo paid a visit to old haunts. She was foolish enough to let a nostalgic wander carry on past nightfall, and in an area no longer inhabited by the happy families she remembered. Running from a mob of girls calling themselves Widgies, she had the good luck to bang on Jamie's door. The gang retreated when he placed her under his protection.

Jamie admitted that he saw only what Clo allowed him to see, but he had the advantage of having been invited to read her earliest writing.

That is, the stories written before she became a successful novelist. Clo kept a journal from the time she learned to shape letters. From these journals, and his personal knowledge, he helped fill in her background.

To me, the most interesting part of her childhood was her connection with the woman she called the red lady.

# Chapter Thirty

To Clo, the red lady was a permanent figure in the streetscape of that part of the inner city. She was short and thin, with hair the colour of those plastic flowers decorating cemeteries, their pigment blanched to a yellowish grey by the sun. She never wore shoes, and she dressed in shades of red, from her dress to the pillbox hat with its mosquito-netting veil. In winter she wore layers of red over maroon trousers. This confirmed the young Clo's opinion that the lady had been, in her younger days, a prostitute. In Clo's child mind, red was scarlet. Women who wore scarlet and trousers just had to be whores, even though the ladies who walked the nearby streets seemed to like black and never wore trousers, much preferring the leg-display of hotpants or miniskirts.

The red lady had no family. At least, none ever visited or wrote. She lived alone at the end of Clo's row of houses, in the permanent shadow of the biscuit factory where most of the mothers and fathers worked. The children would nudge and giggle when she walked the length of the street. They mimicked her mutterings and the shuffling walk until she swung around, screeched and sent them scampering off in a giggling huddle behind the nearest fence.

The men passed her with eyes averted. To the women, she didn't exist. All others who walked the gauntlet of front gate gossipers were hailed by name, greeted with enthusiasm, and the details of their lives exposed when they passed into the sunlight beyond the factory. As the red lady shuffled by, not one eye flickered in her direction.

'She's just different,' Clo's grandmother said.

Clo learned about grades of difference when the Greek families moved into three houses at the far end of the street. Within days the men were on speaking terms. 'Ow yer going, mate', and 'Ullo, mister'. They discussed whatever men discuss in factory work lines, and they tipped their hats when passing each other on the footpath. The eventual mingling of the women never seemed as easy. For the first year or so they greeted each other with a nod, taking in the difference of dress and culture with barely concealed suspicion and a touch of contempt from both sides.

At one end of the street was the quick-fire, cut-word speech of those who had been born and bred there, as had their parents before them. Life beyond the grandparents was never talked about, and probably not known. The conversation at the other end was just as rapid, but the tones more fluted, and strange. Only after their children merged at school did these groups of women speak to each other with less wariness. Once the barrier was down and friendships were formed, Clo discovered that most of the differences were superficial after all.

Lucia Demoska became Clo's best friend, although their friendship might not have begun without the red lady. Lucia moved into the street at a time when most of the kids had grown tired of the aping game. But Clo felt she had a loyalty to uphold. She would not be guilty of desertion.

For a week or two the newcomer was content to watch, and practise on her pathway. That suited Clo fine. An audience brought out the best in the red lady. She added dance to her walk and snatches of songs to her mumble, which made the mime more of a challenge. Yet on the day Lucia tried to join in, Clo hurled a mouthful of insults. She wouldn't admit to it for fear of sounding foolish, but she liked having the lady to herself. In her extended family, everyone shared. Sole owner-ship was a rare thing. It was much too valuable to allow a newcomer to make a claim.

The red lady turned and screeched, making cat's claws with her fingers. They were outside the Demoska house at the time, and the first rule of the game was to hide behind the nearest fence. Clo shoved Lucia through the gate and pulled her onto the ground. After another shove or two, and a half-hearted wrestle, they sneaked around the back of the house to raid Mr Demoska's tomatoes.

Lucia was ashamed of a father and uncles who never went to the pub, never reached the stage of falling-down drunk, and who turned their cobbled yards into garden plots. Clo's shame in her male relatives was for the opposite reasons, even though they, too, merely followed tradition. She envied Lucia's possession of an ancestry rich in legends.

Clo learned that her own background was English and Scottish, with a dash of German from Great Grandma's bloodline.

'But which one is me?' she asked. 'Lucia's grandma says they've got a tradition. What have we got?'

'I s'pose you can take your pick if you really want,' her mother said. 'But it's today that matters, not yesterday. As far back as I know, our family was born here in Sydney.'

For a while Clo and Lucia avoided each other's houses by playing in the wall's shadow. After a year had passed, they decided that their family mythology was basically the same. The tales Lucia heard from her female relatives were of how an uncle was struck down by God for cheating on his wife, how a cousin coped when she lost her firstborn, about the parents' hard times as children and newlyweds. These were much the same as the stories told to Clo.

So Lucia became Lucy, and Clo's best friend. She never lost her as she lost the red lady. That particular friendship began on the day Clo's father returned from war.

His letter promised that he'd be home about ten on Saturday morning. Clo, her sister Janet and others there for curiosity's sake, waited for him at the biscuit factory corner. When George Gatley strode down the street, his wiry figure was familiar to Clo only by her study of an old wedding photograph.

Janet charged at him with noisy glee, and her shriek of 'Dad! Dad!' trailed to a sob as she threw herself into his arms. He replaced her feet on the ground after claiming half a dozen kisses.

Awed by such an open display of affection from an adult, especially a male, Clo stayed behind the grouping of children.

He singled her out, staring at her with eyes piercingly blue and full of laughter, so different from the noncolour blur of the photograph. She barely recognised a face darker than it should have been, and disfigured by a scar made obvious in his turning aside to hide it.

'Don't remember yer old man, do ya?' he asked, and squatted down to match her height.

His stare asked for something she wanted to give but couldn't identify. She searched her pockets, looking for the something to bring the laughter back into those blue eyes. Finding nothing but a pin and a grit-covered toffee, she held them out, not knowing what else she had to offer.

He stood, ignoring the gift. 'Not to worry,' he said. 'You will in a while. You look different, too. But I remember your dress at least.'

'He doesn't remember it on me,' Clo muttered as Janet dragged him off down the street. 'It was hers when he was at home.'

'Isn't fair, is it?' the red lady said from behind a nearby post. 'Even the womb was second-hand by the time you got to it.'

Clo burst into tears and ran without knowing why, but a relationship was begun, a friendship made potent by its secrecy and the fact that it was given only to her, by tales of places and people she had never dreamed existed. The red lady was the only source of fantasy in a world peopled by aunts, uncles and cousins who treated such stories with scorn.

Clo's other main source of delight was the 'Sat'dee arvo cards' held at Great Grandma's home, a two-storeyed house around the corner from Clo's. Great Grandma presided over these Saturday afternoon card games, though she rarely played. As her sharp eyes took in every movement, every change of expression, her large bulk spilled over the sides of the just as huge and equally worn chair which seemed to be grafted to her backside. Clo had never seen her upright or in any other chair. Even when the children arrived on Saturday mornings for their weekly dose of herbs and castor oil, the old lady never moved. The portions she measured out were administered by Great Aunt Jean, the eldest of her six daughters. The term 'Great' was always applied, for there were many Grandmas and Aunt Jeans in the host of Clo's kin who lived in the surrounding streets.

Clo hated the herbs and oil, and still tastes them in oranges today. A half orange was supposed to disguise the medicine's vileness. Yet she never considered refusing. No one refused Great Grandma. That huge bulk, the age-spotted skin, the iron-grey hair pulled back into a tight bun, the breath smelling of stout and peppermint, the slippers slit down each side to allow her bunions room to breathe, and the feel of her iron hard hand as she pulled Clo close to kiss her forehead, these were all symbols of her power. Clo feared Great Grandma as much as the old lady feared her God.

On Saturday afternoons most of the fathers retired to the local pub where they relived the war, their work, their real or imagined encounters with women, and financed the starting price bookmakers. Women with young children gathered to gossip at the local pocket park while watching the 'young uns' at play. Older children found their own amusement. The elders — those women whose children had grown and married, though not necessarily moved away from home — would, at one thirty on the dot, make their way to Great Grandma's house for the card game.

Clo was an exception to the rule. By the age of ten she'd become ashtray emptier, drink and food fetcher, tea maker, and holder of the change jar. She always arrived early to cover the kitchen table with a blanket in preparation for the game. She'd ready the tea-making utensils and chill Great Grandma's two bottles of stout, which were the old lady's Saturday allowance. One was her limit on weekdays. She did not indulge on Sundays.

Clo squatted in a corner of the room under a triangular table. It held a tall vase filled with peacock feathers and a moulting sheaf of wheat.

She watched them arrive, these women fifty or older, and ticked off their names on her fingers. Those not related by blood were considered honorary aunts through long association with the family. A dozen or so usually sat around the table. Numbers varied according to illness and an occasional death.

The game was as professional as any in a major casino. The cards were mixed, cut, flipped and spread without a second's pause or an interruption in the flow of dialogue. Curses rarely used at any other time punctuated the language. Words were abbreviated and merged, and sentences cut off by others' recognition of how they'd finish.

'Y'thinking bout wiping y'bum with that card or y'gunner play the bloody thing?'

'Shut y'gob an what's y'bloody hurry? Pass the whatsit.'

'Y'gunner light that bloody . . .'

'No, I'm gunner suck me tea through it.'

'For chrissake wake up, Dolly. He'll get another job soon enough.'

All accompanied by gestures, smiles, scowls, winks and an occasional brief laying of a hand on a shoulder.

Clo watched intently, fascinated by the flying fingers which dealt, swooped, plucked and ejected, lifted teacups and rolled cigarettes, and emphasised a point in the owner's story. The tone of the voices ranged through the emotions as each woman patched or reattached the parts torn off by the frustrations of everyday living.

For bringing the red lady, Clo was banned until age would allow her return. By then many of the traditions of her childhood had been lost.

The biscuit factory was rumoured to be closing down, and a distant relative of George Gatley had offered him a job south of Sydney. The red lady's entry into the card game was Clo's farewell present to all her adult friends. She felt sure that once the kin became acquainted with the lady and her stories, they'd make her an honorary aunt.

Such an auspicious occasion demanded a touch of drama, so Clo was deliberately late that day. She took the red lady's hand, ignoring the stares as they passed the other houses, and ushered her into Great Grandma's kitchen. The red lady paused at the door to slip on newly bought shoes and to smile around the room. She shrugged her red coat into Clo's arms and turned slowly, displaying a modest brown frock. The shy droop of her shoulders underlined the statement.

Silence descended. Expressions grew bleak. Eyes were hooded as Clo pulled out a vacant chair.

'Good afternoon, ladies,' the red lady said as she sat and fussed with her skirt. 'How are you, Mrs Ade?' she added when the silence dragged on a little too long.

The ladies looked at Great Grandma. Eyes decently vacant, she inclined her head.

'Afternoon, Joyce,' was her meaningfully toneless reply.

With a flourish, almost a bow, the lady reached into the pocket of her shy brown dress and pulled out a scarf. It was a hazy, weightless thing that hung in the air for moments before floating around her shoulders like an aura. Its bright shade of red reflected in her arms and face and throat. The smile remained on her mouth, though her eyes had turned to flints.

'Still the same old rules?' she asked.

Without waiting for confirmation, she began to deal the cards.

No one spoke more than was necessary for the game. The kin remained politely communicative, although the colours of their language were missing. After exactly one hour the lady laid down her cards, gathered her winnings of five pence, her skirt close to her legs, and rose.

'Thank you, ladies. You are kinder than I remembered,' she said.

Clo watched in awe as Great Grandma rose from her chair and escorted the red lady to the door.

'You're welcome,' Great Grandma said, and stood at the steps for a few minutes before beckoning to Clo. 'Off you go,' she added.

'But she knew your name,' Clo accused. 'You know who she is.'

Great Grandma nodded. 'Joyce Trelelan. She ran off with a woman and deserted her child.'

'But she's back here now and she's on her own,' Clo protested.

'She never came back for Agatha,' Great Grandma said.

Before Clo could protest again, the door slammed in her face.

Clo saw the red lady many years later while visiting cousins in Sydney. By then Great Grandma's generation was gone. Those left of the sons and daughters had been moved to the outer suburbs. There they were as alien and lost as any people dispossessed of their tribalism.

The red lady still lived in her house. She gave Clo a cup of tea and polite conversation, but she did not know her.

# Chapter Thirty-one

That first time Curtis saw Clo, the friendship between him and Richard was strained to breaking point by the time they reached the Lawson house. A half-dozen of their schoolmates had joined them, and Curtis laughingly revealed Richard's lust for Maidy Watling. Richard was not impressed by the chiacking that followed, 'Blabbermouth' being his kindest word to Curtis. He was panting for revenge when he saw Henry hiccupping, 'Hup two three four,' and stagger-marching around the yard with a rake dangling over one shoulder.

'G'day, Mr Lawson,' Richard yelled, calling the boys' attention to a sight they might otherwise have missed.

Henry dropped to his stomach, aimed the rake and proceeded to 'Blast you bloody Nips to kingdom come'.

Richard grinned, clutched at his heart and went down screaming. Three boys mimicked his action. The remaining three took cover and fired, reverting back to their little-boy days with the use of an index finger as a firearm.

Curtis jumped over Richard and ran into the yard. 'They're my mates,' he told Henry. 'You're always trying to take my mates,' he yelled, not meaning a word of it, not knowing what he was saying but needing to say something. It wasn't right to be ashamed of your father. Even at the age of fifteen he knew that. Albert had told him that. If people laughed at your father, you belted their bloody heads in but you never felt ashamed. Shame was a parent's right. Kids were not supposed to give a bugger.

'Bugger you, you're drunk,' he hissed, red-faced and ashamed of feeling humiliated.

Henry grinned and swung the rake to shoot him down. Curtis ducked too late. The handle whacked the side of his head. It whacked him again as he shoved it aside. He stared the beginning of an apology into silence. Henry raised a hand as though protecting himself from a blow.

The boys on the opposite side of the street had fallen quiet. At Henry's action, someone sniggered. He looked over and saw Richard's teeth bared in a nervous grimace.

'What's so bloody funny? A man can't have a bit of a muck around, ay?' he roared.

Shoving Curtis onto the ground, he turned him around and planted a boot on his backside. The kick was hard enough to send Curtis sliding face down across the grass, but he refused to cry. Staggering to his feet, he thrust his head forward and glared with enough hatred in his eyes to make Henry quail. They stared at each other, neither wanting to back off. Curtis not wanting to actually speak his contempt. Henry believing that apologies or demonstrations of affection had to be women's business.

'Come on, Curtis. He's drunk again, that's all,' Richard called.

'I'll show ya bloody drunk! Go on you lot, piss off!' Henry shouted, taking a half-dozen menacing paces towards them.

The boys raced away down the street. Their shouts of laughter, which were merely teen bravado after all, sent Henry into a rage.

'You gunner let that toff's kid talk about your father that way?' he snarled. 'You gunner go after him and teach him a lesson, or am I gunner show you what a man woulda done?'

'He just told the truth,' Curtis sneered.

Letting loose a roar that sounded more like a scream, Henry charged. He lashed out with a fist that turned into an open-handed blow at the last moment, catching Curtis across the side of the head. Curtis hit the ground, then leapt to his feet. Henry hit him again.

The dance of contempt versus anger might have continued until Henry lost all control if Agatha hadn't spied them through a window.

'Tea's ready,' she called, and 'Tea's ready now!' in a voice rising to a shriek when Henry kicked Curtis again.

Harry wore a satisfied smirk as he joined her at the window. Albert had his usual deadpan look as he strolled past her into the yard. The look did not alter, except for an inward turning of his bottom lip, as he stumbled on the lowest step and grabbed his youngest brother for support. When they crashed to the ground, his ribs took a kick meant for Curtis.

Swaying with the force of his own breathing, Henry glared from the tangle of his sons to the back door. Albert understood the message and rolled aside, leaving the pathway clear. Curtis stared back without moving. A boot might have connected with his head if Albert hadn't hauled him out of the way. He finished off the movement with a hand clamped over Curtis's mouth to contain a verbal retaliation.

Henry strode through the kitchen, past the table which held his meal of baked lamb, potatoes and pumpkin surrounded by a mound of peas, carrots and cauliflower, all swimming in a sea of onion gravy. Throwing the door shut behind him, he stumbled into the room which children were never allowed to enter. It was the visitors' room, though they rarely had visitors, and furnished with one stiff lounge, two equally uncomfortable chairs and the only radio in the house.

Henry disapproved of radios. His sons were apt to listen to music instead of his football stories.

The pale yellow walls were almost hidden behind old family snapshots: mostly the Lawsons and their vast range of aunts, uncles and cousins. The only representative of Agatha's family was a cameo of Joyce Trelelan. The mantelpiece held three pictures, the central one being a sepia-toned wedding group of Agatha, Henry, his eight sisters and their husbands. On the left stood one of Henry and Agatha alone. He sat to the fore as befitted the man of the family. She stood in the background, separated from him by the bars on the back of his chair and her chin tilted away from his head. Her fringe had been brushed back from the straight line of her eyebrows, showing a slightly puzzled look in her pale blue eyes. Except for her mouth, which was thin-lipped and small, she looked more like Curtis than he did. Or so Henry always said.

The picture on the right was a faded drawing of Uncle Bert on his way to the Boer War. Uncle Bert Lawson, the brother of that western plains farmer, stood tall and straight. No dicky hip or s-shaped spine there.

Henry's stare travelled across the blur of faces staring back at him from every wall. He did not know most of these people. He didn't want to know them. His sisters had always been strangers. When old enough to think for himself, he kept them at a distance, afraid their soft bodies and stroking fingers would turn him into a replica of the man he knew as Father. Mr Lawson had been a wisp of a man who could only make his presence known in a household of women by relying on their compassion.

The only pictures Henry ever studied were those of his childhood holidays with his uncle, aunt and cousins at the outback property known as Lawson's Place. These — around a half-dozen he had managed to coax from his mother — were thumbtacked above the mantelpiece.

There was Uncle Bert cracking a whip. Frank rounding up strays in the scrub. Bob branding steers and Gus looking out at a flat expanse of drought-stricken land. Sam the eldest with Jack the youngest (Jack was sent to boarding school as punishment for being smart), and one of Henry astride a shaggy old horse.

Laughter was always hearty at Lawson's Place. No mocking giggles or a crowding of petticoats there. He was never isolated by his between-legs; 'the little grub' his sisters called it, and ridiculed it, but always tried to sneak a look. He was never spied on at Uncle Bert's. Never pinched or tweaked. At times Uncle punished him, but never by disappointed looks that made him feel like a worm. Uncle Bert gave good whacks. A man's punishment for a man. Henry had once been knocked to the floor for feeding the working dogs. 'An overfed dog is a lazy dog, and the punishment for laziness is a bullet,' Uncle Bert explained. Punishments were always defined. Henry was not expected to know without the telling.

He ran the pictures through his mind, smiling as he greeted each familiar friend. A grin from Uncle Bert, a wink from one of the boys. The thump of booted feet. The deep laughter and jocular insults of that male place. The slow drawl of men's voices that never became high-pitched and spiteful. The silent speeches of Aunt Miriam, who showed approval by a smile or an extra piece of pie. Censure was a cup placed loudly on the saucer, or a stiffening of her neck. Both were instantly noted and the cause of her disapproval removed.

Agatha had been one of those causes. On her only visit to the outback, he'd taken her out in the old truck to share his joy, to let her taste the freedom in a vast expanse of saltbush plains. She'd huddled in the seat and stared at the dashboard. He opened the door and tried to push her out. She clung onto the steering wheel. He lifted her chin and forced her to look through the windscreen. Her eyes faded to the colour of the sun-scoured sky. Beads of sweat popped through every pore of her skin. Her clothes became soaked within seconds.

On their return to the homestead she lay in bed for days, stricken with attacks of vomiting and migraine. Yet she recovered quickly enough when he took her back to Steeltown. Her only explanation was that the Agatha inside her had become lost out there. She was afraid of losing her forever in such an unpeopled place.

There was no room for Henry at Lawson's Place. He'd always known that. Not with Uncle Bert having so many sons. Yet all he ever wanted was a holiday once a year. That would build up a store of peace inside and get him through the next twelve months. Maybe Agatha thought he intended to take up jackerooing or shearing, but he'd known from the day he first clapped eyes on her that she couldn't live out bush. Maybe he should have told her about the choice he'd made, but women never listen to a word men say. They hear only what they want to hear. He'd learned that early in his life.

Drying his palms on the coarseness of his cotton trousers, Henry grabbed a flagon of wine from its hiding place up the chimney. The only way to blur his yearning for Lawson's Place was to soak it in alcohol. After downing two glassfuls with barely a pause for breath, he strode into the kitchen, threw his dinner against the wall then shoved Agatha and Curtis off their chairs with an order to clean up the mess. Agatha kept her eyes lowered as Harry passed her the dishcloth. Henry marched off to the pub.

'He did it, let him clean it up,' Curtis said.

Albert's face held the expression he seemed to reserve for his youngest brother. 'How would that help?' he asked in the tone of someone speaking to a backward child.

'It would just stay there forever,' Agatha said in the voice some people use when helping a little boy to learn his lessons.

'Why don't you leave him?' the boy asked loudly, as if the strength of his appeal could cause the act to be done.

For Curtis to say such a thing was more shocking than a slap in the face to Agatha. She sometimes thought about leaving Henry, but she always kept that thought inside her head where it belonged.

'You don't just up and leave,' she said. 'You don't break up a family like it's a bar of chocolate. Family is more important that anything on this earth. Without your family, there's nothing. I thought I'd taught you that much.'

'He's just a crazy old man,' Curtis pleaded.

'You're the one who makes him crazy,' Harry growled. 'He's all right when you're not around. You've always made him crazy, right from when you were little. He turned himself inside out to make you happy then. You never gave him anything back. You just went running to Mum.'

'So what do you want me to do?' Curtis snarled. 'Kiss his boot when he kicks me, like you would?'

Harry knocked the table over as he threw a punch that sent Curtis staggering backwards across the floor. He would have followed with another punch if Albert hadn't stepped between them.

'It doesn't help,' he said.

Curtis ducked around this oldest brother and slammed a header into Harry's chest. Harry grabbed him in an arm lock, tossed him into the yard then turned away, expecting that to be the end of it. Curtis rolled to his feet and charged back up the steps.

Albert threw him into the bath and turned on the cold-water tap.

# Chapter Thirty-two

Sometime during that night, Curtis decided to leave. The decision wasn't an easy one to make. Thought of living in unfamiliar surroundings made his stomach lurch, as if he'd swallowed something it couldn't accept. But neither could he stomach living in the same house as Henry and his two clones. Bad enough being shoved around by the so-called man of the house. He didn't need those two starting in on him again. He'd had enough of that as a kid.

At dawn he threw a change of clothing into a blanket roll and left. At no time did he try to be quiet. He wouldn't allow them to accuse him of being sneaky. As he clanged the gate shut, a face appeared at the front window. His first thought was of Agatha. There was that same gape-mouth look. Seconds passed before he recognised Albert. He turned and strode down the street, half expecting to hear a voice calling for his return. He couldn't think of a reason why Albert would want to follow him, but still he prepared arguments and slowed to a stroll. He had no idea why his chest tightened when the street remained empty.

Curtis had no sooner reached the highway when a semitrailer lurched to a stop beside his outstretched thumb. He climbed into the cabin muttering a thanks and feeling strangely satisfied when he saw Albert thudding down the road. Settling back against the seat, he blocked out the realisation of what he had done, what he had actually done at last, by staring out at the crowding of houses that were just beginning to stir.

Lights snapped on at windows, as if they were heralding his passing. Their glow was made brighter by a gathering of black clouds that blocked out the rising sun. Dogs checked fences for messages left by their street-wandering brothers and sisters, and an occasional cat streaked across the road, testing the truth of the nine lives legend. Every now and then a yawning man or woman stumbled bleary-eyed through a doorway, searching for newspapers that were usually found embedded in rosebushes and shrubs. The early starters were already pedalling their way to work on bicycles, or jogging to the nearest train station. A milkman put his own life and those of his adolescent helpers in jeopardy when he swung his van in a U turn at the crest of a hill. The truck driver's shouted curse and horn blast were countered with a half-dozen upraised thumbs. The accompanying jeers were left behind as the driver turned off Princes Highway onto Bulli Pass.

Curtis had lived his life below the escarpment. He had never ventured up the mountain before. He regretted that now as he pressed his face against the window, fascinated by the view when the truck began to zigzag upwards through rainforest country. A mist wound around the treetops here, following the pattern set by liana vines coiling around their trunks. A crowding of tree ferns knitted their fronds into umbrellas, protecting the smaller ferns at their feet. Water clear enough to be tinted silver made a dash across the road. There it hissed under and around the pound of rubber before sliding on.

To his right the ocean was shrouded, though gaps in the clouds allowed flickering visions of the contact between waves and sand. A train following the coastline south met with another heading north and stopped to pass the time of day. Cars converged briefly then went their separate ways.

The road moved back from the cliff edge as if nervous of the sheer drop. Curtis stared at thickening stands of towering gums until the truck became horizontal again. Not having to reach for the light, the trees up here were shorter than the ones below. Fire had recently passed through the area and these eucalypts were blackened and lonely. Their newly sprouting leaves mimicked the colour of fire and sun.

'Blinky Bill and gumnut country,' the driver said, relaxing his concentration now they had safely negotiated the narrow bends. Extending a hand, he added, 'Me name's Ned Beattie by the way.'

Curtis shook hands across the steering wheel. 'Curtis Lawson. Been driving long?'

'Twenty years. Nothing much else to do now the missus is gone. Cancer, y'know?' Ned Beattie whispered the word, as if saying it aloud might summon the darkness into his own body. 'She was a real special woman too. Cold and wet today, ay? Either too much rain or not enough, but that's the story of Australia, ain't it? Still got me daughter but. Six kids would you believe in this day and age? Her husband's some sort of foreigner. Don't talk like one, but he's got one of them little mos sticking out from his top lip like a toothbrush, so he must be, mustn't he? But he's a worker all right. Has to be with six flaming kids, what d'you say? Day at the mines and driving taxis at nights, but he drinks a bit and smokes like a bloody chimney. Not me. Not no more. Not after seeing how it got the missus. Though hers started in places a man don't talk about. Know what I mean? Me daughter Hazel give it up too, but now she's swelling like a balloon.'

Curtis closed his eyes and made himself as comfortable as possible against the hard vinyl seat. Ned Beattie didn't seem to expect an answer.

'She's a fine style of a girl as well as being a good mum to them kids. They live in my house, but that's all right because I'm hardly ever there now I've started driving round the country for a living. Got offered five thousand pounds for me house after the wife died, but what would I do with that kind of money? Not as if I needed anything flash, and Doreen would turn over in her grave after all the hard work we put into the place. Started on the front veranda. You know, filling it in to make another room. Went round the garbage dumps picking up bits of lumber. Got the windows when that bookie pub owner bulldozed a few places down to build his bloody mansion.'

The renovations to Ned's home were being detailed in full as Curtis drifted off to sleep.

His head thumping against the side window woke him at one o'clock. The truck was barrelling along mud and gravel, sending a stream of water hissing sideways into trees that were already having trouble keeping their roots in the ground. He guessed by the slant of light trying to prod a way through rain gloom that they were heading west. Before he had a chance to ask, Ned pulled up under a sign saying 'Petrol, Food and Drink'.

Climbing out of the truck, Curtis looked around at a car graveyard crowded with wrecks waiting to be recognised as antiques, and trucks embalmed in black oil. A circle of dying she-oaks was their tombstones. The house-shop-service station was a bilious green weatherboard construction. Behind it, a yard pen of wire added to a wooden shack formed a large cage. From where he stood, Curtis couldn't see inside.

A sharp point plunging into the lower curve of his backside refocused his attention. He swung around to throw a punch and saw Ned laughing, pointing down.

'You've just been given the bird, lad,' he sniggered.

Curtis swore and tried to pull away. The bird hung on.

'Enough! Leave it alone!'

The gander released its hold on his trousers when the high-pitched voice shouted the order. Curtis watched the bird retreat to its harem then turned to thank its owner, who smiled and apologised for the attack. At least, Curtis thought it was an apology. The words were unintelligible. Not one tooth could be seen in that cavern of a mouth, although the smile was a wonder to behold.

The owner continued to chat while filling the truck with petrol, and Curtis stopped himself from staring by strolling forward to stroke a shaggy donkey. The animal stood splay-legged behind a fence, its head almost touching the ground. When Curtis tried to make contact, it moved out of reach and studied him with unblinking concentration.

Curtis leaned against the cage and stared back, determined not to let the beast get the best of this encounter. The moment he touched the wire, something hit his shoulder with enough force to shove him sprawling sideways into the mud. He looked up into shining eyes and saw twin reflections of his own face staring back. He saw talons wrapped around the wire, and a hooked beak flecked with blood. While he finally recognised an eagle large enough to be the king of all birds, it turned towards the donkey. Another eye stared down at him from its chest.

He scrabbled backwards, leaving a scrape of neck skin on a hidden rock, and two rows of hollows where his heels had thrust against the earth.

'Time to come home, Curtis.'

Albert was there, reaching out a hand as he glanced at the bird.

'Pity to see a beauty like that caged, ay? Never seen one up so close before, or as big. Been feeding on that chunk of meat and thought you were trying to take it I reckon,' Albert said.

Curtis clung to the hand, soothed by the hardness of his brother's callused palm. Memories he did not know he possessed came to him, brought out by the strength in that grip. Albert a wall between him and Harry's spite, between him and Henry's frustration. Albert never telling him where or what to be, but always there or somewhere nearby with words of advice. Never angry if those words were ignored or even rejected outright.

Now, at the time in Curtis's life when he was finally certain of the thing he had only suspected, he wished to be close to Albert. He wanted to be his brother in blood as well as name. But while others might think that eagle had a strange pattern of bloodstained feathers on its chest, Curtis saw a third eye.

Albert hauled him erect with a grip Curtis thought of as needlessly strong. There was more than a hint of exasperation as Albert pushed him in the direction of a battered utility truck.

'Saw a name on the semitrailer and rang the owner. He told me where it was going. Got a thermos of tea and some sandwiches if you're hungry.'

Curtis crawled into the ute, not answering a called farewell from the man with the screeching voice. Ned thrust a hand inside the window and he shook it automatically, still squirming around to stare at the bird.

'You're like a bloody sparrow feeding around cats,' Albert said as they drove away. 'I don't understand why you let Pa and Harry worry you. You gotta learn not to take any notice. Anyway, I warned Harry off and Pa won't hit you again. Though he's not too happy with you running off like that. Ma hasn't stopped crying since.'

The eagle was just a part of larger shadows now, but Curtis stared back at it until a heavy downpour blocked his view of the cage.

# Part Two

# Sow and Grow

**Sow**: *introduce for development; seek to extend; disseminate*
**Grow**: *increase by natural development; to become by degrees*

# Chapter Thirty-three

Amanda and Debra astounded everyone by leaving school at the age of fifteen for studies at a secretarial college. It had been expected that Debra would find a job in one of the clothing factories, or behind a counter in one of the major stores. In Steeltown during the fifties, a descendant of coal miners and steelworkers was not supposed to waste time and money on education. Everyone knew she would marry at eighteen and have three or four children in quick succession, then she'd spend the rest of her life trying to make ends meet. During the war it might have been proper for women to work. They were doing so for their country. But in a time of peace they were made to know, and in no uncertain terms, that a woman's place was in the home.

Being the daughter of wealthy parents, Amanda was expected to complete her secondary education then continue on to university or, if she was really daring, to 'do' Europe. After completing her apprenticeship at the usual round of balls and parties, most of which would be in Sydney if she had the right connections, she would select a husband from her own class then continue the set traditions. After marriage she'd become an office bearer in various committees, or gain an executive position in one of the charities run by the society wives.

Anyone breaking from these moulds was considered either too big for her boots or lacking in taste. Yet being the granddaughter of a clergyman gave Debra the benefit of the doubt. In Amanda's case there were upraised eyebrows amid giggles of, 'Oh dear, these modern girls', while everyone waited for her to recover.

'I should never have allowed her to associate with that Watling girl,' Mrs Falls was heard to sigh at least a dozen times.

Amanda and Debra each had visions of working for her intended husband, Richard Rees. His parents expected him to become a lawyer.

'Why would I go through all that rigmarole when I already know who I'm going to marry?' Amanda asked her mother.

Marianne Falls had no answer to give.

Maidy Watling had all the answers. 'For Richard to marry his personal secretary would not be considered beyond the pale. You must pass head of the class then find a job with an established lawyer to gain experience,' she told her daughter. 'Then, when Richard sets up his practice, how could he refuse you? I will never allow you to marry a steelworker like that Lawson boy.'

Curtis had fought against employment in the steelworks, but after a few months of gardening without the necessary tools then working as a labourer in a milk factory, he succumbed to pressure from his father and brothers. He entered the mill as an apprenticed boilermaker with the same heavy heart he'd begun his education. He couldn't see much difference between school and the workplace. The cliques, bigotries and rivalries between the different races and religions were much the same. Immigrants from a hundred countries worked side by side with the Australian born. They called each other 'mate', but rarely mixed outside their place of work. In my opinion this wasn't racism, but a recognition of the differences in culture and family mythology. A lack of common ground. Many of the new Australians lived close to the belching stacks to save the cost of travel. Until they had accumulated enough money to buy better homes in the outer suburbs, that is. They worked as many overtime shifts as possible, despite the debilitating heat of the blast furnaces and plate mill, while more than a few Australian born preferred to live as far from the steelworks as possible. They often refused those extra shifts in preference for surfing, sport, and an hour or so of hectic drinking at their local pub. At that time the hotels closed at 6 p.m.

The immigrants came to Australia looking for a better way of life. They worked hard to get it. A large portion of the Australian born gave no thought to that better, or easier, life. And who could blame them for that? Unlike the immigrants to Steeltown, the Anglo-Australians had never known true want. They had never seen their country or homes invaded, had never watched their children go hungry, had never seen their family or neighbours carted away, not to be seen again. This was the lucky country, and surely the synonyms for luck were happiness and contentment. Happiness was mates, sport, family, a home just big enough to house that family, with a lawn to mow thrown in. Contentment was being happy with who and what you were, and having enough sense not to reach further than your arms could comfortably stretch.

The days of being ashamed of convict heritage were long gone, and in Steeltown there were few Aborigines to remind us that the land we called ours had been usurped. At least, I never encountered any. Those original inhabitants seemed to have moved further down the coast, perhaps confounded and overcome by the prolific number of strange languages. No doubt they were just becoming accustomed to English, or our version of it, when those hundred different nationalities flooded into town. Or perhaps they were driven out by belching smokestacks and air too thick with chemicals to inhale an unpolluted breath. Many more reasons could be given, but those reasons don't belong in this particular story.

Five years passed without much change. When Curtis wasn't at work or with Angus in the garden, he accompanied Richard, Debra and Amanda on various excursions: movies, theatre, sporting events, picnics at the beach. Wherever they were, they rarely went unnoticed. They were a striking foursome. Richard and Curtis were still alike enough to be brothers. Amanda — tall, dark-haired and brown-eyed — walked and talked aggressively and had total control of herself in most situations. Debra, shorter and rounder, had inherited Maidy's striking beauty though not her sensuality.

Although many tried to separate them into couples, it seemed the four were a team. I believed this to be for the benefit of Maidy Watling and Marianne Falls. Each was sure of the coupling, in name only of course, of her daughter and Richard Rees. Curtis was supposed to be with the other girl. Which one depended on which parent. I knew he held no liking for Maidy so I assumed that any tenderness he felt for Debra was driven more by sympathy than attraction. Therefore, I thought he must prefer Amanda. An assumption probably brought about by the fact that I, personally, admired her strong will and outspoken style. What you saw was what you got with Amanda.

# Chapter Thirty-four

Amanda stared into the mirror, and imagined that she was looking through the pores of her skin into a shiny interior waiting to be filled. She decided she was made of plastic, chrome and smoked glass, and insulated with indifference to deflect barbed words, or bounce them back twice as hard to where they came from. Except for her quick temper and acid tongue, she was squeaky clean and boring. Much like Richard, she thought; although his innermost self did have a few shady corners. His walls had been formed from a certainty of always being liked. It would be interesting to see how much would crumble under a barrage of dislike. Still, she'd always been drawn to him. Probably because she could see into his interior without needing to squint. In Curtis all she could see was sky and trees, and he'd never shown an inclination to invite her to examine him more closely.

Damn him, who cared? She had enough to worry about with Debra. Debra with her narrow little hallways and triangular compartments, and odd-shaped spaces locked with invisible keys. After months of persuasion she'd finally hand over the explanation and a door would open, only to reveal the outline of Maidy Watling. Most of Debra's shadows really belonged to her mother.

Debra had the ability to feel excessively guilty about any little thing; while she, Amanda, could barely scrape up a spoonful. How could she be interesting without a reasonable stock of guilt and shame? Even being last in class at that stupid secretarial college hadn't given her more than a few minutes of depression. She was growing weary of all those boring parties and balls, and of the insipid men clamouring for her attention. Why couldn't she bring herself to bed a couple of them, just for the hell of it? Why couldn't she care about her mother's snobbery or her father's philandering? No other girl she knew would shrug away such flaws as natural human failings.

She turned from the mirror, tired of looking at an interior with no stains or spills, no secret compartments containing hidden hates. How could she ever compete with Debra? Especially now that Debra had something that made her sigh and kick the ground and swear, and lie awake all night as if waiting for the end of the world to arrive at any moment. Perhaps today she would finally decide to share her little secret.

Debra brushed with rhythmic strokes, glancing occasionally into the mirror as she divided her pale blonde hair and began a plait. Her face remained expressionless as the bristles released a tangle.

'You have to realise it's for your own good,' Maidy said. 'Amanda doesn't need him.'

Another twist, then she doubled the plait and fixed it with pins. As she checked the glass to make sure each hair was in place, her hands touched her face and were momentarily frozen there. She saw a rubber-sheeted bench against the wall, bright lights and a hard chair. She watched a tiny spider building a snare in the skylight to keep her eyes away from the nurse's sneer.

'Are you listening to me, Debra? Have you any idea of the sacrifices I made to put you through that college?'

A quick dab of a powder puff, a smear of lipstick; a spit-wet finger reproved unruly eyebrows. Debra surveyed the effect without approval or criticism.

'You should never have allowed Amanda to talk you into that job with the dentist. We all know what her motives are. You need to get into a lawyer's office. You need to stop her and that Lawson boy from hanging around you and Richard.'

'I'll wait for them outside,' Debra answered.

Outside the air was fresh with just a trace of chill. She thought about getting rid of Curtis and stared upward, watching clouds racing in from the south, tearing off little pieces of themselves on the way.

The apricot tree was heavy with green fruit. Branches hung over the veranda, ready to carve their initials on unwary visitors. The clouds were blacker now, and lower. She stared down and wondered why the leaves of grass are called blades. Blades are knives, sharp and slashing. Or joined together as scissors.

Amanda was first through the gate. Amanda had always been first. But not any more.

Debra looked beyond her to a mynah bird flitting down, catching movement in a blunt beak. The bird, startled by Amanda, opened its beak and dropped the movement. Debra's thoughts slowed to a crawl.

'I'm pregnant,' she told them.

Amanda strode away. Richard followed.

The dark clouds pushed in front of the sun.

Curtis placed an arm around her waist and led her to the veranda swing.

# Chapter Thirty-five

It was a distinct shock to me when, not long after Curtis's twenty-first birthday, Angus and I heard him confessing Debra's pregnancy to the bonsai. He was bewildered by the fact because, he said, he'd always been careful. I was too stunned to ask for details about his idea of carefulness. Debra had inherited Maidy's determination to be some-body in the social order of Steeltown. She surely wouldn't want to marry Curtis.

'What else is there?' he asked.

What indeed? The year was 1960, but our part of Steeltown had not yet crawled out of the fifties. An unmarried mother was still classed as a slut. Even marriage to Curtis would be preferable in Debra's eyes. Maidy would come after him with a shotgun.

Run, was my advice.

Marry her, from Angus. Angus who never listened to gossip and never gave advice.

'Should we talk about cuckoos and currawongs again?' I snarled.

'He knows where he chucked his bloody seed. Stay out of it, Liona, and let the lad decide for himself.'

Houses were entered, doors were slammed, and Curtis married Debra one week later in a Sydney registry office. Neither of their families attended.

The newlyweds moved into 11 Blackwattle Road, the house I owned on the other side of Angus. Living so close to me was against Debra's wishes, but she wouldn't consider the alternatives of living with Maidy or the Lawsons. My acceptance of Curtis's meagre savings as a deposit ultimately convinced her.

Agatha did not receive the news of Curtis's elopement in the required mother-of-the-groom manner. Many years later, when she and I were much closer, I finally pieced together the jigsaw of her thought process on the day he broke the news.

# Chapter Thirty-six

'Debra and I were married in Sydney yesterday,' he said. 'We're buying the house next to Angus. Liona is letting us have it cheap. We're going to have a baby. I've come for my belongings.'

He waited for an answer. When she had none to give, he disappeared into his bedroom. Agatha listened to the sound of drawers opening and closing while she made a pot of tea. She knew he had more to say. She'd seen it in his eyes. Yet Curtis emerged a few minutes later, shook his head at the offer of a hot drink and walked outside to sit under the eucalypts.

His words worried at the edges of her brain. She shoved them away. Time enough to think about them when he told her the rest. He had a seed, one of those he'd saved when he planted the eucalypts. When he scratched it with a thumbnail, she wondered what he hoped to find. There were no more secrets, she'd given them all; the ones he hadn't already known.

She wiped a breath smear from the window. He glanced up, perhaps mistaking the action as a wave, and shook his head, causing a fringe of hair to cover his eyes so that she, along with everyone else, must break through those golden bars to discover his expression. Many people thought of Curtis as a secretive boy, yet he was just niggardly about sharing his emotions. So different from Harry and Albert, who never thought twice about yelling or cursing, laughing or scowling, whatever the situation demanded. From the day Albert was born, his expression said he'd be tall and big and tough-talking like his father. That was perfectly natural. A man's first son should be his own. She searched Harry's eyes the moment they opened and saw Henry looking out at her again. Both boys were mirror images of their father. Everything they had to say was in their mouths.

For the first few years of their marriage, Henry had been a talker. To fill her silence he told of football games, work and workmates, parents and sisters, and everything he knew about himself. Which hadn't been all that much after all. Yet she married him for his words and family. Now his mother was dead and the sisters had moved to other states, and his words had altered to grunts and shrugs.

Curtis peeled away the casing, shredding the seed slowly, looking for its secrets. He wouldn't find the what and where before it was here. That was like trying to discover where you went after you were gone. Nobody ever did.

She finally saw herself when Curtis was born, and not just in his blond hair and blue eyes. Their affinity could be read in all the bits and pieces. He cried out just once to catch in the air he needed to survive, then he lay quiet and watchful, knowing from the very beginning the secret of being unseen and unheard. He had learned many secrets while he was still inside her. From the hour of his birth, she'd begun teaching him the rest.

As a child she would huddle in a corner, unseen and unheard as the ladies arrived. Aunt made tea and circled biscuits around a plate. Sometimes they sat for hours around that table, yet nothing about those ladies remained idle for long. Everything had their wholehearted and careful concentration. A reason could always be given for their gatherings, a base purpose that differed from house to house. At Aunt Bea's Armidale home, the justification was called rummy.

A full house. Three Jacks, I win. I bet a penny. Sure you can afford it? Deal the cards, dear. I'll open. Did you hear about Mrs Thingummy and Mr Doodah?

At Aunt Violet's house they knitted or crocheted, their hooks and needles guided by hands with spots and calluses and folds of crepey skin. Blue veins rippled with the movement of fingers, matching the click of abacus teeth counting off the neighbours' sins.

Aunt Helen was the youngest aunt with a circle of younger ladies (none admitted to being more than fifty). She had turned her house into a hive for the quilting bees, buzzing around boxes of old dresses and shirts, and even trousers if materials were hard to come by. Needles flashed in slivers of light, drawing the patches together while the ladies spoke of how this man beat his wife or child, or ran away with that woman. Of how the woman in number ten abandoned her children and husband for that man up the road who had money by the ton but not an ounce of morals that anyone knew of. And there was number seven at the age of sixty going off on a fortnight's cruise with forty-five. Number one beat his wife until she died quite young, though he tried to palm it off as cancer.

They spoke of childbirth and incest in the same breath, of rape and marriage in the next. Whether the girl on the corner would be found out again, and if her father would take up the frayed leather belt and beat her until she screamed promises broken the following night.

Those stories raced around and through Agatha's brain like sperm to an egg, conceiving the real Agatha, the one who placed herself in the families and stopped the beatings, the rape, the incest and poverty. She became the daughter or the wife, sometimes the husband or son. She gathered the family together and saved them all. It did not matter if it was only inside her head.

'And it's best to keep it there,' Aunt Jane, the first aunt, had said. 'Nobody will listen if you speak, and it's only what our minds contain that matters after all.'

Curtis buried the shredded seed, every single scrap laid to rest beneath the tallest eucalypt. He then scraped earth from the roots of a seedling, one dropped from the smallest tree. He would have that same half-puzzled, half-sad look as when she told him the life stories of all the families so he could find himself, as she had done so many years ago now.

She cleaned houses, ironed clothes, minded children. She even worked for the ones who frightened her in order to bring back the stories for Curtis. She did try the knitting, the crocheting, and even the cards. The ladies stayed away because of Henry's rudeness. Henry strangled words. She'd seen him do it. She'd seen him walk into a room, take hold of the conversation and kill it. So she went out and discovered the families with beatings, incest and rape. That was all she had to give, except for Liona. Liona supplied the words.

How was she to know that Liona would demand so much in return?

She, Agatha, couldn't tell Curtis about her ancestors. She did not know. Yet everything she was, everything inside her head was part of him.

He was married to Debra Watling. Moving out. Buying the house next to Angus. One of Liona's houses.

He should have asked his mother first. She could have warned him to keep it inside his head. Of course she knew about Maidy and Debra, but Curtis couldn't save them. She had tried that with the man who beat his daughter with the leather belt. 'You beat your child because she goes with those boys, but she goes with them because you beat her,' she'd told him. The man had shouted obscenities and laid the belt across Agatha's back. She still had the three-cornered scar where her flesh had torn.

She must tell Curtis before it was too late. She ran down the steps and joined him in the yard.

'There's nothing here,' he said. 'The seeds could have dropped from any number of trees.'

Agatha pulled up her blouse to show him the three-cornered scar.

'But I know about me,' he said. 'I guess I've always known. I'm too different from Pa and Albert and Harry. Too different from you.'

Her denial formed a ball inside her throat. She tried to scratch out the words in much the same way Curtis had peeled the seed.

'I know you did your best,' he said. 'I know you pushed Harry and

Albert back so I wouldn't feel second best. I know why you told me those stories. It was to make me realise how lucky I am to live with you and Pa.'

He held out the seedling stripped of earth and roots.

'Liona and Angus pretend not to care, but I know how they feel. I know how people gossip. I've heard it all from you. You taught me not to concern myself with what the rest of the world thinks, and I thank you for that.'

'What are you doing? Don't,' he said when she ripped at her blouse, trying to show where his roots began.

That was a Henry look. One she'd seen on Albert and Harry too. Yet different somehow. This child had fooled them all.

She grabbed the seedling and slashed at his ears and mouth.

Not bothering to protect himself, he said, 'I guessed a long time ago,' and strode into the kitchen.

Agatha ran inside and grabbed the wedding photograph, the one of her standing behind Henry. Her pointed chin, not yet doubled, was slightly tilted. Her eyebrows, not then plucked, were a straight line above her nose. A fringe of hair just naturally fell down to cover eyes that were the exact same colour as Curtis's. In this photograph, at the age of twenty-one, she could have been him. Or so Henry always said.

In the hallway she leapt in front of Curtis and shoved the photograph forward, as a priest would thrust a crucifix at the devil. Curtis avoided seeing the likeness by turning away. She lashed out again with the eucalypt, striking his head to make him turn back. He lifted an arm to shield himself from the blows and the portrait, and continued walking.

Agatha slashed her stomach with the seedling, trying to expel the last of him from her womb. The first pain was still greater. She threw the photograph, striking his shoulder like a push with an open palm to attract his attention.

He did not look back as he entered Angus's gate.

# Chapter Thirty-seven

Agatha couldn't forgive Curtis for leaving home. Angus said she'd finally revealed her true self by carrying on like a madwoman. Yet he wandered around with his head down, conversing in grunts for days.

'Something in her eyes,' were the only coherent words he spoke for almost a week.

The silly woman should have known that Curtis would leave one day. She still had Albert and Harry. I doubted if they would ever marry. They were too much like their father, and there weren't too many Agathas around for another Henry Lawson. She waited on them hand and foot, and gave them all her gossip. It seemed to me that she tried to shift the blame of all those years she pampered Curtis onto his shoulders, as if he had used the excuse of being the youngest to ensure her indulgence.

And while Agatha preoccupied herself with fussing around Albert and Harry, Curtis did the same with the coming child. After spending every spare minute of his time scouring the second-hand shops for the kind of furniture he wanted, he stripped every piece back to bare wood, then painted and polished until it looked brand new. When that was done to his satisfaction, he scrubbed the spare room from top to bottom. Then, using a dozen different brushes and countless cans of paint, he turned the ceiling into a cobalt sky, the floor into bare brown soil. He covered the walls with shrubs and trees filled with light. When he'd finally finished, the room resembled his beloved bush on a summer's afternoon.

The ceiling and floor were comfortable enough, although they could have been subdued with a shower of rain, or even just a few clouds. It was the starkness of those trees that bothered me. Their branches were sparsely covered with olive-green leaves, each outlined in gold, and the trunks stood upright, reaching for the painted sky and defying the painted heat. Looking around at summer trapped forever in one small room, I felt my energy drain. My throat yearned for water.

'I hope this child has a strong constitution,' I said. 'If not, the poor little thing will suffer from exhaustion. Can't you add a touch of haze? At least a shadow or two.'

'That's the Mayberry coming out in her,' Angus growled, dismissing me with his idea of an insult. 'I think a few bunches of new growth would brighten up that corner furthest from the window.'

Curtis added the new growth — splashes of red that gave fire to light and heightened the effect of unrelenting heat.

I stashed a tin of white paint in my laundry, ready to create a mist. My plan was to turn summer afternoon to autumn morning whenever the opportunity presented itself. Unfortunately, I never carried out my intention. Had I found a way, I might have saved a life. Or, at the very least, given peace of mind to one small boy.

Occasionally, when we were allowed to visit, Angus suggested adding leaves to a branch or he'd argue over the curve of a trunk. I would set up my sewing machine and stitch weeny sleeves into tiny armholes, using this cover of busy bee to study the queen of the hive. I'd watch her under lowered eyebrows while she eased herself this way and that, trying to find a more comfortable position in her chair. Her butterfly fingers would hover across the mound of her stomach, touching here and there to caress or prod, perhaps outlining the shape of a tiny head or buttocks or touching tiny fingers.

Do all pregnant women sit like this, or was it remembered from her own days in the womb? Did Maidy Greentree Watling touch and prod to seek the face and form of her child, to remember its conception?

I thought that Curtis had inherited Agatha's obsession with family when he became preoccupied with finding a suitable name for his son or daughter. He pored over newspapers and books, and even asked strangers for suggestions. This was after Angus and I refused an invitation to offer up our parents' given names.

'It would be a way to keep one of those names alive, seeing as how neither of you seem to be interested in doing so,' Curtis said.

I told him that Angus and I had decided long ago that we weren't the type to rear children. Angus had said marriage would cause us each to be two people — the one each of us was, and the one the other wanted us to be. The restrictions of church and law would turn our commitment to duty, and neither of us had dutiful natures. We must remain single to be undivided, he said. Children would tear off little pieces to keep for themselves, and a child should not be reared without the comfort of a whole family. People would call them names. A child could not be expected to have our contempt for the opinions of others.

I said I had to agree with him, especially when Angus swore that living with me every minute of the day and night would drive him mad. He was already halfway there. Who was I to chauffeur him the rest of the way?

When Curtis mentioned in an offhand manner that he might call his son Angus, or his daughter after me, I thought Angus had finally reached his destination. He unfastened the peg leg, placed it in a bowl of water sprinkled with manure, and waited for it to sprout. To show him how foolish this was, I threatened to turn my yard into an English cottage garden. Angus continued to stare at his wooden leg and wait for it to multiply.

Curtis eventually decided that the child would be named William or Dianne. He looked sideways at me as he said it, as if I had aligned myself with Angus. Yet I would have been delighted had he named his daughter Liona. He and Debra would produce a blonde, pink-skinned little girl. The name would suit her as it had never suited me. I rather fancied a cute little Liona. But it wasn't to be.

# Chapter Thirty-eight

Debra's pains began at midnight, as birthing pains so often do. Curtis rushed her to the hospital then, at her insistence, telephoned Richard and Amanda. The request was natural enough. Richard was his best friend and the two women had been inseparable for years. Although a certain coolness had developed between them when Amanda walked away from the news of Debra's pregnancy.

At the hospital, Richard paced the floor with Curtis. He related events at university to help block out the sounds echoing through his best friend's brain. Debra might have been of English descent, but she certainly wasn't the stiff-upper-lip type described in certain novels. As the time between contractions became shorter, so did her temper. As the pains became stronger, so did her language. She still blamed and abused while being wheeled into the elevator. Yet worse than any oath or accusation was the glimpse of fear in her eyes as they closed the door in Curtis's face, shutting him out of the birth. The last sound he heard, a whimper from deep down in her throat, was more shocking than a scream. He waited and paced, and heard that whimper time and again, until they finally gave him entry. Richard held him up while they shuffled into her room.

Debra watched them through the screen of her eyelashes. These two men were still alike enough to be brothers, although Richard's expression was as open as it had been when she first began to know him. Curtis was thin of face, and shadows still flickered in eyes which could be as bright as a midsummer sky, but were more often filled with the pattern of wind-blown leaves. A secretive man, she thought, and smiled. She had her own secret now, although it was just at its beginning, nothing more than an ache in her breasts and a feeling without a name. For the first time in her life, she had created something unique. For the first time in her life she had something to belong to. Someone belonging to her.

Richard fractured the handsome picture these two men made by walking to the other side of the bed. His expression said he wanted to give her a hug but he had to wait for Curtis.

Curtis's eyes were sky bright now, and filled with a light she'd never seen before.

'Yes,' she said. 'You have your William.'

He moved forward, wanting to do something, anything, but not knowing what. He felt awkward and gangling — a child in the presence of a maker and mother. He bent and kissed her forehead. Softly, as though she were paper-thin crystal.

She knew then that Curtis had to be kept at a distance. How could the child not love Curtis above everyone else if she allowed him to stay close?

Richard laughed and shoved Curtis aside, engulfing Debra in a hug before stepping back and ruffling her hair, tossing it over her eyes.

'Think you're clever,' he said, but with delight.

Richard always knew what to say. Debra was about to tell him so when Amanda interrupted.

'Congratulations,' she said from the doorway. 'He's a beautiful baby.'

'You've seen him?' Curtis asked.

'In there.' Amanda nodded the direction.

'His daddy should have seen him first, but better late than never. Go see him now,' Debra said, smiling directly at Richard before turning the last of it to Curtis. She avoided noticing his reaction by stretching out a hand to Amanda. 'You will be godmother, won't you?'

Amanda watched the men leave before saying, 'Do you really want me to?'

Debra patted the blanket beside her. 'I really do.'

They lay stretched along the bed, one partly under the covers, one over, their heads touching. A nurse paused at the doorway and smiled before going about her business. Both women smiled back. They knew they looked good together.

'Was it a hard birth?' Amanda asked, reaching up to stroke the pain lines from Debra's forehead. 'Is everything they say about it true?' she added, continuing the downward stroking of cheeks and throat. Her fingers bunched to massage away the tenseness of shoulder muscles.

Debra pushed the covers aside and twined her leg around Amanda's leg, opening and closing her hand to knead and stroke the other's outer thigh while studying the question. This habit of touch and caress had been with them for many years. It was the only way to communicate the sweet things they were unable to form into words.

'Nothing like my mother said, or anything your mother would say. And not like the poetry and prose I've read in the past few months. Those writers left out the pain and being frightened and not knowing what to do. It was hard. But worth it, you know?'

'Not yet. But I will.'

Amanda spoke the words lightly, but they were definitely a statement. The thrust of her jaw showed determination.

They lapsed into a companionable silence until Amanda said, 'I know you've been with them both. Which one is the father, really?'

'Do you really care?' Debra asked.

Amanda tried to care, but she could not. The word was a sigh of disappointment when she finally answered no.

'We're a pretty pair, aren't we?' she added.

'Always have been,' Debra agreed.

'I love you, Deb.'

'Same to you. Pity we couldn't like each other a little more.'

They pressed their foreheads together and laughed into each other's eyes.

Curtis pressed against the glass and peered at a red scalp with downy fair hair emerging from a bundle of blue blanket. Richard tapped the glass, beckoned to a nurse and directed her with a pointing finger. She turned the baby and pulled back the blanket.

The tiny eyes opened. The tiny mouth opened wider and emitted a lusty wail. Richard punched the air.

'Yeah. Wahhh,' he mimicked.

Curtis drew back and studied Richard's face, then he turned again to William. After a few seconds had passed, he strode out, not looking back. His eyes were an eclipse.

# Chapter Thirty-nine

'I remember,' Angus said, 'just walking along, minding me own business. Keeping me eyes peeled for snipers. Dicko on one side of me, Col Burnett on the other. Dave Watling, Toady and Simpson watching our backs. Nobody to watch theirs. Most of our platoon had been wiped out. Then I hear this great thumping big *whumph*! Thought it was in me head for a moment or two. Thought me brain had finally done what it had been threatening to do for years. Next thing I know, we're all flat out in the mud. Dave, Toady and Simpson were dead. They'd copped most of it. Strange thing is, I didn't feel surprised. Been there, done that, somewhere sometime before. No pains or aches or anything. Mostly just a feeling of twitchy irritation. You know, like when a hot northerly wind springs up and rubs you the wrong way, making you wanna smash and break for no particular reason, except you're getting more pissed off by the minute, and mostly at yourself. I felt like bashing Col when he kept groaning on about his gut. Dicko lay back like Sunday afternoon at the beach, looking at something just out of his reach. His bloody arm from the elbow down, would you believe it? He stared at it with this sort of puzzled expression, as if that arm was familiar enough and he should have known what it was and who owned it, but he didn't. Then he looked over at me and grinned. That's when I noticed half me leg had gone. Dicko picked up that flaming arm and tried to toss it over. I couldn't for the life of me convince him that it was the wrong shape. We sat in that mud until the stretchers came, arguing the point on who owned the bloody thing. Never did find the rest of me leg. While they were taking us back, they said we'd been hit by friendly fire. Friendly bloody fire, wouldn't you know? Dicko started crying. Col and me near busted a gut laughing, though Col's gut was already hanging out through his fingers. Bugger died laughing. What a way to go, ay? Dicko went a bit queer after that. Got it in his head that I'd pinched his bloody arm. He ran every time he saw me coming. Friendly bloody fire. Like that out there.'

He pointed to Curtis standing at the front gate of the Lawson home, staring at the pavement while trying to compose his restoration to the family speech. He had already been to see us. Angus sat him in front of the bonsai then walked outside to spade over a garden bed. I followed him out to show that this problem with Debra and the baby had nothing to do with us, although I felt sure Curtis heard everything I left unsaid.

# Chapter Forty

For many years he'd told his troubles and dreams to the bonsai. Now he was mute. For once he couldn't talk to the tree. Its spirit held no comfort on this particular day. He needed flesh to lean against, arms around him. He needed to expose his wounds without being scorned or ignored. Only one person would give him that — the one who had soothed him when Albert and Harry refused him entry into their bond, when Henry's drunken rages had terrified him. She had cried with him, no matter how small the injury, and held him until he fell asleep. He needed that now. At this moment he needed Agatha more than he had ever needed anything in his whole life.

'What can you see in the cement that I can't?' a voice asked.

A pair of shiny black shoes refracted the sun's glare into a leer. One foot tilted sideways as Curtis continued to stare, but the bashfulness of this gesture was immediately reversed by a lewd wink of light. It came from a row of thin gold chains encircling the ankle. In a working class suburb clinging stubbornly to the prim fifties, those chains seemed shockingly wanton. Even more so than the short skirt hugging rounded thighs. A jutting hip was a proposition, although the closed fist resting there promptly withdrew the invitation.

'Try up here,' the voice suggested.

He looked directly into her face. The stiletto heels added to her height. Her hair, cut very short in opposition to the current mode of cute ponytails, echoed the colour and parlance of her shoes. She was smooth-skinned and very pale, in opposition to the current trend of suntanned leather. Her bark-brown eyes regarded him with a waiting expression.

Clo Gatley was five years older than Curtis. Although he did not know her, he knew her reputation. He turned away, not wanting to play her games; not wanting to admit to the pull of her aura, even to himself. It was then he noticed that the eucalypts no longer threw their shadows across the Lawson home. He shoved the gate open and ran.

Clo hesitated, looking from the lawn to her stiletto heels, then pulled off the shoes and followed.

A dozen suppurating stumps poked up from patchy grass like abscessed teeth. Untidy piles of bleeding branches lay scattered around the yard. Henry stood beside the body of the largest tree, one foot resting on its trunk while he shouted orders to Albert and Harry. They were heaping the bonsai's children into bonfire shapes. The smell of freshly let sap had already faded to a mulch odour. Gum tips had dropped from the sawn-off branches in vast quantities, as if the slaughtered trees thought they were merely in drought and were shedding copiously to ward off dehydration. To Curtis, the rustle of falling leaves was a scream.

Turning away from the massacre, he watched Agatha descend the stairs. She walked forward swiftly, ignoring him to stare at Clo's curly dark hair, at the shoes in one hand, at the bare feet with their declaration of slim gold chains. A flimsy red scarf floated from Agatha's hand like an echo of blood from a deliberately sliced palm. She held it out, an offering. All she offered Curtis was her silence.

Henry barred her way. 'What d'you mean bringing that slut to my house?' he roared at Curtis.

Curtis's hands tightened to fists. Clo had seen the expression on his face as he stared at the trees, so she knew the gesture was not in protection of her. Shrugging, she stepped back from the reek of Henry's beer breath.

'No man raises a fist to his father,' Albert stated quietly.

'He never wanted to be a son to me, no matter what I did. Never could please you, could I?' Henry snarled.

'What are ya doing here anyway?' Harry asked. 'You haven't been back since ya left, not even when Pa took sick and the steelworks laid him off for three months. Never thought about us then, did ya? Not even to buy him a bloody beer.'

Agatha brushed past Henry, squatted on the ground and arranged the scarf to cover Clo's bare feet. Clo looked into her face and quickly looked away.

'Bloody trees. Can't get clothes dry on the line. Bloody magpies attacking a man if he comes home from the pub before dark. Not even welcome in me own backyard any more,' Henry muttered.

Clo tugged at Curtis's arm. 'Let's go. There's nothing for you here.'

'Reckon I'm old and useless, don't ya?' Henry shouted. 'They don't have to laugh at a man because the blasted country wanted pink cheeks and straight backs.' His voice dropped to a whine. 'Don't have to shove me away when I'm just trying to show what a good father I can be. Don't have to do that to a man. Don't haveta.'

He wiped a shirt sleeve across his mouth, leaving threads of saliva hanging from his chin. His head lowered and swaying while he glared at the piling of dying trees.

'Come on. Come on, Henry,' Agatha said, leading him to the back door. 'There, it's all right.' She wiped his mouth, stroked his face, still leading, supporting his weight. 'You have a nice little nap while I make tea. It will all look better after you've had something to eat.'

Clo sensed the anger building in Curtis. It was powerful enough to intrigue and excite her. If not dampened soon, it would have to explode.

'Look,' she said, touching his neck with a pointed finger. 'Over there. A seedling.'

She turned his face to a scrawny plant lying sideways in the imprint of a boot. Its leaves were shredded, but the main stem hadn't broken.

'If you do something now, you'll be able to save it,' she whispered.

Albert and Harry shambled up the pathway, following their parents indoors. As they passed Clo, Harry sneered. She smiled into his face and flicked up a middle finger. Albert cut off any possible retaliation by clamping a hand on the base of Harry's neck.

Clo dropped her shoes and helped Curtis ease out the plant. They placed it in the red scarf and carried it to his yard. Curling her arms around the clumping of dirt and roots, he whispered something she couldn't hear, some kind of assurance not meant for her. Fossicking among a pile of garden tools for a spade and a watering can, he dug a hole just inside the front gate and lowered the eucalypt into it, using all the gentleness one would normally use lowering a baby into a bath.

'Synthetic,' he explained tersely as he rolled the scarf into a ball and tossed it onto the path.

Fully engrossed in the procedure, he carefully tamped soil around the seedling's roots then refilled the can, eking out a little at a time, and watched the water being slowly absorbed into the ground. Clo couldn't decide whether a healing was taking place or if he was forming a scar. She stood back, expecting him to say something to honour the occasion.

His only words were, 'Now you can grow if you've a mind to it.'

'My name's Clo,' she said when he tossed the watering can aside.

He nodded. 'Clo Gatley. You work at the Oxley pub. Your family used to live in Steeltown but your parents divorced and moved away. You live in a flat up the other end of Blackwattle Road.'

'I've heard about your mother,' she said, and picked up the balled scarf before following him through the gate.

Agatha ran onto the road and placed the black stiletto shoes on the centre white line, one behind the other. Clo shook out the scarf, flicked away a few grains of dirt, and tied it around her neck. Reaching for Curtis's hand, she continued walking.

At three o'clock the next morning she sat up and looked down at him, using her fingertips to rediscover the shape of his face. She remembered his hair shaken forward over his eyes, and wondered how much of himself he kept locked away from others. He'd been hard and hurtful at first, but she knew his ruthlessness wasn't directed at her. She had felt the same kind of fury many times.

Later had been different. Other men might have called him feminine then. They certainly would have been contemptuous of his tears. He cried while she stroked his cheeks and hummed a song of her child-hood, and he fell asleep with his face pressed into the soft hollow of her shoulder. She continued to hold him until her arms ached, then she placed his head on the pillow and snuggled down to sleep. Now it was time for him to leave.

She switched on the bedside lamp. 'Wake up. It's after three.'

His eyes opened instantly.

'Time to go home or Mumma will spank.'

'Yours or mine?' he asked.

She pulled the blanket up to cover her breasts. 'Takes a special kind of kid to wade through the muck they heap on you if your parents aren't spotless. You can't do that to your son.'

For a moment she thought he wanted to hit her. She frowned, wondering why.

Curtis grabbed the bottle of whisky he'd bought but she hadn't allowed him to drink, and headed for the door. He'd almost emptied it by the time he staggered into the main street of Steeltown. He thought about going to Angus, but Angus would smell the whisky and the sex. Curtis didn't want to explain. Not even to the bonsai.

A patrol car pulled up alongside him. He smiled. This would provide a bed for the rest of the night.

'Curtis Lawson isn't it?' one of the officers asked. 'Never known you to hit the bottle. Bad as your old man.'

Richard's blue sedan pulled up behind the patrol car. Amanda climbed out. 'A celebration,' she explained to the policemen. 'Debra presented him with a son last night.'

Curtis allowed the policeman to shake his hand and pummel his back. He even promised to buy them a beer, but he baulked when Amanda led him towards the blue sedan.

'Richard's gone back to uni,' she said.

Curtis wanted to say something bad about Richard, but he couldn't think of anything. He shrugged and climbed into the car.

'Your place or Flagstaff Point?' she asked, offering a payback to Debra and Richard.

Too late, he'd already spent his cheque with Clo.

'Screw you, then,' Amanda said pleasantly enough as they drove slowly along the main street. He passed out before they had turned the first corner.

# Chapter Forty-one

The heat woke him. Someone had emptied a birdcage into his mouth while he slept. Or so his tastebuds thought. He couldn't breathe. Someone had to be holding a pillow over his face to keep the foulness inside. Lashing upwards with a closed fist, he heard more than felt the crunch of his knuckles connecting with something solid. He tried to sit up, but fell back when his forehead smacked against another solid object. Tears of pain washed the glue from his eyes. They opened, and he stared into a tunnel of light. He'd read about these post-death experiences. Long-dead loved ones would be waiting at the end of the tunnel to guide him to the other side. He could see one now, an angel clothed in white. Her halo was the essence of gold.

'Curtis Lawson, what do you think you're doing? Debra is worried sick.'

The angel was Maidy Watling in a white housecoat. The coffin was Richard's car. Curtis looked cross-eyed at a steering wheel, and laughed.

'I'm glad you find this amusing,' Maidy said haughtily. 'Debra expected you at the hospital last night, and now Marianne Falls tells me you were with Amanda. Have you no decency at all?'

Curtis managed to avoid bashing his forehead again by sliding sideways before sitting up.

'What time is it?' he asked.

'Eight-thirty. Why are you in Richard's car outside my house?'

'Christ, I'm late for work.'

'What about Debra?'

He switched on the ignition. 'She has her son and he has a name. What more do you want from me?'

Not one of his co-workers at the steel plate assembly area expressed surprise when Curtis arrived late for work. Each section of the steel mill was similar to a small village, where gossip travels as fast as the speed of sound. Everyone knew about William being born, so how could they be surprised that Curtis had turned up with a pallor that would have shamed a ghost? Most of those men knew about the cost of hospitals and babies. They knew he'd need every penny to pay the bills.

They laughed and thumped his back while he staggered around in a post-drunk haze. They even brought aspirins to switch off the jackhammer in his head. He thanked them nicely and thought them kind, but he'd forgotten the traditional jokes played on anyone who wasn't aware. Newcomers and apprentices were their usual targets — or those like Curtis, whose whisky-stunned brain had to send signals via nerves made numb by a massive hangover. While he surrounded his brain with nonthought to keep his mind on the job, they welded the cleats of steel on his boots to the metal plate on which he stood. After that, he managed to look reasonably alert and snarl his workmates away.

'Been giving yer a hard time, 'ave they?' Joe Phelan sniggered while Curtis prepared to leave at the end of shift. 'They worked out a few good uns, but I talked 'em out of it. Got to look after Henry's boy, haven't I? Been 'is mate for nigh on thirty years.'

With these kind words and a kinder smile, Joe reached out in a friendly gesture and grabbed the back of Curtis's neck. Curtis hadn't noticed the roll of electric welding lead on the floor, or the bare patch of wire concealed by Joe's boots. Yet he did notice Joe's fingers on his neck completing the circuit. Seventy volts rattled his teeth before he fell in a heap.

'Guess the blokes ain't too happy with yer, neither. You bought the last lot of lottery tickets and we were one off. If you hadn't been in such a hurry to get home to the little woman, we might have won it.'

It was an old joke and, like the hand on his neck, not all that amusing. But when Curtis arrived home, he couldn't resist looking up the winning number in the morning newspaper. 2792. He fumbled a ticket out of his wallet, the one he had bought in his own name. 2792. He had won twenty thousand pounds.

His first thought was to rip the slip of paper to pieces. He had enough worries now. That sort of money would be a load. It would make a difference. To Debra it would. But his fingers slid away when he tried to make the first tear. He stared at 2792 for an hour or more before deciding to look for help. Angus's laughter shook him.

'I can't see the joke,' Curtis said. 'Joe's already peeved about the shared ticket being one number short. The men are going to think I've cheated them in some way when they find out that I won the first prize.'

'I wouldn't worry about Joe,' Angus laughed. 'You've done him the biggest favour of his life.'

'But I've got the number. Just me. The shared ticket was one off.'

'Yair, and that's better than winning the jackpot for old Joe. For the rest of his life he can rail against the cruel hand of fate. Joe's never seen more than fifty pounds at one go. A sixth share of that ticket would have meant fame and fortune to someone like him. Respect and envy, and blokes shouting him beers. But one off means every rotten thing he does, or gets done to him, wouldn't have happened if he was rich. Can't you see it? Every time he pisses against the wind and it comes back in his face, it'll be because Curtis bloody Lawson was a second too early to buy the winning ticket. You've even given him someone to hate, someone more useless than his own self. Better than a jackpot to old Joe Phelan.'

Curtis recognised the logic in Angus's words. 'But what will I do with so much money?' he asked.

'Wave it around and you'll have half of Steeltown coming here with stories that would make a brick wall weep. Other half will hate your guts for having such luck. Sock it away somewhere safe and don't tell nobody you got it.'

'Maybe you could use a few pounds.'

Angus considered the offer. He was independent, but he wasn't stupid.

'Ruin me lifestyle,' he said at last. 'And I don't wanna be beholden.'

'A gift,' Curtis said.

Angus shook his head. 'Me father come into easy money like you. But with him it was jewels, and it never did him any good. Just you don't let it all slip away into nothing, like he did. You gotta do something smart with it. Invest it.'

'What about Liona?'

'What would Loby do with more than she's got? She's not short of money, you know. The first thing you should do is buy something nice for Debra and the boy.'

'It's nothing to do with them,' Curtis stated.

'Nothing to do with me neither. Now get the hell out and let a man get some bloody sleep.'

Like Joe Phelan, Curtis had never seen more than fifty pounds in his life. He could give a few thousand to Agatha and Henry to pay for his childhood upkeep, but a large amount of money would frighten Agatha, and Henry would stay drunk for a year. He needed advice from someone who knew their way around. Only one name came to mind.

He tapped on the door softly at first, then thumped. It opened abruptly.

'I have to talk,' he said.

Clo turned away, leaving the door open. She had wrapped herself in a robe that had seen better days, and her eyes were hung with sleep. She almost fell into the refrigerator while taking out a bottle of orange juice. Yet her aura hit him with the force of a softball bat. By then he had noticed the two suitcases and the empty look of her flat.

'I'm not hanging around to play whoops-a-daisy because you're pissed off with your wife, if that's what you're about to ask,' she said.

'I've won the lottery,' he blurted out.

She raised an eyebrow.

'I want to put the money with someone I can trust. Someone who won't tell the world about it,' he explained.

'Jamie Blake would know,' she said after a few minutes thought.

'Blake,' he echoed, trying to recall where he had heard the name before.

It was a common surname, but it had a bad connection in his mind. Something Agatha had mentioned. Headlines in the newspapers not long ago. He remembered that a Don Blake had shot his own father.

Curtis spoke the memory aloud. Clo ignored it.

'Jamie's a friend of mine,' she said. 'I stay with him when I'm in the city. His uncle is an accountant. Good with money, and he knows how to keep his mouth shut. Come with me to Sydney. I'll introduce you.'

Two hours later Clo and Curtis met Jamie Blake in a Sydney restaurant. No questions were asked about whether or not Curtis wanted to add quickly to the capital, or if he'd prefer a blue chip investment. After the sum was stated and a few papers signed, they agreed on a verbal accounting to be made over the phone, and at least five years before the capital would be touched.

If Jamie was surprised by Curtis's reluctance to discuss plans, hear details or even accept the fact of having the money at all, he gave no sign. At three o'clock he left with an arm around Clo's waist, leaving Curtis to find his own way to the railway station. He couldn't help being surprised that Clo allowed him to walk with his arm around her. She usually objected to being touched in public.

'Men think of it as a badge of ownership,' she always said.

He knew the intimacy was a show for Curtis Lawson, but he didn't ask why. Clo rarely answered personal questions. She'd tell him to mind his own business.

When Curtis could no longer see them, Clo pulled away.

'Look after his money, he's a nice bloke,' she said, and took Jamie's hand to keep him at a distance.

# Chapter Forty-two

Jamie Blake is a cousin on my mother's side. His grandfather and my grandmother were brother and sister. I discovered this fact when I became interested in piecing together various family connections. The information was obtained at the Register of Births, Deaths and Marriages.

Jamie's family was on the black sheep side of the Blake bloodline, but this fact never worried me. There are some murderers who are praised by family and friends for their kindness and generosity, and though Jamie was sometimes on the wrong side of the law, he certainly wasn't in the murderers league. As far as I was concerned, Jamie Blake was essentially a good and decent man.

He had the kind of wiry body which is never accused of being skinny. He also had the kind of reddish hair usually accompanied by freckles, and he owned more than his share of those. His eyes reminded me of the ocean on an autumn day, when clouds crossing the sun change the water from cobalt to sinkhole green, and to the various green-blues in between. His habitual expression was one of mild surprise. A perfect poker face, so Angus said. It was Angus who told me that the man was a crook, although not necessarily a criminal. I never quite knew what he meant by that, and Angus wouldn't elaborate except to hint at shady deals done in the city. Suffice to say that Jamie's wallet always bulged while he never seemed to be overburdened with work. When asked point-blank, he'd say he worked for an uncle who had interests in real estate.

'When I was young,' Jamie told me, 'I didn't know enough to get out of me own way. The eldest of four kids, I was also the puniest for many years. Me old man used to beat the hell out of me. Me old man beat the hell out of everybody until me brother put him out of his misery. I was born in Newcastle you know. Lived there for a couple of years until me parents moved to Sydney. I went back when I left home. I would've been around sixteen at the time, and I wanted to look at the old place again to see if it was anything like I remembered. Nothing ever is.'

# Chapter Forty-three

The once grand residence for men and women of refinement showed its age like a time weary whore, sagging at the balconies and trying to cover hard times under numerous coats of paint. The rose garden had almost disappeared under a passionfruit vine, which had dropped its seeds and multiplied, sending shoots to weave around the beds like telephone wires carrying gossip. The pathway had become an untidy shadow almost hidden under foot-scuffed grass.

The vegetable patch had disappeared along with the henhouse, but the dogs still threw themselves against their chains until they were almost strangled senseless. They were a younger lot of mongrels now. Jamie ignored their furious attempts to reach him and ran quietly up the back steps, along the hall and past the staircase to his old room. He stood with one hand on the knob, remembering the desert and the dreams.

There was just Jamie and Ruby his mother then, living here with Grandma and Grandpa. He remembered cuddling up in the great tent bed, dreaming of more free space than he'd ever seen in the waking world. Grandpa, still in the force then, had had Jamie's father beaten senseless and run out of town. Ruby pined for him, only knowing Joseph Blake in those early days as strong arms holding her, and soft words she'd never heard before. Grandpa ignored her, and Grandma seemed to regard her as the cause of old age creeping up. She dressed Ruby in little girls' clothes even after she turned sixteen, but good old Joe Blake saw through the lace and bows to the woman underneath. Within a few months he'd got her pregnant and got himself run out of town. Life would have been good for Jamie then, if the old man hadn't sneaked back a few years later and taken them off to Sydney.

Remembering that day, he turned the door handle with a savage twist, as if that tarnished brass knob was his old man's nose. He kicked the door as if it were a shin.

They had turned his room into a storeroom filled with boxes, bins, old furniture and stacks of newspapers. All were coated with dust, as if they'd stored that too. The floor was still the remembered yellow, the walls a sun-blanched blue. But they'd built a paper city in his desert and ruined it with pollution.

'Hey you, what do you think you're doing, ay?'

He didn't recognise Grandpa Blake at first. The once great stomach hung almost to his knees in one soft drape. The flesh on his shoulders, chin and backside created an illusion of limp curtains drawn around a hospital bed to hide a dying man. His face, grey-stubbled and ash-coloured, appeared as a blob of melted skin. His eyes were squinted and dull, as if they'd given up hope of sighting anything worth the strain of looking. His words were blurred, his voice sucked dry of intonation.

'It's me, Grandpa. Jamie. Jamie Blake.'

'I know who you are. And I know they got married and had more kids. Won't make no difference. He'll never get his hands on this place. Ah yeah, and where is he then, that no good father of yours? And your stupid mother?'

Ruby Blake might have been a bit slow, but she'd never been stupid. Not like this old fart of a man who danced around Grandma as if she were the Queen of Sheba.

Jamie swallowed a sharp retort, despite a feeling that the old bloke hoped for a hostile answer. The guesthouse needed a handyman, a young man with vision and guts enough to restore it to its former grandeur. He could be that man. He could be the son his grandma never had. Even living with this flabby ghost of a tough cop would be better than returning to the greyness of a life in Sydney.

He forced a quiet, low voice as he asked, 'Where's Grandma then?'

The man who used to be proud of keeping his town clean of thugs, thieves and bludgers gave a wheezing grunt, as if he'd been hit in the stomach with a mallet. His hands trembled and flapped like a couple of dirty old bedsheets thrown over a line and stirred by a weary wind.

'Dead these past three years,' he said, and turned to shuffle away.

'Hey!' Jamie called. 'I thought I might stay on for a while.'

'Get on back to your mother, boy,' the old man called over a shoulder. 'You're nothing to do with me.'

If Jamie had detected a hint of anger, he might have stayed. But even a fifteen-year-old boy could see that Jack Blake was nothing more than a pile of flesh and bones entombed in a monument to the already dead. Living with the shades of happier times might have been bearable, but he had a feeling that those ghosts had slipped away. Laughter had long since turned to mildew. The damp and mould had even swamped his desert oasis — although if Jamie had known the tale of Madam Basha, he might have thought the contamination had spread from that room. Perhaps madness can flake off in little pieces and lie in waiting, in cracks between the floorboards or underneath a mattress.

He headed back to Sydney, not really wanting to be there but not knowing where else to go. He lingered on the way, searching for work. All he found were a few odd jobs which barely paid for his food. Prospective employers laughed at his skinny legs and told him to come back when he'd finished growing.

He finally managed to hitch a ride in a semitrailer heading south. It passed over the Harbour Bridge during a midmorning of August, 1945.

There was a war going on. Jamie knew that. He couldn't help knowing when everyone's mouths were full of it. He'd played battle games with the kids on the block. He'd cut out scenes of victory and pinned those cut-outs onto his walls. He'd seen candles at windows, widows weeping, men coming home minus a limb or two. Yet even when the Japanese bombed Darwin, that war had seemed a world away. He had his own conflict, the one in his own home — watching the old man's eyes for that telltale tic, his mouth for the sudden twist that said it was time to head for the trenches. Crockery and fists had whizzed around Jamie's head like bullets. The old man's flying boots could cause as much damage as a grenade if you didn't know how to dodge them. So when he climbed down from the cab of a semitrailer in Sydney and heard everyone yelling an end to the war, Jamie thought for a moment his luck had changed and the old man had dropped dead.

The truck pulled away trailing a horn blast, leaving him to be swamped by a tide of people. Joy washed over and around him, hand pumping, back thumping, surging forward to envelop him in a heaving bosom, wet lips on his face, dragging him along and tossing him around like jetsam on a crest of bliss. At the next corner another wave of frenzied people dumped him into the gutter and his head hit the concrete, hard.

Struggling to a sitting position, he put his hand to the back of his neck and felt a wetness there. A vision flashed of a wall of water holding him down, filling his eyes, his ears, his mouth; darkness seeping into his lungs until there was no room left for air. Blackness filtered through his skin, clogging his heart and stopping his breath.

At the moment of letting the darkness take hold, he opened his eyes, waiting for two arms to lift him. He waited for fists pummelling his back to force the salty water out in a gushing jet. He saw the face, Ruby's face but not hers. The lips thin like hers saying, 'You're all right now, boy.'

He was sitting in a gutter. A tall thin man with sandy hair and cankered skin sat beside him.

'Are you all right, boy?' the old man was asking.

The face might have been right, but the place and time was definitely wrong. He wasn't on a beach, and he wasn't two years old. He'd turned fifteen a month ago. And this man was older. Older than who? The memory of his near drowning had already slipped back into the recesses of his brain. He was sitting in a gutter on the corner of Market and George Street, Sydney.

'Gotter stay out from under them boots or they'll trample yer for sure,' the tall thin man grumbled. 'Silly buggers ain't got the sense to know that when yer get rid of one war, there's always another waiting round the bend.'

Jamie felt his clothes. Of course they were dry. That other thing, the drowning thing, must have been an hallucination brought on by hunger and the whack on his head.

'Yeah,' he said. 'In a grey house around the corner from a biscuit factory wall.'

'That yer home?'

'Was.'

'Right then, yer better come to mine,' the tall man said.

'Why's that?' Jamie asked.

'Because yer need to get that gash on the back of yer head tended to. It's still leaking blood yer know. Besides that, you remind me of family I lost a long time ago. What's yer name, boy?'

'Jamie Blake.'

'Blake, ay? Right. People round here call me Jock.'

Jamie followed when Jock walked away without saying another word. Wherever he went had to be better than going home, and there was something about the old geezer's face that reminded him of the tent bed, the dreams of open spaces and the cuddling. Jock reminded Jamie of his mother before Joe Blake came back to spoil her.

# Chapter Forty-four

The little back room in Jock's Newtown house was a working man's cottage, small — twelve foot square — with a wardrobe and a narrow cot, and the odd flake of paint dropping onto his head throughout the night. Jamie lay on a lumpy mattress congratulating himself for the end to combat. Not the fight between nations. That, he felt, had nothing to do with him. It was his private combat that he'd finally won. Or if not actually won, at least he'd executed a lasting peace by his withdrawal from the house where his father lived. At that young age, Jamie truly believed that out of sight was out of mind.

He stared at the ceiling, refusing to look down at the peak formed by his erection under the blankets. Jamie was determined not to make this night, this start of a new life, like every other night for the past three years. The peak gradually dwindled while his hands were still firmly clamped under his armpits. This second triumph confirmed the fact, in his own reckoning, that he'd finally become a man. Surely self-restraint was a sign of maturity. Although when he deliberated on this concept, he realised that he'd never known a man or woman with that particular trait. The adults of his acquaintance did as they liked, within the bounds set by their purses anyway, while the children had to constantly restrain their words and actions. If he followed the examples set by the adults in his world, they'd call him a hoodlum.

He couldn't remember ever being a child. As a toddler in his grandmother's house he had carried messages, fed the dogs and hens, gathered eggs and performed the role of buffer between his mother and her parents. From that grey house around from the biscuit factory wall he ran messages for everyone in the street. He cleaned shoes, minded children, worked the paper route and continued in the role of buffer, this time between his father and the other members of the family. The odd days at school were islands of peace he never thought of spoiling by knuckling down to learn things he couldn't use. Yet he had learned how to fight, and how to gather a gang around him as protection from the older boys. He'd learned how to win the liking of teachers, and a penny from those kids with one to spare. 'Spare' meaning they hadn't been sensible enough to spend it on their way to class.

Jamie turned over in bed and listened to a cat yowling her way around the yard. It was Jock's cat, a big grey tabby with marmalade-coloured ears and paws. Jock said he'd found her under the apple tree, half starved and big with unborn kittens. He fed her with scraps from the table and she thanked him kindly by shredding the skin on the back of his hand.

'I keep her because she gets up Emmie's nose,' Jock said when the tabby spat at Jamie as he tried to stroke her. 'You'll like her for the same reason when yer meet Emmie.'

Emmie, Jock's housekeeper or boarder or whatever, had gone into her room and slammed the door the moment Jamie entered the house.

A series of spits and snarls interrupted the cat's howling, which descended to the deep-throated growl that usually heralded a successful mating. Jamie pulled the pillow across his face to muffle his laughter when a window grated open and a woman screamed a string of curses. The language was foreign, but he knew by the tone that the words had to be oaths. The cat yowled defiance, and the war of sound between females continued, somehow changing in tone as the feline seemed to be yelling abuse while the woman howled frustration. A man's shout and a window slamming shut abruptly ended the duel.

Wide awake and restless, Jamie crept onto the back veranda. The tabby leapt up the steps and rubbed her body along his legs. He knew she would be kittenish and carefully gentle for perhaps an hour or more, until the urge to mate again sharpened her claws and temper. He stared down at her, wondering if pleasure or pain was the reason for loudly announcing the act of coupling. He wondered why Lottie Anderson had never uttered a sound when he coupled with her against the door of the Anderson laundry.

Thought of Lottie sent him scurrying back to bed, groaning at the knowledge that this night would be exactly like the last three years after all.

After an early breakfast Jock led Jamie to Foley Brothers Bacon Factory and talked the foreman into giving him a job. The work was back-breaking at first, but as months went by it put flesh on Jamie's bones. It broadened his back and hardened his muscles. Regular pay and a promotion halfway through the year gave him confidence, as did the twice weekly workouts at Marrickville Boxing Club. Two after-noons a week and Saturdays, he drank beer with workmates at the local pub. Sundays were rest and football, though not necessarily in that order, and never both at the same time. At night he went to the movies, or he sat and yarned with Jock. He would have been content if not for Emmie.

He could never be sure who Emmie was or why she lived at Jock's house. A small dark woman about forty years old, she had a quick-fire way of talking, never using a word that Jamie understood. He thought she spoke Spanish, but Jock swore that the language was an invention of her own.

'She cleans and cooks. I give her food and clothes and a few shillings a week. She mostly spends that on paints and brushes. Fancies herself as a bit of a painter I reckon, though she never lets anyone see what she's doing. I let her stay because she reminds me of a bird of a bloke I knew a long time ago,' was Jock's explanation of her presence.

Emmie spent a large part of each day inside her room with the door shut against inquisitive eyes. At times she disappeared for a week, emerging only to cook and eat and give the house what Jock called a lick and a promise. Jamie laughed at the complaints of unwashed plates and corner dirt, and told him to try living at the Blake house. Emmie usually offered a broom and threw the dishes into the garbage.

Jock worked six hours a day, five days a week as janitor at Foley Brothers. He shopped for food on the way home, then he usually spent an hour or two playing dominoes at the local park with other old men. His favourite pastime seemed to be chasing the local children. They liked to disrupt the domino games with a barrage of cheek and water-filled bags. Jock had never been known to actually catch a child, but he did help colour their language. Late at night he gained revenge by rocking roofs or knocking on doors then disappearing before they opened. These childish acts were naturally blamed on children. On Saturdays he sat around the Golden Barley pub watching others spend their wages on slow horses and alcohol. Jock never gambled or drank anything stronger than a lemon squash. Sundays he read the weekly papers and shouted himself hoarse at every Newtown rugby league game, no matter where the Blues were playing. The nights he felt too lazy for revenge, he listened to radio plays.

Sometimes, and to Jamie these were the best times, he made himself comfortable on the lounge. With a cup of tea in one hand and a stack of evil-smelling cigarettes by the other, he talked for hours. He'd spent time in most states, in outback places, in fishing trawlers. He had even lived for over a year with an Aboriginal tribe in the Northern Territory.

Emmie usually sat cross-legged in a corner, listening intently. Her eyes would fill with a yearning for something Jamie could not name. For a while her body would grow limp. The hard lines of her face would smooth and soften. Her fingers fluttered, as if they were passing on an unspoken message. Then, for no reason apparent to him, a shrill whistling scream would force its way through her lips. Shadows of doubt or dislike would turn her roundness into sharply jutting edges. If Jock noticed, he grinned. Then she would jump up and spit on the floor at his feet. At the door to her room she'd glance back at them, not bothering to hide a wet shine in her topaz-coloured eyes. Although tears on her dark skin appeared as drops of jet — which Jamie always thought of as solidified malevolence — he never quailed from her glare. It always seemed to be directed inward.

She had never wanted Jamie in the Newtown house. Her silence made that plain. That unintelligible gabble of hers met him coming home from work every afternoon. His entering the kitchen stopped the words in what always seemed to be midsentence. She'd serve up a dinner laced with olives and garlic, then she'd sit with her arms folded watching his every bite. He usually finished his meal on the steps of the back veranda.

Jock's only comment was, 'If yer play the game the way she wants, she'll beat yer every time.'

Arriving home late one night and not bothering to switch on the light, Jamie did not see the changes to his room until the following morning. Rocks of all shapes and sizes, from tiny round pebbles to jagged stones as large as a loaf of bread, lay scattered across a floor painted the colour of wet sand. The walls were a mural of rolling waves, and the window resembled a porthole. After just one look, Jamie raced outside for a gulp of air. That night he rolled up in a blanket and slept on the old sprung sofa smelling of stale milk and cat's urine.

The sofa became his permanent bed when waves began creeping across the ceiling of that little back room. Fish and eels circled the walls. A slick brown seal flopped across the top of his wardrobe, and strands of seaweed twined around the rocks.

Jock threatened to throw Emmie's paint tins into the garbage. 'She'll end up putting the whole place underwater if I don't stop her,' he growled.

'It gives her something to do and I don't mind the sofa,' Jamie argued.

But he knew he had to leave that house when he woke to see the veranda floor painted yellow. Water oozed in shiny droplets from the bottom of the sofa and his blankets. Emmie wanted him gone, and she'd have her way even if she had to drown him in the process.

A week later, coming home from a night out at the movies, he almost slipped in a stream of water snaking down the front stairs. He turned the key slowly, shoved the door open and jumped back, half expecting a torrent to rush out and swamp him. Prodding the wet carpet with the toe of his boot every few inches, he moved down the hallway one step at a time and shouting for Jock, although he knew he wouldn't receive an answer. It was a dark and moonless Thursday. A perfect night for wreaking childish revenge.

Emmie was in the kitchen, totally naked except for a coating of pale grey paint. As Jamie stared at her, she threw a bucket of seaweed across the linoleum floor, forming a pathway to the sodden carpet. Smiling slightly, she drew up a strand of the weed and wrapped it around her small breasts, pausing occasionally to rub a hardened nipple or slide one hand downwards to the matted grey pubic hair. Her smile widened as she draped the strand over one shoulder, dipped the end into a large paint pot then drew two rows of teeth across the mound of her stomach. She began to undulate, moving with the sensual rhythm of a belly dancer keeping time to slow music. Her fingers played imaginary castanets as the shark's teeth opened and closed.

Jamie could hear the blood ticking through his veins when the beat quickened and her movements became wilder. He fled when she dropped to her knees on the pathway of weed and began to unbutton his trousers.

He could still hear the echo of her laughter as he booked into an inner-city hotel and paid for a month in advance.

After work the following day Jamie bought a middy of beer and sat on the front steps of the King's Head Hotel, thumbing leisurely through the newspaper that would switch his life to a new direction. There, on the third page from the front, was a picture of his old man. Joseph Blake had been arrested for armed robbery of his brother, George

Blake, head of the accountancy firm Eastman, Blake and Associates. Jamie drew in a sharp breath and almost passed out as he tried to read the article while he choked on his own spittle. His shock wasn't caused by his father's attempted robbery of family, but by the knowledge that George Blake existed. Big bad Joe had always claimed to have run from an orphanage at the age of ten. He had never known his parents, he'd said, and never had kin worth talking about. Not that being without kin had ever stopped Joseph Blake from talking.

'If I did have kin, I wouldn't talk about the kind of mongrels who'd turn their backs on someone just because they didn't like his friends,' he'd say. 'Hah hahh, coo-wee, the kind of friends who paid me bloody good money for running a few messages and being a lookout.'

Joseph Blake was over six feet tall. His shoulders were broad, his chest wide. Most people called him handsome despite his habitual sneer and never-still eyes. He had a long fall of shiny dark hair, which he liked to toss back when punctuating a story with that teeth-displaying shout of 'Hah hahh, coo-wee!' His shout of laughter often thundered around the bar of the nearest pub, turning heads in his direction. Others were unable to resist laughing with him. Good old Joe Blake, good old bloke Joe. A happy sort, the sort of bloke who's the life of every party.

'Hah hahh, coo-wee!' he'd shout, claiming everyone's attention. 'I died ya know, on the day me wife's old man beat me up. A heart attack they said. That big old bruiser had another bloke lined up for her. You know the sort. Hardworking, school at nights to get ahead. Talking like a bloody toff when he wasn't no better than me.'

Another flick of hair, another beer bought for him, and he'd go on with the story.

'Popped me cork I did. Kicked the bloody bucket. But the man upstairs took one look and shot me back. Knocked back by God. The ultimate rejection, that toff talker said. Hah hahh, coo-wee, but I come back and got her pregnant. How do youse like that for a comeback! Got another beating and kicked out again for me trouble, but the comeback kid come back again and this time she went with me. Her big fat father put the cops in every town onto chasing after us, but none of them got within grabbing distance for six months or more. When they did and they took her back, she trashed half his bloody mansion before she run again. How's that for the ultimate rejection?'

'Those were the good times,' Jamie's mother would say, and cuddle up to the old man, forgetting yesterday's black eye. He hit her time and again, but a few soft words and a hangdog look would have her coming back for more.

As Jamie remembered that hated voice and his mother's black eyes, he couldn't hold back a shout of elation. No more petty crim, Joseph Blake had hit the big time. Correction. Ha ha, coo-wee. Had tried to hit the big time. Armed robbery would mean at least five years, and that wasn't counting the time in jail waiting for a trial!

Tearing the paper into strips, he threw the pieces over his head and performed a couple of cartwheels which took him into the bar. He danced a jig on the counter while ordering drinks all round. Most of his mates thought he'd won the lottery. They were glad to open their wallets when he couldn't pay the bill, sure they'd get double their money back the moment he picked up his win.

Perhaps it was just as well that Jamie never returned to Foley Brothers Bacon Factory, for those former mates continued to shout the bar after he left. To visit his mother was his plea to get out of that place, while in fact he headed for the accountancy firm of Eastman, Blake and Associates to get the story first-hand, and to meet a formerly unknown uncle.

Uncle welcomed him as long-lost kin, if only because of Ruby.

'I met her first and loved her first,' Uncle said. 'My brother wormed his way into her affections just to spite me. But I've kept my eye on them in case she ever needed my help. Help I've offered time and again without it ever being accepted.'

'You can't imagine my shock,' he went on to say, 'when Uncle Jack died six months ago and named me as the sole inheritor of his property. When Aunt Nell passed away, the old man let the guesthouse go to rack and ruin, but I sold the land for a fair enough price and I offered the money to your mother. She turned it down, which I thought she would. A fact that made your father very unhappy, to say the least. When I refused to hand the money over to him, he tried to take it by force. Unfortunately for Joseph, he made the attempt while two police officers were making enquiries about an illegal betting ring. It was supposedly operating in a warehouse belonging to my partner. Of course I had no knowledge of such things and I couldn't help them.'

'Of course,' Jamie said, covering a grin.

'But I can help you with finance for a house, and I can provide a job paying more than you'll earn anywhere else, taking into account your lack of scholastic qualifications. I have an opening for someone who is street-smart, has guts and a buttoned-down lip. I think you could fit the bill,' he said; and Jamie did.

# Chapter Forty-five

When Joseph Blake went to jail, Ruby decided that the only way for her to earn a living was to take up cleaning houses. To do that, she had to travel to the other side of Sydney. Yet she too often missed a bus or a train, and if she did arrive at the required hour, those other-side ladies rarely invited her back for a second try. Ruby's motto for cleanliness — out of sight is out of mind — did not meet their specifications.

At home Ruby wore a floral cotton frock and a faded cardigan. She never wore shoes around the house, and her hair was usually kept out of her eyes with plastic rollers. Except for a thin smear of lipstick, she rarely wore cosmetics. All that was exactly the look those other-side ladies raised on clichés expected to see. Yet on her cleaning days Ruby donned a severely styled suit from Beatrice's Pre-Loved Clothing and, carefully painting her face to make it look pale and unpainted, brushed her hair into a pageboy style. The result was a trim, attractive woman (a little too short to be chic) who appeared, to the average northside visitor at least, more classy than her employer. She had that European old money, nouveau poor because of the war look. The intention was to appear too genteel to be asked to perform tasks below her former station.

This maid's game was considered to be the epitome of one up on the posh. It kept Ruby's neighbours amused for hours. They didn't mind buying her a few drinks while she told the tale, and the beers numbed her to sleep despite the cold half of the bed during nights that seemed to go on forever. It was all very social and pleasant enough for her, but working just a few days a week meant she barely earned enough to feed her family.

Jane and Hannah Blake, still at school, managed to stay agreeably plump by babysitting for the local mothers. This provided snacks from their refrigerators, a few pence for hamburgers, and the added bonus of keeping them out from under their own mother's feet. Yet they were tired of wearing second-hand dresses and cast-off shoes, and sitting on the porch half the night waiting for Don to come home. Ruby — as pissed as a parrot, or so the neighbours said — could never be wakened to let them in.

Don Blake, just thirteen at the time, sold newspapers during the early morning, bread through the day and sweets at theatres at night. He was considered too young to earn a man's wage, and half the wages he did earn were slid across the counter at the corner pub as payment for cigarettes and booze. Without these essential items, Ruby could not have borne the squalor of her life, she said.

So it was hardly surprising when, on the day Jamie arrived at the door with the deeds to their house, his family welcomed him with open arms and the honour of being their regular provider.

The Blake house had three bedrooms running alongside a narrow hallway ending in a lounge room, which opened onto a dining room and kitchen. Laundry and bathroom were through the kitchen door and down three stairs. Ruby had the front room to herself, the girls had the middle, and Jamie claimed the third room. Don had to make do with a sofa in the lounge room.

Although nobody complained about this crowding, Jamie knew they were cramped enough with five living there, but he couldn't stop thinking about Jock. He didn't feel right about leaving the old bloke in Emmie's clutches. That first wave of fear, which had driven Jamie away in a panic, had turned to shamed derision directed at himself. He decided to make amends by inviting the old man to move in with the Blakes. Emmie could take care of herself. She would have to one day. She was a whole lot younger than Jock.

Still trying to be as different from his father as possible, Jamie told the family of his plan and asked for a show of hands.

'Just like your old man,' Ruby said. 'He always asked, then did what he wanted anyway.'

Jamie won the vote by four to one. Don and the girls were not taking chances on a cut to their pocket money by voting against him. Ruby showed her thoughts by sitting on her hands, yet when the taxi arrived to take her son to the Newtown house, she climbed in beside the driver and threatened to yell blue bloody murder if they tried to throw her out.

As they arrived at Jock's open front door, a vague impression of something wrong flared to a certainty of disaster. Jamie burst into the kitchen just in time to catch Jock and Emmie halfway through their dinner.

'The prodigal returns,' the old man said. 'Lot of blokes at Foley Brothers looking for you. I told 'em you'd be back to pay yer debts.'

Everything Jamie wanted to say waited to pour out of his mouth, but he was afraid to open it. Surrounding him, hanging on walls and propped on boxes, were squares of Masonite board covered in rolling waves. Seals and fish swam in every direction. His knees buckled and he might have fallen if Ruby hadn't propped him up with her shoulder

'Thought it was you,' she said to Jock. 'Felt it in me bones.'

The old man sagged in his chair. For the first time in his life, Dougal McLean couldn't produce a wisecrack answer.

Ruby nodded, aware of this fact. She prodded a little further.

'You let all this go on,' she said, waving a hand at the paintings, 'knowing about his fear of the ocean.'

'How would he know?' Jamie asked.

'He pulled you out of it once. Years ago, when you wasn't much more than a baby.'

'Who are you, then?' Jamie asked, standing away from his mother's support and looking directly at Dougal.

'I thought you and Emmie would learn to get on,' the old man said. 'Never thought for a minute that you'd run.'

'You did.' Ruby's voice was an accusation.

'I told her right from the start that I wasn't having marrying or kids. And Jack Blake was there, waiting to take over. Had been for years, waiting, before I happened along.'

'That's a man's answer,' Ruby said.

'I followed yer back after you come looking for me. He had me run out of town.'

'I had you run out of town.'

'I was drunk, Ruby. Too drunk to see who you were.'

'You were winning at cards. Money was more important.'

He shook his head. 'Money's never been important. If it was, I'd never have been a gambler. Don't yer see that yet? And I've never gambled since. Never drank anything stronger than a lemon squash.'

'You were always too late.'

His voice rose. 'And you were too busy screwing that no-good to see yer boy being drowned.'

'You're a fine one to talk, Dougal McLean,' Ruby sneered. 'You screwed everybody. Like you're screwing her. Letting her carry on naked in front of a half-grown boy like any horny old slattern. Letting her run Jamie off. Like you'll run off from her.'

Emmie erupted into a barrage of gabble and catapulted from the chair. Jamie's mother bunched a fist and caught her on the chin with a blow that laid her out cold. Ruby had learned to fight man-style when she'd first run off with Joe.

'He's Jock and he's Dougal McLean,' Jamie said. 'Now will you tell me who he is?'

'Nobody important to us,' Ruby said. 'But you're old enough to make a choice, and that's what you have to do. You come back with me to your rightful place, or you stay here and learn to tread water.'

Dougal McLean, for only the second time in his life, chose in someone else's favour. Pushing Jamie aside, he hauled Emmie upright and into his lap.

'Go on, boy, go off with your mother,' he said. 'This is the only family I've got and she already give yer the message.'

# Chapter Forty-six

'For the second time in her life, Ruby Blake stood up for herself and deliberately forced an issue,' Jamie said. 'My old man always said she was a true socialist. She might put up a hand to make an objection, but no matter what her opinion, she always went along with the mob. That was the old man's idea of socialism. People going along with the mob rather than following their own direction. A coward's way, he said; and that was the only time ever I agreed with his way of thinking. Yet the first time she stood up for herself, she ended up with my father. A frying pan to fire situation if ever I saw one. But this second time was different. Somehow it gave her strength. She turned to being a mother. Handing out orders like fairy cakes, expecting every one to be swallowed without a word of objection. She stopped taking money from Don because she'd stopped drinking and she'd cut down on cigarettes. She wouldn't let the girls out at night until they turned fourteen and were old enough to get jobs. Even then she checked out their boyfriends and chucked out the ones who didn't meet her standards. The old girl was no more than five feet tall, but she threw a punch like a man. And by the time Jane and Hannah had grown out of being little, there weren't too many men willing to go up against me. By then I was Uncle's right-hand man, and Uncle had connections.'

A few weeks after the showdown at the Newtown house, Dougal arrived at Uncle's office to say goodbye to Jamie. He didn't know what he was going to do, or which direction to head. He just knew it was time to be gone.

Luckily for Dougal, Uncle knew a bloke by the name of Colin Jensen who owned a farm out Mudgee way. It was an inheritance from his parents. At that time Jensen dealt mostly with agistment — a few beef cattle, a few sheep and horses — so the property virtually ran itself. Yet he had a continuing problem with squatters in the homestead, which was a large sandstone house built by convicts around 1839. Jensen offered Dougal a small wage and free rent, electricity and phone just to keep an eye on the place and count a few cattle. Dougal grabbed the offer and left on the next day's train.

Jamie breathed a sigh of relief as he waved goodbye from the platform. He knew that if Dougal had stayed in the Newtown house, he would have gone back to see him. That would have meant trouble with Ruby. With Dougal gone, the only source of contention had disappeared. Now, as Uncle's right-hand man earning a steadily growing wage, he could settle down to the style of living that he'd always wanted.

This upward turn in the Blake family's lives might have continued indefinitely if the well-meaning people who decide these things hadn't granted Joseph Blake his parole. Good behaviour was the excuse and condition they made. Jamie's old man, a reject even from jail, returned to take his place as head of the family. Rejected once more, for Ruby said he'd selected the wrong end, he tried to enforce his claim the only way he knew how.

Jamie happened to be visiting Jensen's property at the time, but using reports from doctors, welfare agencies, family and neighbours, he managed to piece the story together.

# Chapter Forty-seven

The first blow was a battering ram, an elbow slamming her into the back of the seat. Ruby ricocheted into the dashboard as the second blow, a closed fist this time, smashed against her cheek. The bone cracked and she tasted blood. Two hard jarring thuds, then his signet ring ground into her top lip, splitting the flesh against an already broken tooth. She swallowed convulsively, gagging on a thick flow. A flurry of open-handed slaps were almost kind, yet terrifying in their promise. One arm rose instinctively in protection while she scrabbled for the door handle and kicked out to keep him away. The first flush of rage had left his face. His eyes were glazed as if he did not know her, as if he was watching a horror movie and was fascinated by the special effects. The corners of his mouth lifted.

That tiny smile created panic. She grabbed the door handle and shoved. Her face hit gravel, one arm wrenched back, caught by the handle, caught by him as he swung across the seat, his boot aimed at her back. She jerked free, elbowed across the dirt, then was up and running, heaving against blood and bile, clawing hair from her eyes.

Twin headlights flared into high beam, paving the gravel with tiny gold nuggets. Sparse bush growth leading to the beach darkened to an impenetrable wall, a tunnel leading to a void. Instinct screamed at her to dive away, to run the gauntlet of bramble and gorse. Instead, she turned, and night became a blinding glare that pinned her. A vision flashed of a small brown rabbit held in the laser beam of a spotlight, its head lifted, its eyes filmed with light. She had pleaded for that rabbit. He had smiled while he shot it.

Dropping to her knees, she bowed her head. Her elbows dug into her thighs, her fingers were spread over her face while she tensed for the thud of impact. There was no sound except the pounding of the surf.

Glare became a roomful of light peopled by white coats and blue uniforms. The dirt road became a rubber-sheeted bed. She listened for the rhythm of waves but heard a murmur of voices instead. One called her name while she turned away to deny her own existence. Her nose was swollen and distorted in a grotesquely blackened face. One eye refused to open, the other was no more than a blue iris centred in a pool of blood. Fingermarks necklaced her throat, and her chin was cleft with a ragged line of stitching. She stared at a mirror in mute horror. There was too much pain in crying. The pills numbed. They blessed her with the luxury of not caring.

But that was the last time. This was here and now. Now the headlights still glared. The car hadn't moved.

When Joe walked towards her, she cringed away from his darkness.

'Oh Christ, Ruby. I'm sorry. I don't know, I just couldn't hack you telling me to get. The kids ganging up on me. We've been through a lot together, you and me. It won't happen again. I swear it.'

Covering her head with her arms, she twisted sideways and cried out for him to please just leave her alone. On the third 'Please' he stumbled away into the tunnel wall.

Lifting the hem of her skirt to staunch the flow of blood, she staggered erect. Anger stirred, but faded when she couldn't find the energy to keep it alive. She climbed into the car and sat behind the wheel. The motor purred. She'd never learned to drive, but still she grabbed the steering wheel with one hand and trod the accelerator.

The car gathered speed, hurtling along the dirt road before skidding across grass. Wheels spun, throwing up a spray of sand. The engine roared, then coughed and died. Scrabbling for her purse, she opened the catch using the undamaged side of her mouth, and spilled its contents. The little miracles of unemotion weren't there. He'd taken them, the last two. That was the reason he'd gone so meek and mild.

'Bastard,' she whispered. 'Bastard. Bastard. Bastard.'

She screamed at last. It began as a grunt, gradually building to a wail, tearing her throat, locking her jaws open, strangling in its intensity. It ended in a gargle as a fresh flow of blood cut off her breath.

Her reach for air gentled to a shallow panting while she listened to the sound of waves. Her body swayed in rhythm as she breathed the smell of petrol and blood. She had no difficulty in slowing the staccato of her thoughts.

A night-bird called, answered by its mate as Ruby walked slowly down the beach, holding the comforting dark around her. Breathing was an indulgence. The throbbing pain throughout her body didn't exist in her mind as she pulled off her skirt and blouse.

The first wave broke across her legs, drawing a gasp at its icy clutch. The second wave hit harder. The third slammed into her stomach and forced out a cry. Salt stung her wounds. As she began to swim, the coldness numbed. Turning onto her back, arms and legs outspread, she felt the water over and under her, building its cocoon. One day she would climb out, she thought, a changed woman with soft white wings like those pictures in her Bible.

Something brushed her legs. It was no more than a touch, but it travelled throughout her body with a scratching, tearing sensation. She sat up and went down. The water clamped over her mouth and nose like a strangler's hand. Thrusting back with her elbows and feet, she shot to the surface. The scratchy thing clung to her legs and thighs like children's hands.

She had to go back to her girls. They needed someone to watch out that they didn't tie up with the wrong sort, those sort of boys with their slick looks and slicker hair who latched onto nice girls and filled their bellies every year, tying them down to kitchen and cooking and caring with never a minute to themselves while they, the slick boys, ran around with nice younger girls and spent all their money on beer and horse racing. And Jamie, Jamie needed family. He'd run away again and get into God knows what kind of trouble. And don't forget about Don, all defiance and hate, ready to take on the world, or at the very least his old man. But that wasn't his place. She, Ruby, was the mother.

She stroked harder and stronger until the waves eased her onto the sand. Kicking free of the clinging seaweed, she stamped along the beach to warm herself and find the point where she had entered the water. She found her clothes, dried herself on the skirt then put it on, tied the blouse around her neck and headed for the dirt track. The blouse flapped around her back and shoulders like wings as she tramped to the highway.

One bus and two trams later, Ruby walked up the street to her house. Her shoulders stayed straight, even when she saw the car outside her gate. She had expected to see it there. He couldn't leave it on the beach. It didn't belong to him.

'He owns nothing,' she yelled, letting them all know, the ones who thought her a fool for trusting him, for going off to the beach in a borrowed car in the first place. To get him away from the kids, she'd said. But she had never been able to say no to Joe. Not when he said the words nobody else ever said. Not when his eyes were filled with her, when his mouth was all soft and hanging open from wanting. Not when he talked about the good times they'd had, the authorities they'd defied. But that was the old Ruby.

He'd be waiting at the dining room table, staring up the hallway to the door, ready to pull down the lines on his face the moment she stepped inside. Head down and pleading as always, he'd be confident of success. His knowledge of her had never failed him before.

He was there all right. He even managed a few tears. She flattened him with one blow. A king hit out of nowhere was the only way. Fair fighting's a mug's game, Joe had always said, and his physical strength would beat her if she tried it. Before he had a chance to open his mouth, she busted his head with a rolling pin and bum-rushed him into the street. He staggered away, dripping blood and cursing.

He came again later, drunk, as she knew he would.

A neighbour had yelled a warning that Joe was downing whisky as if expecting prohibition at any moment, and everyone knew that spirits made a beer man mean. Ruby waited for him with a poker this time, even though she had trouble staying on her feet. She was still half-blind and vomiting from the punches she'd taken in the car. The girls were hiding out at a friend's place, and Don had disappeared. He had begged her to call the police, but if Joe didn't get to her first, the locals would tar and feather her if she brought cops into their part of town. She answered Don with a sneer and she hadn't seen him since.

Ruby's breathing was too harsh for her to hear her second son as he trembled and wept beneath the front veranda. That was his favourite hiding place, the one he and Jamie had used when they were small. The old man had never been able to get to them there, although he knew about the scooped-out hollow lined with chaff bags. He knew about the pistol. On the day the police had stormed the house and arrested him for assault, Joe had given a gun to Don and told him to hide it, fast.

Ruby clutched the poker firmly when a protest from the gate announced Joe's arrival. Spreading her backside against the table for support, she watched him stagger up the pathway. She knew there was no sense in closing the door. He'd only bust it down, and that would cost money to fix. She'd make her move when he entered the hallway. Her size was a bonus in cramped spaces. He'd have no room to swing.

Her fingers tightened until the knuckles cracked as he stepped onto the veranda and stood underneath the grime-yellowed light, looking down, shaking his head like a wet dog. He looked up at her and grinned.

'Hah hahh, coo-wee,' he mouthed, and sunk down onto his knees, placing an eye against a knothole in the floorboards.

'That you down there, Jamie?' he whispered hoarsely.

Don shrieked. The gun roared. Joe raised up, then fell in a salaam to his gods of violence.

Ruby stamped up and down the veranda as if play-acting a giant in one of those old nursery stories.

'Thief!' she screamed. 'I'm the mother. You had no right.'

The floor was old and rotten. Two boards caved in. She dropped to her knees, pulling and tearing until the hole became large enough for the sixty-watt bulb to shine its dirty yellow light down onto Don. He crawled a few paces forward, then stopped to cry out his bewilderment and guilt into the mouldy earth. Ruby reared back as if its sour stench, mixed now with fresh urine, was a physical blow. As if Don's face when he turned to look at her was another.

'Come out now, Donnie. I need you here with me,' she whispered, handing over her newfound strength without a second thought.

# Chapter Forty-eight

At this point Curtis knew nothing about Jamie or his family; though later, when they became friends, I allowed him to read the part of my journal where I'd recorded Jamie's story. I suppose I did that so he could see how good his life was when compared to my cousin's. But at that time Curtis had problems with his own family.

The day Debra arrived home from hospital, she snuggled William into his cradle then stamped into the yard where Curtis was stirring the compost heap.

'You're nothing but a cur,' was her greeting.

I liked the sound of that. Something interesting was about to happen. I strolled out of Angus's house and sat in the shade of a tree that grew alongside the fence.

'Do you know how people are talking? You haven't been near me since William's birth. Ten days ago, Curtis. Ten days.'

I couldn't hear his answer.

'Amanda told me. You might have known she would. The night William was born, you were out there screwing around.'

'She knows about screwing people around all right. How did she know about me?' he asked.

'She might have been drunk, but not that drunk. She said you even pretended to be Richard until you got her where you wanted her.'

'And where would that be?' Curtis asked in a voice completely devoid of emotion.

'Do you deny making love to Amanda on the night William was born?'

'How do you define making love, Debra? Those short bursts of energy you displayed once or twice before telling me you were pregnant?'

'Do you deny it?' Debra screeched.

Curtis didn't answer, which was to be expected.

There should have been an ache in Debra's voice, but the pain she should have felt was missing. I detected a note of triumph when she continued.

'My father died young. I don't even remember him. How would you like to be reared by a woman like my mother? And I was an only child, Curtis. Just me. You had a father and brothers to make you feel like you belonged to something, somewhere. Someone.'

She sounded like Maidy Watling.

'I'm your wife. You owe me. The least you owe me is a loving home.'

'I don't owe you a bloody thing,' he said as he walked around the side of the house and through the gate. He stopped just once to say goodbye to the eucalypt seedling.

'And don't bother coming back,' she screeched after him.

# Chapter Forty-nine

Curtis stayed at my house that night. The following day he moved into Flat 2/138 Blackwattle Road, which was the one Clo Gatley vacated when she left for Sydney. That was around the time Henry lost his job.

The steelworks had introduced shiftwork into their mills, and Henry headed the line of volunteers for the 3.20–11.20 p.m. roster. He was proud to be one of the forerunners, and he liked the idea of a shift allowance added to his pay packet. Yet later hours meant he would miss the usual afternoon drinking sessions with his mates, which he considered to be a well-earned break from the duties of earning a living. Those few hours of freedom in a smoke-filled bar, swapping insults and yarns, and arguing about everything from politics to the price of eggs in a fish market, were the only upswing in days that were growing more downward as the years piled up behind him. An added bonus was the alcohol buzz that numbed the yearning for Lawson's Place, and the anger directed at Agatha for being no different from his mother and sisters. She was the one who kept him away from the outback where he belonged. She was the one who stood between him and Curtis. The outback and Curtis were waiting for him, if only he knew how to claim them. Without that numbing buzz of alcohol, he had difficulty in restraining himself from bashing down the barrier standing between him and what he wanted. He needed a drink to get him through the day, to get him through the next few hours. To stop him from hitting that face, the one so like Curtis's; both of them hiding their eyes behind the golden bars of their fringes, but not trying to hide the knowledge of what he was. A bench warmer. A bum and a bloody reject.

A few beers before the starting whistle was the way to go.

'The whole flaming thing began as a joke,' Angus said. 'Henry had this habit of peeing where he shouldn't. The urinals are a fair walk from the fabrication shop where he puts in his time, so old Henry would go round the corner and take his leak against one of the steel-plate racks. The other men didn't care for that much. When they had to cut one of them plates and they hit it with a bit of heat, they'd get a full whiff of Henry's beer piss. They decided to teach him a lesson by sticking an electrode against the back end of the first plate in the rack. When Henry sprayed it, he got hit fair in the old fellow with seventy volts. Must have rattled his teeth.

'Anyway, the shock mixed with those afternoon beers must have spun his brain. He's there where they're rolling plates into a cylinder, directing the bloody operator, and the stupid old bugger gives the wrong signals. The plate shoots off the roller and just misses taking off Reg Wilson's legs. Reg does what any normal man would do. He drops Henry on the spot. Foreman comes over to break up the fight — although how you'd call one king hit a fight, I'll never know. He smells the beer on Henry's breath and that's the end of it. Tells him to come back in a week and pick up his pay.

'Albert and Harry tried to stir up the union. There was a lot of talk back and forth, but not even the union could get Henry out of that one. Now the silly bugger's going round saying there's a conspiracy against him. Reg Wilson was supposed to be a mate of his, so even his mates were in on it, Henry says. That would be right too. What did I tell you about friendly bloody fire?'

Henry gave up his afternoons at the pub. He wouldn't drink with a bunch of liars and backstabbers, he said. He began to visit the bottle shop twice a week before the workers arrived, then stagger home with a flagon of wine under each arm. With that, and the beer Albert and Harry supplied, he managed to stay comfortably drunk most of the time. The square build which had once made him appear so macho, soon turned to mucho fat. The little-boy sulky look became a permanent sneer. His dicky hip became even dickier, and often refused to support his weight; or so he said each time he fell flat on his face. He even stopped talking about his glory days of football. Albert and Harry tried to keep their eyes bright as they begged for stories, but they were discouraged by the usual epilogue of tears.

Henry's descent into deterioration might have become a plummet if six weeks of psychiatric care had not made him pause midrung. His stint in hospital — in what was termed Ward Twenty by the doctors but known as Troppo Ward by the locals — began when baby William was twelve months old.

# Chapter Fifty

'You're not to go,' Henry said for the fifth time, although even he had become aware that his roar had sunk to a nag.

'There's nothing else for it,' Agatha said as she packed the old cane basket. It held two aprons, assorted cloths and cleaners, and scrubbing brushes to reach into every crack and crevice. Underneath everything else, she had tucked a notebook and pencil. Not that she ever needed them. Agatha's memory was amazing.

'You shouldn't have told them down at the government office that we didn't need help,' she added, covering the basket with an embroidered cloth. It was backed with the remnants of an old raincoat to keep the polishing rags dry.

'No Lawson has ever been on welfare,' Henry said, 'and no snot-nosed pansy is gunner tell me that I'm bloody unemployable. I was working twelve hours a day while he was crawling around in nappies.'

He threw back the old army blanket, climbed out of bed and poured himself a Vegemite glass of wine.

'I'm not having people talking,' he growled. 'They tell enough lies as it is.'

'I don't ask for much,' Agatha quavered as she watched him pace, 'and I don't think it's right for you to stop me. I know people talk about me being away from home most days while I'm out cleaning, but

I'd go mad sitting around doing nothing all day. Since the boys have grown, there's nothing here to do. It's all right for you being smart and reading all those books.' She indicated his box of war novels. 'But what about me?' she snivelled. 'They know we've got enough to live on, with your severance pay and savings and Albert and Harry's board. Those vegetables are from their gardens, and the other stuff is just what they'd throw out anyway.'

'Still don't look right,' he muttered.

'We'd be fine if you hadn't sent that money to your sisters.'

Realising her tongue had betrayed her again, she added hastily, 'But you're the man of the family. If they ask, you have to give, I can see that. Not having family makes me ignorant about family matters.'

Watching him pour another glass of wine, she knew she must leave now or he'd never let her go. The savings and severance pay had long been spent, and she hated taking so much of Albert and Harry's money. Without her wages, they wouldn't be able to manage. But she couldn't tell Henry that. He'd say she was just trying to make him cut down on his drinking.

Shuffling through the door, she kept her head lowered and her eyes averted from his sneer. He was mollified by such meekness, as always, and did not call her back to make the bed. Placing his sandwiches and a thermos of tea in the centre of the table, she kept her pace to an amble until she was through the door and out of his sight. When she reached the footpath, she ran.

Henry fell back onto the bed and slept. Waking around midday, he began to drink in earnest. He couldn't eat the sandwiches. The salmon had soaked into the bread. That was the trouble in letting a woman go out to work. She neglected her rightful duty. He must have told her a dozen times to put lettuce leaves next to the butter. If she was at home where she ought to be instead of gadding about the place, she'd be able to make them fresh. But it was his own fault for giving in to the whims of a woman.

He passed out again around four o'clock, then revived at seven to refuse the meal Agatha had cooked, and to switch from wine to beer.

Albert and Harry crept outside when he began to mutter. If they were out when his mumble became a snarl, they couldn't be expected to explain the unexplainable. Agatha sneaked off to bed when he started shuffling through his war novels. When he couldn't find the one written about him, he threw the books across the room and bumbled outside, not noticing his eldest son across the road. Harry and Albert took turns keeping an eye on him, especially at night.

Two streets away he met Colin, Paul and Jimmy Lee returning home from roller hockey practice. Their sticks were tucked under their arms. Their skates hung from laces around their necks.

The Lees' ancestors had arrived from China during the gold rush days almost a century and a half ago and had made their way to Steeltown to begin a transport system. The family business had diversified into many areas but still specialised in people. A Lee drove nearly every bus in town. They were well respected and liked, for they never laughed then trod the accelerator if they happened to see someone running for a bus, as seemed to be the practice in other towns.

Jimmy Lee at fifteen years of age had reached what was fashionably termed the teen rebellious stage, when the young rich despise their families for being wealthy, and the young poor detest their parents for not having money. On this particular night he felt even more hostile than usual. He read, wrote and thought in Australian, but his parents insisted he learn Chinese speech and customs. His brothers slipped from one language to the other, and often used a mixture of both. They had done so tonight while A team played the B team. When Jimmy answered in kind, their coach had called him a bloody wog. He was still fuming when he saw Henry sprawled face down on the footpath.

'Drunk as a skunk again,' he sneered.

Colin and Paul knew the vengeful nature and powerful fists of Albert and Harry Lawson. They were sure that one or the other was, and perhaps both were not too far away. Their instructions for Jimmy to shut his mouth were spoken in the language of their forebears.

Henry rolled over and pressed against the fence. He'd seen the movies. He'd read the books. He knew the enemy always attacked at night.

'Learned that much in training camp even before I made sergeant,' he muttered. 'Enemy always attacks at night. Bloody Nips are swarming all over the place. Ambush for sure.'

Now he could see them. Boots around their necks. He knew about these things. They liked to sneak around barefoot. And they had rifles, he could see that too.

'Probably a machine gun in that dark patch to the left. There's a nest of the mongrels. Gotter get them before they get me mates.'

If he died in action, so be it. Curtis would have the medals to boast about his dad.

'I'll take them on with me bare hands. Scrawny little cowards are no match for Henry Lawson.'

Jumping up, as light as a feather on the balls of his feet, he grabbed the rifle from the first soldier and smashed it across the side of his head. That one fell with barely a grunt, but the others were coming for him. He lifted the rifle and raced forward, aiming his bayonet at the sergeant's heart. He had to take them out before they warned the rest.

Something twisted around his foot. He fell, bounced up and turned. It was another enemy soldier. A big bugger, but never too big for Henry Lawson.

He charged at Albert, who regarded him open-mouthed and went backwards with the hit. Albert's face crumpled in disbelief, and a pain which had nothing to do with the hockey stick in his chest.

Henry turned, yelling, muttering, yelling again, and charged at Colin and Paul as they bent over their brother. Colin sidestepped and swung out with his stick, catching Henry across the cheek. Henry sprawled sideways, bounced once and lay still.

Albert crawled across the footpath and wiped the blood from his father's face with a pulled-up shirt tail.

'Jesus, Dad.' To Colin. 'Call an ambulance.'

'I'm calling the cops,' Colin snarled, and sprinted to the nearest house.

Jimmy groaned, but he managed to stand. 'What's going on, Albert? Your father called me a Nip. That's old slang for a Japanese person, isn't it? Was he a prisoner of war or something?'

'He's gone crazy. I don't know. He wasn't in the war. My dad was never a soldier.'

Henry rolled over and vomited into the gutter.

Jimmy Lee had not been injured, so no charges were laid against Henry. The police hauled him away to Ward Twenty, where he remained for many weeks as the alcohol drained from his system. With it went a dramatic loss of fat. When finally allowed to return home, he was loose-skinned and sallow, and wracked with a permanent cough. He then stayed close to the house, except for an occasional daylight stroll with Albert or Harry. They thought he was slowly recovering, getting a little better each week, until the day after Michael Falls was born.

# Chapter Fifty-one

Curtis was on the point of leaving his flat when the doorbell rang. If he hadn't stopped by a kitchen window to admire the shadow patterns in an old eucalypt, he might have already left. As he opened the door, Henry pushed his way inside. Albert, Harry, Maidy Watling and Marianne Falls were close behind him.

'A man should run you out of town,' he greeted Curtis.

'You have a lot of explaining to do,' Maidy added.

Marianne Falls burst into tears. 'The whole world is turning upside down,' she sobbed. 'I will never survive the shame.'

Curtis had no idea why this visit had been inflicted on him.

'Randy little bugger,' Harry growled. He shot his older brother a frowning look and tried unsuccessfully to cover a smirk. Whatever the problem was, Harry secretly approved.

'Amanda had her kid last night,' Henry managed to say between patting Marianne's back and trying to block Maidy's view of a row of knives.

Marianne moved out of his reach. Even in this, her hour of grief and shame, she could not forget her position in Steeltown. Henry Lawson was a nobody.

Curtis managed to hide his surprise. Nobody had told him of Amanda's pregnancy. He did not think she was married, though her parents would have done their best to force her into it. But Richard was still playing scholar at university, and she wouldn't marry anyone else if the archbishop himself arrived with prayer book and licence.

'It's no good denying anything,' Harry said. 'Even at a few hours old, little Michael is the spitting image of William.'

'Where's Agatha?' Curtis asked.

'And when did you start calling her that?' Henry roared.

'Where's Mum?' Curtis amended.

'Crying again. You got any idea what you've done to her with all this carrying on?'

Curtis welcomed a surge of rage. Not the white heat of fury he had experienced when Henry destroyed the backyard trees. Nothing as clean as that. This was a destructive mound of ice. He could feel it growing, filling him until he shivered. He looked at the man he had once called Pa and snarled, 'How many times have you made her cry, did you ever stop to count them? All her life she's had to put up with your browbeating and bullying. Didn't want you in the army, did they? Couldn't hang onto your job, could you, old man? How are you living now, hey? On her house-cleaning wages. On Albert and Harry's charity. You're nothing but a bum.'

Harry and Albert tried to save their father the only way they knew how. Albert launched the punch that knocked Curtis to the floor. Harry laid in the boot. But it was all too late for Henry. Threads of saliva ran down his chin, and each of his muscles softened until his bones would no longer support his weight. He sunk to the floor and squatted beside his youngest son, who shoved his outstretched hand aside. He rolled with the shove and lay full length along the floor, not once turning away from Curtis.

'You bloody-minded whelp,' Maidy said, glaring at Curtis. 'If I were a man I'd take a strap to you. No boy should treat his father in such a way.'

'Go on, tell her,' Curtis ordered. 'Tell her you're not my father.'

'A bloody bench warmer,' Henry groaned. He put up a hand when

Harry raised his boot for the second time. 'Enough now,' he whispered. 'I won't feed the dogs again.'

'You'd better phone for a doctor,' Maidy told Harry. 'Come on, Henry,' she added, kneeling down and lifting his head. 'Get up now. Your boys will take you home.'

Henry's chin slid to his chest. 'Not to that house. Take me to my place,' he said when Albert grabbed his armpits to haul him up.

'What place is that, dear?' Maidy asked, taking his hand. 'Harry, help your brother get him out of this one.'

'After I smash your face in,' Harry snarled at Curtis.

Curtis wiped blood from his mouth and crouched, ready to transform ice to fire. Albert stopped a fight by stepping between them and hoisting Henry over Harry's shoulder. Curtis swung his anger to Maidy and Marianne.

'Have you ever really looked at William?' he asked. 'Have you really compared him to Amanda's baby? Go and look again, then find Richard. Everyone says we're alike, but our faces aren't the same. Our eyes are not the same.'

Marianne found refuge in her position in Steeltown. Drawing her rather plump body up to its full height, she glared at Curtis with all the contempt she could muster. Maidy just looked stunned.

'What's the matter, Mrs Watling?' Curtis asked as he walked out. 'Richard been in your pants too?'

He tried to make his exit more dignified than his parting shot, but he missed the second step and sprawled flat out on the pathway. As he sat up and rubbed an elbow, he noticed the blue sedan parked out front. Richard was behind the wheel.

Richard locked the passenger door as Curtis charged. Curtis kicked in the side panel and continued to kick, moving around the car. When he reached the driver's side, Richard finally climbed out and stood, fists up, ready to protect himself. But Curtis was defeated by the fear in his old friend's eyes. He slumped onto the kerb.

'Is this because of Debra?' Richard asked as he sat in the gutter beside him. 'I never hid anything from you. You always knew about her and me, and about Amanda. You always acted as if you didn't care. You always knew.'

It was true. Curtis had always known. But he'd wanted to put himself into Debra's family and save her. Perhaps if he'd minded his own business, she would have learned to take care of herself. Amanda had managed to avert gossip by dumping her shame onto someone else. The townspeople would now feel sorry for the two women wronged by that strange Curtis Lawson, and Debra would gather sympathy around her like a cloak of respectability. He hadn't saved Debra. Amanda had.

'I'm sorry,' Richard said.

Curtis had painted summer trees in the spare room, and bought baby furniture while he thought about names for his own seed. Right up to the very last, he could tell himself it was for a continuation of the happiness he found with Liona and Angus. But although Debra had never denied him as the father, he'd seen the truth in William's eyes. He couldn't love someone else's child as his own. He couldn't do that to the child.

'Jesus, Curtis, don't cry. I came to warn you about them coming here but I was too late. I'm sorry, mate.'

He was surprised to find his head resting on Richard's chest. He jerked away and stood.

'You're a mongrel, mate,' he said, but he patted Richard's back to contradict any real hostility in the words.

Richard sprang erect and grasped his hand, taking his strength from sunny faces, as always. Curtis smiled, but he had no wish to resume the friendship. There was less complexity in caring for his trees.

# Chapter Fifty-two

'How could you possibly go through two-and-a-half years of war without making one mate?' I asked Angus on the morning after Anzac Day. He had again refused to march. 'I thought that was the attraction wars had for men. Making mates while you kill people.'

'You read too many books,' he growled. 'It's about not making mates. That way they can't take bits of you down when they get themselves killed. Switch that load of old rubbish off.'

I had been listening to highlights of the Anzac march on my radio, having finally caught up with the times and bought one. Angus hated radios, but he suffered one inside my house because, he said, it kept me away from gossip. In fact I heard very little gossip now, except for all the delicacies newsreaders liked to give us for breakfast. For many months I had wept and hated and pitied and mourned, until the eternally shocking events wore the edges off my umbrage and numbed my imagination. Horror ceased to touch me unless I could place it in the life of someone I knew. But my local source had dried up. Agatha had quit her housekeeping jobs to stay at home with an ailing Henry.

Curtis visited my home most nights, and weekends when he wasn't planting trees around the neighbourhood. Yet he still spent much of his time in Angus's garden. His retreat from the world of family and friends had turned to flight since Richard Rees began visiting Debra's

261

house, and Michael and William seemed more at home in Agatha's yard than in their own.

On the day Henry decided not to get out of bed again, Curtis began climbing trees. He lay full length along a limb, his head tucked into the vee where branch met trunk. At times he was almost invisible, as if the bark had spread to surround him. He'd lie for hours, unseen and unheard by anyone except Angus and myself. Not that he was much to see, being as thin as a stick, and untidy. He wore old mismatched clothes and he refused to shave. He had even developed a stutter, as if he needed to think carefully before allowing words out of his mouth. Angus shaved his own beard off in a protest against Curtis's foolish behaviour. He did not stutter; but then, he rarely spoke.

During the last two years Curtis had grown more like Angus every day. They were both tanned almost black by working outside clad only in singlets and shorts. Angus was dark while Curtis's hair had been bleached white by the sun, yet their similarity amazed me. I think Curtis worked hard at resembling Angus. God alone knows why. Angus has never been handsome. Individual, you might say. If you were kind.

'Then why do they take their kids and grandkids along?' I asked Angus, reverting back to the subject of old soldiers.

'Politicians,' Angus said. 'They want the kids there. Conditioning in case there's another war. If those mothers had any sense at all, they'd keep their kids away.'

'Are you saying those men aren't heroes?'

'Of course they're bloody heroes. They went through a war without running away, didn't they? But it was the same on the other side. All a game to the blokes up top.'

I was afraid Angus planned to parade his list again, yet I had to say it. 'You must have made one mate at least.'

'They're all dead, aren't they? Except for Dicko, and what bloody good is he with only one arm? He's probably still blaming me for that.'

I decided to change the subject by asking why he had dressed in his old brown suit. He had even combed his hair and shined his shoe.

'I'm going with you to Henry's funeral. If others we won't name won't go, then I have to take on the responsibility. Somebody's got to look out for Debra,' he said as he left the room.

By then Debra had sued for divorce. Harry paid for her lawyer to prove that at least one of the Lawson family could accept responsibility. Or so he boasted to his cronies at the pub. Finally, the judge granted Debra the house and an allowance for William. She refused anything for herself. A matter of pride, her mother said. Amanda had moved in with her and they earned their keep at the steelworks canteen. Amanda worked during the day and Debra at night so one of them could always be at home with William and Michael — although the children could usually be found with Grandma Lawson. The relationship seemed happy enough. The two younger women had always been close, and Agatha had always possessed a martyr complex. Nobody thought to ask the boys if they were content.

Angus reappeared in the doorway. 'Henry will die a second death if you don't go,' he said to Curtis. 'There was enough trouble the first few years of your life because you wouldn't go to him. You can't do it again. Can't do it to Agatha, neither.'

'He won't know whether I'm there or not,' Curtis said.

'You real sure about that, are ya? Know all about every dimension in heaven and earth, ay?'

'It's nothing to do with you,' I said.

'It's to do with respect,' Angus said quietly. 'Henry and Agatha raised him. They did their best by him. He owes them for that. He owes Agatha the comfort of seeing him there.'

'They wouldn't let me see Henry before he died. They won't want me there now,' Curtis objected.

I sat up at that. Curtis trying to see Henry was news to me. And although I agreed with Angus, I was amazed to hear him speaking out.

'Don't matter what your stupid brothers want. You got about twenty minutes to get cleaned up. Do it now,' he said.

Curtis's resistance vanished. For the first time in his life, Angus had given an order. Curtis was not only willing to obey, but he seemed pleased to do so. As he strode up the road, he gave the appearance of having gained a victory over Angus instead of the reverse.

I prefer not to remember the day of the funeral. I had watched Albert and Harry grow to adults without having once seen them cry. Now they wept as copiously as Mary Mayberry had before she found her jaguar man. No doubt they were more than half drunk from the Anzac Day celebrations. Henry had died as old diggers began streaming into town to gather at Steeltown's numerous hotels. I was sure he would have found comfort in his name being forever linked with a war that refused to have him. If he'd had a say in it, he would have insisted on a ceremonial viewing at the local pub. Not that I approve of that peculiar custom, where the cadavers are elaborately preserved to give an illusion of being peaceful. Death is denied, even in its presence. Survivors are supposed to take comfort from bright cheeks and lips and an expression never worn in life. In all the years I knew him, Henry had never looked serene. I have no doubt he was glad to go, but at least the mortician could have made him seem a little sorrier. In my will, I insist they leave me with an appearance of a fight on my face. Death won't take me without a battle.

Yet when I entered the chapel, I thought it rather a shame that they had closed the lid of the coffin. For the first time since Henry left his mother and sisters, he was the centre of attention. He was in everyone's mind. If he'd sat up and spoken, everyone would have listened intently. Nailing the lid down seemed to me an unkind stroke. Although I'd never liked the man, there were depressing moments in my life when I realised that he may have been closer to me than I would care to admit. They were the days I had to fight against the knowledge that semen-and-egg was truly the only method of conception.

Agatha was there in body, if not in mind. I was sorry for her, and annoyed by how much I did not know — how much Curtis wouldn't tell me at the time. I could understand why Debra, Richard and Amanda were present, yet the mystery of Clo Gatley and Jamie Blake tormented me for quite a while.

# Chapter Fifty-three

Curtis arrived at the crematorium as the mourners edged into the chapel. The size of the crowd surprised him. All of Henry's old workmates were there with their wives. Even a few of his old football team were present, those not killed in the war. There was Reg Wilson, who had king-hit Henry and cost him his job. His expression revealed a shame that endured throughout the service, despite the fact that Albert and Harry had shaken his hand. Joe Phelan and the rest of the regulars from the corner hotel were grouped around the publican and two barmaids. Albert and Harry's cronies filled two rows, as did a variety of people whose houses used to be cleaned by Agatha. It seemed that all one corner of Steeltown had gathered on this day to mourn the loss of a man they had never really known, or particularly liked.

Curtis wondered if pressure had been applied. Agatha had intimate knowledge of the personal lives of most of these people coughing and mumbling their way to the nearest pew.

Agatha sensed his presence and looked back. The gratitude in her eyes unnerved him. As he slumped into the seat next to Angus, he was surprised to see Debra and her mother in the second pew. Amanda and Richard sat in the third. He was even more surprised when he noticed Clo with Jamie Blake seated across the aisle.

The lump in his throat grew and spread until he thought it would choke him. He rubbed it with both hands, fighting a temptation to shove a finger along his tongue to rake it out, to retrieve the words he had hurled at Henry on the evening Michael was born. He pressed against the back of the seat, forcing his chin down to stop himself from throwing up. Staring at a mound of pink flowers covering the coffin, he tried to arouse his anger.

'They should've known that pink is the one colour Henry wouldn't like,' he whispered to Angus. 'A girl's colour, he would have said. Red was always his favourite.'

He slid his stare to the minister's face and buried an elbow in Angus's ribs. 'Why is he raving about God? What use is any of that now? How does he know Pa's going to a better place? Why is he calling him Ronald?'

'He was a Ronald before he became a Henry,' Angus hissed. 'Shut up and listen.'

'I've never heard anyone call him Ronald. Even Agatha' — when did you start calling her that — 'always called him Henry.'

On the back of his eyelids he watched Henry kick a football around the yard, lost in the days of glory before a hip injury forced him off the playing field. He saw Henry weeding around the eucalypts when he believed Curtis to be away from home. He heard Henry's shouts of rage at something one of his boys had supposedly done. In reality, they were yells of frustration at not being able to help them with their homework. He felt the texture of a work-callused hand squeezing his shoulder when he laughed at one of Henry's stories. The grip tightened and the voice trembled when he asked for another. The watery eyes had become even wetter on the few occasions Curtis wrapped his arms around Henry's neck. He felt again the shock, but not of resentment this time, as he was roughly shoved away after the hug. This time he saw Henry's eyes belie a voice telling him not to be a bloody girl.

Curtis thumped his shoulders against the back of the seat and wondered why the hell he was here. Henry wouldn't know, and who cared about the rest? Looking up as one of Agatha's female employers covered a yawn, he imagined punching the back of her head. Not one of these people knew Henry. They didn't belong here. It was nothing to do with any of them. He half stood, about to tell them so, when Angus grabbed his arm.

Music swelled. The coffin slid towards a curtained opening. Someone muffled a ragged sigh. Agatha cried out a denial, though he didn't understand why. Albert and Harry's harsh breathing scratched across his nerve ends. He held his breath until his face crimsoned, but still his chest began to heave.

The tightness in his lungs reminded him of the time Henry had flung him across the yard then planted a boot in his backside. He remembered Agatha's pleas, heard through a thin wall, when Henry came home drunk and threw her into bed. He remembered the bruise in her eyes next morning, her pleading denials when Henry blamed her for keeping him away from his place. Henry's place — somewhere he wanted to be. A place where everyone liked him was all he'd ever said.

Well then, perhaps he'd finally made it.

The mourners stood. Agatha, supported by Albert and Harry, walked up the aisle. She sought Curtis's eyes while he stared at his brothers to avoid being caught. Harry's glare was fierce, and his face denied Curtis's entry into the trio, as always.

Curtis glanced across at Clo, who winked a brazen invitation. She had seen the brotherly exchange.

Albert turned to wait at the doorway. 'I'll kill him,' he said quietly. 'Eyeing that piece of baggage while Pa's being put away.'

'You and me both,' Harry growled.

'No you won't,' Agatha said.

The command in her tone was like being hit with a bucket of cold water. Agatha asked or pleaded. Agatha never commanded.

'You're both just like Henry, and he loved you both. But he loved Curtis more. That's why you're angry. He wanted Curtis most because he knew he couldn't have him.'

Eyes averted from their youngest brother as he passed them, Albert and Harry leaned against each other for comfort. They couldn't argue with their mother. How could they doubt her? Henry had always wanted what he couldn't have. Harry was the first to break into heaving sobs.

Debra barely glanced their way as she shoved through the crowd, watching Curtis walk towards a red sports car with Clo Gatley. Richard headed her off and stood directly in front of her, deliberately blocking her view. Amanda heard the grinding of teeth and coughed to hide a smile.

Maidy Watling tried to place herself between the two young women. They held firm, keeping her on the outskirts of their friendship as they stood with their arms around each other, staring at the back of Richard's head. She did not notice the arched necks and flaring eyes as Debra and Amanda mentally circled and threw out challenges, like two cats claiming territorial rights.

Maidy fiddled with her handbag in an effort to ignore the older Lawson boys. Others were pointedly looking away, as if the sight of two grown men so obviously distressed was an obscenity. Finally, she could no longer bear their sobs. Marching over to them, she drew their foreheads onto her chest.

'There there,' she whispered. 'Come now, your mother needs you.'

She turned their faces to Agatha, who was nodding at a proliferation of words which seemed to bewilder more than comfort her. Harry drew in a breath and howled louder.

'Enough!' Maidy snapped. 'Look at her eyes. Look, I tell you, and stop being such selfish children.'

Albert and Harry looked, blew their noses and hurried to their mother's side.

'You're a kind woman,' a voice informed Maidy as she watched them go.

She stared at a reddish-blond man about ten or more years her junior, and recognised the look in his eyes. Maidy had seen this same expression many times, though not so often since passing forty-five. She was grateful, until she remembered his companion.

'You're with Clo Gatley,' she accused.

'Yes,' he said. 'You remind me of her, but I think you're even more beautiful.'

Maidy stalked away, but she turned to watch through slitted eyes as her admirer climbed into the car with Curtis and Clo. He lifted a hand in salute as they drove slowly down the gravel pathway.

# Chapter Fifty-four

Curtis watched a bag of groceries being dumped onto the table while he wondered about Clo's motives. She never worried about such mundane matters as food. When she appeared for one of her visits, they usually went out for Chinese.

'My dear old mum once told me that babies arrive when they're ready,' she said while sorting through the contents of the bag.

The comment did not surprise him. Clo often introduced a subject through the back door, especially if she couldn't be sure of its reception. On her last visit about two weeks ago, she had twice opened the door to her mind with a seemingly random thought, only to close it again before the essence could be revealed. The problem still waited to be presented. She proved its presence by throwing groceries into the garbage. Her mind had been elsewhere even while she shopped.

'You know, maybe they took William out before he was ready,' she added as she shoved food into the refrigerator. 'Maybe he was angry with Debra for forcing him into the cold. Then with you when the nurse pulled him out of his nice warm place for a second time, just so you could check him over. Maybe he'd already checked you over.'

'Maybe,' Curtis said, and the tone was as neutral as the word.

'I suppose you've heard that Debra and Richard are getting married?'

Curtis studied a slab of steak as if it were something new and mysterious.

'So what's all this leading to?' he asked warily.

'I'm pregnant,' Clo answered abruptly. 'She's due in July.'

'She? How do you know it'll be a girl?'

'Because I want a girl.'

'And Clo Gatley always gets what she wants?'

'Reaction at last,' she said, hearing the slash of exclamation before he had time to curl the sentence upwards into a question.

'What do you want from me?' he asked.

'I want a baby, and I want to have her before I'm old enough to be a grandmother. I don't want to marry or settle down, but I do need help until after she's born. I'll do the homebody bit, washing and cooking and all that nonsense, if you feed me and keep me company while I'm getting fat and ugly. In a year's time we can call it quits and go about our own business.'

'Sounds good to me,' Curtis said.

'No ties,' she added. 'No standing in the way of what either of us wants to do. We can call an end to it at any time.'

'I get the idea,' Curtis answered slowly.

'Good, but I don't want you getting the idea that either me or my daughter can't get along without a man.'

For just a moment he thought he saw a little girl looking out of those bark-brown eyes, and he had already learned his lesson. You can't help by going into their family. Yet still he nodded agreement.

'Right,' she said. 'I won't be long. I'm going for Chinese.'

As Clo walked out, he wanted to call her back. He wanted to stroke the slightly rounded dome of her stomach where a seed was beginning to grow. He wanted to ask her face to face whether or not it was his, as he should have done on the day Debra confessed her pregnancy. His need became so great that he squatted on his haunches to stop himself from running after her. He turned his face to the floor and counted slowly.

By the time Clo returned, he was seated at the table reading a newspaper.

# Chapter Fifty-five

'I'm moving out tomorrow,' Amanda said, 'into a townhouse a few blocks away. I start work on Monday at the university bar.'

William and Michael stared at each other across a stack of building blocks. At five and six they were around the same height, shape and colouring. Yet if one looked closely, they were really nothing alike.

'So you can hang around campus and pretend to be one of the students?' Debra asked.

Her dulcet tone didn't fool William. Such sweetness usually heralded the beginning of an argument. Usually the boys would wander off and wait for the quarrel to blow over. This time William signalled for Michael to stay. He wanted to hear more about this business of moving out.

Amanda might have been speaking to a rather backward child as she said, 'I've managed to wangle my way into a creative writing course at the technical college. I'm going to be a poet and a freethinker. I'd advise you to try it, but of course nothing about or around you could ever be free.'

'I wondered why you were wearing those crappy jeans and faded old shirt, and the sneakers tied with broken laces. But of course it's the writer's uniform and you're trying to get a start by looking the part.'

Amanda smiled. 'How nice of you to notice. Would you really like Michael and me living here when you and Richard get married?'

Debra nodded. 'I really would.'

'Why? So you can keep an eye on us?'

'My best friend and my husband?' Debra pretended to shudder at the thought. 'Never.'

Amanda lowered her voice. 'You whined to him about a fatherless son until he gave in and offered to marry you. That's how you did it, I know.'

'Are you jealous that you didn't think of it first?' Debra snapped.

'Why did you wait so long? Was it to make sure Richard wouldn't be able to remember dates and put them together, or is it because of Curtis and Clo Gatley?' When Debra lowered her face and refused to answer, Amanda added, 'I could never figure out why you drove him away. I know how you've always felt about him. Is that what it's all about? Marry Richard to get at Curtis? He won't care, you know.'

'Tut tut, cat's claws,' Debra said, her voice now cloyingly sweet. 'I didn't think you'd take it so hard. Not now you're so wrapped up in your poetry and that university professor. And we made a bargain years ago that there'd be no hard feelings, didn't we? Have you forgotten that?'

Amanda shook her head. 'Of course there's no hard feelings. Especially when I know it'll never last. I can wait. I just hope your marriage will give you as much satisfaction, both mentally and physically, as my professor gives me.'

The women laughed to signify an end to the exchange. The sound was a little too raucous, but still they snuggled together on the sofa and whispered words that made the laughter louder. An argument did not eventuate, but Amanda and Michael moved out the following day.

That night William sat alone in his room watching the eucalypt through his window. When he was small, that tree had been just another one of a million things discovered around the yard: the slimy feel of frogs, the maze trails left behind by snails, the sting of bees, and ant bites. He was four years old the first time he actually studied the shape and size of the tree. That was on the day Grandma Agatha told him that Curtis had planted it to celebrate his birth. He stood and stared, seeing it so much taller than him, and imagined how he would grow when the time came.

From underneath, the eucalypt appeared as a ladder going up to the clouds, although the rungs jutted out from the middle. Every time he tried to see to the top, his eyes grew wet and sad. How did it get so big when he could only just manage to grab the bottom rung? Angus said the tree would still be there when he was long gone, but Angus never did explain where he might be going.

'It didn't do it on purpose, it's just a tree,' Angus said on the day one of those little finger-sticks poked into William's neck and made him bleed. He said the same thing when the tree clouted William over the head.

William had grabbed the lowest limb and jerked it up and down as hard as he could, using all his strength to break it off. It wasn't that he intended to be mean. He just wanted to know whether he could. The branch snapped with an abruptness that threw him onto the ground. When he put out his hands to save whacking his nose, that eucalypt's limb slipped out from under his body and reattached itself to the trunk. William jumped up and grabbed it again to wrench it away. That's when he found the thorns. They jagged his hands with a viciousness matching his own frenzy. He watched blood drip onto the ground and slide into the roots. The tree grew a few centimetres, and one of the high thin branches thudded onto his head.

His mother pointed out that only humans were capable of planning revenge, and such a thing as a eucalypt with thorns didn't exist. Branches fell because of wind or rot or boring insects, she said, and they couldn't be blamed if they happened to drop on someone standing below. The scratches on his hands had been caused by the roughness of the bark, and anything else he saw must have been an hallucination caused by the knock on his head.

Everything she said made sense, but William never went near the tree again. He always climbed the fence or squeezed between the palings whenever he left the yard. Yet the eucalypt hadn't forgotten. At night he'd stare through his window at its twisted shape, watching the branches sway to and fro without a wind to help them. He'd hear the creak and groan of its roots trying to pull free of the ground. He'd lie in bed and listen to the rustle of its leaves.

It would come for him one night, it said, when Michael wasn't there to keep it away. When William was alone.

This night, Michael had gone. This night William was alone. Yet being almost two years older and wiser now, he no longer believed that trees could lift up out of the ground. Provided he never went underneath it through the gate, it had no power to hurt him. He challenged the shadow with a grin and settled back to think of something nicer, like Richard moving in. Richard knew how to kick a football and throw a stone straight. Richard never kissed him in front of the other kids or sent them home, or refused to speak for a week if he asked about Curtis.

'Are you asleep?' Debra asked from the doorway.

His mother had been crying for most of the day. She did that at times — cried for no reason that he could think of. Then he'd have to say he loved her again and again, as if repetition could make words real and true. Of course he loved her, but saying the words over and again turned them into a times table chant. If he stayed quiet, she'd take a couple of pills and sleep like a log until morning.

He steadied his breathing to an even tempo as she bent over the bed. She kissed his forehead and wandered off to her room, leaving him to the excitement of invention.

Imagination had taken him past the point of kicking a football around the yard with Richard. He'd won the under-seven backstroke race in front of a cheering crowd at the swimming pool when the scratching began. It was then he remembered the way the eucalypt leaned towards his house, the way its branches hung over his roof.

Keeping his stare fixed on the ceiling, he crawled to his mother's room, staying as low to the floor as possible. No matter how hard he pushed and strained, her door wouldn't open more than a few centimetres. Its bottom had jammed on the dressing gown she'd shrugged off on her way to bed. He yelled through the crack, but there was no answer except that scraping sound. It was louder and closer now, and directly overhead. He couldn't actually see the process taking place, but he knew those gnarled fingers were peeling off the roof tiles one by one, forming a tower of tiles to prop up the armpit of a limb as it reached through the roof and grabbed him.

He fled through the back door and squeezed through the fence into next-door's yard. Angus's yard, and Angus was working in the garden.

'Good on ya, mate,' Angus said. 'Full moon tonight. Best time for planting beans is the morning after a full moon. Give us a hand, then six to eight weeks and I'll give you the best beans you ever tasted.'

Angus asked no questions. Angus never did. He handed William the small spade made long ago for Curtis. They worked side by side, pulling up weeds and telling each other stories. William listened to yarns of sun and sand and camel caravans. Angus heard about a claw-like scratching on roof tiles on dark and lonely nights.

'It's the bird, you see. It's gone to the wrong place,' Angus said. He wouldn't elaborate further.

William sneaked home at dawn. He stood on tiptoe and circled his house three times without finding sign of a bird.

That night, the night before Debra's wedding, the scratching returned at exactly the same time. It was louder now, and accompanied by a thumping noise. If that tree couldn't claw its way in, it would break the roof in two.

William ran to Angus's garden. He found the yard empty and the house dark. He stood at the steps and screamed.

'It's all right, Will, I'm on top of things,' Angus called down from a nest of bagging on the roof beside his kitchen chimney. 'I'll be here watching every night. The minute I see that bird, I'll send it about its business.'

William wanted to yell the truth, but he knew Angus had birds on the brain when the old man explained away the tree's shriek of laughter as nothing more than a screech owl. The boy ran again, through Angus's gate and along the sidewalk to Agatha's treeless yard. She found him by the sound of his sobs and took him into her house.

'Sleepwalking,' she said on the phone to Debra. 'But he's wide awake now and listening to the wireless. I'll bring him back after the wedding. He can sleep in Harry's room.'

Richard Rees Senior had consented to pay for the ceremony that would bind his son to Debra. As Elizabeth Rees planned *the* social event of the season, she sent out invitations stipulating that children should be left at home. Debra agreed that children tended to get underfoot and call attention to themselves, taking the spotlight from where it rightfully belonged. William had fully expected to be left at home alone. He was more than content to be handed over to Harry. He spent the night in his uncle's bed and slept sounder than he had for years.

While most of the street attended the celebrations, to which Agatha was the only Lawson invited, Harry decided to solve the problem of the roof monster by trimming the eucalypt's branches. He promised to load every last twig onto his ute and carry the lot away when the trimming had been completed. He would have cut the tree down if Angus hadn't objected.

'It doesn't belong to you,' Angus yelled from his perch beside the chimney. 'You lay a blade on that trunk and I'll bloody well have you arrested.'

'It bothers the boy,' Harry called back. 'The kid's got to get his sleep. How can he do that with possums using his roof as a springboard?'

'It's the bird that's bothering the boy,' Angus shouted down. 'But you go ahead and trim those branches back from the roof. I'll come over and help if that's what you want, though it won't make a skerrick of difference.'

Possums and birds. Grownups could always find a way of getting around a truth that didn't suit them, William thought from his vantage point in the bedroom. He wanted to watch Harry at work but be well out of the way of flying branches. This room might not be the safest place in the world, yet the eucalypt had to find a way through the roof or the thickness of brick walls. Which wasn't impossible, William knew that, remembering last night's thumping and scratching. But this time he had Harry and Angus for protection. Still, he locked the window to make sure the truth wouldn't sneak in that way. Watching through his own breath fog as Harry wielded a chainsaw, he shrunk back as the tree groaned and gnashed as if it was being shaken by a storm, though the day was clear and windless.

'Got you. Got you!' he whispered.

'Timberrrr!' Harry yelled to Angus standing below. He grinned as one thick limb, thicker than his own leg, toppled towards the ground.

His grin disappeared in a hurry when greenstick fingers grabbed for the roof and clung on. The butt end of the branch crashed through William's window. Harry yelled a curse and almost fell. He managed to grab the trunk and slide down, leaving scraps of shirt and skin along the length of the eucalypt. He heard William's scream and he ran, hurling a string of curses over his shoulder at both Angus and the tree.

William threw himself sideways as the window caved in. He escaped the tree, but he wasn't fast enough to dodge the explosion of flying glass. He lay on the bed, wiping blood from his face and staring at the branch. It hung through the wall of his house as if it had found a new trunk. He could clearly hear the rustle of its laughter.

'You missed,' he managed to say through a mouthful of blood.

That was when he discovered that trees had more power than he'd ever imagined.

William stared at the midsummer bush painted on his walls and felt the heat of it, as he'd never felt it before. He could feel the glow burning his skin. The trees swayed as if they were blown by an unseen wind, creaking and groaning as they tried to pull free of the wall. He heard them call to the branch hanging through his window. He screamed as a flurry of leaves blew across his face.

Harry and Angus pushed and shoved each other up the hallway. They found William unconscious under his bed.

After being carried to the Lawson house, the boy was swabbed, stitched and given a tranquilliser. The doctor said he was lucky not to have lost an eye, but scarring would be minimal. William sobbed when they tried to take him home, so Debra allowed him stay with Agatha until the honeymoon was over and Richard had settled in.

# Chapter Fifty-six

Maidy Watling knew she should regard this day as one of the bullseyes of her life. There was her daughter being married in the proper way, in a church filled with flowers and the social elite of Steeltown. Mr and Mrs Rees and all their cronies had arrived in limousines. They were dressed in furs, diamonds, and Italian suits more in keeping with the opening of an art gallery, those expensive costumes being the much admired works of art. Maidy herself was the centrepiece, stunning in a sea-blue suit matching the colour of her eyes. Her thick blonde hair, still without the aid of a permanent wave or a tint, was as perfectly manicured as her hands. Although she might have faded a little with age, she still had the power to turn men's heads and women's lips. Despite Debra's youth, Maidy had no doubt that she would outshine her daughter, as always.

Then Richard appeared at the dais, watching the aisle with that same expectant look he usually reserved for her. What others had supposed to be a dewy-eyed pride began to overflow. She could not make herself care if the tears ruined her makeup, even though it had taken hours to apply as she mourned each new wrinkle and noted new depths to the old.

The tears became a flood when Debra strolled down the aisle, supercilious and smug in pale cream lace. By the time the wedding party reached the reception, Maidy was well into the swing of an all-out crying jag. Amanda's barely controlled rage, and the ill-concealed jealousy of Marianne Falls, had no effect. Nor did the contempt underlying the Rees family's display of sympathy for the distraught mother of the bride. Maidy hid in the powder room to avoid their assurances of Debra's devotion, but even a brand new toilet roll pressed to her lips couldn't muffle her howls. Elizabeth Rees's whisper through the keyhole — 'You are not losing a daughter, my dear, but gaining a son' — merely served to make her howl louder.

Still swollen of face an hour later, she was asked to charge her glass and toast the bride and groom. No doubt she would have managed such a simple task if Richard hadn't tried to show his support with an arm around her shoulder. Perhaps her hand shook, or perhaps Debra's grasp on her elbow was a little too firm. Whatever the reason, the crystal goblet missed her mouth and its contents poured down the front of her silk jacket, accenting the indignity with a spreading wet stain. To compound this unforgivable social error, when she tried to cover her embarrassment with an arm flung across outlined nipples, the glass slipped out of her hand. It bounced off Richard Rees Senior's rather prominent nose and shattered on the floor.

Maidy could think of no other course of action. Kicking off her shoes, she fled through the diners, oblivious of the chaos she created. Chairs were overturned as men jumped to their feet to get a better view of her progress. Tables were up-ended. Gowns worth a small fortune were splattered with food. Women who were not supposed to know such words shouted vile curses. Luckily for them, Maidy's screams of rage, horror or frustration — or perhaps a combination of all three — drowned their oaths. They had no trouble denying them later.

An arm's length away from the doorway and freedom, a waiter ducked her swinging handbag and tried to grab her around the waist. She punched down with both fists, sending him to the floor, and shrugged clear of her jacket when he clung to its tail. Using full lung power to accent her resentment, she leapt down the stairs and ran to Richard's car.

Two young men were decorating the windows with tins of shaving foam. Fortunately one had stolen the spare key in order to sprinkle the seat with condoms. She noted, but without the usual satisfaction, that his stare remained on her exposed breasts as he placed the key in her outstretched hand. He continued to stare as she started the engine and careered away up the street. The other young man saw Jamie Blake swing his sports car in a U-turn and follow her.

Richard's blue sedan roared down a stretch of dirt road, leapt out into darkness through the turning circle and thudded onto the beach. The wheels spun frantically before the engine coughed and died. Maidy thrust the door open and fell face forward into the sand. She licked her lips, spat out the grit and crawled towards the sound of the surf.

The first wave struck her squarely on the breasts. She jumped to her feet and backed away as the breath of a cool breeze curved around her ears, more shocking than whispered abuse. Her toes curled inwards, grabbing the sand as another wave broke around her knees and turned seaward, promising to numb with needles of cold.

'I don't want to die,' Maidy said as the wave curved around her feet. 'I don't want to live, but I certainly don't want to die.'

'I thought about it once. I was up at Flinders Lookout at the time,' someone said from behind her.

Maidy had sensed another presence a few moments ago. She would not look. That presence might be an avenging angel. Perhaps even God Himself. Or the devil. Perhaps they'd arrived to fight over her soul as the scriptures promised. Lightning and fire would scorch her body. The smell of brimstone and confirmation wine would take away her breath. A halo would battle horns — the story of her life. Or being just Maidy Watling, they might play cards for her soul despite the lack of light.

She smiled at that ridiculous thought. God and the devil could make their own light.

'The other side of Flinders where the cliffs are sheer,' the voice continued. 'But there would've been nobody left to take care of my mother.'

'My mother died a long time ago,' Maidy said. 'Quite young at the time, if I remember rightly.'

He draped his coat over her shoulders when she shivered.

'My father too. You're Jamie Blake, aren't you? Your brother went to jail for killing your father.'

'Don's out now,' Jamie said. 'He went north a few months ago.'

'I thought everyone always went west,' Maidy said.

'No, Don went north. There's a blanket in my car.'

Maidy glanced back. 'I've never made love on the sand, or in a car.'

'Then my timing is perfect,' Jamie said.

She decided he was probably the devil and God hadn't bothered after all.

She woke just before dawn, curled around Jamie Blake among the condoms on the reclined seats of Richard's car. Jamie hadn't been able to close the top of his convertible, and the wind on their naked bodies had been cold.

'Are you a religious man?' she asked when he stirred.

'Can't say I am, but I have read the Bible,' he said as an each-way bet.

'If a woman makes love with a man and that man later marries her daughter, will she go to eternal hellfire for the sin of incest?'

Jamie opened an eye. 'The woman or the daughter?'

'Of course you're right,' Maidy said. 'The woman was first, after all, even if it was only in her mind.'

Jamie lifted his coat off the floor, wrapped it around her shoulders and asked, 'Can you remember what we did with the rest of our clothes?'

'I'm years older,' Maidy said.

He opened the other eye. 'I live in King's Cross now. They don't care about race, religion or age there.'

'Do you think your mother will like me?'

He shrugged. 'She's in a home out in the western suburbs.'

'I knew most of them went west,' Maidy said as she followed him to his car. 'I made a fool of myself, you know. I'll never be able to look anyone in the face again.'

'I saw you leave that place. Striding down the steps to the car, head up and eyes blazing. I saw that bloke hand over the keys and I saw the way he stared at your breasts. You looked magnificent.'

His version sounded delightful.

'I hit some people, and I threw food around. I whacked Mr Rees with a goblet. I don't care about him, but it's Debra. She looked very concerned.'

'For you, or for herself?' Jamie asked.

Maidy nodded. 'We'll just go back to my place while I grab a few things and lock up the house.'

She wrote a brief note which she pinned to the door for Debra.

*I've gone away*, it said. *I hope you'll be very happy. Please give my love to William. And stop refusing Curtis's money. I believe he has more than you realise.*

# Chapter Fifty-seven

I could not, would not, did not want to believe my eyes or ears when Curtis walked into Angus's house that Saturday morning, in the full light of the sun, and told me that he and Clo were living together without the benefit of clergy. Or anything else for that matter. And that she was pregnant. I must admit to a slight umbrage — Curtis had given no hint of an association with this woman. Which had nothing to do with my instant dislike of Clo Gatley. Distrust would be a better word. No doubt she was smarter than the average wanton. She had even managed to fool Angus. A fact that caused me pain, for my esteem of him dropped a level or two. I had always been certain that no one could ever induce me to think ill of my Angus. Yet I detected a certain light in his eyes, one I had not seen for many years, even as he lay in my bed. He said Clo reminded him of Maidy Watling.

My relief at this statement was short-lived when I spent hours searching his list and found no trace of Clo Gatley, or Debra and Maidy Watling. The absence of the Gatley name didn't surprise me. I had no reason to believe he knew of its existence. But Debra? After the way she had treated Curtis? And most people hated Maidy Watling. I remembered then that I had never liked her. Furthermore, I found my own name on almost every page. On each occasion it was scratched out or inked over, but the cover-up was usually effected in a different coloured ink. When I taxed him with this fact, he laughed in my face. I allowed the wounding to show.

'Don't be like that, Loby,' he said. 'You've given up and given over all your years to me. Lots of people might think the years of a strange woman don't mean much, but I know you made yourself strange for my sake. That means more than anything to me.'

'You being as you are, it couldn't mean much then,' I snapped, although his words had appeased me. Angus doesn't often speak so gently, and the gift of my years had been a selfish one. I would have been miserable without the return gift of his. If I had borne him a child out of my own body, my life would have been perfection.

Perhaps Angus read my mind. He often did.

'Be content with what you've got, Loby,' he told me. 'You've done some unforgivable things in the getting.'

I refused to invite further criticism by continuing the conversation. Instead, I looked through the window to where Clo and Curtis were admiring the eucalypt at Debra's gateway. I watched him turn to her and laugh. He had plastered back his hair so he wouldn't have to look through the bars of his fringe. I'd never seen him do that before, not even for Angus or me. I cursed the cabbage eaten for dinner last night as my stomach rumbled loudly. It felt hollow, yet my lungs were tight and solid. I suspected another bout of flu.

'I'll make you some toast to sop up the bile,' Angus said.

'All right, I'll admit to being worried about what Clo and her baby could do to Curtis,' I said as I chased Angus into the kitchen. 'But how do we know she's not after his money? How do we know she doesn't know about that lottery win?'

'And how do you know about it?' Angus asked.

'I listened through the wall the night he came to tell you.'

'Jesus, Loby.'

'Jesus has nothing to do with it. Why shouldn't I listen when you were very kindly refusing money on my behalf? And how do you know how much I might or might not have?'

'I know you've got more money than you can spend in your lifetime, yet you never offer anyone a help-out.'

'The Lord helps those who help themselves,' I told him.

He nearly choked on that one.

'If anyone knows about that, you do,' he said.

As I sniffed and turned up my nose, he added, 'I never knew anyone who could know so much about everyone except themselves.'

I let that pass. He was trying to lead me into the jungle of his overly fertile imagination, and he was the better bushman. There were days when Angus would safari on no matter what, shooting down anyone within his line of fire. This happened to be one of those days. For some reason, this thing with Clo had upset him. I saw the look on his face when Curtis broke the news, and I'd been foolish enough to believe he would line up with me against the usurper. I believed he would understand, although my feelings were beyond my own comprehension.

Ah Liona, there you are, trying to read those bark-brown eyes and seeing the stone angel. Afraid she would take everything you had, not knowing then that you only had yourself.

'She'll take Curtis away you know,' I said.

'Away from what, Loby? We're his friends.'

'Do we have so many that we can afford to lose one?'

Angus's eyes grew darker as he stared at me, sighting me, his finger tightening on the trigger. I could feel my lungs solidifying. I coughed to clear my throat, and couldn't stop. I began to choke on my own gasp for air. He brought a glass of water and stroked my back.

'It's nothing to do with us, Loby.'

'Perhaps not,' I agreed when I could speak. 'But does he know that you're encouraging young William into your yard?'

'I like the boy. He reminds me of Curtis.'

'Anyone with eyes can see that he's the image of Richard Rees.'

'Was it you who put that idea into Curtis's head?'

'Don't yell at me,' I shouted. 'Didn't Curtis tell us so?'

'You're worse than strange, Liona. You're a bloody meddler,' Angus snarled as he grabbed his crutch and hop-jumped into his bedroom.

He had stopped wearing the wooden leg after deciding that it made him look like Long John Silver. He'd always hated that story.

I yelled, 'Yo ho, my hearty,' or some such similar nonsense, and skipped outside. Some people have a talent for bringing out the child in an adult. Angus always brought out the childishness in me.

'I suppose we'll be hearing wedding bells again,' I said to Curtis.

'Not unless you're going to make an honest man of Angus,' Clo said sweetly.

I wanted to say something to put her in her place, but I wasn't sure where that might be. The laughter in her eyes was disconcerting. I made my distrust easy to read. She didn't appear to notice, so I waited for Curtis to wander away before making it plain.

'I don't know if I like you or not,' I told her.

Pussyfooting, they call it. That was another mark against Clo. She gave that knowing grin, which made me feel the need to tread softly.

'Yes you do,' she said. 'But it's because of Curtis, so that's all right.'

Her laughter followed me as I stamped away.

Getting even was easy enough. Clo wasn't jealous of Debra. Or if she was, she hid the fact well. Yet sometimes, when she and Curtis called on Angus and myself, William would be playing by the side fence. I noticed Clo watching Curtis to see if he watched the child. This told me that she believed the boy to be his. I would call to William and invite him into the yard. He'd climb between loose palings and take up the small trowel, the one made for the young Curtis, and kneel in the dirt. Occasionally glancing at Angus for an encouraging nod, he would carefully turn the soil.

Curtis made a comment only once. 'Seems to know which are weeds,' he said in a tone that could only be called indifferent.

If he did watch the boy, it was only after he'd shaken down the bars of his fringe. Yet within minutes, Clo became fidgety and urged him away, even though William rarely acknowledged his presence. The boy was painfully shy, and obviously had no idea who Curtis might be.

I should have been content with these small triumphs, yet I was not. Whenever Clo and I were alone, I would paint glowing pictures of William's charm and intelligence, and speak of Curtis's rapture in the first six months of his marriage. I would laugh about how he had bored us with the name business, and about the hours he spent readying the nursery and caring for Debra. I very cleverly connected my stories with Clo's pregnancy. If she commented on something Curtis had said or done for her and the coming child, I'd answer with a laugh and 'I remember . . .'

Had I known Clo better, I might have refrained. I honestly believed she was aware of the game I played. She always laughed; and I think she always liked me, despite the grudge she carried for many years.

I might have refrained, though I doubt it. Like Jamie, I have a certain viciousness in my nature. Perhaps it runs in the family. So many things do.

Clo repaid me in kind by moving Curtis many kilometres away not long after Ellie was born.

# Chapter Fifty-eight

Curtis sat on a bench under a eucalypt in the small yard of their flat. Ellie lay along his upper legs, her head resting on a balled blanket, her feet against his stomach. Hunched over, he stared into her face, fascinated at seeing his likeness there. She had the same colouring as Clo, the same shiny black hair. But that pointed chin, and her straight eyebrows with barely a break above the bridge of her nose were definitely him. Now and then she opened her eyes and stared back, as if she were making sure he hadn't gone away. He swallowed occasionally, as if he'd been drinking in the sight and smell of her. Glancing up at Clo standing beside them, he smiled a slow, quiet smile.

In the two weeks since Ellie's birth, those two words described Curtis perfectly. Slow and quiet. His movements were fluid, his voice soft enough to slur. The stutter had disappeared, and the sometimes jerky movement of his body — which Clo thought of as an impatience in his muscles — had stilled. At first she thought he had trained himself to be this way so he wouldn't startle the child. For the first few days Ellie had been jumpy and quick to tears. Now Clo realised that these two had a quietening effect on each other. She knew she should be pleased. She wanted to be pleased. But a baby's initial bonding was supposed to be with its mother.

'The sun's too hot. I'll take her inside,' she said.

Curtis reached for Clo's hand and pressed her palm against his cheek before gently pulling her onto the bench. He moved the baby to lie across both their laps, joining them. Clo had read somewhere that a baby's vision is blurred for the first few weeks, yet she felt Ellie's direct and solemn stare.

'She's the image of you,' Curtis said. 'A miniature Clo Gatley.'

Clo wondered if he were making comparisons. Men always wanted a son. Or so Liona had said.

'I want to take Ellie to meet Agatha,' he said.

'Didn't Liona and Angus make enough fuss?'

'Angus said that all babies look like skinned rabbits when they're new. Said she looked more like you than me, then went on with his gardening. He couldn't see the special qualities. Neither could Liona. When I tried to point them out, she said she had to agree with Angus.'

'I don't mind if you want to show Ellie to your family, but I won't go with you.'

She hoped he would insist and he could feel the wish, but he said nothing. Clo would create a disturbance. She wouldn't scream or yell, that wasn't Clo's way; but the more Agatha repulsed her, the more vulgar Clo would become.

Clo watched as he shook down the bars of his fringe. She knew all his defences, as he thought he knew hers. As he did know when she used them on others yet never recognised when they were applied to him.

'Take her now,' she advised. 'Her next feed isn't due for three hours.'

Curtis tucked Ellie into her pram and walked the few blocks to the Lawson home. He paused at the fence to watch Albert and Harry kick a ball around the yard for William and Michael. Michael's chase was a series of stops and starts. William ran fast but often fell. If he didn't jump up immediately, Albert or Harry lifted him onto his thin little legs and whispered encouragement. Curtis wondered why he hadn't experienced such gentleness from them at William's age.

The front door burst open and Agatha ran to the fence, stumbling in her eagerness. He cleared his throat before saying, 'I brought Ellie to see you.'

She ran through the gateway and knelt beside the pram, gently lifted the blanket and stared. 'She's dark. Not like you, Curtis.' She glanced up and added quickly, 'But when I look close, I can see that the shape of her face is yours. She's pretty. Clever too, I can see it there already.'

Curtis looked up when the backyard noises stopped. Harry and Albert walked forward, Michael trailing, William hanging back. Albert glanced at Harry then stopped. Curtis felt a sudden affection for his brothers. He beckoned them over.

'So that's her. I heard,' Albert mumbled.

'Looks like her mum,' Harry added.

Michael thrust an arm through the palings to touch the pram. His fingers couldn't quite reach, so Albert lifted him while Curtis lifted Ellie.

'She's only little, but nice,' Michael decided, looking around for affirmation.

Curtis studied the solidly plump little boy. His liking was instant and without reserve. Michael grinned and held out both arms, wriggling impatiently while Curtis shifted Ellie. He had difficulty holding the child, his arm and shoulder sagging under the sturdy weight of him.

'Yep, nice,' Michael repeated.

'So are you,' Curtis said, and smiled when Michael nodded agreement. At that moment, the lingering hostility towards Richard Rees disappeared, banished by Richard's son.

Michael grinned satisfaction. 'Let's play more ball,' he demanded of Albert.

As Albert assisted him back over the fence, Agatha turned to William. 'Say hello to Daddy,' she instructed.

The child's look became mulish. He turned away and wrapped his arms around Agatha's leg. When she tried to turn him back, he shrieked.

Ellie jerked. Her eyes flew wide. She held her breath until Curtis shook her in panic. Then she screamed.

'Just like a bloody girl,' Harry laughed.

Curtis glared. The laughter died.

'Well, what did you expect?' Harry asked. 'You don't take any notice of the kids you already have, and now you come round here expecting us to cheer about another one.'

He grabbed William and marched down the yard to join Albert and Michael.

Agatha wrung her hands. 'Don't take any notice of Harry. You know what he's like. Like your pa. He doesn't know how to say things properly. It's just that him and Albert are fond of the two littlies, even though anyone can see who Michael's real dad is. They worry that William will start spending more time with Richard's family now, then I won't get to mind him so often and we'll hardly ever see him.'

Realising that her words had turned to a babble she bit her lip to keep the rest inside. If she allowed them to roll out, anything might follow. Words she did not want to say.

'Mind him?' Curtis asked.

'Oh yes. I'm not working now you know, not cleaning houses or anything like that. Albert and Harry take good care of me. I mind Michael and William when their mums have to work. Or go out somewhere, you know?'

Curtis wanted to tell Agatha that she should not spend her time or love on Richard's children. It was nothing to do with them, and she shouldn't make the same mistake a second time.

'Maybe you could mind Ellie now and then,' he said. He felt the withdrawal. 'Why not? Because she belongs to Clo?'

'That Clo, she'll go away one day, you know. She'll go away and make you leave your child.'

'Why don't you like her?'

'It's nothing like that, Curtis, don't you go saying such things. But you have no claim on this baby. Remember what I told you about Winnie Radnor marrying that American and taking her two littlies off to the other side of the world? Remember what I told you about Cecil Martin? He was never the same. Those kids were rightly his, but he had no claim. Now he lives in that old shack near the town dump, dirty and half crazy.'

Ellie whimpered again when the shudder passed through Curtis.

'I'd better take her home,' he said. 'She's probably hungry.'

'You mind, Curtis. You take care. This baby doesn't even look like you. She's little and dark, not like you.' She turned and beckoned to Harry, who was standing by the corner of the house with William. They approached reluctantly. 'You see? William has your colour. You see how his hair falls over his face like little gold bars?'

'Open your eyes, Agatha,' Curtis said coldly.

She pulled back when he called her by name.

'Look at him and Michael. They're like enough to be twins. Anyone can see they both belong to Richard,' Curtis added.

'I promised Ma I'd be nice if you came here, but I'm buggered if I'll stand and listen to this,' Harry roared. 'This is what you did to Pa. Now you're doing it to your son. You'll break him like you broke our pa, and when that day comes, I'm going to break you into little pieces. You listen to me, Curtis, because I'm making that a promise. Now you take that little chit back to where she belongs and don't you bring her around here again.'

Curtis dumped Ellie into the pram and lifted his fists. The baby screamed. Agatha turned on Harry and slapped his mouth — quick, frantic little taps to keep the words inside. He pushed her aside and strode to the gate, ready to sink his fists into the flesh of this favourite son, ready to finally relieve grief for his father the only way he knew how. He imagined Curtis's face pulped, the secret in his eyes blackened, the lifetime of sneers smashed with his teeth. The pale good looks gone forever. Then maybe his mother would see her real sons. Maybe all the pretty women who treated him and Albert like dirt while they mooned over Curtis would see who the real men were. Maybe Debra would see Harry at last.

'Albert!' Agatha shrieked.

Albert ran when he heard his mother's call. He stumbled to a halt when he realised the cause of her panic. Curtis was no match for Harry, but they'd been leading up to this fight for as long as memory. Maybe if Harry finally gained satisfaction by knocking Curtis down, he would settle into not hating any more. Maybe two black eyes would help Curtis see that this middle son had grown tired of being last in everyone's affections. Yet Albert was confused by William's sobs, by the little girl's wails, and by Michael howling behind him. And Ma was starting to tear at her tongue again. He leapt the fence and grabbed Harry's arms.

Clo slowed her approach so they wouldn't notice that she'd been running. 'Well, it's nice to see the family getting together,' she said. 'Am I in time for a cup of tea?' She placed a hand on Curtis's shoulder, feeling the tightness of muscles that matched the hardness of his face. She recognised the same fury she'd seen when his family cut down the trees. 'You're supposed to be looking after the baby, not playing with your big brothers,' she added casually. 'Ellie's not accustomed to all this friendly exuberance.'

Ellie was crying in jerky spasms. When Curtis lifted her, she screamed. She would not be quietened until he handed her to Clo.

'It's time to go home,' Clo said as she walked away.

Curtis followed, and when they reached the corner she placed Ellie into his arms. The little girl snuggled into his chest. He felt all tension fade.

Agatha glared at her remaining sons. 'That's enough now, off you go.' She spoke as if they were children again. 'Harry can take a shower while I put the kettle on. Albert, you see to Michael. I'll tend to my grandson.'

Her eldest sons obeyed her orders, as usual. She sat cross-legged on the grass and held William close.

'Now now,' she soothed. 'Aren't they silly arguing like that? Just silly men being silly. Your grandpa was the same. A silly man being silly. But not my little William, ay?'

He nestled closer, quietened by her tone, and by her hand brushing the annoying fringe of hair out of his eyes.

'Your daddy's being silly too. Oh yes, Curtis is your daddy,' Agatha continued. 'I'm your grandma, aren't I? And you have Uncle Harry and Uncle Albert. You're part of our family because Curtis is your daddy. No matter what they say, what anyone ever tells you, my Curtis is your daddy. He'll show it one day, just you wait and see. But don't you tell your mum I said that or she'll keep you away from Grandma. We'll have our little secrets, you and me. One day I'll tell you all the things I told your daddy when he was six like you, when he was mine. But for now we'll go and have some biscuits and juice and make a cup of tea for your uncles. Then you can play ball with Michael again. Won't that be nice?'

William hiccupped and nodded solemnly.

'He's a sweet little boy,' Agatha said, 'but he's not my William, is he? Grandma loves William best.'

He wound his arms around her neck and kissed her cheek.

Curtis saw the kiss and stumbled under a backwash of depression. Proximity was the key to her affection.

'What did she say to you?' Clo asked. 'I was on the other side of the street so I couldn't see your face, but I could see she'd hit you with something.'

'Will you marry me, Clo?'

'Do you really believe that marriage is a good way to spite your family?'

'Remember why you kicked me out of your flat that first night?' Curtis asked. 'You said kids have to be special to take the muck heaped on them if their parents aren't spotless.'

Clo shrugged. 'It's too late for Ellie. She has me for a mother.'

'They'll forget about the things they said once we're married.'

'I don't give a blue blazes what they say,' Clo snapped.

'Would it be so bad being married to me?'

'And have you telling me for the rest of my life that I'd hooked you through Ellie?'

'It's me who's trying to hook you,' he protested.

'What about our deal? No standing in each other's way if we want to cut out for any reason?'

'We've been okay, haven't we? We're good together.'

'We're not married.'

Though she had long passed the point of being able to walk away.

'Then let's get married,' Curtis said.

'All right,' she agreed abruptly. 'But there's a condition. I want out of this town.' She held up a hand to stay his objection. 'Jamie has a friend called Colin Jensen. He owns a place in the country that he inherited from his parents. Old family home, you know?' she sneered. 'Colin runs beef cattle, so the work isn't hard. A pensioner lives there to keep count of the cows, but Colin is looking for someone younger who'd handle the repairs. Free rent, electricity and phone. Are you with me?' Curtis nodded. 'Jamie told me about it because I said I was getting tired of all the finger-pointing around here.' Tired of Liona, she could have added but didn't. 'He thought we might like to give it a try.'

Steeltown was home. Curtis had never thought of living anywhere else. He had never thought of moving away from Angus and Liona. But Ellie's background would be clean in another town.

'Lots of native bush on the hills,' Clo said. 'The nearest neighbour is a couple of kilometres away. Six to the nearest village. Jamie said the first settlers made a thorough job of clearing the land and now Colin's having trouble with erosion. You could put your knowledge of tree-planting to good use out there.'

Curtis placed Ellie into the pram. She was sleeping peacefully.

'Fresh air and home-grown food would make a difference to her,' Clo added.

'You're hard selling to a willing buyer,' Curtis told her, 'but I can't picture you living so far from a city.'

Clo looked into his eyes without blinking. Her voice was quieter as she said, 'For Ellie.'

He grinned. 'Let's phone Jamie. We'll ask him down for the wedding.'

Clo shook her head. 'Registry office. Just you and me.'

'Jamie can be a witness. And your parents.'

'Her, not him. But nobody else.' Clo forestalled him. 'Not even Angus and Liona. We won't tell anyone until after it's done.'

'They probably wouldn't come. Angus wouldn't. He hates weddings.'

'And politicians. Taxi drivers. Street sweepers. Clean floors. Dirty floors.'

They continued the list, laughing, as they strolled back to the flat arm in arm.

# Chapter Fifty-nine

Curtis had walked the streets for hours saying goodbye to Steeltown and the hundreds of trees he'd planted. Now he was heading up a steep slope towards a cement water storage tank. The hill was dotted with shrubs and old horses. The eucalypts reached outwards instead of up, happy to have such a large area to themselves. The trees below fought houses, streets and people for their few metres of soil. This hill belonging to the Water Board would remain home-free forever.

Once at the top he looked out and around, and realised that he'd never really noticed distance before. Always, even when on this hill, his eyes would focus on the nearest tree. He had often stood on another high point, a smokestack ladder or warehouse roof, and looked out across the ocean to the giant ships — sometimes a dozen or more waiting their turn to fill their maws with coal and iron ore. He had watched the fishing fleet chugging seaward, or homewards with their holds overflowing with silvery protein. Once or twice he'd even admired a sunset or sunrise. Yet always the splash of colour on a flowering shrub, or the crimson glow of gum tips would refocus his eyes. He'd stare around at the oaks, elms, pines, maples — at all the European trees and plants which had replaced native gums, lilli pillies, banksia, casuarinas, silky oaks. He would see the soft, pretty hues and deep greens of Europe and long for the silver-grey, olives, umbers and gold that were the true seeds of this area. Then he'd vow to bring them back again.

Curtis often wandered along the mountains that curved around Steeltown like a giant arm. He roamed through the pockets of rainforest while enjoying the tree ferns, maidenhair and birds-nest ferns, and the cool greens and straight trunks of towering trees. Yet he always knew a deep, singing pleasure when leaving the shade and mulch smell behind as he walked out into the woodlands — called bush by most Steeltowners. 'The bush' was an Australian term used for any natural environment, from coastal scrub to saltbush plains, but his bush was the woodlands. It had eucalypts of muted olive or grey, tipped with red and gold and clumps of feathery blossoms. Weird shapes and even stranger flowers and seeds; bottlebrush of all sizes and colours; the slashing leaves of grevilleas protecting flowers dripping with nectar. Great gaps between the gums shared the sunlight with other plants. Here was every colour, size and shape in imagination.

Thinking of his bush now, Curtis wondered how he would adapt to the treeless plains soon to be his home. Clo had wanted to visit the small beef property before making a commitment, but he had refused. It was better to make a clean break. If a back door was left open, he would probably retreat. He'd slammed that door by signing a two-year contract with Colin Jensen, a big bluff man with a secretive smile which instantly won him Curtis's dislike.

He reached the water tank as the sun began its ascent out of the Pacific Ocean. Ignoring a No Trespassing sign, he climbed a ladder and forced himself to look beyond the eucalypts. The ocean was just beginning to glitter, and the pattern and sparkle of streetlights was dimmed to inconsequence by scarlet-fringed clouds and a golden glow. In this light, at this time, the steelworks had its moment of glory — towering chimneys and black, symmetrical shapes outlined in red. To the west the mountains were darkly sombre against the skyline.

Something shifted within him. For a moment he perceived further than his own eyes could see to an outlook beyond comprehension. Out there were ever-changing forces that could destroy the world as he knew it. If he opened to them, he would again become a little boy listening to Agatha's stories. Staring around him, he shivered, and wanted to hurl himself from the heights of this man-made mountain. He crouched, ready to spring as the sun finally hauled itself out of the ocean, dripping red fire to light up the coastline, the houses, the steelworks and the mountains; to show him a familiar vista, each object plain and clear as he'd perceived it all his life.

The surrounding eucalypts watched their corner of the world, seeing all and knowing everything without ever becoming involved. They had no secrets, no perversities. They showed all their colours and moods, holding nothing away from him and only their protective branches over him. Drawing their familiarity around him like an insulation, he slid to the ground.

Angus had once said, 'Take no notice of me or anyone else, sonny. You look and listen and draw your own conclusions.'

Curtis had tried, but he was always left with a collage of other people's negatives. Dabs of his own creation were muddied from too much mixing, too much overprinting. On those treeless plains to the west, the nearest neighbour would be kilometres away. He'd know nothing about the families in that area. They would know nothing about him. Out there Ellie could develop her own colours without others' imprints to cramp her style.

He ran down the slope, ignoring the pain in his back, eager to be with his daughter when she woke for her breakfast bottle.

# Part Three

# As you sow, so shall you reap

**Harvest:** *the product or result of any labour or process.*

# Chapter Sixty

The car shuddered, gave one final sigh and ceased to breathe. Curtis thought they were out of petrol. Clo swore it had died of old age. A strange grating noise had developed as they drove over the mountains, and she'd rebuked him for not getting something a little more modern. Curtis knew nothing about cars. He had thought this one a good buy at the time.

'A real bargain at the price, practically a steal. But I am overstocked,' the salesman had said while counting Curtis's money.

So many car yards and so many salesmen: hearty men in dark suits and pastel shirts, their hair neatly combed, their teeth and eyes reflecting the gleam of their nicely shined cars. They fidgeted and smiled as the words flowed fast, none making sense to Curtis. He bought this car because of its unshined state, and because that particular salesman hardly spoke at all. Curtis was fooled by a shirt tail that hung over baggy trousers and formed a white flag surrounding a threadbare jacket.

When Curtis was seven years old, a talkative and well dressed door-to-door vendor had cheated Agatha out of a week's wages. Angus said it served her right for trusting such a person. Since then, shabby and subdued had formed a connection with honest in Curtis's mind. The car salesman had shown a definite lack of interest as prospective buyers walked around kicking tyres, so Curtis just naturally thought of him as a man to be trusted.

He explained all this to Clo when she rolled her eyes at first sight of the dingy old car. She was not impressed. She was even less impressed when its sigh turned to a cloud of blue smoke and the engine fell silent. They were many kilometres past the last town. They'd been lost for almost half an hour. Clo blamed that on him, too, even though she held the road maps.

Curtis leaned forward and peered through the windscreen. If shabby and lazy had any connection with honest, they were now in a righteous place. Prickle weeds and tree skeletons dotted the paddocks. Cows lined the fences, seeking shelter from a hot sun beneath the meagre shade of a few scraggy roadside eucalypts. A small mob of sheep stared into each other's fleeces. Not one of them looked up when Curtis accidentally pressed the horn. A magpie called a protest from a nearby she-oak, but apart from that, the only sign of life was a scurry of rabbits. Which merely proved that the owner of this property couldn't be bothered clearing the many burrows.

Clo and Curtis climbed out of the car and leaned against each other for comfort. Until now, the furthest either had ventured from Sydney or Steeltown was a walk along the escarpment. Compared with the woodlands there, these yellow grass paddocks were desolate. He kissed her forehead and mumbled something meant to be reassuring, although a growing depression formed a question mark at the end of every sentence. She screamed when the magpie took umbrage at his breaking of the silence for a second time, and ran when it made a swooping pass over their heads. Her flight took her through an open gate and she managed to regain her dignity when the magpie flew off to less populated spaces.

Cursing the bird and Curtis's choice of cars, she marched down a slight incline, up over a rise then down again towards a homestead flanked by English trees. Curtis grabbed Ellie and followed. He thought that with a bit of luck they could beg a ride to Jensen's Place. Without luck, they would at least get a drink of water.

A tall skinny old man with a patchy white beard came out to meet them on the veranda.

Clo introduced herself, then said, 'That's my husband Curtis and my baby Ellie. Our car broke down and we'd like to use your telephone, if that's all right. We're looking for Jensen's Place.'

'And you've found it,' the old man said. 'I suppose you'd better come in and have a bite of breakfast,' he added, tossing the invitation over a shoulder as he shambled back into the shadowy hallway.

The house bore no resemblance to the weatherboard farmhouses they had passed that morning. This one was longer, wider and taller, and built of sandstone blocks. It had a feeling of history and richness, even to Curtis who knew nothing of such things. He had always felt that this type of building looked down at him with a sneer. He couldn't decide whether to take his shoes off at the door or turn back to the road. The car might be unshined and apparently dead, but at least it was a part of home. Homesickness could be the cause of its collapse. If he could get it wheeled around and headed east, perhaps he could bring about a resurrection.

'What do you think?' he asked Clo, inclining his head towards the highway.

'You can't possibly think of reneging now,' she answered, but doubtfully, as though the same thought had occurred to her.

They might have turned and headed for home if Ellie hadn't objected. Raising her knees to her stomach, she kicked out as hard as she could, almost throwing herself through the door. Curtis tried his best to calm her, but still she squirmed and sobbed as if she understood their intention. When a voice called from the gloom, 'Are youse coming in or not?', Clo took the baby from Curtis and strode into the house.

The old man cocked a thumb towards a refrigerator. 'I'll have two eggs, a bit of bacon, toast and a cuppa tea when you're ready to make it,' he told her.

She would have spoken her curses and walked out if not for another wail from the travel-weary Ellie. Resentment was no match for anxious mother. Clo soothed the baby and turned away to find a bed, leaving Curtis to make their breakfast.

The old man slumped into a bum-worn chair, angled in such a way that he could look south-east through the open door, south-west through a fly-specked window.

'They do that, yer know,' he said, pointing to the frying pan without attempting to leave his seat. 'They have yer kid then use it to make yer feel guilty. That way they can have a lie-down while you do all the work. Woman's work that is, making breakfast.'

With the expertise of long practice, Curtis broke six eggs into the pan one-handed. He hid a grin at the expression on Clo's face as she re-entered from the hallway.

'Then where's the woman who usually makes yours?' she asked. Her tone sounded more like a snide remark than a challenge.

'Left a good while back,' the old man growled, 'and me being a sensible bloke, I never bothered looking for another. Which I reckon you know well enough. Jamie told me all about you, so I suppose he had the hide to blab my business as well.'

Clo shrugged away Curtis's accusing stare. 'I thought he'd be gone by the time we got here,' she said.

'That right, ay?' the old bloke asked. 'And where might I be going?'

'That's hardly our problem,' Clo snapped.

Curtis sensed her dislike as nothing sudden or new. Whatever she had learned about this man had determined her attitude before they arrived. He felt sorry for the old bloke despite his abrasiveness, but there would be no peace while he remained.

'Yer right about that at least, and I'm not the kind to stay where I'm not wanted,' the old man said, grinning up at Clo. 'Honest to goodness, missy, yer can take my word on it.'

He raised his palms in surrender, but no more honesty and goodness resided in the gesture than in his sly look.

'Or me name ain't Dougal McLean,' he added.

The rays of a newborn sun spiked through the open door. It lit an old faded map of a face complete with hills and valleys that were lumped, cracked and guttered by erosion. Curtis studied the map and knew he had travelled that country before.

'But I've been here for a fair pile of years now. Guess that makes me part of this place,' Dougal continued. 'A sort of a first come right, yer might say. Though I suppose yer can stay if yer keep the kid out of me hair.'

'I've been hired to run this place,' Curtis said. 'I can kick you out any time I want.'

He knew the words were childish, but this old bloke had that effect on him.

'What's stopping yer then?' Dougal asked casually, as though he had no real interest in the answer.

'If you're Dougal McLean, you have to be Angus's uncle.'

'Angus, ay? That would be Sparrow and Polly's boy. Angus McTavish,' Dougal said with a snort of laughter, the way most people said the name. 'And what relation are you? I can see the McLean in yer. In that kid of yours, too. Mostly in the shape of her eyes and chin.'

Curtis's belief had always been firm, but he'd never said the words aloud. He couldn't say them now. 'She's the image of her mother,' he said instead.

'And who was your mother before she became a Lawson?'

Guessing the old man was referring to Agatha, Curtis shrugged. He did not know. She had never mentioned her maiden name. Only Liona had told him family stories. He filled Dougal's cup from a freshly made pot of tea, ignoring Clo's sniff of derision and the old man's satisfied smirk.

# Chapter Sixty-one

Clo hated the place at first. Hated the darkness at night, the air smelling of cow dung, pollen and sometimes rotting carcasses. She loathed the flies, the loneliness; the quietness most of all. She hated Dougal and called him a cranky old shit more perverse than any male she had ever known. He rarely moved from that bum-worn chair, yet if there was even a sniff in the air of work to be done, he disappeared in an instant. When challenged, he said he had just gone for a stroll and anyway, working was definitely none of his business.

'This property's been rotting away too long to worry about it now,' he said on their second day at Jensen's Place. 'Ask the ghosts if yer don't believe me. Come night and they're wandering everywhere.'

To keep Curtis's mind away from cleaning, Dougal began listing the number of convicts who had died in this place, detailing who they were and why they'd been sent to Australia.

'Thieves and murderers,' he said, 'with a few political prisoners thrown in for good measure. But if politics then was the same as now, who's to know the difference? The ghost at the creek, he got drunk and fell off a horse. The one in the front room, that's a woman. The streak of blue in the little maid's cell on the front veranda, that was a poor little bugger died in childbirth. The red one out back is an Irisher. He killed three Protestants before they flogged him to death. The ones way back and beyond the creek, they'd have to be Aborigines. They're the reason why the drunk bloke fell off the horse. Coming home from a party at a neighbour's place he was. Three or four miles that way.' He nodded towards the south. 'Creek was in flood at the time. Flood changes a creek's direction, did yer know that? There used to be fifteen-odd convict graves this side of the creek, but most of them got washed away during the floods. I suppose yer noticed that the boss cocky's family graves are up on the hill. But I was telling yer about that drunk bloke.'

Completely taken in, Curtis listened to tales like that for hours. They ended when Clo asked Dougal how he had acquired his information.

'Made most of it up,' he answered promptly. 'But yer have to admit they're bloody good yarns, and listening to me telling them is better than busting yer gut fixing up somebody else's house. Like I said from the start, this whole place has gone to rack and ruin, and that's exactly where it belongs.'

Curtis left the house feeling foolish. He spent the rest of the week mending fences and counting cows, leaving Clo alone to bear the brunt of the old man's temper. Dougal hid if something upset him, hunching down in a chair or in a corner beside one of the wardrobes. Usually he could be traced by the sound of grunted curses.

'I'm a grown man,' he said when asked to refrain from using obscenities in Ellie's presence. 'I can swear if I bloody well want to. Learned it from kids anyhow, while I was living in the city.'

He moved his bed to the old disused shearers' shed at the back of the house a few weeks after the Lawsons moved in. 'Dust is best left to lie,' he said when they began shifting years of it into the yard. 'Can't see the sense of tossing it into the air to get up a man's nose and spoil his view. The man upstairs invented spiders to keep the flies down, and mice to tidy crumbs off the floor. Not right for anyone to go poking their noses into God's business. You'll pay for it one day.'

'What's he doing now?' he asked when the house was finally clean and Curtis began ploughing the ground.

Clo had been roaming aimlessly around the place, wondering

what the hell she was going to do with the rest of the day, the week, the year.

'Seedling beds,' she said. 'Eucalypts I suppose. That's what he does.'

'Yer not talking about trees, are yer?'

'Do you have something against trees?' she asked.

'Did yer ever take a good look at one?' He pointed to an ancient eucalypt growing alone in a nearby paddock. 'Look at her there, spreading out, taking up a lot more room than she needs. She drops her seeds, see there? Those couple of sorry little saplings. Squats over them like any clucky old mum, sheltering them from the heat and wind and cold. Looking after them, yer think, ay? But the only ones to live will be the ones who got away. The ones underneath will die because she's taking all their air and space. Never did like trees, lest they be in a forest where all things are equal. Or worked into something useful, like tables and chairs.'

'I'd like to hear you repeat those views to Curtis,' Clo said softly.

Dougal's answering grin said he wasn't that much of a fool.

She remembered the twitch of his hands and the squint of some-thing strange in his eyes when the first crop of seedlings died after two days in the sun, when the second lot never sprouted.

'You did something to them, didn't you?' she asked, bailing him up in the shearers' shed. She stood hands on hips in the doorway so he couldn't slide outside and avoid the question.

'I got used ter living on me own in open spaces. Don't like the idea of people and trees everywhere I look,' he said.

Looking past her as Curtis joined them, he added, 'There's not much difference between them yer know.'

Curtis could have given a dozen reasons for disagreeing, but he merely smiled and nodded.

Clo's face darkened. She couldn't understand why he wanted Dougal's liking. 'Talking about being on your own, what happened to your wife?' she asked.

The question seemed blunt enough, but the look in her eyes suggested that she was ready to cut into the old man at any moment.

'Never found one silly enough to take me on,' he said after a long sad sigh.

Self-effacement was too foreign to this man to fool Clo. When he added sloping shoulders and a basset-hound droop to his face, she became even more annoyed.

'But then I suppose you're talking about Emmie.' He glanced at Curtis, giving a slight shrug that said, man to man, they both knew women had to be humoured. 'I brought her here and looked out for her for a year or so, then she just up and disappeared. She wanted the city. The ocean near.'

'Jamie told me how she made him leave that little house in Newtown,' Clo said. 'I'd say she's one very clever lady.'

'You don't know the half of it,' Dougal agreed. 'That night Jamie brought his mum around really got Emmie moving.'

Curtis edged past Clo and sat on the end of the bed. Dougal lit one of his evil-smelling cigarettes and settled back, ready to talk.

'I started getting fish or crabs and stuff like that for breakfast, dinner and tea. All the green vegetables tasted like seaweed, and the potatoes like clams. The house got wetter every day. I swear that every time I looked at those fish on the walls, they were swimming in a different direction.'

'Hah!' Clo snorted.

'You know about every dimension in heaven and earth, do yer?' the old man asked.

'I've been on this property long enough to recognise bullshit when I see it.'

The tightness of Dougal's face now accented the gentleness of his voice as he persevered. 'The crunch came on the night I found her standing stark staring naked in a bucket of seaweed. All I could see at first was her flesh. Give me a bit of a jolt, too. In me young days, I was as eager as the next bloke. But I never laid a finger on Emmie. That's not what we were about. She cooked and cleaned, I paid the bills, and that was it.'

'Oh yes, and then she suddenly decided to seduce you,' Clo said.

He pretended to miss the note of sarcasm and shook his head slowly, as if he still couldn't believe that moment. 'You just picture her in that flaming red bucket, those seaweed strands waving around her bosoms as if she was sitting at the bottom of the ocean. Me standing staring. Everything had a saltwater smell, like old fishing bait. I turned around and went for me life when water started dripping off the ceiling.'

'If all that's true, which I have to doubt, how did she come to be here?'

'I thought when she moved away from the ocean she'd get out of all that nonsense. I thought she'd start painting nice dry landscapes. Knew it wasn't going to work when I woke up one morning and found a shark along the length of me bedroom wall. That's your room now, and if yer shove that big old wardrobe aside, you'll see it.'

Clo straightened her hands then clenched them into fists. Curtis recognised this sign of a rising temper.

'Did you ever ask her what she wanted?' she said in a deceptively mild voice.

Dougal scowled. 'I didn't ask her to come. She followed me.'

His voice matched her fists. Clo's eyes gleamed.

'You brought her here to cook and clean, and for company in your old age.'

'Cooking and cleaning was good enough for me mother,' Dougal snarled.

'The mines were good enough for your father, but you didn't follow in those footsteps.'

'A woman does what something inside tells her to do. A man thinks with his brains,' he shot back at her. 'And mine said I didn't belong in a black hole under a mountain.'

'You sound just like my father,' Clo said scornfully. 'He could always justify his rotten behaviour too.'

'I've seen people like you plenty of times,' Dougal said, matching her scorn. 'Everything wrong in yer life yer blame on your past, without ever owning up that you was the one who made it. Just like Emmie, trying to find meanings where there weren't any. Not wanting to know

313

that things just happen, that people are what they are and not what somebody else wants them to be. I told her to take it or leave it, and she left.'

'She left because you stopped her from doing what she wanted, just so you'd have someone to wash your dirty socks and do your cooking.'

The old man and the young woman faced each other. Although the width of the room separated them, they could have been toe to toe. Tension resembled jagged streaks of electricity as bark-brown eyes stared into watery blue, as their voices took on the sound of cracking stockwhips.

'You tell me why the man's always gotter do what the woman wants.'

'When did that ever apply to you?'

'And you tell me who's choice was it to come out here to the country, ay? Bet it wasn't his.' He jerked a thumb towards Curtis. 'Bet it wasn't that little girl's neither.'

Curtis knew he had to find a way to make peace between them before Dougal gave Clo an excuse to move back to the city.

'Where's this Emmie now?' he asked loudly.

'Making a million with her bloody painting,' Dougal snarled. 'And keeping the millions to herself, though if it wasn't for me she never would've got started.'

'Emmanuelle Costa,' Clo said. 'She paints ocean scenes. Whales, dolphins and seals. She's been exhibited overseas. That house in Newtown and its little back room would be worth a fortune now, if someone hadn't destroyed her paintings.'

'She did that herself, the night I told her I was leaving for the country,' Dougal said when Curtis frowned at him.

'Then why did she follow you here?' Clo asked.

'To punish herself for not being able to keep the dolphin alive. Or maybe to punish me.'

The slope of his shoulders and the droop to his face had returned. This time even Clo could see that his appearance wasn't a pretence to win sympathy, or even to prod her into anger. His voice became more wearier than the look of him as he added, 'She was mad, yer know, or madder than most. She thought she was born from the sea. Hang on a bit. I'll show yer something.'

Dougal eased himself onto the floor, pausing now and then as his creaking bones reset to another position. Reaching under the bed, he dragged out a metre-square board — wood-fibre pressed into a sheet, commonly known as Masonite. Struggling upright, he sat it on the bed.

'She thought this was her mother. Painted it before she left. To remind me of how we met, she said.'

The colours of the ocean hit Curtis with a wave of homesickness. Swathes of greenish blue in a deep channel hedged by a sandbank on one side, beach on the other, took his breath away as if he had plunged into those waters on a wintry day. As he stared at what seemed to be a simple seascape, a shape formed from cloud shadow. Indistinct at first, it gradually grew darker and stronger as his mind confirmed its presence. The ocean receded to a sketchy background behind a sleek, perfectly formed and fluid sea creature. Its colour was a dark blue-grey to pale grey underneath. Beside its breathing hole was another opening surrounded by black burn marks. The look in the dolphin's eyes was a scream.

'I was past seventy when I first met Emmie. And feeling every day of it,' Dougal said. 'Maybe because the only job I could get was janitor at Foley Brothers. Maybe because Iain's letter had caught up with me at last.'

Dougal read the letter three times to make sure there hadn't been a slip of the pen and Iain meant sick. Never dead. Not Ma McLean. Friend, foe and fighter, there was nothing in her face or voice to suggest she would ever die. One day maybe. Everyone has to go one day. But not Ma, not yet. He didn't know her exact age, but he felt sure she couldn't be old.

He thumped the letter onto the bed and looked at himself in the cheval glass, wanting to see the part of her in him. He had inherited Da's height, build, general features and skin; but the colour and shape of his eyes, the crooked smile, his way of looking through his fringe of hair, these had been handed down from Ma. He stared at himself for five minutes or more, hardly believing what he saw. The purple heather eyes had paled to a watery blue. Their shape had been altered by sagging lids. The smile remained crooked, but one or two blackened teeth, and a few more missing, gave his mouth the appearance of a gargoyle's not too friendly grin. Fine wispy hair, always too long, caused no impediment to the view as his gaze travelled downwards to a bared chest with crepey skin. And even on him, a working man all his life, sagging muscles and pouchy breasts. His nipples had turned inwards, like eyes unable to accept the vision of old age.

Is this what had happened to Ma? This sneaking, creeping of years ignored until now, hidden by work to be done; by blaming laziness for shortened breath, and the shine of memories for an inclination to sit and daydream instead of making more.

He put his boot through the cheval glass and continued kicking until not one piece remained large enough to throw his reflection back at him. But still he felt old and left out of it. Now Ma was buried and gone, he had no kin to speak of. A daughter who wouldn't own up to him. A kid brother on the other side of Australia. Might as well be the other side of the world.

'I wrote to Iain and he wrote back asking me to visit,' Dougal said. 'Maybe I should've gone, but Iain didn't know me any better than I knew him, and Polly was there by then. Polly and me never got on. She was too keen on herself to care about anyone else. But I needed lifting up out of meself, so I decided to take a week off and go hunting.'

He grinned at Clo's snort of disgust.

'As a young bloke I liked the feeling of walking an animal down then cutting it down. Some blokes I lived with for a while up north talked me out of that. They showed me how killing for no reason took away me power and gave it to the animal I killed, besides being a waste of good meat. Those blokes spent most of their lives killing and eating, but there was sense to what they did. Still, I liked hunting, so I went after rabbits and cats gone wild. Rabbits eat out the land,

and a feral cat's worse than a bloody weed and no good to anyone, not even to itself. But the sight of rabbits filled with man-given disease made me puke. And you kill one cat and some numb-brained mongrel dumps two more. By then I'd worked me way back to the coast, so I took up fishing. It's hunting just the same. Knowing the right bait, the right place to throw a line. Fighting to haul in the fish, then nine times out of ten yer can slip the hook and let it go about its business. Maybe not too much the worse for wear, and maybe a bit wiser the next time.'

The sky was scoured of colour but high, as if the sudden snap of winter cold in autumn had sent it outwards and up in search of the sun. Dougal packed his wet-weather clothing, although he knew the rains were a week or two away. The nylon jacket and pants would keep out the icy wind better than any store-bought jumper. The days of chunky hand-knits from Ma were gone forever.

He oiled his reel and checked the line for knots, then stowed his gear into the dicky seat of the dark green '32 Chevrolet he'd been driving since it was new. A breakfast of porridge, sweet black tea and toast dripping with cocky's joy, then he was on his way, aiming for a stretch of beach down south past Mollymook. The swinging winds in April there caused riptides that built up a sandbank and formed a channel parallel with the beach — always a good place for fish of a decent size. He stopped off at Lake Illawarra and pulled up a can of squirt worms. A creek a few miles further south surrendered a bucket of sprats without argument, or too much work. It was almost a shame the way those little silver streaks jumped into his scoop, as if they sensed his need for companionship.

Driving slowly, ignoring the curses from those in a hurry to get to their next resting place, he admired the countryside, still unspoiled by too many houses, while he remembered Ma. The Sunday hat with its prodding pin. The sturdy brown brogues. The stories she told of the old country. Remembering the heather blue eyes and baby soft skin, he was almost glad he hadn't seen her in those later years. Not when age and worry and grief had sandpapered off the brightness. He hoped she'd forgive him for that.

He turned off the highway onto an old fire track as yet undiscovered by tourists. The bush showed its presence by scratching at the paintwork of his car, by shoving up roots to tear at his tyres and bounce him around until his teeth rattled. It occasionally rewarded his stubbornness with a patch of brilliant flowers, a couple of cheeky birds, or a tree so twisted by years that he had to admire its tenacity. The odd echidna or wombat waddled away from his wheels as if they had all the time in the world. Which of course they did.

The camp site hadn't changed. Coastal gorse and scrub and a few storm-blasted lilli pilli trees still battled swinging winds and creeping sand dunes. Mulga as warped as a murderer's heart mingled with salt-scarred eucalypts and she-oaks. The bull ants were as big as always, but cold weather had chased off the sandflies and mosquitoes. On one side of a gully sheltered from the wind by a tangle of lantana, he built a roaring fire to keep him warm. After a few minutes searching, he found a dead tree of the required size and age to keep the flames going throughout the night. Nearby was his cooking fire ready for the Dutch oven damper, and for the three wood pigeons he shot while the flash and flare died to a glow of embers.

As the birds cooked in the way he'd been taught by those blokes up north, Dougal lay back in the fire-warmed sand. He watched the day slide into night while he dreamed of the clan McLean. One by one, led by Ma and Pa, they came to shake his hand.

The old folks still in Scotland, blurred by the fading memory of drawings pinned to bagging in a shack at Mount Tumblebee. His brothers, every one except Iain forever under forty. Two sisters, little and thin and pigtailed, the forms of the women they had become just out of reach of his mind's eye. Beyond them, a small half-circle of nieces and nephews he'd never met. A daughter with her back turned to him, hustling her children away.

After they'd been and gone, he sipped hot black tea and repeated every vile oath he'd learned in his long and lonely life.

As he sat down to eat, Emmie appeared, enticed by the smell of freshly broken damper and just-cooked meat. She stayed drooling at his every bite, so he placed a hunk of meat on the nonburning end of the tree. She broke off a piece of damper and sat opposite him, eating slowly and delicately in small, even bites. She sometimes rolled her eyes to show appreciation.

He didn't know where Emmie came from, and he never found out, but he knew she was alone. She had that defensive look of someone always alone, even in a crowd. When she finally spoke, it was in a language he'd never heard before. The alien sound reminded him of Sparrow. He remembered his little mate and mateship, and he gave the memory to her. Emmie accepted his gift with a gracious smile, then repaid him with a song. Her voice was low and husky and not particularly tuneful, but it was filled with the sound of the ocean, the waves, the sea and sand, and the whisper of wind through trees. The pictures she painted with her voice and hands were as comprehensive and unique as the pictures she later painted in oils.

That night she slept on the front seat of the Chevrolet. Dougal rolled up in a blanket beside the fire.

When he woke next morning around five o'clock, Emmie had disappeared. At first he thought of her as a phantom sent by Ma to ease his loneliness and grief. Ma had known Sparrow, so she'd know the look and feel of a person most likely to bring comfort to her son. But Ma would also know that when the phantom disappeared, as all phantoms do, then Dougal's loneliness and grief would have an extra edge. Punishment for his neglect could be her reason, yet Ma's love had never been reasonable. If his mother had sent the dark-haired, dark-eyed female to be his mate, then mate she was and would be. He crawled around the car until he discovered the imprint of small bare feet. The tracks led east, directly to the water.

He found her up to her armpits in water, as blue as the deeper sea and close to passing out. She was trying to push it out, the dolphin — whispering her pleas, trying to reason it back to where it belonged. There were no wounds or marks on that silvery skin; but death was in its eyes, and in the way it tried to roll over and present its underbelly to the killing sun. Her death too, if she didn't give up and get out.

'Leave it,' he said. 'It's near gone.'

'Help me,' she tried to yell, tried to be fierce; but hopelessness and helplessness robbed her voice of its scream.

He grabbed her armpits and dragged her up the beach. She lay quietly, too weary to fight him. Yet the moment he let go, she crawled back to the water, talking to the dolphin, trying to push it out to sea, back to where it belonged. He knew she'd keep trying until it killed her.

He went to the car, took out his rifle, marched back to the beach, put the barrel beside that dolphin's blowhole and pulled the trigger. The look in Emmie's eyes, when she looked at him, was a scream.

'I thought she'd go then, back to where she belonged. She did disappear for a while. But later, after I'd fished for an hour or two without any luck or heart for it, she came back and sat in the dicky seat without saying a word. Didn't talk to me for near a week. When she did, she never mentioned the dolphin.'

'Why did she stay with you?' Clo asked.

He shrugged. 'You tell me what goes on in a woman's head.'

She nodded. 'Or a man's. Ruby told me about you.'

'So you think I'm a right mongrel for walking out on me kid, even though I would've made a poor bloody joke as a father. Even though nobody asked if I wanted to be one in the first place. Nobody can see it but me, but at that time in me life, being tied to a wife and a kid would have been the same as working in the mines.'

'I can see it,' Clo said as she left the shed.

'I'll call it quits if you will,' Dougal called after her.

Curtis looked from one to the other. He had no understanding of their words, or of what had passed between them.

# Chapter Sixty-two

After a summer month of roasting in the corrugated-iron shearers' shed, Dougal moved back to his old room in the homestead. Curtis ploughed seedling beds further away from the house; and while he reaped what he sowed and covered the land with eucalypts, Clo spent large chunks of her days sitting with the old man, staring out at the hills, listening to Dougal talk about the old days.

'Them mongrel dogs scared the hell out of the little bloke. But then, there wasn't too much that didn't scare him. Not long on guts was Sparrer, but yer can't have everything, can yer? It didn't surprise me none when I heard he pulled his own string. Women can do that to yer. Women and kids. They always want yer to be more than yer can be. I thought Jack would be a good father to Ruby, but he had nothing left. It all went to Nell yer know.'

He spoke of Ma and Da, of Mount Tumblebee and the mine. He described the digging and the coal dust until she could barely breathe. She cried with him in memory of dead McLeans, and the words he used to describe Ma evoked a yearning for Great Grandma and the clan. She listened intently to his tales of wandering the countryside; reminded him of Emmie, or so he said. But unlike Emmie, Clo talked about herself. Not as a gift to woo him, or to win his sympathy or dislike. She wanted to hear her story told aloud, to remember it without the distortions of pain and blame. He listened intently, in the same way she listened to him: just giving a nod and making a cup of tea when a particular part of her story ended.

If Curtis made his presence known, Dougal would turn his bum-worn chair around and stare out at the hills. Clo would wander into her room and sit for hours scribbling in her journal.

Throughout that year, she became almost housewifely, although Curtis never felt that her efforts were for him. He did not understand why the approbation of an unrelated old man should mean anything to her, but he refrained from asking questions. Clo was city to the core, yet she displayed no sign of the restlessness he had expected. Grateful for that fact, and for her gentle, almost obsessively tender care of Ellie, he stayed quiet and enjoyed a sweetness that had not yet begun to ferment.

On the day before what Dougal claimed was his ninety-second birthday, the old man disappeared after breakfast and did not return for lunch. His chair was cold to the touch and his favourite seat on the veranda was empty — which hadn't been all that uncommon during the past few months. Since age had started making his body increasingly more infirm, his mind was turning inwards. He often sat for hours staring at the wall or floor, and he'd curse them aloud if anyone interrupted his train of thought. Sometimes he hid in out of the way spaces.

'To be on me own for a change,' he'd snarl if Clo sought him out.

Although she understood his need for time alone, she worried when he forgot to eat.

'He's much too thin as it is,' she'd whisper to Curtis.

Clo looked in all the usual locations: the walk-in pantry, the two tiny back rooms still inhabited by the ghost of a convict servant (or so Dougal said), the outdoor toilet. The only sign of life was sunlight pouring in through leaded windows. She strolled outside, expecting to find him soaking up the sun. The weather had turned warm, with just the suggestion of a breeze stirring the high yellow grasses.

There were two places Dougal went when he felt like being antisocial. One was the shearing shed which housed his cache. He liked a beer in the afternoons these days, but Clo refused to have alcohol in her home. So he sneaked up to the shed and drank his beer warm, even though he paid for it later with a belly full of wind.

She glanced at her watch. Three o'clock. His happy half-hour normally began at four. He would be down at the creek under the willow, she decided, writing poetry on scraps of paper.

Dougal spent hours composing sonnets in memory of mates lost to wars, both worldwide and personal. He would bury the poems and mark their resting places with piles of stones. The little cairns rarely lasted longer than the first heavy rain. When they were washed away, he started again.

Clo glanced up at the shed then turned towards the creek. 'Too early for his beer,' she said as Curtis followed her down the track.

'Dougal, where the hell are you?' she shouted.

He rarely answered when she called. 'I'm not a dog to come a-running when you yell or whistle,' he'd growl at her. Five minutes later, he'd make her a cup of tea. She recognised that as his version of an apology.

Clo ducked as a magpie swooped down from a eucalypt and flapped by over her head. Picking up a rock, she hurled if after the bird, swearing it was the same one that had frightened her on the day of their arrival. 'And every nesting season since,' she insisted when Curtis accused her of being cruel.

It flew in a straight line to the largest willow tree, and now they could see Dougal sitting with his back against the willow's trunk. Clo waved, but he didn't acknowledge their presence.

'Dougal, why don't you ever answer me?' she sighed.

Curtis stared past the old man to the creek. In a pond deep enough to swim in when the rains came, a square of Masonite board nudged the opposite bank. Clo was too busy with Dougal to notice. She grabbed the old man's arm, meaning to hoist him back to the house if she had to. He fell sideways, and lay without making a sound. She listened to his chest, sat up and thumped his shoulder. She thumped him again, harder, when he didn't move or breathe.

Curtis carried Dougal back to the old shearers' shed then telephoned Colin Jensen. They arranged to have the old man buried in the homestead cemetery — the boss cocky's graveyard up on the hill — so he'd be safe when the rains came.

Clo cried off and on for the next two days, but on the morning of the burial she was dry-eyed and peaceful, as if something more than old Dougal McLean had been laid to rest. She cried again when she discovered the square of Masonite in the creek. By then the dolphin had slipped off into the deep-water pond.

# Chapter Sixty-three

My first impression of Curtis's new home was definitely unfavourable. My first emotions were disappointment and a feeling of being cheated. From the movies I had gone out of my way to watch, I anticipated being moved to a pioneer frame of mind. I imagined myself being close to nature, possibly dressed in a ground-sweeping brown gown and a wide-brimmed hat. I had dreamed of communing with fauna both tame and wild, and breathing unpolluted air while being spellbound by soaring eagles or vast stretches of rippling wheat that would remind me of the ocean.

The women I met wore floral cotton frocks. Except for the absence of seagulls, the native birds were much the same as those in Steeltown (I never saw an eagle), and most native animals had been driven out by cows too stupid to commune with anything but their cuds. The unpolluted air was heavy with the stink of dung and an occasional carcass, and thick with flies determinedly crawling into every available human orifice. I could not find one paddock of wheat. The lucerne was pretty enough, but riddled with snakes and insects, and surrounded by barbed-wire fences to keep out the cows. If they ate wet lucerne, they would swell and burst and die.

Instead of the expected picturesque countryside, I saw a vast emptiness that made me feel claustrophobic. It was as if the vacuum created by a lack of people on those yellow grass plains could close in around me and steal the breath out of my lungs. And having read every story and poem by *the* Henry Lawson, I assumed every man I met would be either tough but softly spoken, or a happy-go-lucky larrikin with a wonderfully dry sense of humour. The women would be either perpetually afraid, completely invisible, or stark staring mad. They'd spend their days dreaming up ways to make their men miserable. Imagine my initial discontent when I encountered men and women no different from the average Steeltowner.

Yet the people I actually met were friendly and hospitable. The plains were in reality valleys surrounded by hills topped with spindly gums, she-oaks and thick scrub. Beyond the hills, many densely wooded areas had not been cleared by the early settlers. In many places real bush lined the road leading to the farm. It was much like the bush beyond the mountains above Steeltown — eucalypts galore. This surprised me. I think Curtis was more surprised. Pleased, of course, but surprised.

He always seemed delighted when I visited Jensen's Place, yet he somehow managed to make me feel not quite welcome. If I tried to impart stories of friends and family, he cut me off and steered the conversation to more impersonal channels. I found this very frustrating. There was much to tell, and Angus wouldn't listen either. Angus was too busy meddling in William's dreams.

# Chapter Sixty-four

The grownups wouldn't listen. They never do when a kid tries to tell the way things really are. William had found that out almost before he could walk. When he tried to reveal the truth about the trees on his walls, they insisted he was having nightmares. When he tried to run from those trees, they said he was sleepwalking. They fixed heavy mesh on his windows and locked his door. He kicked and screamed until his mother took him into her bed. That's when the fights began. His mother and Richard yelling, throwing things, juggling accusations. He wanted to tell them that it wasn't their fault, but he was afraid if he did, the blame would shift onto him.

His ninth birthday happened on a day when their looks had grown longer and colder. Words had turned to icepicks chipping away, digging into cracks and forcing them further apart. He knew if he cut the eucalypt down, all would be back to normal. But his mother stopped him the moment he began to chop.

'If we get rid of that tree, he might find something better to do than stand staring at it,' Richard said.

'Perhaps if you took him out occasionally, he would have something better to do,' Debra said in the sweet low voice which always foreshadowed an argument

'Please don't start fighting. Listen to me, just listen for once,'

William begged. But of course they didn't hear him.

Richard's polished black shoe thumped down on the head of the axe, holding it against the ground as he nudged William back from the tree.

'You didn't have to push him,' Debra shouted.

She tried to shoulder him away. Richard moved with the shove. As Debra fell, William grabbed the axe and swung at the trunk. The blade slid across its bark and bit through the polished black shoe.

As blood oozed into the ground, the eucalypt throbbed. William could feel it and hear it. He looked into its leaves and screamed.

Debra rolled between him and the tree. Recognising the fear in her eyes, he clenched the axe tightly, demonstrating his willingness to protect her. Yet she knocked it aside as if she were afraid to take it out of his hands.

Richard stepped back, staring silently from her to him to the tree, and this was a different kind of silence. This time William wasn't caught in the vacuum between his mother and Richard. This time the absence of sound had lodged between him and them. His head drooped as Debra put her arm around Richard and helped him to the house.

The front door was cold against William's face, as icy as their silences. He slid down and sat with his back to the wall, listening to a faint mumble of voices from inside.

'He just doesn't like you,' Debra said. 'You try to be his mate when what he really needs is a father.'

William squeezed through the palings into Angus's yard. He ran along the side fence, onto the footpath and through the Lawsons' gate to tell his tale of nightly haunting to Harry.

Harry didn't laugh or swear, or point out the true nature of trees and inanimate paintings. Growing up with Henry and Curtis had taught him the futility of applying logic to nonsense. He calmed William by listening solemnly to his story. They agreed that Debra would never allow him to cut the eucalypt down, but now its branches had been trimmed it couldn't reach the roof. Provided William never went under it through the gate, it had no power to hurt him.

They walked to the beach and back while pondering a practical solution to the problem of the bush in William's bedroom. Harry finally banished the nightmares with two tins of Snow White interior gloss paint.

And while Angus sat on his roof watching them through William's window, I sat at my window watching him. I couldn't help wondering about the mind of this man as he apologised to the summer trees at every covering stroke. It was my firm belief that the boy merely wished for a little attention. The nightly haunting hadn't begun until Michael moved out. The nightmares did cease when his walls were painted white, but that was also the day Richard left and Amanda returned with Michael. It was also about the time that Maidy came back to Steeltown.

# Chapter Sixty-five

Maidy and Jamie lived in a surreal world, alternating ecstasy with exhaustion. She was very inventive, and her instincts were amazing. To make sure he gave her the same pleasure, Jamie viewed pornographic movies. He did not reveal this fact to Maidy, for he'd begun to know the curiousness of her values. Sex could be enacted, but never debated, read or viewed. She believed such practices to be disgusting, if not actually evil. This had been learned on her parents' knees. Pastor Greentree and his wife had never discussed the performance, except to preach that it couldn't be condoned except within marriage, and then only with a view to producing children.

At the end of twelve months, when satiation had set in and Jamie seemed to be always away from the house on mysterious 'jobs for the boss', Maidy began to wonder what the neighbours were saying. This introspection led to the natural progression of wondering what Debra and Steeltown were saying. Thought of Debra reintroduced the memory of dourly religious parents, of Sunday school and church, of hellfire and eternal damnation. She cleaned and cooked, scrubbed and washed, and prayed every hour all the hours Jamie stayed away. This was her idea of a daily penance.

He felt the cooling of her ardour as shame interfered, and he mourned the certainty that he would lose her to old habits and guilts if something wasn't done, and quickly.

'Let's get married,' he said one afternoon at the end of their thirteenth month together.

Maidy didn't know how or what to answer. She said the first thing that came into her head.

'I don't know what you do when you're not with me.'

'I'm a sort of private detective,' he replied. 'I work for my uncle and a couple of insurance companies.'

She tried to reason whether or not this would be a respectable way of earning a living, but her knowledge of his line of work was limited to Carter Brown.

'It's the neighbourhood we live in,' she said. 'The people are strange. They're dangerous I think. I read terrible things in the paper, and I hear things through the walls. Yet they never bother us.'

'I know people,' Jamie said.

She was afraid to ask about the kind of people Jamie knew. They were the kind who invoked respect from pimps, prostitutes, mobsters, petty criminals and the young muggers who seemed to abound within the area Jamie called home. Maidy was afraid of them. She'd become afraid of herself.

She debated the matter for a week or more, but she couldn't make up her mind to leave until Jamie revealed a side of his nature she hadn't seen before.

The doorbell rang. Maidy's toes curled inward and the hairs on the back of her neck stiffened. This was her usual reaction when those chimes echoed through the house. Most of the visitors who came to whisper through the door had this effect on her.

'I'm not expecting anyone,' Jamie said, as if he expected her to open the door.

Maidy stayed in her chair. Most of his callers were unexpected.

'Come in if I know you. It's not locked,' he yelled, forcing Maidy to move.

She opened the door a crack and peered out at a tall, short-skirted, long-legged woman with a beer-blown, slatternly look.

'Jamie there? Tell him it's Liz.'

Jamie appeared behind Maidy. Liz straightened, primped, and produced a coy smile. 'Hullo, love,' she said. 'We've got a bit of a problem you see. It's your mum. She's round at our place and we can't get her out.'

'What's she doing there? When did she arrive?' Jamie asked.

Liz shrugged. 'An hour or two. She reckons it's her house.'

'I thought she lived in a home out west,' Maidy said.

'You had her put there, did ya, love?' Liz sneered.

'She's there because she can't look after herself,' Jamie said.

'Tell that to Adrian,' Liz snorted. 'When he tried to chuck her out, she decked him with a rolling pin.'

Jamie's expression became flat and still. His voice carried an inflection which sent a shiver up Maidy's spine as he asked, 'Adrian tried to throw my mother out?'

'Come on now, Jamie. It's our place,' Liz whined. 'You sold it to us when you moved here. We paid a good price. We can have anyone in it we want. Or not have, if ya know what I mean.'

Jamie banged on the wall of the house next door. A tall, thickset man with an overgrown mane of frizzy blond hair appeared on the porch. Jamie curled a finger. The man Maidy knew only as Priceless strode onto the footpath and slid behind the wheel of a brown sedan. Jamie beckoned to Liz and slid into the seat beside him.

'I'm coming too,' Maidy called.

Jamie gave her a long hard stare, then shrugged.

Within twenty minutes they had reached a seedy little house set in a row of equally dilapidated buildings. Jamie glanced along both ends of the street before frowning up at cracked windows and peeling paint.

'Let it go a bit, haven't you?' he said to Liz.

She pretended not to hear by watching two girls stroll by. One slowed to smile an invitation. Jamie gestured curtly and she hurried on. Motioning for Priceless to wait in the car, he strode into the house. Maidy trailed Liz to the veranda then stopped, glancing nervously from Priceless to the open door. Liz shoved past Jamie and ran down the hallway to a young man dressed only in undershorts. He was leaning against a wall, holding a bloodied towel to the side of his head.

Maidy studied the woman seated at the kitchen table. She was short and plump, and had the pallid look of someone who rarely sees the sun. Her thin, greasy hair hung over eyes which stared unwaveringly at the young man. One sleeve, hanging by a few threads, flapped against an arm too thin for the size of her body. Buttons had been torn from the front of her dress, showing a good measure of breasts hanging empty and loose without the uplift of a brassiere. A dark red mark on one cheek would soon turn to a bruise.

Maidy bit down on a lip hard enough to draw blood. This Ruby, this woman Jamie's mother, was just a few years older than herself. When would she look like that?

Ruby turned and stared at Jamie. No gentleness or recognition touched her eyes.

'Mum? It's me, it's Jamie.'

'I know who you are. You're the one who put me in that home for old people.'

Maidy shuddered.

'Not old people, Mum. For sick people.'

'Old and sick in the head. You'd never have done that if my Joe was here.'

'You wouldn't talk to anyone.'

'Who would I talk to? Don who killed his own father?' Her eyes flicked Maidy then rested again on Jamie. 'I was the mother you know.'

'Don only tried to protect you,' Jamie protested.

'You think I don't know that?' Her voice slid into bewilderment before strengthening again. 'I knew why he did it. That's why I stopped talking. So I wouldn't say the things that would make him turn the gun on himself. You think I don't know me own kids? But I'm the mother.

333

It was me should've killed Joe. Not Don or you or anyone else.'

'Why didn't you tell me this before?'

'You were hell-bent on putting me away so you wouldn't have to look at me.'

Jamie shook his head. 'I couldn't take care of you, Mum. I had to work.'

'You paid good money to keep me in that place, but you couldn't pay someone to look after me until I got me head straight?' Ruby asked.

Maidy's shudder was not as strong or as apparent as the shudder passing through Jamie.

'You sent Don and the girls away so they couldn't take care of me neither,' Ruby added.

'Don went to jail, and the girls didn't want to stay here. Uncle sent them to live with the Eastmans.'

'Him!' Ruby spat. 'He's the one who had your father put in jail.'

'Uncle set the girls up with good honest men,' Jamie said. 'They didn't want to stay here.'

'Course they wanted to stay. He put them away like he put my Joe away.'

She was uncertain now. Her voice slid in and out of a scream and ended in a quaver. Jamie's head jerked, as if she had slapped him. He'd thought she had found her strength again. Now he wasn't sure.

'What is it you want?' Maidy said, trying to be his strength.

Ruby flicked her a look of malice before turning back to Jamie.

'And who might she be, ay?'

'My, um, fiancée,' he answered.

'Her?' The cackle overflowed with scorn. 'Why would you be putting your mum in an old people's home then putting another old bag in her place?'

Jamie avoided looking at Maidy. 'What do you want, Mum? Tell me and it's yours.'

'This young bloke here tried to chuck me out. Look at this.' She displayed the ripped sleeve, the open seam of her dress, the reddened cheek. 'Your dad would never have let him get away with that. Your dad might have hit me sometimes, but he never let anyone else.'

Jamie's face regained that flat, expressionless look as he turned to the younger man.

Adrian held his ground, although a nervous tic appeared over one eye. 'I bought this house fair and square,' he said defensively.

'That's all right,' Jamie almost cooed. 'I'll just buy it back. Give you ten percent on what you paid.'

'It's my house,' Ruby yelled. 'You look out there on the veranda. That's my Joe's blood on the boards. You can't see it now, but it's there. Only way I can be with him is in this house.'

'It's not for sale,' Adrian said stubbornly.

'Tell you what, Adrian,' Jamie said, cutting off his mother's protest. 'I seem to have caught you at a bad time. It's not nice to be undressed like that in front of ladies. You go and throw on some clothes and we'll talk.'

Liz and Adrian disappeared into a bedroom. Jamie smiled at the sound of a hoarsely whispered argument behind a closed door. He strolled up the hallway and signalled to Priceless.

Ruby winked as Maidy slumped into a chair. 'You just wait,' she whispered. 'Now we'll see who Jamie Blake really is.'

Liz returned moments later, sullenly defiant. 'It's our house,' she stated loudly, as if shouting would make it a truth. Her eyes already showed surrender, thus declaring the lie.

'It's my family home,' Jamie said in the same reasoning tone he'd used with Adrian. 'I should never have sold it, you do see that. It's up to me to rectify my mistake, and up to you as a friend to help me.'

'Working for Mr George don't make you nothing. It's our place and we're keeping it. Why should we hand it over to your crazy old ma?'

Liz turned and ran. Her mouth was open as if chasing the words, hoping to swallow them back before Jamie had time to hear them. She hadn't reached the door when his fingers buried in her hair. One look at his face choked off a cry for help. He released his grip and she cringed, covering her head.

Jamie stepped aside when Adrian rushed him from the bedroom.

The young man sprawled over Liz, but recovered immediately. He wasn't quick enough. A large ring on Jamie's middle finger broke his nose. A hand chopped down. The youth lay still.

Liz sprang to her feet and grabbed a carving knife, ignoring Ruby's cackle of laughter and Maidy cowering in the chair.

'You've lived too many years to start being stupid now, Liz,' Jamie pointed out. 'Put the knife down or I'll cut off your ears with it.'

The knife fell. He nodded approval.

'That's a good girl, now go and pack your bags.'

'What about Adrian?' she whispered.

'We'll just go for a ride and talk a little business. He'll be all right, won't he, Priceless?' Jamie asked as the big man shambled into the room.

Ruby clutched Maidy's arm. 'Come on,' she hissed. 'Into the car before they go without us.'

Priceless hauled Adrian across a shoulder and, after a quick glance along the street, threw him into the back seat of the sedan. Ruby lifted the youth's head onto her lap and wiped blood from his face with the hem of her dress. She explained why he should pay for his bad behaviour; but gently, and to the tune of a nursery rhyme. Maidy cringed in a corner while the car turned east.

Priceless's expression of bland good humour never changed as cars cut in and around him, slamming on their brakes inches away from his bumper, filling the streets with blue smoke and insults in the way of normal city traffic. His grimace was neither a smile nor a sneer, but just his way of whistling with a curved tongue between his teeth as a backup to Ruby's lyrics.

He pulled up beside a gateway. There he sat patiently waiting for further instructions as Jamie surveyed the scene. They had reached the Gap park, a pretty place above sheer cliffs with a magnificent view of the ocean. The street was deserted, as was a narrow path leading to the cliff top. Dusk hadn't quite arrived, but all the sightseers had left before the shadows lengthened. The Gap had never been a comfortable place after dark.

'Wakey wakey. Time to get up,' Ruby crooned as Adrian shook his head to clear his vision.

Before the youth could recognise his surroundings, Priceless hauled him out of the car, banged his head against the roof and bum-rushed him up the pathway. On the brink of the cliff, Jamie placed a hand under each of his armpits while Priceless grabbed his legs.

'I'll count to three,' Jamie said.

Adrian surrendered after the second swing, when the fingers began to slip from under his arms and the number three was much too close for comfort.

'All right, ten percent,' he yelled.

'We'll make it eleven to prove how fair I am,' Jamie said. 'You won't mind finding your own way home, will you? Give you time to consider the consequences if you're thinking about changing your mind.'

Priceless walked Adrian back to the street. He draped an arm around the younger man's shoulders to show that no personal affront had been intended. He was just doing a job that had to be done. Adrian had to agree, having done much the same job more than once for much the same employer. They parted friends, as workmates should. Adrian hurried off to telephone Liz and prove he was still alive. Priceless slid behind the wheel and waited for Jamie to finish admiring the view.

Jamie stared down at the rocks below, remembering another time and place like this. Then he had sat at the edge of Flinders Lookout for hours, blaming himself for Don going to jail. Jamie was the eldest. He should have done the deed. He should have killed the old man and saved his family. Guilt had almost thrown him over the cliff that day, but someone had to look after his mother. Yet he'd put Ruby into a home because he couldn't bear looking at her. And when Don made parole, Jamie sent him away to live with his sisters. He couldn't bear looking at any of them. They had all killed Joseph Blake, not caring that when the old man died, someone had to take his place.

'But not me. Not now and not ever,' he snarled, turning away from those grinning rock teeth which reminded him of his father.

He strode down the path and climbed into the car, sitting rigidly against the seat while trying to control his shaking hands. He had not realised, until this moment, just how much he'd wanted to watch Adrian sail over the cliff and onto the rocks.

'Well?' Ruby asked. 'Are you going to tell me what happened?'

'It's okay, Mum,' he said wearily. 'The house is yours.'

'Hah hah! Coo-wee!' she shouted, tossing back the fringe of her hair. 'I knew one of my boys would have Joe in them. Say it for me, Jamie. Say it. Hah hah, coo-wee.'

Not waiting for an answer, she ran up the pathway and dropped onto her knees at the edge of the cliff in a salaam to Joe Blake's gods of violence.

# Chapter Sixty-six

'I'm going back to Steeltown,' Maidy said that night. 'I have to make arrangements about my house.'

'There'll be a lot of talk, Maidy.'

'I have to see Debra,' she insisted.

Jamie could only hope that a few days abstinence would make Maidy remember old frustrations, or that Steeltown gossip would drive her back to him. He wasn't very hopeful when she shrank away from his kiss.

'Have I changed so much?' he asked.

'What I saw today was always there. Maybe it just takes someone like Ruby to bring it out in you.'

'You'll never see it again if you stay,' he promised.

'What are you going to do about your mother? Is she capable of taking care of herself?'

'I telephoned the home. She has her good and her bad days.'

'Was today good or bad?'

'Today was Joe Blake day,' he said wearily.

On the day Maidy returned home, she packed the rest of her belongings and hammered a For Sale sign into the front lawn. A glance up and down the street at fluttering curtains had convinced her that she couldn't stay. She couldn't live with the stares and whispers, not while the touch and feel of Jamie was in every crevice of her body, while his smell still inhabited the pores of her skin.

Debra arrived as Maidy locked the front door. The neighbours had telephoned her when Maidy refused to return their greetings.

'Well?' the daughter demanded. Her arms were folded. Her eyes glared.

'Yes, I am, thank you. Very,' the mother assured her.

'You can't leave me again at a time like this. Not so soon after Richard and I broke up. I'm miserable and it's all your fault. Everything you taught me was wrong.'

'I can't come back, Debra. You must see that. If they talk about me, they'll talk about you.'

'I told them you were visiting relatives. And then, when you still didn't come home, I said you had to have an operation. Women's problems, so they won't ask. Marianne Falls phones every second day, and Richard's mother wants you to work on her committees.'

Maidy could see her mother and father, the Church, God and the gossips standing behind Debra. She had already discovered that Jamie was the Devil. A return to that little house at Kings Cross meant turning her back on all the years of her life. She was too old to allow her previous years to be called a waste. She was almost as old as Ruby, and she did not want to be put in a home for old people sick in the head. She'd been weak, but her daughter had made her strong. Maidy Watling would return to the fold and forsake the Devil. The angels would sing. God and her parents would forgive her, and the people of Steeltown would look up to her if she served on Elizabeth Rees's charity committees.

Writing a brief note to Jamie, she enclosed it in a Bible and sent it COD.

# Chapter Sixty-seven

The years dragged on, as quiet years tend to do. The only event to mark the passing of time was the marriage of Albert Lawson to Lucy Demoska, who had been Clo's best friend during their childhood days in Sydney. Lucy had arrived with her parents, Charlie and Stella, a few months after her husband was killed in a car accident, leaving her with four children stepped in age, plus seven-year-old twins. The Demoska family bought 6 Blackwattle Road, a house with a small vineyard out the back. Our front doors faced each other.

The weekend that began more than one relationship began a few months after Amanda and Michael moved back into Debra's house, the one next door to Angus. There were four of us — Lucy, Agatha, Albert and myself — each on our own veranda watching Stella Demoska crawl around her yard. Her short plump body, clad in a brown woollen dress, was hunched in a squat. Head tucked, backside jutting, she moved over the lawn with an awkward shift of feet. At first glance this seemingly purposeless movement appeared to have no obvious destination. But as she swung back towards me, a half-step to the left and squat again, I noticed the short garden spade in one hand. She was removing bindi-eye and flatweed. Not once did she look up as she reached the path and swung around, half-step to the right and squat, and began the ritual again.

Stella had once told me, in fractured English helped by talkative hands, that physical activity was the only way to relieve a troubled mind. I knew the house must be spotless for her to venture into the yard on this particular day. Charlie had been suffering from a kidney disease for years, but he had remained confident that a organ donor and good health would arrive at any moment. Today was his day of reckoning.

Remembering this, I speculated on who would have vandalised his vines last night. More than a third of the plants had been smashed and the grapes had been trampled into the ground. Anyone in our corner of town who knew Charlie, and almost everyone did, also knew that he'd been rushed to hospital the day before. A donor had been found, a kidney implanted and Charlie was fighting his body's rejection of the new organ.

While inventing and discarding possible motives, I observed a procession of preschoolers and their mothers marching up the street. These children visited the Demoska property most weekends for the wine-tasting sessions. Grape juice of course, but the little ones didn't know the difference. A table and chairs were placed under the passionfruit canopy at the side of the house, and Charlie would pour the drink into glasses while Stella fussed over plates of biscuits.

Angus said this benevolent act was just as another way of averting future raiding parties, but the Demoskas' beaming faces showed a love of children.

Sometimes on a hot summer's night, Lucy wandered across the road looking for the kind of peace never to be found in a house full of children. We would stare out at the dark together while she spoke of something troubling her, or talked for the sake of being listened to. I rarely offered an opinion. She didn't seem to mind.

Through Lucy's ramblings, I began to know her mother. The flat picture of this dark-haired, stocky woman gradually became three-dimensional as I learned of Stella's upbringing. Her marriage to Charlie had outraged her extended family, who made up the bulk of her home village. She had been betrothed to another man at an early age. I guessed that outrage was the cause of their voyage to Australia, although Lucy insisted that her parents had journeyed here to make a future for sons who had never eventuated. This was told with an expression of guilt, as if Lucy felt she was somehow to blame for their lack of success. She was an only child.

She spoke, often with derision, of her mother's strange superstitions. She seemed puzzled by the fact that no clashes occurred between these ancient beliefs and a devout Christianity. Both parents were pillars of their church. I also wondered how Stella managed to separate the ancient earth goddess from the Christian god. I could only assume the merger, or careful division, to be similar to the blend of old country and new world in Lucy.

The procession of preschoolers, many of whom were also an integration of different cultures, lined up at the Demoska gate that weekend, all freshly washed and self-consciously pretty in their Sunday best. Each carried a bunch of flowers or a package. Stella continued to weed, ignoring them as they placed their gifts on the path then ambled away. She finally looked up when they were almost out of sight. Perhaps it was a trick of the light, or a reflection of the sun, but the red glare in her eyes jolted me.

'You didn't have to be so rude. Those kids wouldn't have smashed the vines. And anyway, these things aren't for you, they're for Poppa,' Lucy shouted at her mother.

Stella hunched closer to the ground. For a moment she was a boulder, all smooth curves and hidden crevices. A shudder ran through her body, opening her shoulders and lifting her head, and forcing out a groan from somewhere deep within. I moved further into the shadows of my veranda so she wouldn't have to avoid noticing me.

That afternoon, another procession marched up the street. These were older children and parents armed with hoes, scissors and baskets. Lucy had taken the family to visit Charlie, so I thought this second group would also disperse. Yet after a brief consultation, they filed into the vineyard. They worked all afternoon — tying up vines and picking the damaged grapes and placing them in a pile to be buried later.

As Lucy's car pulled into the driveway, Stella screamed at the workers in a shrill voice. Her grandchildren cut off the abuse by dragging her into the house. I drew back into the shade, but Lucy had felt my stare. She crossed the street and called out from the gateway.

'I thought Mumma would be furious when we found the wrecked vines, but she actually seemed relieved. That man, the kidney donor, was killed in a car accident. Mumma feels sure that it's bad luck to benefit by someone else's loss. You know, like tempting the gods. She says those people should leave well enough alone.'

'They are trespassing after all,' I said. 'She has a right to throw them out if she doesn't want their help.'

'Thank you,' Lucy said as she turned back, as if I was attempting to find excuses for her mother's behaviour. Yet I meant every word. I wouldn't think kindly of people invading my privacy, no matter what their reason.

Somewhere around 5 p.m. the workers filed down the slope from the vineyard. Stella, dressed in flowing black, met them with gestures and words to match her garments while she invited them to eat. Under the passionfruit canopy she had spread a feast large enough to feed an army. Very much the cordial hostess, she offered encouraging smiles and exquisite cuisine until her guests were sated with food and gratitude. I hadn't seen this side if Stella before, and I must admit that her stately graciousness astounded me. It comforted me to know that one need not be tall and willowy, or gorgeous and sensual, to be beautiful. And beautiful she was, enough to bring tears to my eyes and a clamping sensation to my chest.

An hour later, as she watched her guests depart, I sensed her satisfaction. Everything had been eaten. When the empty dishes had been cleared away, she paused at her door and looked over at me. I lifted a hand and inclined my head. She nodded acceptance of my message and walked inside.

Lucy scuffed across the street again and leaned against my wall.

Angus had joined me by then, but she didn't seem to notice him. Nor did she see Albert leaning against the fence, or Agatha's face framed in a bedroom window.

'Poppa's still the same. The doctors will know by tomorrow if his body will reject the new kidney,' Lucy said with a sigh. 'Mumma thinks the broken vines are some sort of payback,' she added, looking down at her feet. 'She thinks those people are forcing her to renege. Like lighting a candle at church then blowing it out to save buying another one tomorrow. She fed them as payment for fixing the vines. That cancels her debt and doesn't interfere with the sacrifice.'

'Maybe she's right,' Angus said, surprising me.

'Crap,' Lucy snorted. 'I feel like shaking her for being so bloody stupid. And I feel like taking down Poppa's old shotgun and shooting the mongrels who did all that damage. Which is exactly what I'll do if I ever catch them. Poppa thinks of those vines as something almost sacred. They're his only connection with the old country. He was a farmer there, and he's never lost the yearning to be one again.'

She burst into tears and strode away.

I couldn't be sure how Lucy or her mother would cope if there was another attack on the vines, so I decided to keep watch until Charlie had turned the corner in either direction. I had sworn to call the police if anyone so much as looked at the Demoska house. Around midnight, a barking dog sent me scurrying to the phone.

'Wait,' Angus said. 'A false alarm would only make matters worse. Let's find out for ourselves.'

We were halfway across the street when Agatha joined us. I hadn't seen or heard her until she appeared at my side. She darted an almost-smile at me before turning the last of it to Angus. He gave a brief nod, and her tread on the gravel became firm enough to be heard as we crept along the path.

Lucy stepped out in front of us. Placing a finger to her lips, she pointed towards a movement by the side of Charlie's garden shed. A hunched figure dressed in black was heading for the hill vines. We

345

followed as it flickered between the rows of plants, almost hidden by cloud shadow.

I barely managed to pull back a scream as the moon shoved its cover aside. Its light revealed Stella throwing off her own covering — an old black dressing gown I'd seen Charlie wearing on Sunday mornings. Beneath the robe she wore a cheap nylon nightgown made sheer by its copy of the moon's colour. Stretching her arms upwards, she whispered something in her own language and the words were followed by a keening wail. The sound reminded me of a fretful wind. Dropping onto her knees, she lifted her face and the palms of her hands to the sky. Her fingers curved, cupping the moon's shape. She knelt that way for a minute or so then, removing a short garden spade from the pocket of Charlie's gown, she began the beetle crawl.

Angus led the way back. I watched his heels to avoid looking at the shine of tears on Lucy's face. We had barely reached the passionfruit canopy when Albert appeared out of the gloom.

'Go home, Albert. There's nothing for you here,' Lucy said.

Albert placed a long-handled hoe in her hand and pointed towards Stella. Lucy closed her eyes for a moment, nodded slowly, then turned back to join her mother. Agatha took a pair of shears from her apron pocket and followed Lucy.

'Superstition,' Angus said disparagingly.

'Like birds with three eyes,' Albert said, looking at me.

I agreed, but refrained from saying so. For once I had nothing to say. Albert had truly surprised me. Staring across at him, I realised that his face was a coarser, stronger version of Agatha's, and it held the same expression — as though he viewed the world, or those close to him in it, and was forever disappointed by what he saw. Whether she knew it or not, Albert was the son Agatha had always wanted.

# Chapter Sixty-eight

A few months later Lucy and Albert were married, and Charlie's new kidney had decided it liked its new home. He was back to working in his vineyard two weeks after the wedding.

Albert gave up drinking and settled down to being a good husband. He worked every overtime shift available so Lucy could quit her job as cleaning lady at the university, allowing her to stay at home with the children. He joined the PTA, the Friends of the Children's Library, sundry committees affiliated with child sports, and he coached the under-nine rugby league team. Along with Harry, he was seen every weekend attending various football, hockey, basketball and swimming competitions. Albert became portly in his content, while Harry trailed him like an evening shadow. Harry was a father and husband by association only, which could not have been very fulfilling.

Out on the plains beyond the mountains, Clo continued her house-wifely duties in fits and starts. When she needed relief from the day-to-day dullness and lack of a social life, she took off for the bright lights of Sydney. Curtis and Ellie managed well enough without her, and she always returned after a week or two. Once at home, she'd retire to her bedroom and write. One journal became two, three, four, ten, a boxfull. More boxes were filled with quarto-sized paper after she brought a typewriter back from one of her trips to the city. At that time she considered most of her writing to be a learning experience, with bits and pieces that might one day lead to something better. These bits and pieces were folded into files and tucked away in boxes under Jamie's bed. It was as if she knew those years in the country were only a marking of time, and the stories she wrote merely a honing of her talent.

She and Curtis were happy enough, though sometimes they fought — more for a change of routine than from any particular animosity. Clo accused him of being a passionless man, saying she'd need to sprout leaves and a sharp smell to attract his attention. Often he thought she was right, yet the accusation was still a blow to his ego. He would yell at her, she'd break a plate over his head then they'd tumble into bed, still shouting. When the yells became moans and sighs, Ellie unlocked her door and proceeded to make dinner, or breakfast, whatever the time dictated.

Their twelve years of country living jolted to an end when pink marble was discovered in Baldy Ridge, a hill not far from the homestead. It was a stony, ridged and useless hill, unable to grow enough grass to feed cattle even in the lushest of years. Only the stunted eucalypts could find nourishment in such a profitless place. With no thought for these trees — or for the older, stronger gums which barred the pathway of trucks and machinery — the owner leased one fifth of his property to Amalgamated Quarries Pty Ltd. Curtis left on the day he discovered what Jensen had done.

When the homestead burned to a shell that afternoon, when fertiliser was discovered in the dams and cattle in the lucerne, nobody blamed Curtis. He had simply grown tired of living in the country, the neighbouring farmers said. It was time for Ellie, a charming and intelligent child, to begin high school. The private city schools had a better academic record, as everyone knew, just as they knew that Clo preferred city life. The 'accidents' were blamed on the louts working for Amalgamated Quarries — which began a feud lasting for as long as the marble.

# Chapter Sixty-nine

Although I am tempted to leave that last picture as it was framed, I realise upon a second viewing that this glossing over of unpleasant details cannot go unremarked. To reveal the true facts of the pink marble affair, I must go back to the time of my last visit to that small beef property on the western plains of New South Wales.

It was a long visit, intended to punish Angus. He had made an unkind remark about what he termed my 'bloody hypocritical sticky-beaking' when I could no longer bear the mystery of Maidy Watling. Her intermittent disappearances happened quite frequently during the two years following her first absence. Although these vanishing acts had gradually lessened to just six this year, I couldn't bear the enigma. I once tried to read an Agatha Christie novel, but I turned to the last page before reaching the third chapter.

Maidy's story of a religious retreat had been widely accepted, mainly because she always returned with a renewed fervour towards her church. Yet I noticed that on her reappearance she possessed a strange lethargy, even though her eyes seemed brighter and her skin glowed with a youthful elasticity. I suspected beauty treatments or a health clinic, though I could not substantiate these suspicions. During friendly telephone conversations with ladies who attended the same prayer meetings as her, I did learn that she travelled by train. To where and with whom, nobody knew. So I joined one of Marianne Falls's charity committees in the hope that lady might be in the possession of private information, via Amanda via Debra. It was this fact that got up Angus's nose.

I assumed that in my absence he would be forced to deal with the public to sell his plants. Unknown to me at the time, he enlisted the aid of Agatha Lawson with whom, also unknown to me, he'd begun a wary association. This was brought about when William began sneaking into Angus's yard at all hours of the day and night. If Agatha knew he was there, she'd select a corner of the garden then sit unheard and almost unseen until the child was ready to go home. Angus appreciated a woman who knew how to keep to her place, and when she grew bored with doing nothing and offered her services as a saleswoman, his nursery became the most popular in town. Agatha had the advantage of being well liked in Steeltown, especially since Henry's demise. Her new daughter-in-law had many relatives, and those relatives had many friends. They all took the opportunity of stocking their gardens while viewing the town's eccentric. Angus even managed to be polite occasionally, and offer expert if curt advice on garden management.

Back at the property known as Jensen's Place, I enjoyed myself immensely. I joined the Save Our Historical Beginnings Society and discovered, to my intense pleasure, that the elderly women in the area had their city sisters beaten hands down when it came to gossip. Within weeks I knew everything about everyone, including the little titbits about Curtis and Clo that I managed to worm out of their daughter. This proved to be of benefit to Ellie. When chastised by her parents on their discovery of her loose tongue, she learned the advantage of keeping it within her cheek.

A few weeks of my company was all Clo could bear. When Curtis disappeared on one of his sporadic walks and wasn't seen for two days, she decided on a trip to Sydney. She left on the noon train, arriving back a week later in a white sedan driven by a large and hearty man.

'This is Colin Jensen. He owns the place,' she said in an offhand manner after Ellie had been kissed, hugged and studied for signs of resentment.

I did not know how to react to this statement, so I made a pot of tea. Between munching biscuits and sipping from my cup, I endeavoured to discover where Clo had stayed during that visit to Sydney. She remained smilingly though decidedly uncommunicative, and my curiosity bordered on the importune. I ignored Colin Jensen, deciding that the man was a little slow-witted when he merely stared in answer to my questions. Driven to desperation, I finally asked Clo the question without bothering to add the usual frills.

'Where did you stay while you were away?'

Before Clo had time to answer, Mr Jensen cut in with, 'This is interesting. Where did you find it?'

He was studying a large rock which I'd been using as a mud-scraper at the back doorway. Caught up in my concern for Clo's welfare (I hated to think of her wandering around a dangerous city like Sydney on her own) I forgot that Curtis had instructed me to throw the rock away and forget where I'd found it.

'I picked it up in the village,' Clo said before turning to me. 'As a matter of fact, Liona, I stayed at the Cross with Jamie.'

I did not doubt her. Clo never lied. At least, I had never caught her in a lie. And I knew about her friendship with Jamie. I knew about Curtis's business association with Jamie's uncle. In fact, upon hearing of the success of that association, I arranged for the uncle to invest my small capital. I am not materialistic, no more than the next person, but I hope to live a long life free of monetary worries. And I know a good thing when I see it.

All this had nothing to do with those current events, but I am trying to make the point that I was sure Clo had told the truth. She knew I had no equal at worming facts out of people like Jamie. Although street-wise, he was exceptionally naive when confronted with a master in the art of devious questioning. She knew Jamie and I had become friends. He often stayed at my house when he had business in

Steeltown. He had taken a liking to me because, he said, I reminded him of his mother. I was aware of Ruby Blake's questionable mentality, but I also knew he was very fond of her, so I accepted the compliment at face value.

Clo smiled at me and added, 'At the Cross with Jamie and Maidy.'

'Whereabouts in the village?' Colin Jensen wondered aloud.

'Maidy? Maidy Watling?' I asked.

At that time I had no inkling of the Maidy and Jamie affair. I decided then and there to patch up my differences with Agatha. No doubt she knew all the bits and pieces.

'Where did you say?' Mr Jensen persisted.

'I found it on a hill over that way.' I gestured vaguely. 'You do mean Jamie Blake?' I inquired of Clo.

'He's the only Jamie I know,' she said.

I knew the relationship couldn't be platonic, not if Maidy Greentree Watling was involved. Maidy had been cute as a child, stunning as a young woman, and even now had not deteriorated into handsome — as most people like to call a fading beauty. In my opinion, a woman like that just naturally had to have a sluttish disposition.

Mr Jensen had the audacity to grab my arm. 'Where exactly is this hill?' he demanded.

I shook him off. 'That way. Baldy Ridge or something. Is Maidy staying with Jamie?'

Clo cut in. 'Baldwin Ridge, I assume. On the Hillson property the other side of town. Yes Liona, Maidy often visits Jamie in Sydney.'

'Baldwin Ridge. Never heard of it,' Colin Jensen said. 'This is pink marble. Worth a bloody fortune. Where's Baldwin Ridge again?'

'Maidy and Jamie, fancy that. Baldy Ridge is behind your west dam. So that's where Maidy goes when she disappears,' I said.

Clo took my arm. 'We'll take a stroll and I'll tell you all about it. And Colin, I really think you should leave now if you want to miss the peak-hour traffic.'

I looked from Clo to Mr Jensen and finally realised that I had spoken out of turn.

'Yes, it does get busy. You could be held up for hours,' I said. 'Not here, really, but when you reach Katoomba.'

'Then I'll take off. Don't mind if I borrow this rock, do you?'

Glancing from Ellie's questioning eyes to Clo's barely concealed anger, I sought an escape route. 'Look, Mr Jensen, Colin, would it be putting you out to ask for a lift to Sydney? I can catch a fast train from there. Angus will be worried about me. I should have returned weeks ago.'

'I'll second that,' Clo said nastily.

I was already hurrying into the spare room to throw my belongings into a bag.

When I telephoned the next afternoon, Ellie answered my call. The girl knew something was wrong, but she had no idea what. Curtis had arrived home some hours after my departure, tired and dirty from days in the bush, and more annoyed by Clo's leaving Ellie alone with me than by her coming back from the city with Colin Jensen. Ellie could not understand why her mother screamed something about spending the week with Mr Jensen. She knew Clo had stayed with Jamie. They'd had a three-way conversation on the phone every second night.

Once or twice, when Curtis had gone bush before, Clo later confessed to being with Mr Rigby. Ellie had instantly recognised the lie. Ellie had stayed with her friend Candice Rigby many times, including the night Clo was supposed to be there when the family were supposed to be away. And once Curtis said that he was with Mrs Rigby when Ellie knew this to be another lie.

She did not know why these false confessions hurt her parents so much. She couldn't understand why they lied. She only knew that they did, and their house would be cold and strangely quiet for many weeks. She decided it was a grownup thing, this biting and scratching at each other with words, and learned to stay out of the way by retreating into her bedroom when the battles began.

The worst battle, the one that returned them to Steeltown, began a few weeks before Christmas.

# Chapter Seventy

Curtis lay sprawled under the shade of a eucalypt, staring into the heat haze. On a day like this, when the temperature hovered around forty degrees and a gathering of black clouds signified a coming storm, his mind would wander into fantasy. He pictured a bush baby in every gumnut. He saw ancient warriors in the shadows, and a nightmare monstrosity in the round-legged straddle of a small goanna. The banksia seeds were eyes belonging to flickering, stick-like little people who cared for the lost and lonely. He could feel the rich velvet of their clothes in some leaves, their spears and daggers in others. The colours of their party cloaks were in the gumtips.

A crow fluttered down to investigate the goanna. The bird saw Curtis at the last moment and launched itself into the air, uttering a caw of protest. The lizard flattened and became absolutely still. It stared at Curtis with unblinking eyes, reminding him of the way Ellie sometimes chose a corner of the room to sit quietly when an argument erupted. Clo was the crow, forever squawking. Whenever he went walking in the bush, she abused him for going then in the same breath said she was pleased to have him gone.

Life on the property did have its drawbacks. They were constantly in each other's company, with no one to force politeness or cause a diversion when they grew bored. With little to do except count a few cows, mend a fence occasionally and tidy the house, this happened often enough. Ellie had school and friends to keep her occupied. Curtis had his plants and planting. All Clo had was her scribbling, which became annoying when it kept her locked in a room during the days he wanted to talk. Every so often an argument would erupt. Usually over nothing in particular. Then Clo would take off to the city for a week or two and return brimming with easy conversation. Or Curtis would pack a backpack and wander the bush. Without these separations, their life would be one long fight. They had nothing in common except their love for Ellie and each other. They needed to be apart to renew their need.

He'd been gone for over a week. Lovemaking would be new and good again, and Ellie would want to hear everything he'd seen and done. It was time to go home. Grabbing his backpack, he set out at a run.

An hour later, he paused at the highway gate to collect the mail and was surprised to find a letter from Colin Jensen. Jensen usually phoned.

Curtis tore through the envelope. The words in the letter tore through him. Baldy Ridge would be leased to Amalgamated Quarries. They were going to mine the pink marble.

He strode through the door of the homestead. His tone accused as he said, 'Colin Jensen is leasing Baldy Ridge. They're going to quarry the marble.'

Ellie opened her mouth, but Clo shouted her down.

'And how do you think he found out?'

'Was it before? Or after, when you go all soft and cosy?' Curtis sneered.

'Colin complained about being down to his last million, so I told him how he could make a fortune from this stinking dead hole of a place,' Clo snarled.

Curtis turned away. 'You won't be bored any more. We're going back to Steeltown.'

'So you're using this thing with the marble as an excuse to run back home. Don't like the idea of William being so close to Agatha, do you?' she shouted.

He swung back. 'At least his mother doesn't go bed-hopping every time she's feeling itchy.'

'What do you know about mothers? What do you know about parents? You helped one to die and you treat the other as if she's dirt, then wonder why she's not interested in you any more. She has William now. She admits to her own blood.'

'They're going to quarry the bloody marble!' he shouted.

'That isn't my problem,' Clo said, quieter now, knowing he'd refuse to talk of anything else. 'I'm going to Sydney and I'm taking Ellie with me.'

'Like hell you are,' Curtis snapped.

'Like hell I'm not!'

'Please don't start fighting,' Ellie begged. 'It wasn't Mum's fault.'

Curtis finally saw the look on his daughter's face.

'It's all right, baby,' he soothed. 'We'll get together at Steeltown. You'll like it there, just wait and see. The schools are better than here. Mum likes the towns better, you know that, and Dad just wants to go home.'

'Mum didn't tell Mr Jensen,' Ellie began, but Curtis was already striding away.

When he was sure they had gone and couldn't stop him, Curtis herded cattle into the lucerne paddocks and dumped barrow loads of fertiliser into the dams. When that was done he gazed thoughtfully at a narrow creek running through the property. Ruining its purity was beyond his power, but the quarry would manage that. Just as they would destroy most of the trees with machinery and human pollution.

Later, alone in the house, he used the image of Colin Jensen and Clo to build up his rage again. Upon that he piled images of Clo with a parade of faceless naked bodies. He heaped them into a bonfire shape, helped along with papers, broken chairs and old boxes. Kerosene drowned the smell of sweat and sex. Thought of those trees on Baldy Ridge erased any guilt he might have felt. If Colin Jensen could destroy the history in those trees, it was only fair to destroy the Jensen history in this house.

Curtis threw a match onto the pile and walked away, not staying to watch it burn.

The highway became no more than a memory of blinking white lines as he looked down from the Steeltown escarpment, deciphering the dots of houses, the dashes of lawns and the scribble of roads leading up to the crowded scrawl of the city proper. The lighthouse stood guard over white-capped water resting its edges on sand and spreading to the haze which hides the edge of the world. Over a dozen iron ore and coal carriers waited to enter the harbour. Their mammoth size dwarfed the fishing boats, which were made to look cumbersome by a fleet of white-sailed yachts. The lighter blue of the lake to the south was framed by ocean, land and the mighty sprawl of the steelworks. And there was home, just a few kilometres away. Buried among hundreds of other ant houses, but it was there. Home. He turned and sprinted to his car.

# Chapter Seventy-one

The day after her hasty departure, Clo borrowed Jamie's red convertible and drove back to Jensen's Place. She was determined to have it out with Curtis. This business of accusations and counter-accusations no longer amused her. It had been fun once. It gave them an excuse to be away from each other for a while, which was something they had always needed, and the reconciliations led to hours of glorious sex. But if he knew her at all, he must know that she wasn't interested in having affairs. Not since their marriage. Not with Jensen or anyone else. Somehow, some way, she must convince Curtis that it was time to have peace in their lives. For themselves, but most of all for their daughter. Ellie was the one being hurt.

In contrast to her usual lead-foot style, she kept to the speed limit as she drove, planning what to say. Yet Clo knew better than anyone that as far as Curtis was concerned, setting a plan was a wasted effort. It all depended upon whether he was feeling sorry for the things he'd said, or if he had worked himself into one of his obstinate rages.

At the turn-off to the homestead, she slammed on the brakes, amazed to find the main gate open. If the cattle wandered onto the highway they were going to cause a horrendous accident. The speed limit on this road was a hundred kilometres. She distinctly remembered closing that gate yesterday. Luckily, there wasn't a cow in sight.

Driving down the track, she glanced to her right and saw the trampled lucerne paddock. The cattle had broken in. Or someone had let them in. How could this happen?

Even before she turned her head to the left and saw the homestead, she knew. She wanted to scream and cry and curse him with every vile curse in her vast vocabulary of curses, but all she felt was a strange kind of numbness.

The sandstone walls, the chimneys and the veranda floor had endured, although they were blackened and scarred. Clo wondered about the ghosts — the woman in the front room, the maid, the Irisher out back. Dougal had never stopped insisting that they existed. Would they wander this place now, or would Curtis's vandalism (for what else could you call it) have freed them? Perhaps they had gone with him. Perhaps they would stay with him forever and make his life as miserable as theirs had been. It was a gratifying thought.

Whoever had fought the fire — probably the neighbouring farmers — had pulled away the twisted iron roofing sheets to search for anything that might have survived. Nothing had. The fire had been too fierce. She could smell the kerosene.

Trudging through the ruins, Clo poked among the charred furniture for the skeletons of a twelve-year marriage. She found nothing to prove it had ever existed. Even photographs recording the events of Ellie's childhood had been destroyed. Nothing remained of her life with Curtis.

She tried to cry. She could not. Her mouth was as dry as her eyes, but she could do something about that. She ran down the track, urged on by her thirst and a need to be away from the devastation behind her. He hadn't been able to spoil the purity of the creek. Grateful for that, she gulped down handfuls of water until her stomach rebelled. When it did, she threw up most of what she'd drunk then lay in the deepest part of the creek, scrubbing her clothes and hair with eucalypt leaves until the smell of smoke and kerosene and vomit had been washed away.

Clean of these stinks at last, she staggered to the nearest willow tree, curled up on the grass and slept. Though later, when she'd had time to think about it, she decided that her mind had simply shut down for a while. Self-preservation, she thought.

An hour or so before dawn, she climbed the hill to the settlers' cemetery and sat on the end of Dougal's grave. It was then the tears came, and she cried until a magpie perched in the tree over her head and sang the sun into existence.

Staring up at the magpie, she remembered the one that had dive-bombed her head on the day of her arrival at Jensen's Place. She remembered the bird who had led her to Dougal on the day he died.

'So it's you again, is it?' she told it. 'Well I hope you're satisfied, because I'm going and I won't be back. But maybe you know that already. Maybe that's why you're singing.'

Turning its head sideways, it studied her for a moment then, after one last yodel, flew off in the direction of the highway.

'I get the message,' Clo said, smiling tiredly.

Wiping her face on her skirt, she stood and stretched warily, groaning at the pain in stiff limbs, in a head that felt as if it was stuffed with straw. When she could walk without it hurting too much, she cut across the lucerne paddock to avoid the homestead. Keeping her eyes averted from the blackened ruin, she climbed into the car, swung it in a dirt-spraying circle and flattened the accelerator.

# Chapter Seventy-two

On the day Curtis returned to Steeltown, he came straight to me. I would not allow him to blame Clo for the pink marble affair, although I couldn't give him an alternative. Truth might have been in my memory, but I refused to remember. Aside from Angus, Curtis was all I had.

Had Angus not been in the garden with William, Curtis might have had the advantage of an alternative viewpoint. Angus might have flattened the mountains into decent sized molehills. He might have read the lie of the land and altered the direction of darkness and light with his own perceptions. But Angus was in the garden with William.

I did not point out the For Sale sign on Debra's front lawn with any notion of spiting Clo, or of clinging to Curtis. My motivation was the salvation of the eucalypt by the gate. I knew he had a particular fondness for that tree. I also knew that an unsympathetic buyer would cut it down. It towered over the footpath and house, filled the guttering with debris. Occasionally, for no apparent reason, it dropped branches on unwary joggers. A pair of aggressive magpies had nested among its leaves.

Curtis approached the house where Amanda and Michael now lived with Debra and William. Amanda answered the door and invited him in with that same half-curious, half-knowing smile he remembered so well. Michael greeted him with a grin and a handshake before leaving for football training. Curtis was struck again by the boy's similarity to Richard.

He made a generous offer for the house, and Debra agreed without hesitation. She was sure he could afford to pay a good price, although she had no idea just how rich he'd become. Even Curtis was only vaguely aware of the extent of his assets. George Eastman Blake had invested wisely.

Noting the eagerness of her acceptance, Curtis realised that neither Amanda nor Debra was financially stable. Amanda had gained recognition for her poetry, but food and clothing are not purchased with accolades. Debra had refused any help from Richard, and she now stacked shelves at the local supermarket. So Curtis added another two levels to the offer. Fifty thousand dollars extra if she would sell the contents along with the house, and a weekly allowance for William's clothing and education. When Debra hesitated, he offered the same allowance for Michael. Amanda agreed without coyness. She'd been born to a wealthy family. Money had no special meaning to her. Amanda pleaded poverty for the sake of image, but she'd never known want.

The contracts were signed, and Curtis sent for Ellie and Clo. Ellie arrived with Jamie the following evening. Clo stayed away for weeks. On the day she finally arrived to meet the brick wall of his expression, she told him to go to hell.

# Chapter Seventy-three

To go back in time was impossible. This was here and now, and the here and now had to be surmounted. Here was back in Steeltown where Clo had never wanted to be — and in a house holding the paraphernalia of another woman's experiences. The paintings were that other woman's choice. The wallpaper was her taste. The marks on the furniture belonged to her ghosts.

Clo wondered if a three-cornered stain on the lounge could be coffee or wine. More stains on the old-fashioned doilies were evidence of food spilt years ago. Dozens of figurines decorated every nook; all preciously pretty and useless, as if chosen by a child. Rows of smudged watercolours and childish drawings of dogs, cats and rabbits hung on the hallway walls.

Perhaps she, the other woman, had hidden them away years ago and only brought them to light when she found a place of her own.

The linen press held a large box containing more watercolours. In these paintings of dogs, cats and rabbits, every animal was horned and clawed. A rolled bundle of pencil drawings depicted a tree as the background to a large man and an even larger woman, both holding the hands of an undersized child. In each of these drawings the tree grew progressively more towering.

Clo knew these things had been deliberately left behind as proof of previous ownership. She couldn't be sure whether the claim was on Curtis or the house. She realised that she didn't really care. She'd come back for Ellie's sake, and for that last little flicker of hope that she and Curtis could make their marriage work. If they could go back to the early years of their relationship, then the effort would be worthwhile.

The second bedroom, the one allocated to Clo, was a cold bare room. The scratched and scarred floor showed chips of brown beneath white paint. A wind whistling through the gapped and twisted floorboards carried a smell of mildewed earth. The furniture had been painted white to match the walls, with no decoration to lift the hospital look. Security mesh on the window cast shadow patterns of bars and whorls on the shiny white plastic blind. The first time Clo entered this room, she noticed that the locks were on the outside.

Who needed to be locked in, she wondered, and why am I allowing myself to be locked away now? You know the mother, Jamie; do you know the daughter? Did she paint those pictures or do they belong to William? He rides past this place on a bicycle, always fast and never looking, at least a dozen times a day. I called out to him once, but he wouldn't stop. Ellie says he's a shy boy. And what can I say about Curtis? Better if he were like other Australians and looked to bushrangers or sportsmen for his heroes, instead of giving his reverence to trees. Visit me, Jamie, as often as you can. I could go mad in this house. Depressed and miserable like her. Or is it him?

Clo shrugged as the question bounced back from the bare white walls. She was talking to herself again. A sure sign of madness, they say. But who else did she have to talk to until Jamie came? And he would. Jamie never failed her. He would be picking up on her now, listening to her mumbling to herself as if she were talking on a phone. Jamie with his perpetual look of surprise. Jamie with those thin strong fingers rubbing her neck, her shoulders, her back, prodding and poking until they hurt, but somehow untying knots which were really somewhere else. Thank God she only loved him in a loving way and not that other way, the one to do with wanting and sweating and thorns and flowers and thunder. The way she had once loved Curtis.

# Chapter Seventy-four

A month after arriving back in Steeltown, Curtis bought a hectare of ground close to the mountains. Days later he began a nursery specialising in native shrubs and trees. He organised a Save Our Local Flora Day, decorating three large floats with waratahs and wattle, flame trees, cabbage palms and all the various shrubs and ground covers which had been usurped by plants introduced from other countries. The parade ended at the beach and a free carnival for the children. It was an unqualified success; the council combined it with a Buy Local and Save Our Jobs Day and turned into an annual event.

He planted casuarinas, banksias, silky oaks, lilli pillies, melaleucas and grevilleas in local parks and gardens at a nominal cost. Those who would plant eucalypts were given free trees (labour for planting supplied). Pensioners with a gum tree by their gate gained a dinner every six months, courtesy of Curtis Lawson Landscapes. Schools with a stand of eucalypts in their grounds won the installation of free alarms.

Angus accused Curtis of trying to fill Steeltown with trees in the hope of crowding out the people. When he growled about the competition, Curtis bought him out and made him gardener-in-charge. He was paid a good wage, he never had to deal with the public, and Curtis always asked his advice in all things pertaining to plants.

They worked well together, as they always had — digging, weeding, sowing, and arguing over the amount of peat and sand to be added to the soil in order to gain the best results. They discussed pest control, pruning, grafting, and how to properly mulch a backyard garden. In fact they talked about everything except people. Curtis avoided this particular topic, just as he evaded personal contact with everyone except Angus, Ellie and myself. Yet when Michael began calling in on his way home from school, he was greeted affably enough, unless William happened to be with him. Then Curtis would find something to do on the other side of the nursery. After three or four visits when he was politely but firmly ignored, William began to leave Michael at the gate. Sometimes I would see him riding his bike along the highway which wound up and over the mountain.

# Chapter Seventy-five

William hid his bike in the long grass and jogged away at right angles from the road. Workmen had straightened a sharp bend on the highway, leaving the original layer of bitumen to form a wide black scar running alongside the cliff edge. Between this disused remnants of a road and the cliff top stood piles of gravel, and boulders which hadn't been bulldozed over the incline. William threaded his way through this debris to a machete-cleared trail cutting down and across the slope. This track ended at his special place: a shallow tunnel dug into the mountain by a long forgotten hermit.

When William had found this place, he'd cut down the surrounding saplings to form a clear space. He then carried boxes into the cave to store his sketchbooks and diaries. During the past few months this place had become his home away from home. It was somewhere he could sketch or read without being disturbed, or just sit and let his mind wander. If he did any of those things in his mother's house, she'd accuse him of being bored. Then she'd insist on sitting close and talking. That always ended in tears after she'd worked herself into a frenzy over the loneliness of her life since Amanda started spending most of the week at Sydney University. The tears usually turned to a harangue against Ellie and Clo. 'Blaming them for her own bad choices where Curtis was concerned,' Amanda had said.

William had grown up without a physical father, yet everywhere he looked he saw Curtis. Curtis showed in his mother's waking dreams, in her face staring through the window at the eucalypt, in her shrill cries and pummelling fists. She had never hurt him, not with the blows. They were mostly aimed at his back. She stopped hitting his head after Angus caught her in the act. William didn't know what Angus had said, but her blows had been kinder after she talked to Angus. Hours later, she came back from that talk and cried on William's shoulder.

William realised long ago that she loved him more than she'd ever loved Curtis. The trouble was, she blamed him for what she said was the Curtis in his eyes.

Thoughts of his mother receded to the back of his brain when he reached his place. He hadn't been here for over a month. In that short space of time terrible things had happened. Tree roots had reached down into his cave, trying to discover the who and what of William Lawson. And the saplings were springing up again, closer and thicker. If he allowed the eucalypt's friends to move in, he was back to nowhere and nothing.

He grabbed up an old machete rescued from the local dump. He had spent hours honing its blade to a razor-sharp edge, and it rewarded his care by fitting snugly into his hand.

'My place. Mine!' he yelled as the blade sliced through the saplings, cutting their trunks close to the ground. But the ease of the killing blunted his perceptions. The smell of leaking sap turned his usual watchfulness to a frenzy.

Sprinting to the ledge above his cave, he attacked the wind-twisted gum squatting there. He knew it reached down with its toes, learning about his dreams so the eucalypt could invade his nights once more. The blade bit deeply, but when he tried to pull it out for another blow, the tree refused to let go. William shoved and pulled, using all his weight. The machete snapped cleanly just below the handle. A flurry of leaves scratched across his face.

That tree thought it had beaten him, but William wasn't so easily defeated. Careful not to stray beneath the old, wise eucalypts, he gathered armfuls of dead leaves and hauled a rotten log across the clearing. He tore up his diaries and sketchbooks, not wanting them now that the tree had seen them. Onto the crumpled pages he added the termite-bored wood more combustible than paper. Building a mound large enough to fill the cave, he threw a match to it then continued adding sticks and logs. The tunnel became a huge oven, baking the mountaintop until the earth rumbled a protest. As the nearby trees hissed and crackled, he capered and danced and matched their groans with laughter.

William underestimated the spirits of those trees, although he couldn't be sure whether the fire tumbled out of the cave, or the old gum leaned forward to take the flames onto its head in a willing sacrifice.

The tallest eucalypt, a four-hundred-year-old creature with more twists and gnarls than a madman's mind, exploded with a roar of triumph. The heat intensified, sucking William's skin dry before he had time to break into a sweat. He could smell his hair singeing. Blisters erupted along his arms and legs. He screamed in fear of this monster he'd released, knowing it was closing in on him. Yet he dared not run among the trees.

'Run, you bloody idiot!'

Two youths around his own age raced across the clearing, grabbed his arms and pulled him along a narrow track he had never explored. The only path he'd ever dared to tread was the machete-cleared trail from the highway.

'Run!'

The yell came again as he stumbled and fell. A hand hauled him upright and shoved. He stared fixedly at the back of the boy in front so he wouldn't see the monster trying to outpace them. It chased them down the mountain, swallowing bracken and bush in great gulps and spreading sideways in an effort to outflank them. It leapt across treetops to bombard them from above. It shot fireballs from the cannons of exploding eucalypts in an effort to cut off the forward avenue of escape.

They hurtled down the narrow track, stumbling, sliding, falling; ducking tongues of flame licking out at their heads from overhanging branches. Twice they leapt through a small space between meeting flames, thinking they were safe as they raced across thick dead leaves which had not yet begun to smoulder. Each time, the flames raced in from their left, trying to turn them back to the heart of the fire. They veered and sprinted and leapt again, urged on by the roar immediately behind them.

The cleared acres of a new subdivision saved their lives. The fire brigade saved the homes beyond the subdivision.

William and his new-found friends continued to run until they reached the first row of houses. One of the youths — a tall, fair-skinned boy now covered in blisters — grabbed a hose and turned its spray into the air. They sat underneath it, passing the hose from hand to hand like a bong at a Saturday night party.

'Look at that!' the fair boy yelled as he shook a fist at the fire. 'I've had those plants for two years now. They've all gone up in smoke.'

The other youth — short and dark and wearing little more than a stunned, disbelieving look — held up a hand.

'Listen! I can hear somebody screaming.'

'The only screaming I can hear is me bloody weed crying for help. I've been taking care of it like a baby,' the blond boy groaned.

'The trees are singing,' the other youth said before he passed out.

The blond shot William a look of disgust. 'Why wouldn't they be singing?' he asked. 'I know six guys got their weed planted up there. And that's only the ones I know. The flaming mountain's as high as a kite. Half its bloody luck,' he added before he too passed out.

But William knew the real reason the trees were singing. They thought they had taken his place.

A week later, as he walked up the trail shown to him by the marijuana growers, the blackened trunks and denuded arms barely noted his passing. That's when William discovered that, next to men with axes, fire was the greatest enemy of trees. If the monster could be tamed by a cleared space, and held on the leash of good management, its flames would be his friend. So he widened the small clearing to make a new place, and he held back the trees with fire.

Sometimes, when his mother flew into a frenzy after sighting Clo in the home that had once belonged to her, he thought about using his new ally there. Two foes with one match — the other woman and the eucalypt. Three things stopped him. The first was his respect for fire. If it was feeling particularly nasty it would swallow the whole block, including Angus's and Liona's houses. The second was Ellie. He knew she was somebody special. He could tell by the way Curtis smiled at her. The third was a promise that Grandma Agatha had made many years ago. That one day Curtis would know him.

# Chapter Seventy-six

Had Curtis been poor he might have been called crazy, but a man with the Midas touch is called merely eccentric. Within five years he had nurseries throughout the state. He funded a local centre for the study of Australian flora, another to research the growing of hybrids to suit all countries and climes. He set up trust funds to provide scholarships for anyone talented in the protection and analysis of the environment. Despite the fact that he had never studied horticulture at any academic level, and he'd never been even slightly interested in the advancement of humanity, he became known as a landscape architect and philanthropist of the highest degree.

Although fast becoming one of the wealthiest men in our city, he continued to potter in his nursery, which now covered far more ground on the lower mountain slopes. The original site was a storehouse for seedlings ready to be sent interstate. He stocked an old tin shed tucked away at the back of this store with various tinned and boxed food, a few old pots and pans, enamel plates and mugs, cutlery that looked as if it had been scrounged from the local garbage dump, and two canvas camping beds.

Angus stayed in the hut occasionally, yet more often than not it was Curtis who spent his nights in that place. To get an early start or because he was finishing late, he said if asked, although most questions were frowned into apologies for being impertinent.

Sometimes Ellie stayed with him. Learning the trade, she said. At other times Michael Falls occupied the second bed. Except for Angus, and possibly Jamie, Michael was closer to Curtis than any male since the friendship split with Richard Rees.

Since she'd become a university student, Amanda barely acknowledged her son. Although his postal address was the townhouse shared with Debra and William, he could usually be found in the house where Clo and Ellie (and sometimes Curtis) lived. Michael and Ellie were often seen together, joking and laughing in the manner of brother and sister. Yet very few people thought of them as siblings. Amanda's series of lovers had weakened her claim against Curtis.

More surprisingly, at least to me, was the camaraderie that existed between Michael and Clo. He made no secret of his admiration, leaping to defend any slur against her name with the caustic tongue inherited from his mother. Clo accepted his attention as she accepted most things — with a teasing disregard or casual indifference, as if his affection could only be a temporary whim. Yet except for Lucy Lawson, and Jamie of course, for a number of years he was probably her only friend. I suppose I could add my name to that extremely brief list, but my connection with Clo was more a meeting of minds than hearts.

The seven trunks of books, passed down from Constance Mayberry to my mother to me, were now a mere fragment of my collection. Most walls of my rather large house were hidden behind piles of novels — literary and mainstream of every genre — and every possible classification of nonfiction. When Clo discovered what she called my treasure trove, her visits to my house became frequent. She would browse for hours, and sometimes borrow. Every so often we would while away an afternoon conferring on what she had read, or what she might like to try next. Of course we endeavoured to avoid those conversations bordering on the personal, but philosophical discussions too often slid in that direction. Although only in a shadowy way, I began to see in and out of those stone angel eyes. And I believe

Clo came to see in and out of mine. We didn't always like what we saw, but we did develop an understanding.

Jamie continued to visit Steeltown every fortnight or so, sometimes staying for days at a time. He occasionally dined with Angus and myself, but his nights were invariably spent next door. This delighted the gossips, even though his long association with the whole family was generally known. For a year or two, as the rumours thickened and became multilayered, Clo added a few of her own. No doubt she hoped to force Curtis into staying at home. But as the months ticked by and he continued to spend more and more time in the shack at back of the store, she seemed to lose all interest in him.

# Chapter Seventy-seven

The years had gone, more than five now, and she was still where she had never wanted to be.

'Throw Debra's things into the shed out back,' Curtis had said; and so she did, along with most of her own possessions.

The walls in her room were still bare and white, but she'd coloured the wardrobes blue to match the new carpet. She did consider taking down the mesh covering the windows, but she rather liked the shadows it cast. One day, when she found the time, she would fill in those patterns with colours to match her bedspread.

Clo had spread her bed with the quilt she'd made from bits and pieces of her life. Sometimes she'd sit for hours, running her hands across patches of her red wedding suit, the green skirt worn on the day Jensen's Place burned down, the white dress she wore to her mother's funeral. A piece of her mother's cream wedding outfit was there, stitched to a strip of the dress she'd worn on the day Clo demanded to join her in this world. Bits and pieces of Ellie were as easy to see as the sun — Ellie's favourite colour being yellow.

The once bare room now contained the paraphernalia of Clo's life. The quilt, the curtains Great Grandma had made from fragments of the clan's life, the desk, the typewriter and paper, journals and pens; these were all she needed. And she possessed her own phantoms now — the real ones, and the others from her imagination.

Sometimes she saw them clearly, the ghosts of things and people left behind. Kids throwing balls against the biscuit factory wall. A magnolia tree swarming with bees and an overpowering smell she had never liked. Great Grandma, solid as a rock, with her great grandmotherly backside spread across that huge chair while she measured out the herbs. Only the herb smell could prevail against that of the magnolia. Eva Gatley, her mother, who still made Clo cry when she thought of all the things they hadn't done together.

Her father was there, but he was hardly more than a recollection of blue eyes in a sun-brown face. He'd walked out on his family when Clo was twelve. She'd never found out why.

There were enough men to make her feel abashed at their number, and sometimes as horny as hell. Dennis Robertson had been her first lover — if an awkward fumbling in the dark could be called an act of love. Yet she could never quite see his face. The other men were distorted reflections of Curtis. Yet staring at the mirror returned her through the years. She could look at these men out of the face of various ages, all the way back to fourteen. Wrinkle free then, with the waxy skin and shining eyes of a girl just discovering the secrets her body. She had succumbed to Dennis's pleas from simple curiosity. Now she saw the outline of his face turned from her in shame at himself and disgust at his seed shining on her legs. They had not held hands or talked, and when he left her at the gate, she was glad he'd gone.

Closing her eyes, she could easily picture the white dress with its tiny mauve flowers and the back stained with blood; stained with the metallic smell of blood and Dennis's juice, sticky on her fingers as she rolled all of it — the dress, the bras and panties — into a ball and shoved the bundle down among greasy chop bones and vegetable peelings in the garbage.

She told all this to Jamie and he listened quietly, never commenting while he rubbed her neck and shoulders with those unknotting fingers.

The phantoms from her imagination were less hurtful than the ghosts from her past. Although at times they kept her awake at night, arguing with the plot, refusing to do as she asked, insisting that the words she had written were not their way and she must find a more natural path for them to follow. Old friends were annoyed at being pushed aside for others, the ones in short stories being published more frequently now. Yet those old friends were always there, waiting to come forward and fill her mind with thousands of words to form into a novel. When she was ready, they would fill their places in her mind, her heart, on paper. And one day, on bedside tables and bookcases.

'Don't shut out your living friends,' Jamie had said as she drew into herself, shutting them out, not wanting to wear their burdens or share herself with them.

Yes, there was Jamie. Always Jamie. And Ellie not yet her friend, but who would one day be as close as Clo should have been with Eva and Janet. Michael Falls, not much more than a child, but who could resist those eyes filled with admiration? And Amanda Falls, closer in kind than either cared to admit. Literature was their link, their conversation; but each saw parts of herself in the other. Lucy Demoska, Lawson now, would not be turned away. And strangely enough, Liona and Angus and Albert. Even stranger was a growing affection for Agatha.

Hungry for details about Curtis's life in the country, Agatha had forced herself to tread Clo's path to the porch. After an hour of thrusts and quick withdrawals, and the tentative word play usual between women who did not know each other, they had drunk tea and spoken of scenery and Ellie. On the second visit they spoke of Clo's childhood friendship with Lucy, and Agatha's fondness for the whole Demoska family. Through marriage, that family belonged to Albert, too.

On the third visit their sparring session was shorter, and milder now as neither had much heart for it. At first annoyed by Agatha's turning aside verbal barbs by pretending not to hear them — and by knowing they weren't thrown with the intention of wounding but just for the hell of it anyway — Clo realised that the older woman's expertise had been gained through years of practice. Agatha was an attractive woman. She had been a pretty child. Such a child raised by mostly unattractive elderly spinster ladies would need to invent a shield at an early age. A blank look and a sudden lack of hearing always proved the best buffer for a pretty girl. Clo had used this defence many times. Usually against street-corner boys, cafe cowboys, Curtis and her father.

By the fifth visit, the shields and barbs had been put away. The long silences narrowed to pauses for breath. Agatha spoke of Curtis as a child — a subject that often led to talk of Henry, Albert and Harry. To her surprise, a surprise that showed, the act of talking about them (and Clo's often uncomfortable questions) revealed facets of their personalities she had not perceived until now.

To Clo's surprise, and it showed, she discovered that talking about her own family also revealed knowledge she had never considered before. For a reason she couldn't explain, she told about Dougal and Emmie, about Dougal and Jamie and Ruby. Agatha had a way of sitting unseen and unheard until Clo believed she was speaking her thoughts to the sky.

Agatha never asked about Clo's personal life, nor did she discuss her own for six months or more. By then the visits had increased to once a week. They increased to twice a week after the second anniversary of Stella Demoska's funeral.

The gods hadn't accepted the sacrifice of the vines. Or perhaps Stella had been right all along, and those who tried to help had made the offering worthless. As Charlie's body bloomed with a second life and the vines bore more fruit than ever before, Stella's health declined. She lingered in bed for years, growing thinner and paler and, in her final year, terrified of being alone.

'She could see it, you know, that cancer inside her,' Agatha said. 'She showed it to me, that shadow creeping through her stomach and out about her body.'

Clo looked back to girlhood days and nodded. She knew about shadows.

'How could she tell you?' she asked.

Realising that the question was meant literally, Agatha shrugged. 'I listened to her and Charlie talking to the kids and Lucy, and to the answers they gave. It wasn't hard to pick up. It's a pretty language you know. And that last year, all Stella wanted was me. Albert and the kids and Lucy moved into my place with Harry. I took Lucy's old room. That's the one next to the passionfruit vine. They're nice you know, they help you relax — the patterns that vine makes on the walls. The afternoon sun coming through. Especially during late afternoon when the light seems to slide along the leaves. After a while I believed that room belonged to me. I never felt like that before. As if something belonged to me. Maybe it was because of that room that I took on her family as well. The day she died, she said I could keep them. For looking after her, she said.'

Reaching back to childhood for the small village and her relatives there, Stella had listed each one in the correct order. She had given them all to Agatha, along with their virtues and sins.

Agatha repeated the list for Clo, sometimes going backwards to retrieve a lost child, a short-lived mother, a grandfather gone away. She described their characteristics, the way they looked, their relationships to each other. She brought these relatives out and paraded them before Clo, introducing each one proudly, enumerating their attributes, laughing at their follies, apologising for any bad behaviour. Finally she wept, grieving for the loss of the two things in life she had ever wanted: a best friend, a large family. Both were gone with Stella to the grave.

Clo, crying with her, took one of her losses away. 'Albert married into the family, which makes them yours without the gift,' she said.

Agatha left abruptly, taking Clo's words to study in the privacy of her room. After turning them over in her mind, she consulted with Albert and Lucy — then (to my surprise followed by relief and pleasure) with me — and delighted in our agreement. She would have liked to ask Charlie, but she knew what his answer would be. Marry me and make sure, or words to that effect. Twice now, Charlie had proposed. She had put him off without actually turning him down.

Agatha had discovered desire. It was an enormous and a greedy thing, far greater than the sometimes pleasure she had found with her husband. Its strength, and the pictures it placed in her mind, shocked her enough to make her beg for time to grow accustomed to her own sensuality. She wanted to enjoy anticipation for once in her life, and to grieve for the fact that such passion had never been there for Henry. One day she would allow Charlie to fill her mind and her body, then she might discover who was to blame for the lack of lust in her marriage. But for now she had a family to consider.

She pondered the size of her family, remembering names, giving them faces, gloating over their presence. She then returned to Clo with words of her own. Slowly, giving Clo time to write the words down — and sometimes finding difficulty in matching Greek to English — she reconstructed Stella's stories of the time when Earth was goddess.

In return Clo presented her with Great Grandma and the clan. Slowly, giving Agatha time to file the words in her mind — and sometimes finding difficulty in matching the heat-ripened inner-city vernacular to a language born in ice and snow — she told of the closeness and the culture which had died almost as it began. The factory wall, the card games, and the difference of people like the red lady.

'Curtis married into my family. That makes them yours, even without the gift,' she said.

Dazed by the hundreds who now belonged to her, Agatha related her meagre memories of Joyce Trelelan and Abigail Hind. By the time that story was told, Agatha was almost Eva. Clo was almost the daughter who had never been born.

'Would my mother like me now if she knew me, do you think?' Agatha asked. 'Would the red lady remember the songs I used to sing, as I remember hers? Would she see the difference in my children?'

'My cousin Abigail stole your mother from you and I'm sorry for that, but I never stole your son,' Clo said.

'I know. That wasn't you. That happened before you came,' Agatha replied.

They remained in comfortable quietness for a long time, considering the frailty of kinship threads woven by marriage or belief.

Clo shifted slightly when William paused at Angus's door to stare back at her through the bars of his long fringe. She widened the gap between herself and Agatha by turning away as his hand lifted. The gesture may have been the beginning of a wave, or an attempt to shade his eyes from something he couldn't quite believe.

He'd gone inside the house by the time Agatha looked up at Clo's head turned away from her, at the pale neck showing through a vee of dark hair, at the disbelief in the younger woman's body language. She read the withdrawal as a retreat from their new-found liking.

'Maybe it's what you want to believe that counts in the long run,' she said.

'William,' Clo answered, and although the word was merely an indication of his presence, it had the sound of an accusation.

'William is family too,' Agatha said. 'There has to be a place for him.'

The lack of reply turned comfortable quietness into a silence between them. Agatha leaned forward, grunting at the pressure placed on a stomach only just turning to flab, and unbuckled her shoe. She held out her foot to Clo, presenting its paleness, the pink half-moons on nails that had never seen the sun, the soft sole which had rarely touched the ground.

Clo swung around and thrust out a leg, showing the contrast of suntan, roughened nails and a thick pad of calluses.

'More differences,' Agatha stated after comparing the two. 'But both of them the same when all's said and done. Just things put there to save us from crawling around on our knees.'

Their laughter was a rejoining.

'William is family too,' Clo agreed at last. 'There has to be a place for him.'

# Chapter Seventy-eight

William dropped an armful of wood by his fire and climbed onto the metal stool he had brought from home. Its purpose was a high point to stand and survey his place: this small clearing on the escarpment above Steeltown.

The mound of fuel beside him had been gathered with care, allowing for size and quality. The branches had to be free of sap, but dense enough to gain maximum burning time. Smoke would bring rangers, or the youths with a personal supply of marijuana plants hidden among the natural bracken. Wood bleached for too many seasons flared for a few minutes and was gone. The fire itself had to be small enough to remain manageable, but large enough to hold back the ever-present trees.

As he jumped down from the stool and hunched over the tepee-shaped fire, he remembered the day flame had become his friend. He looked up at the nearest tree, challenging it with a grin. Others might think the answering rustle of leaves was caused by a sudden breeze, but William knew the sound of a eucalypt's curse. He had traded curses before, standing on a rock and daring them, watching them bend and sway, gnashing their branches to whip up a wind to blow him down the mountain. If angry enough, they summoned a storm like the one approaching now.

A huge cloud wandered across the sky, leaving a trail of black crumbs for others to follow as it passed across the face of the sun, heading for gingerbread-coloured hills to the north. The cloud's shadow crept over the ground, silencing birds in midcall. Treetops frowned and dulled their beacons of red. William looked around as darkness altered the colours of his view. To one side a straw-coloured pod fell to the ground and scattered seed across the clearing.

Another one of their threats, he thought. But he was too smart for them. They'd never get his head. Yet as the darkness passed over and away, it left a tinge of greyness in his face. It was then he heard Michael answering a call from Ellie.

'If you don't hurry we'll never get to the top.'

'I can't see where you are,' she called back.

'There's a trail. It's faint, but you can see it if you look.'

William saw a flash of yellow dress over to his left. He heard Michael's voice to his right. Not wanting to face either of them, he dived into a clump of the white flowering shrub locally known as snake-bush. Michael entered the clearing as a branch snapped from a eucalypt, shattering on the ground at William's feet. William glared upwards, promising to counterattack when the intruders had gone.

Michael prodded the fire with a stick, dividing and stirring it as if he expected to find an answer for it being here in the flames. Their redness found an echo in William's face. He grabbed a length of the fallen branch and came out of the snake-bush at a run. Michael swung around and fell, scrabbling backwards as the club descended in a sweeping arc, thudding onto the ground between his feet.

'Will? What the hell are you doing?'

'This is my place. You go and find one of your own,' William yelled, and lashed out again. The blow missed Michael's head by a breath as he threw himself aside and away from the club.

'I wasn't trying to take your place,' Michael shouted. 'I thought our place was together until you started running away from me.'

'You started going around to their place.'

Michael did not flinch or turn away as William raised the club again.

'I asked you to come with me. You wouldn't, so I went alone. If that's a crime, then you'd better kill me for it now.'

William looked down at the shock of blond hair and remembered the fallen seed pod. The trees were too many and too clever. One day, one way or another, the eucalypt would win. He dropped the branch and ran, ignoring Michael's call for him to wait.

A half-hour later he climbed into the Lawson's old utility truck, the one Harry had inherited when Albert bought a family wagon. The keys were in the ignition as usual. Harry was too honest to lock anything away. When the engine finally started, William headed west.

Tall trees became dwarfs, then ground-hugging shrubs. An occasional mulga hunched low to hoard its own shade. The straight ribbon of road disappeared into the horizon, seeming to plunge over the edge of the world. A mirage of bridge and buildings finally solidified into a little town signified by a drunken, pockmarked sign. William drove over bitumen-painted logs then pulled into a service station. An old man propped up a sagging doorway with a shoulder while he swore at the slate-coloured sky. William opened the utility truck door and stepped into a furnace.

'Bit hot today, ay?' the old man acknowledged through barely moving lips. He watched with critical interest while William fumbled off the petrol cap. The words took longer than the action and slurred into, 'I'll do that, if you like,' although the offer was not accompanied by any sign of movement.

William filled the tank and proffered a twenty-dollar note that was almost the last of his savings. He had enough food for two days if he ate sparingly, and forty dollars tucked inside his wallet.

'Anywhere around here I can get a job?' he asked.

The old man snorted, 'City bloke, ain't ya?'

'Was once.'

'Once is always, cobber. Could try Broken Hill. Lots of city fellers there.'

'How far to White Cliffs?'

The old man snorted again. 'Foller your nose a ways, then a sign going off to your right. Ain't nothing there, though. Too bloody hot this time o' year. Not even opals anymore if you arx me. Better be sure that's where you wanna go, ay? It'll rain tonight so you won't get out for a day or two.'

William waved through a haze of dust and tiredness as he swung the ute back onto the highway. Around three o'clock he arrived at Whitecliffs: a pub, a few shops, the open doors of houses hidden underground. Hill after hill of white mullock reflected sunlight into his slitted eyes; his sweat-soaked clothes dried the moment he opened the car door. The heat and glitter, and the uninterested stare of two dogs, repulsed his approach. The glare reminded him too much of the midsummer walls of his old bedroom. He fell back into the seat, started the engine and drove onto a dirt track leading away to his right.

A bullet-ridden, split-wood sign whose directions were no more than a whisper led him to another track, slightly wider, then another that could pass at a pinch for a road. Even the treeless plains had ceased to comfort him by the time he reached another sign pointing to something called Mootwingee. Rain and dark arrived to greet him there. He knew he was driving uphill by the angle of his headlights, but that was all he knew. The ute had flattened out again when a torch flagged him down.

'Can't go any further by car,' a disembodied voice said as he wound the window down. 'Camping ground is to your right. Cold showers and a toilet, but not much else. If you want hot water for tea, come on over to the quarters. You won't be lighting a fire in this.'

The voice gained form when the flashlight was muted with spread fingers and held upwards to outline a jacket and face. William recognised the uniform of a ranger.

'I'm a bit lost,' he said, trying to smile. 'Wasn't sure which way I was heading.'

'Well you're here. Mootwingee.' The tone implied there was no-where else. 'Want some help with your tent?'

'Thanks anyway, but I'll sleep in the ute. Just here for the night. A look around tomorrow maybe.'

The ranger smiled and nodded. He indicated the way to the camping ground with his flashlight.

William walked the hills of Mootwingee from dawn the next day without pausing to eat or rest. He could feel the heat pounding down on him, but this heat did not burn like fire, or try to suffocate him. Not once did he break out in a sweat as he rambled along the eroded monuments of this ancient seabed: sand, mud and pebbles deposited millions of years ago and transformed under pressure into sandstone and shale.

From the lowest point, his starting point, he stared up at the range rising above a dried sea floor. Its rockholes and crevices were the result of uncountable years of weathering. Pitted and cracked with sudden dips and ravines, the surface resembled mudflats, although its mosaic had firmed to shale. Colours changed with the movement of the sun, from dun brown to gold-brushed violet, and overlain with a sheen of silver where narrow waterfalls spilled down the slopes. Most holes were filled with water left by a week of intermittent rain. The sandy gullies, thick with grass and flowering shrubs, held clear deep pools.

At first he found the silence unnerving. The trees of Mootwingee were aloof. If they did speak, their language wasn't the whispers and muttering he knew. The eucalypts here did not hunch over him, or grab out at him. They did not crowd together to bar his way but stood apart, gracefully allowing his passing. He stopped listening for abuse, and heard their sighs. He knew they were unaware of his presence. They dreamed of another time, or waited for a time yet to come. He found peace in their disregard of him, and pleasure in a sky devoid of cloud again, its colour an intense, solid sheet of blue.

He wandered over ridges towering out of deep gullies, not trying to avoid the white cypress growing on red sandstone bluffs. He hadn't bypassed the giant river gums following the creek below. Keeping to a track winding steadily upwards through stunted eucalypts battling for a foothold in sand-filled cracks, he trudged around a man-made dam and on to the top of a t-shaped promontory. There he looked out and around, surveying the surrounding saltbush plains where the soaking rain had given life to stored seed. A carpet of yellow daisies and Wilcannia lilies reached to the horizon. Drought evaders, they would blossom, seed and wither within a few weeks. But while they lived, the plains glowed with life.

The creek below flowed into occasional ponds where animals drank their fill and birds clustered in river gums to wait for their share. He watched a family of shaggy-haired euros hop along the side of a hill, wary of the larger kangaroos. He laughed at the magpies guarding their nests against anyone who dared intrude on their domain. The smaller birds fought and called, as indifferent to his presence as the trees.

William sat on a slab of rock in the full glare of the sun. He closed his eyes, allowing the heat to wrap around his mind and body in a sea of orange. It reminded him of the times he had lain spread-eagled in deep blue water while the Pacific lapped around him, filling him with its peace. This time he drifted in an ocean of light.

A smile stayed on his face as he looked out across the plains, feeling at home for the first time in his life. Many thousands of years ago a tribe of Aborigines had settled here. He felt what had called them, and understood why they had stayed. Their presence was engraved on huge slabs of rock throughout the whole of Mootwingee. He wished the artists were here now to share their stories of this place, and to grant permission to make it his. This was where he wanted to be. Yet he couldn't stay without their permission. He could ask the rangers, but they were only caretakers hired by a white government. They watched over the carvings and the camping ground, and kept out vandals and shooters. Their love of the work, the place, was obvious in the way they talked and touched and smiled; but they were not the rightful owners. Only heirs of the original inhabitants could grant him the right to stay. They'd gone, the rangers said, but one or two came back occasionally. William decided to wait, and while waiting he'd create his own drawings to help make this place his own. Below him and away to one side was a shallow cave decorated with a winding snake. He would begin with this, the art of another time.

The charcoal stick shattered between his fingers. He chose a freshly sharpened pencil. The lead snapped the moment he put it to paper.

Recognising the rebuff, he turned away to stare at another promontory looming over the plains to his right. To him, the piling of rock shale resembled the form of a huge bird with closed wings. Its neck was extended, its head stretched forward as if to watch for trespassers.

He tried a biro. The ink had dried. Another pencil slid across the blank white surface of his page, as if one or both had been greased.

His lips tried to shape a prayer, but the only ones he knew belonged to houses and narrow streets, to men trudging bitumen on their way to work, to children playing on foot-scuffed grass. To women waiting for life to somehow take a turn for the better.

The sketchbook slipped off his knees and fell face down. He picked it up and placed it back on his lap, dusting off the earth with a shirt sleeve. The reddish brown dirt spread in two sweeping swings. The promontory had taken flight on the pages of his book.

He knew suddenly and without a doubt that he wasn't welcome here. This could never his place. This place had been taken thousands of years ago. He didn't try to stop the tears or muffle his sobs as he stood, staggered and fell face down in the dirt.

The rangers found him there as the sun slipped into an ocean far to the west.

## Chapter Seventy-nine

William screwed his eyes shut and tried to rebuild last night's dream. It was on the tip of recollection — a vague shimmer of treeless plains below. He could feel the wind rushing past, pulling at his hair, his skin, as if it were trying to strip him to bone. The pleasure was intense enough to border on anguish.

'Are you awake, William?'

He stared at the back of his eyelids, trying to turn her voice into the same shapelessness as his thoughts and allow his memories to take visual form.

Debra entered his room, not trying to be quiet. She knew what he was doing. They were starting again, the nightmares. The moment she'd picked up the phone and talked to that doctor from a hospital in Broken Hill, she knew this would happen.

'Heat exhaustion,' the doctor had said. 'He's all right now. He'll be back with you by the middle of next week.'

William wouldn't say where he had been, or why. Even before he walked through the doorway wearing the look of an old and weary man, she knew she'd lost him. She'd been losing him since Curtis returned from the country; since Michael began staying at her place, Clo's place, leaving William alone to dream. Next he'd be sleepwalking again. She would have to surround him with bars.

Her distress oozed through and around his dream like treacle, dragging it back into the bog of his subconscious. He opened his eyes and saw his mother hunched over him, staring up at the window. He studied her sagging jaw, the puffy eyes. He saw her fear. His dreams had always frightened her. He would never be able to convince her that they weren't nightmares, just a different world from the one she inhabited.

'They're my friends now,' he told her.

She jumped back as if he had thrown a punch.

'Trees can't ever be friends to people,' she shouted.

He tried to tell her that he did not dream about trees any more. She wouldn't listen, as usual.

'It's that Agatha Lawson. And these.' She grabbed a handful of magazines. 'Stories about things that never happened. She's going senile, that old woman. And what else can you expect from her!'

She jabbed a magazine with a stiffened finger, scratching it with her nail, as if by tearing away the name she could rid herself of the person.

*Shadowland.* 'A richly inventive story both comic and chilling. Another compelling yarn by Clo Gatley. You won't want it to end.' Or so the front cover blurb promised.

William sat up and hugged his knees to his chin. It was better not to think, or speak. His mother would never believe his words, and his thoughts were becoming more and more like dreams.

A hand on each cheek forced him to look up. Her nails dug into his face, reminding him of those poking eucalypt fingers. He banished that memory by dragging forth another, that of a large brown bird with outspread wings surrounded by a treeless desert. He couldn't remember where he'd seen that bird, but he knew it as a friend. One day it would take him away to a place of his own. If he concentrated, if she would just leave him alone, he'd be able see it clearly.

'William?' Debra's voice held a note of panic.

'I'm just tired,' he said soothingly.

She looked at her watch. 'I'm going to be late for work.'

He turned and stared through the window beside his bed. The darkness of a tree outside turned the glass to a mirror. A shaft of sunlight pierced the branches, creating a line down his face, splitting it in two. One was his face, the other was Curtis. Or was it Angus? Difficult to know. That side was in shadow, and the two men looked so much alike except for their colouring. One was his friend, the other his father. Perhaps if Curtis would admit to him, he'd have a place at last.

'You're doing it again,' Debra said. 'Going off somewhere in your head as if I'm not even here.'

'You're my mum. We don't need anyone else.'

Those words comforted her, as always. She tousled his hair, tossing his fringe down over his eyes, and kissed his cheek. 'I'll be late for sure. What are you going to do with your day?'

'Look for a job. Time I had one, then you wouldn't have to worry about being late.'

She kissed him again, showing her love. It was all for him, and sometimes much too much.

'Want to meet me for lunch?' she asked. 'We'll splash out. Go somewhere posh.'

'I'll make it here. Posh but cheap.'

She grinned, kissed him again, and was gone.

William dressed in jeans and a T-shirt and shoved a few pieces of fruit into his backpack alongside a notebook and pencil. Throwing water over his face in the bathroom, he happened to glance up at the vanity mirror. His eyes were bloodshot and circled with dark rings, like the age rings of a tree. Shuddering at that thought, he ran through the doorway, aiming for Angus's house.

He strode around the house looking for Angus in the garden, but he couldn't help glancing across at the eucalypt. It's just another tree, he told himself firmly; yet he distinctly heard a rustle of leaves sounding suspiciously like a chuckle, as if the tree knew something he didn't. Steeling himself, he glared with all the defiance he could muster, allowing his stare to travel slowly up its trunk. As always, his eyes grew wet and sad. About to turn away, he noticed Clo and Agatha side by side on the veranda steps. For a reason he couldn't name, that closeness hurt. He entered Angus's house so he wouldn't have to look at them again.

Angus sat in his usual chair at the kitchen table. The surrounding floor was covered in potted plants, as usual. He wore his usual old shorts and singlet, and appeared as thin and worn and grubby as he had always done. Angus hadn't changed from the day William first began to wander into his yard.

He had to fight an urge to engulf the old man in a hug. He knew from experience how long that would last. Angus had never been one for hugs. Yet somehow William knew this man had always loved him.

'The wanderer returns,' Angus drawled. He asked no questions. Angus never did.

William fought the urge, stronger now, by strolling to the window.

'Been about a week,' Angus prompted, still not asking.

William rubbed a hole in the dust-smeared window pane and stared out at Clo and Agatha. They were comparing feet, and laughing.

Angus misread his drooping shoulders. 'Trees can't pull free of the ground, you know that. Not even if they want to. I suppose they know a lot, but none of their knowing is for such paltry things as humans.'

'Maybe you're right,' William said, although he didn't believe a word of it. At least, not regarding this particular tree.

'You can run to the ends of the earth and back, but no matter where you run, you'll find them. There's no deliberate harm in none of them. Sooner you know that, the sooner you'll settle down.'

'I went looking for a desert too hot to grow trees. I found one, I think.' William frowned. 'Too hot for me, but there were trees. These ones didn't even know I existed.'

'No trees in a desert. Unless you mean palms.'

He looked squarely into Angus's eyes and asked, 'Do you think Curtis will ever own up to me?'

'Loby's the one you should be asking. Not much that woman doesn't know.'

William gulped in a deep breath before asking, 'Do I belong to him?'

'I can't give you an answer, boy. Would if I could. Why does it mean so much, the knowing?'

'If he owned up to me, I'd have a place.'

'There's others who love you, son.'

'I need to know my roots, my blood.'

'Then be satisfied with your mother. Nothing wrong with being a branch of the Greentree family.'

Angus noted William's shudder at the word 'branch', and added, 'That why you run? From that bloody tree?'

William almost smiled. Angus was asking questions.

'Your mum said rangers picked you up from a place called Mootwingee.'

'I don't remember much,' William said slowly. 'Except in the dreams, and they're not clear. All I remember is a bird who comes back every night, but I can't recall its exact size and shape. I only know that it's brown and huge, and it wants to take me somewhere.'

Angus stared at him with a mixture of shock and what appeared to be fear. He stood, almost fell, grabbed his crutches off the floor and hopped to the back door. He fell at last, down the steps, flat out on his face.

'Leave me!' he ordered when William tried to lift him.

William heard the eucalypt's laughter, and ran again.

He roamed the streets for hours, becoming conscious of his surroundings only when he heard the thunder of nearby surf. He remembered Angus once saying that people were drawn to the ocean because it held their beginnings. William was drawn by the lack of trees. Not even the greedy eucalypts could find a footing in that blue expanse, or in the fine white sand leading down to the waves. Even here, in the park where he now stood, the only signs of growth, except for the tussock grass, were two salt-scarred and wind-battered Norfolk pines. They were the survivors of a dozen or so planted long before he was born.

He wandered towards the pines while admiring their tenacity. These trees had dug in and held on, taking everything the elements could throw at them without surrendering their places. Yet they did not mind sharing with the occasional picnickers who sheltered beneath their branches. Unselfish things, pines. Maybe even friendly, William thought as he headed for the nearest one.

As he approached, the shade turned to shadow and stood. His first reaction was relief when he saw a dark-haired girl. She pushed against the trunk, shaping her shoulders to fit its curve, moulding against the rough bark until she became a part of the tree. As he shook his head and backed away, his heels tilted down into a ditch worn by scraping feet under a v-shaped pipe — all that remained of two swings. Arms flailing, grabbing at air, he hung for a fraction of a second before falling. Breath chuffed from his lungs as he sprawled backwards in the dirt.

A pale face appeared above him. 'Didn't mean to scare you,' she said. 'I was just, you know, fooling around. Mike told me you have a thing about trees.'

William stared up at the angles of her face. No one could ever imagine she belonged to anyone but Curtis. She had his way of regarding the world around him through a fringe of long hair. Her smile was Curtis's smile. Not large or bright, but personal and warm.

Her glance skimmed the beach behind them, the scrappy grass underfoot, the piping over his head.

'I'm Ellie Lawson,' she finally said.

'I know.'

'I know you know. I've seen you watching me at the nursery when I'm with Dad.'

'Does he see me?'

'He doesn't see anything much. Why do you go there?'

He gestured vaguely. 'Just to look around.'

'We didn't know that was your place, Michael and me. You know, the clearing. Michael said you were angry because you thought he'd taken your place. We were just passing through and we haven't been back there since.'

'It's all right. It's not really my place. I've got another one now.'

'Where's that? I mean, if you don't mind saying.'

He grinned and pointed to his head. She nodded, understanding immediately, as he somehow knew she would.

'Why don't you ever talk to me?' she asked.

'I'm not supposed to.'

'Yeah.' She scratched her chin and looked around again, moving from one foot to another. 'Going to the football picnic on Sunday?'

'You?'

'Said I would. To help with the little kids and the food.'

'I'm waiting for friends,' she added to fill the silence. 'We're going for a swim. Want to come?'

He thought of her friends. Giggling girls looking at him sly-eyed, nudging each other and whispering.

'I've got to go,' he said, already walking away.

She flicked her hair and marched off in the opposite direction.

William turned and watched her out of sight before entering a shelter shed, eating the fruit from his backpack while allowing the memory of her face to settle. He could clearly see the grin, the half-smile, the nose-wrinkle of disgust when he walked away. Each expression was firmly fixed in his mind. Pulling out his notebook, he made a dozen sketches — an eyebrow quirk, lips full then thinned; her hair outspread as if it were caught by a breeze.

At one o'clock exactly, the automatic alarm went off in his brain. If he wasn't home before his mother, he knew there would be hell to pay.

The old ute with Harry behind its wheel stood outside his house.

'Just called in to see if you'd like to help us out on Sunday,' Harry called. 'Albert's in charge of the kids' races. You can come with me if you like.'

Harry's mission in life seemed to be getting William to join football games, family picnics, anything to do with mingling.

'Yeah, sure,' William decided. 'But I'll go in the bus.'

Harry studied the answer for a rebuff.

'With the others. Michael and the team,' William added to send his uncle away with a smile.

Harry drove away, grinning broadly. 'See you on Sunday,' he called back as he turned the corner.

# Chapter Eighty

'Bus'll be here soon,' Michael called from the front veranda.

The yell jerked Clo's mind out of its backward travel. Her second lover, transformed to a Bryan Brown lookalike by wishful thinking, became just another flyspeck on the glass. The eyes in the mirror unglazed and stared out from the face of an over-fifty. The tall willowy girl in floating white, who had never existed except in teen fantasy anyway, shortened and plumped to Clo Lawson here and now. She grimaced at the image, finished combing her hair with her fingers and stepped out of a daydream onto the hall carpet.

'Ellie!' she shouted through the kitchen window.

The call started low, wailed upwards then ended in a sputter of coughing when she saw Ellie a few metres away, standing on the bed of weeds jokingly called a lawn.

Serves you right, Ellie's look said as she dropped a foot onto the upsmiling face of a daisy and slowly ground it down. If you're going to sit up all night boozing and fagging, it just serves you bloody well right. But she called, 'I'm coming,' just the same, and gave the daisy another twist hard enough to pull the plug out of her thong.

'Busted it,' she said to Michael, and ran inside for her sneakers. She brushed past Jamie without looking at him.

Clo lifted the esky off the kitchen table. Yanking it along the hall, she shoved it across to the steps as Jamie walked onto the veranda.

'You can still come if you want,' Clo said.

He shook his head. 'I'll finish off that business for Curtis and head back to Sydney tonight.'

'Coward,' she accused.

'What's at a football picnic except flabby-gutted men getting drunk and their wives gossiping?'

Her expression became sour. 'It's not you they're talking about.'

Which wasn't true. They did talk about Jamie. Michael had told her that much last night. He'd suggested, in the roundabout way he told her everything, that Jamie shouldn't sleep in this house on the nights Curtis stayed away.

'To hell with the lot of them, let them talk,' she'd snapped, although Ellie was the one being teased at school.

'I can't for the life of me understand why you're going,' Jamie said.

'I promised Amanda,' was Clo's reason.

'I can't understand what you see in her either, or why you should fill in when she's not interested enough in her son to go.'

'That's the reason I'm going. Because she's not interested. Somebody should be. He's a good kid. And except for Liona, Amanda's the only person I know who can discuss books.'

He grinned. 'Stick to murder mysteries and you've got me.'

She pulled a face and turned away.

'Here,' Jamie said, shoving the esky at Michael. 'You're the big football star, *you* carry it onto the bus.'

Michael avoided looking at Jamie as an orange bus pulled up with a squeal of brakes. He grunted something unintelligible as Ellie pushed past him. She threw herself onto the front seat so she wouldn't have to look at the dozens of eyes staring through the windows at Jamie and Clo.

Clo followed Michael up the steps, looking above the heads in the crowded bus but feeling the eyes fixed on her. She gave a toothy grin and would have added a flourishing bow, if the idea and the sight of William hadn't hit her at the same time. His frown, so like the scowl

Curtis wore when she deliberately called attention to herself, shocked her with its familiarity and made her feel a little foolish. As she turned to sit, she noticed the three-year-old Becker girl receiving a smack on the leg for squirming on her mother's lap.

Mrs Becker was secretary of the Ladies Football Auxiliary and treasurer of Friends of the Hospital. She knew children should be seen and not heard, even her own. Especially her own. But when Clo winked and the little girl held out her arms to be rescued, the mother unwillingly allowed the child to be taken.

All the mothers were aware of Clo's prickly nature. They never suffered her past the outskirts of their friendship, afraid the tightness of their closely knit group might be torn apart by the sharpness of her tongue. She regarded them collectively as they regarded her: as a threat to a way of life supposedly honest and without pretence.

Little Amy Becker snuggled into Clo's soft contours. The child knew that a giggle or a few tears would turn the cactus into a succulent. Clo kissed the toddler's head and waved to Jamie, grinning widely when he glanced along the row of staring faces then casually scratched his crotch. She pretended not to notice the flare of scarlet on Ellie's cheeks.

The large mirror above the driver showed William staring at the back of Ellie's head. His expression revealed a wistful yearning, and it crossed Clo's mind that he might be wishing the red stain travelling around to her daughter's neck had been caused by an awareness of his presence. Clo watched him slide a sideways glare at big Lance Becker, the team manager. No doubt big Lance was fiddling with himself again. His hand seemed to automatically reach for his crotch whenever he looked at her. The women were all talking about Clo Lawson, she thought sourly. Their men were all wondering if she could be as easy as her mouth, and fiddling with their crotches.

William shoved hard against Lance Becker Junior, making room for Michael. Young Lance's resistance lasted no more than a second. He slid over in a hurry when William planted an elbow in his ribs.

Michael dropped into the seat without speaking. Clo supposed that neither had much to say.

'A picnic at Reiner's Gorge for the under-nineteen football team is like rubbing in the fact that we were wiped off the map in the final,' Michael had told Clo last night. 'Thirty-six ten they beat us. But having a picnic makes the dads feel better. They'll get drunk and talk about what might have been and how great they were in their day.'

'And how they'd like a bit of Clo Lawson,' Jamie said, and grinned at Michael's snort of disgust.

'You've been coaching Michael's team now and then, so you have a legitimate reason for being at the presentation. Why don't you come with us and give them something to talk about?' Clo had laughed.

'It'll take ages to get there, then we'll just wander about for a while, eat, then wander about until it's time to go home,' Ellie had said before Jamie had had a chance to accept the invitation.

Four hours after getting off the bus at Reiner's Gorge, Ellie was lying back on a blanket, staring up at patches of sky between spiky leaves and wishing she'd stayed at home with Jamie. But at least lunch and the presentations were out of the way at last. She'd be going home in another hour.

An ant nipped her shin. Gathering the threads of boredom into a ball of anger, she sat up and swore, flicked the ant into the air and looked around. Glancing from a group of men and women supervising various games to another group stretched out on blankets, she remembered the way Clo had summed them up before she'd walked off into the bush.

'The I wills and the I ams,' she'd said.

The 'I wills' were taking part in the ball games. These were the males, mostly dads, who were team managers, coaches, referees and linesmen, who cleaned the football grounds, marked lines and drove minibuses filled with smelly kids. The 'I ams' — the men who occasionally attended games to abuse referees, kids and coaches — had gathered around their eskies. They were getting slowly pissed while the 'I will' women shepherded the younger children away from the cliff top. These were the females who ran the raffles and kiosks, who drove car loads of kids to training, who soothed and bandaged, and cheered no matter who was winning.

'The "I am" women are much the same as their male counterparts,' Clo had said, and denied belonging to either group.

'To any group,' she emended. 'I'm not the grouping kind.'

Funny how she never mixed with other women. Not that Ellie blamed her. She wasn't much of a mixer either.

Jumping to her feet to escape the ant's army of friends, she walked along a narrow trail to the gorge and found Michael standing at the edge, throwing stones at the treetops below.

'Having fun?' she asked.

'Just waiting to go home.'

'Where's the rest of the team?'

He shrugged. 'Got a cricket game going. I couldn't be bothered.'

They looked at each other, looked away and looked again. She picked up a handful of stones and began to throw.

Eucalypt leaves are cold to the touch. How do they stay cold on such a hot day? They warmed immediately in Clo's hand. She reached for a sprig of leaves from a different tree, rubbing their velvety smoothness between her fingers while listening to the shuss of wind overhead. As if on cue, it stopped. Someone called. The voice seemed to be kilometres away. She wondered how far she had roamed from the bus, and tried to shake off a feeling of isolation. Hostility was in the sharp points of leaves, the slashing edges of grass, the harsh dry feel of bark against her back. The chainsaw buzz of wasps sounded a constant threat. She opened her mouth, ready to call for anyone who would answer. The call dissolved to an exhale of air as she looked through the trees at William.

He stood at the edge of the cliff, staring away to his right at something she couldn't see. The McLean strain was there in the shape of his jaw, the long thin nose, the curl of his cowlick and the colour of his hair. Except for height, youth and the lack of stoop to his shoulders, he could have been Dougal.

She watched him raise his arms. For a moment she thought he could and would ascend into the sky and soar above them all. Yet as he lifted his heels and stood poised on his toes, imagination saw him plummet earthward. Her involuntary cry of horror caught his attention. He half turned, still with arms outspread, and looked at her over a shoulder. She wanted to call him back from the edge, but the McLean in him left the words in her throat. He must have heard the call in his mind's ear, for he stepped back and lowered his arms. She nodded and walked away.

Michael held out another handful of stones to Ellie. As she lifted a pebble, one of his fingers closed on hers. He leaned forward and she jerked back, then forward again. Their noses bumped, turned, bumped again and moved in opposite directions. Her mouth was dry-hard. She moistened her lips to take away the tension. Now they were soft while his were hard. She pulled back and looked down at her feet. He released her fingers. As she turned to throw another stone, her hand brushed the front of his shorts.

He knew by the flush colouring her neck and ears that the touch had been accidental, and he expected to feel disappointment. Instead, he remembered the way men looked at her mother. He placed the back of his hand against hers. The stones dropped as she turned her fingers into his palm. They looked down at the mass of trees and boulders below. She glanced at him and smiled. He kissed her again. This time they both got it right.

Clo's foot caught in a twisted root. She jerked forward, grabbed a branch and brought herself to a jarring halt. The rough bark scraped her palm. Nursing the graze against her breast, she looked around and thought about being lost here, about being alone in the dark here.

'Is something wrong, Mrs Lawson?'

Big Lance Becker slid out from behind a nearby tree. He stood squarely in front of her, blocking her way to the track. His grin was an insult. She looked at the thickness of his build, his wide shoulders and well-muscled arms, and knew she'd found trouble. She would never fight her way out of this. If she screamed to bring people running, she'd be the one to blame. More talk to embarrass Ellie. The widening of his grin proved that he had read the thought.

'Hi, uh, Mrs Lawson. Ellie asked me to give you this,' William said.

He offered her a bottle of cola as Lance Becker backed away and moved off down the track. Clo glared after him before turning to William.

'Thank you,' she said slowly.

He looked down at his feet. 'I saw him following you.'

'Why would you care? You've never spoken to me before.'

'My mother told me not to.'

'Where is she, anyway?'

He shrugged. 'Says these football picnic things are too common.'

Clo snorted laughter. 'And she's right. What were you doing back there?'

He answered with a one-shoulder shrug.

'You were watching something.'

She didn't know why the thought popped into her mind. Probably the memory of his arms outspread.

'An eagle?' she suggested.

He looked up at last. 'Sometimes they look like animals with wings.'

'But there aren't any clouds.'

She frowned, not understanding his expression. He seemed to expect her to know his mind. He was disappointed when she didn't.

'Those drawings at the house. They're yours, aren't they? Nightmares or shadows?' she asked.

'Dreams maybe. One day I'll see it clear.'

'Sometimes dreams aren't as friendly as they seem.'

He smiled and nodded. He had expected her to know, and she did.

'I've read some of your stories,' he said. His feet shuffled in the dirt before he looked her in the face. 'I've been to your *Shadowland*, but my shadows are in trees. Like the ones in the treetops down in the gorge.'

She wanted to say the story was a fantasy, but she couldn't. He'd know the lie. 'I'm in your old room,' she said instead.

His face darkened. 'You should be careful. They're there, behind the white paint. It stops them from getting out, but they are there.'

She looked into his eyes and saw a world of shadows.

'Why did you come?' she asked. 'Today, I mean. You don't play football, do you?'

'To see Ellie. Grandma Lawson says we're related.'

Recognising the question, she nodded.

'It's a bloody mess, isn't it, William? A brother and sister have every right to know each other.'

His smile was a song. Somewhere, not too far away, soft words brushed their ears and were gone. Clo walked away so she wouldn't cry.

'Yo!' A yell from the picnic area shattered the silence. 'Everyone onto the bus!'

Ellie nodded towards a patch of orange seen through the trees.

'We'd better be going,' she said.

The trail was too narrow to walk side by side so Michael followed, his hand stretched forward, still in hers. Ellie saw her mother strolling along the track just ahead of them. She broke away to catch up, to walk arm in arm. Clo looked at her daughter's face then back at Michael, seeing him wearing the same half-surprised look as Ellie. She remembered the girl in this morning's mirror.

Ellie smiled into her face. Clo's eyes moistened again. Ellie hugged her arm. She hugged even tighter when William appeared at a bend in a track next to the one they were on.

'I've been talking to your brother,' Clo said as he joined them.

Ellie's smile was a hymn. She leaned forward and kissed William's cheek. He grinned and looked down at his shoes, but he backed away when a sound of bootsteps on the pathway became louder. Clo and Ellie ran, watching the trail ahead for hidden snags, but laughing like children at each stumble — for no particular reason except the pleasure of knowing they could.

Michael licked his lips, still tasting Ellie there, and kicked a stone. It rattled across the track and rested among a pile of leaves. He stepped forward and kicked them into the air. Through the shower of leaves he saw big Lance Becker staring after Ellie and her mother.

'Look at the old pervert. Wonder it doesn't fall off,' William said.

Michael realised that William had seen him with Ellie. His fists clenched, waiting for an attack.

'All old blokes are the same,' William added. 'I'm gunner shoot meself when I get to that age.'

He punched Michael's shoulder as they ran along the trail.


Mother and daughter were last on the bus. Clo sank into the front seat and stared through the window, thinking about what to have for dinner and the ironing piled up and waiting. Ellie grabbed the railing and swung up the steps, glancing just once at Michael and William. Watching eyes stared away any sign of recognition. She flopped into the seat beside her mother, hugged her chin to her knees and smiled at the road.

The bus pulled up with the usual puff and chug. Jamie crossed the road to meet them.

Ellie glanced back into the dim bus, seeing the tight lips of women and the narrowed eyes of men.

'Hey, Jamie,' she shouted, making sure they all heard. 'Give us a hand with the esky.'

Clo laughed aloud when Ellie tried to jostle a way past her. Thrusting with a hip, she pushed her daughter back into the seat, and jumped out.

Michael swaggered down the steps. 'Got the trophy for most improved,' he said casually.

Jamie winked. 'Knew you would. I coached you, didn't I?'

'By next year you should be able to get him best and fairest,' Clo said.

'And have them winning the final,' Jamie agreed.

'Thirty-six ten our way,' Michael said, and punched Jamie's shoulder.

Ellie led the way across the road. Michael followed closely. She jumped a patch of daisies then turned back and looked at William. He was watching her through an open window.

'Why don't you come for dinner?' she shouted.

William felt the eyes turn to him. Every single one held his mother's expression whenever Ellie or Clo's names were mentioned. The song shrunk to a whisper.

'I thought I'd have a family barbecue, and you're family, aren't you?' Clo called from the footpath.

He jumped up, ran down the aisle, not caring who he thumped against, and leapt out of the bus. They walked across the road, he and Clo with Ellie between them, their arms around each other. He passed under the eucalypt without looking up.

# Chapter Eighty-one

When Albert's family wagon pulled up at the Demoskas' front gate, Clo shouted an invitation for the Lawsons to join the party. Albert brought Harry, and after a little stiff-legged sparring, Clo made him welcome. She grinned broadly when Agatha and Charlie wandered in.

William, Ellie and Michael sat on a bench while they joked and laughed. I joined them as they were talking about the careers they fancied most.

'I'm thinking of going to Hawkesbury Agricultural College,' Ellie said. 'Either that or do horticulture at the local tech college. Maybe engineering at Sydney uni if my marks are good enough to get me in. Then again, I wouldn't mind nursing.'

'Good to see you've made a firm decision,' Michael said sombrely.

She pulled a face at him. 'Just because you know what you want.'

Before I had a chance to ask, she and Michael chorused, 'Teaching.'

Ellie turned to William. 'If you're serious about your art, you have to go to Wollongong uni.'

'The creative arts degree,' I added.

Harry's rising voice cut off William's answer.

'You say anything to him, just one word, and I'll bash your bloody head in! Just get out!' His words turned to a near scream. 'Get out now!'

Without looking, I knew Curtis had arrived. Only Curtis could send the usually imperturbable Harry into such a state of apoplexy.

'It's my house. My yard and I say who —'

Before Curtis could say who, Harry swung a punch. If the fist had connected, Curtis would have been laid out cold. Luckily for him, Albert shoved him aside and Harry's punch turned into an air swing.

'Hah!' Curtis mocked, which enraged the middle brother even more.

'You can laugh,' Harry said, 'but you know I'd beat you to a pulp if Albert wasn't here for you to hide behind. Like you've been hiding behind him for years.'

'So you could beat me in a fight. So that makes you into a big man, eh?' Curtis sneered. 'But not a big enough man to get Debra to take a second look at you.'

'More of a man than you'll ever be. Man enough to admit when I'm wrong about something. Man enough to own up to me own father. Me own son!'

Lucy and Albert pushed between them, but the argument grew hotter and louder — words turning to daggers drawing blood as they slashed and stabbed.

Michael, pale-faced and grim, walked away from it all. William sat mutely, fighting a compulsion to vomit when Curtis yelled, 'He's nothing to do with me'.

Agatha blocked the flow of words by slapping her youngest son's face.

'If you don't want him, then he's not yours,' she said coldly. 'And neither are you mine. Go back to your nursery, there's no place for you here.'

The silence swelled like a balloon, threatening to explode at the merest prick and destroy them all. It was Angus who provided the pin. He hobbled down the pathway, a crutch under one arm and the bonsai under the other. Brushing past Curtis, almost a shove, he went directly to William and placed the stunted eucalypt in his lap.

'Yours now,' he said, glancing back at Curtis, his expression another shove. 'Always reckoned I'd give it to kin when the time came.'

Looking into Curtis's eyes was akin to looking directly into the sun. He moved in front of William and placed both hands on Angus's shoulders.

'It's between you and me. He's nothing to do with us,' he said.

The bonsai slipped off William's lap as he stood, edged around them and walked slowly along the path. He paused under the shadow of the eucalypt at the gate. A snarl of victory from the tree answered his challenge. He watched a heavy limb part company with the trunk.

Angus heard a screech and saw the shadow swoop. He threw himself forward to catch its attention. 'Run, William,' he yelled. 'Run while I keep it with me.'

He watched, open-mouthed and helpless, as claws tore at William's chest.

# Chapter Eighty-two

The following morning I happened to be on my front porch when Debra stormed up the steps of the house that had once been hers. The sound of curses and smashing crockery could be heard two streets away. Proof of a vicious fight could be seen later in her blackened eye. Clo finally ran up the street in an old black negligee which had been her house gown for the past year or more. Debra chased after her with a hatchet for almost a block before striding back to the house.

An hour later, as Clo reappeared with Curtis and Ellie, Debra was being driven away in Harry's utility truck.

'Are you satisfied now?' she screamed through the window at Curtis. 'William's up there on that machine, no more than a vegetable. Just like one of your trees. Now you can call him your son.'

Curtis, Ellie and Clo stood and stared at a forty-centimetre gash circling the eucalypt's trunk. Ring-barking was a legal if slow way to kill a suburban tree.

Dishevelled and dirt-stained in the tattered black negligee, Clo marched around the house to the garden shed. Returning with a shiny-edged axe, she handed it to Curtis. He swung, biting the blade deep into the groaning tree. When the eucalypt crashed to the ground, they walked away, not once looking back.

# Chapter Eighty-three

Agatha sat in the waiting room with Albert and Harry seated on either side of her. Maidy and Angus were glaring at each other over their heads. I stopped at the door as Angus said, 'You're the only one who can talk any sense into Debra. You have to convince her to switch this bloody machine off.'

'That would be murder,' Maidy said.

'He just needs to be let go,' Angus pleaded.

'All we can do is pray. It's in God's hands now.'

'Don't give me that crap, Maidy.'

'It has nothing to do with you!'

'Listen to him. Please listen,' Jamie begged.

Maidy backed away from him as he joined me at the door. Only the look on his face prevented her from reaching for the crucifix around her neck. She warded both him and the look away with an outstretched palm.

'It's not in me, Maidy,' he said softly.

'I don't want you here,' she snapped. 'You'll bring God's wrath down on my grandson's head.'

Jamie's expression was not meant for outside eyes.

'I sent for him,' I said. 'None of us can get through to Debra and I thought he might be able to make you see what you have to do.'

I waited for Angus to call me a meddler, but Jamie had his attention. His face showed an empathy I couldn't comprehend.

'What right did you have?' Maidy demanded. Her tone dribbled down my face. 'How did you know where to find him?'

'Jamie is my advisor on monetary matters,' I answered coolly. 'He sometimes stays with me when he visits Steeltown.'

Remembering the absence of her name on Angus's list, I added, 'Jamie has a liking for old women. Although the whole town knows your friendship with him is more intimate than mine.'

She managed a right to my stomach and a left to my cheek before Jamie restrained her. Angus stood and watched.

Jamie grabbed Maidy from behind, pulled her close to the curve of his body and rested his chin on her shoulder. I could not believe he loved this old woman, this social climber, this pharisee. Yet when she wrenched away then spat in his face and ran from the room, he stood as if frozen. He did not wipe the spittle from his face.

Ten minutes later, after I'd applied an icepack to my cheek, Curtis halted at the doorway. Clo, with Ellie behind her, stopped his attempted retreat as he saw Angus talking into the glass half-wall, looking through it to the tubes and machines surrounding William.

'It's oversupply, that's what it is. When there's so many around, people just stop looking after them. They stop taking good care of them like they used to. You can't just leave them to grow willy-nilly.'

I rubbed Angus's shoulder to distract him. He frightened me, going on and on like this. He looked at my face without seeing me.

'Yair, it's oversupply,' he said. 'Too much spreading of seeds and not knowing where they land. But that isn't the point, is it, Curtis? You don't take away a bloke's happiness just when he's doing so good at it. You don't make him feel like a lump of shit just because you made a mistake, isn't that right? Jesus, Curtis, I don't know how all that sourness doesn't bust right out. I don't know how it doesn't make little nobs and nodes like you see on the eucalypts when something's eating at them from the inside. But there's no two ways about it. You gotter pull the plug. You're the father and Debra won't do it. All she knows is how to hang on. That's all she ever knew. It's up to you to switch this bloody machine off.'

I rubbed a hand over my face, feeling the map of lines with all roads leading to pain. But the pain was for Curtis, not for William. William was past the point of feeling anything, but for Curtis to do what Angus wanted of him would be tantamount to acknowledging William as his son. That was something he'd always refused to do. For William's sake, he'd said.

'Father and son, mother and son should never be divided. Best to know where your true love and loyalty lie right from the start,' I'd heard him tell the bonsai.

An infant had lain across my stomach. His fists and eyes closed, his knees up, his elbows tucked into his groin. They say it is only from semen and egg that such immortality is created, but I heard the violin. This is a Trelelan, Agatha said to me, and I took her words as a gift. A godsend, Angus said. A man is not a man without a son.

'You're the legal father,' I said softly to Curtis. 'He bears your name. That's what matters here, not divided loyalties.'

I heard Agatha's hissed intake of air, but I did not look at her. I had too much to lose. I loved Curtis as I loved Angus. They were my life.

'You put those ideas in Curtis's head, Loby,' Angus said loudly. 'When he was no more than a little boy. Ideas about how he wasn't like Agatha when every bit inside him is her twin.'

Curtis stepped between us, ignoring me, facing Angus. His expression, his hands beseeched as he said, 'You gave William the bonsai because you thought he belonged to me. I always reckoned I'd give it to kin when the time came, that's what you told him.'

'A long time ago I had a fling with Maidy. I stayed with her for nearly a week,' Angus said, staring at me with that trigger-happy gleam in his eyes. 'You were driving me mad, Loby. Going on about Curtis. I knew what you were up to.'

'That's why you ran away to war. So she'd marry David Watling,' someone said.

I'm not sure, but I think it was me.

'I couldn't marry Maidy,' Angus mumbled.

I waited for him to say he couldn't marry Maidy Greentree because he couldn't live without me. Instead, he added, 'She wouldn't have me.'

A hand rested on my shoulder then rubbed my arm. I think it was Agatha.

'There's enough been said for now,' she told him, but once Angus started, he couldn't stop.

'I knew all along that Debra was mine, but I couldn't show it because of the bird. I never thought it would know my grandson. I wasn't sure until it came for him.' And, 'You should've told Curtis that my mum and Agatha's mum were sisters, Loby. You should've owned up to the fact that you and Henry probably had the same dad.'

'You've been reading my journal,' I accused him, not knowing what else to say.

'Yours, and the one you kept from me all these years,' he said. 'The one that tells my father's story and his rightful name.'

'You knew that?' I asked slowly. 'Then that nonsense about not wanting to change my name was all a lie?'

He ignored the question to add, 'If you'd told him everything that you'd written down, then Curtis would've seen where all the likenesses came from. He wouldn't have broken Henry, who loved him more than I ever did.'

I saw horror become revulsion as Curtis looked at me. I saw Angus fold his arms, repulsing my outstretched hand. I watched my Curtis and my Angus turn away from me, these two who had never been mine. I had stayed, gashed and half stripped like that eucalypt, and let Angus cut into me. But he'd cut too deep and I had weapons of my own. For just a while, a while lasting for days, I hated with a heat which burned and scarred like William's fire.

'Yes, Agatha is the daughter of Joyce McLean. Just as you are Polly McLean's son,' I said coldly. 'And Dougal McLean, their brother, is Jamie's grandfather.'

They were the last pieces of a jigsaw puzzle, an explanation for the family resemblances staring at Curtis from so many eyes. But where did they fit?

I sharpened my hatchet. 'Tell me, Angus. Has Maidy ever admitted to William being your grandson?'

'She doesn't have to.' Angus was arrogantly sure I couldn't cut him down. 'I know by the bird.'

I shook my head, about to deliver the final blow. Harry beat me to it.

'You people think of nobody but your own selves,' he said. 'You, Angus, trying to make out that Debra and Curtis are cousins, making William some sort of crime against God's law. That's all bullshit. Debra's dad is Dave Watling. Ask Mum if you don't believe me. She knows it for a fact.'

All eyes turned towards Agatha. She nodded slowly. 'Debra is the spitting image of Maidy. Her colouring, her eyes. All of that. But she's the same build as Dave Watling's mum. Even has the same birthmark. A big brown mole on the right hip.'

Harry continued. 'You can twist and turn it all you like, talking about three-eyed birds and trees that walk until your faces turns blue. It's all a load of old tripe. Those things just don't happen. In the end, you gotter admit the truth. All you gotter do is go down that hallway to the second door on the right. Colin Lee's down there, getting over the heart attack he had when William walked under his bus.'

'None of this matters right now. Don't you see that? William's the only one that matters,' Agatha cried out.

But as William was so fond of saying, grownups never listen.

Curtis stared from Angus to Agatha to Jamie. He scrutinised William intently, then turned and studied Ellie — her face, her eyes, the tilt of her head. She had the same colouring as Clo, the same shiny black hair. But that pointed chin hadn't been passed down from Clo. Nor did the hang of her long fringe, her eyes, the straight eyebrows with barely a break above the bridge of her nose. Except for Ellie's colouring, he could be looking at the photograph of Agatha as she stood behind

Henry on her wedding day. Or he could be looking at a female version of a young Dougal McLean.

'The same family tree, but to which branch does Ellie belong?' I murmured.

'Does it matter?' Clo asked Curtis.

Her eyes showed a waiting. She knew what his answer would be.

He wanted to say no, but he couldn't.

'Is she mine or Jamie's?' he asked.

'You can go to hell,' Clo said as she turned away.

I expected her expression to be one of grief and accusation as she looked at me. I saw an acceptance of defeat.

'Clo, I'm sorry,' I pleaded. 'It was never meant for you or Ellie.'

She nodded. 'Neither was he. I think you've done us a favour. You've given me the final reason for leaving.'

Curtis strode forward and stopped just a few paces from me. His lip curled before he snarled, 'What are you doing to me? What have you done?'

Years too late, Agatha stepped between us. I expected abuse from her, but she faced him, holding out her arms as if to protect me.

'You believed what you wanted to believe,' she said. 'You always did.'

'It makes no difference if he's yours or not. Don't you see that, Dad?' Ellie shouted. 'It's not what you are, but what you believe.'

'It's only what our minds contain that matters after all,' Agatha added softly.

'I'll call the doctor,' Jamie said to Curtis. 'You'll have to sign a paper.'

Ellie held out a pen. To Curtis it had the appearance of a hatchet, and he'd already cut down his tree. Before that, he'd cut down his father. He would not, could not bear to believe that he had done the same thing to his son.

# Chapter Eighty-four

'Maidy was right,' Angus said the following day. 'None of it makes any difference to William. He's already gone.'

'Then why are you sitting by his bed?' I asked.

'I can't talk to him once they plant him in the ground.'

I had to ask the question that had kept me awake all night.

'When you first came home from the war, did you go to her before you came to me?'

'I saw so many dead men lying around the beaches and paddocks. Blokes from both sides who'd never get to see their kin again. The bird's shadow was over me every hour of the day and night. I thought it got me when they dropped the bomb that got me leg, but nothing's ever that easy. I had to find out if I had kin for it to go after next. I couldn't tell by looking at Debra, just little then and looking so much like her, and Maidy wouldn't say. She called the cops to chuck me out. The bonsai was in the garbage, so I took it with me.'

And.

'You're not missing out on much, Loby. Not by missing my love. It wasn't enough to stop her from marrying someone else. It didn't keep my father or William alive.'

'Why did you stay with me all these years?' I had to ask.

'Because you wanted me to, if only because you didn't have anyone else.'

I tried to think of an example to prove his lie.

'You came back to me after your father died. My parents were still alive then.'

Angus's raised eyebrow asked for a better example. Mary and Leslie Amadeus Trelelan had managed to ignore me all the years of my life.

'You came back from Western Australia. You left Iain to be with me,' I begged.

'I came back because Polly didn't want me there. I came back to be with Curtis. I knew you'd convince him that he belonged to me.'

He could have lied. He could have said he came back for me. But he did not lie, and he didn't see Curtis standing in the doorway. Even then I might not have ringbarked them both, if they hadn't been so wooden-faced as they looked at me.

'You could have stopped me,' I said to Angus. 'You could have stopped me at any time. All you had to do was tell Curtis the truth. But you didn't know whether Debra was yours or not. You used Curtis to fool the bird. All he was to you was a false trail to keep it away from her.'

I felt no remorse when I perceived the beginning of a slow dying on their faces. Nor did I need a mirror to know that my face held the same expression.

# Chapter Eighty-five

Curtis's last act before leaving town was to buy the lots at the back of my home and bulldoze the houses down. He planted eucalypt stands, named the area William Lawson Park after the boy who had hated eucalypts all his life, then handed the park over to the local council. He disappeared the following day, but not before his brothers sought him out. Harry beat him to within an inch of his life. He might have caused permanent damage if not for Albert. Albert managed to point out the fact that not once had Curtis raised a hand to hit back.

Between them, Albert and Harry carried their brother to the hospital. They stayed while he was stitched and patched, Harry crying all the while.

When you long for something all your life, and when the deed is finally done, there's only grief in having nothing left to anticipate.

Jamie came to me a few days after William's death, but not to vent anger over the words I'd used on Maidy, as I half expected when he turned up on my doorstep.

'You were only being Liona,' he said, 'and because you are Liona, I know you'll grant me a favour. Only you can do what I want without stirring up more gossip around the town. I promised her, you see. I swore that I'd never let her go to a home for old people sick in the head.'

He placed an amount of money in my care so I could arrange and oversee a nurse for his old lover. A succession of nurses, actually. None stayed with her for long.

Maidy Greentree Watling, the woman who spat on the man she saw as the devil. Does she know that the devil pays to keep her in the home that had once belonged to her parents? A home steeped in a tradition of anti-sin and anti-lust which had seen the upbringing of a girl with an aura. Touching men with her hands and her smile and her aura. At twelve years of age boys turned to stare, perplexed by the then new feelings she created just by smiling in their direction. Now they laugh and call witch to her face at the window.

'Maidy Maidy old witch lady, watch out for the witch, dirty old bitch, nits in her hair, nuts in her stare, muck on her leg, see her beg, watch her cry, there in her sty. Chuck her the old browneye, hey!'

Maidy Greentree Watling, turning her body this way and that, flicking her golden hair, running from men until she caught them. Until she herself was caught with the seed in her womb — which, whether he liked it or not, was not put there by Angus McTavish. Maidy has lost 'it' after all. Now she must be constantly watched and restrained. Her hands are wrapped in gauze so she cannot tear at her face and body. She still turns this way and that, trying to escape the bands tying her to the chair and holding her back from the window. Her hair, unflickable now, is thin and thready, and dull from lack of washing. Her face has collapsed in wrinkles, her body in fat. She spends her days in that chair by the window, screaming at the boys capering at her gate. She empties her bodily wastes into her silken underwear and spreads the excreta over her legs. She has to be spoon-fed, always from behind so she won't spit into the face of the feeder.

All those juts and curves and hidden crevices marked by highlights and shadows, the haloed blondness of her long hair promising the pot of gold at the end of a rainbow — all hidden away from prying eyes, no more than a pig in her sty. Poor Maidy Greentree Watling. My heart bleeds for her.

She does not know that Harry paraded his jealousies and hurts before Debra. For each he presented a clear and logical reason. Nothing in this man indicated that he might ever spend hours, or even minutes, agonising over what could have been, what may be, what was possible or even probable. There are no hidden depths to plumb in Harry Lawson. Everything either is, or is not. What you see is what you get, and Debra got married to Harry on the day Agatha wed Charlie Demoska.

Nor does Maidy know that Richard Rees finally asked for Amanda's hand in marriage. She danced him around for a while, but finally relented, as I knew she would. Richard and Amanda are now the social elite of Steeltown and the apples of their parents' eyes. On the fourth Sunday of every month they visit Michael, who now lives in the city with Ellie, Jamie and Ruby. And Clo, of course — who has recently published her second novel.

# Chapter Eighty-six

Curtis's landscape is almost complete. For the rest of his life he will not add to it, but he will continually trace back every line and brushstroke, trying to discover at which point he could have made a change in the overall picture. There were many such points — the last being the day he refused to sign that paper, thus completing his denial of William.

Steeltown never saw him again. If asked where their brother has gone, Albert vows that he has bought a island off the coast of Queensland and lives there now like a native. Harry swears that he has emigrated to America and is now running an Australian plants nursery somewhere in California.

In truth he has gone to his special place, a shallow tunnel dug into the mountainside by a long-forgotten hermit. Once a fortnight a certain Martin Phelan, who is the late Joe Phelan's son, leaves a supply of food and sometimes a blanket or two at the beginning of an old disused trail — the same trail Martin's son dragged William along the day the mountain caught fire. One of Curtis's philanthropic acts before leaving town was to present that particular family with the local supermarket.

And Angus? What happened to Angus, you ask?

Angus and I fought every day of the weeks that passed before William finally died. We made up, of course; we always did. But he

422

never called me Loby again, and I began calling him Fred.

I might have cut him out of my life right then, if not for the sickness that struck him on the day Curtis left town. It began with a quickening of his heartbeat and constant vomiting attacks. He couldn't eat or sleep. He rarely spoke. His mouth became ulcerated, his gums bled. The doctors offered no cure as his teeth fell out, beyond calling this malady by the name of pyorrhoea. No doubt he would have blamed the bird, if he hadn't lost faith in its existence.

I pointed out that his sickness began on the day he spat poisoned words at Curtis and me, who were the only ones who had loved him for most of his miserable life. I tore at his mythical bird as it tore at him, ripping and shredding his heart as I ripped and shredded his fantasy with true facts and observations.

'You kept that stupid bird myth alive because you couldn't bear the thought of Mack committing suicide. But you did it for your sake, not his. You didn't want to believe that he'd willingly leave you, but you never once stopped to realise that he'd just had enough. There's only so much anyone can take, you know.'

With that, I left him lying on his kitchen floor, clutching his chest and daring the bird to come and get him then, hoping to prove me wrong. I went to my house, packed a bag, placed both journals in a safety deposit box at my local bank, then flew to Europe the following day. After touring every country I had read about, and many I hadn't, I spent a month in Greece with Agatha and Clo as my guests. Ellie and Michael joined us during the Christmas university break. When I finally returned to Steeltown, Angus had disappeared.

I miss him and Curtis of course, but I fill my hours happily enough. Every Saturday afternoon Agatha, Debra, Clo, Ruby and sometimes Amanda and Lucy visit my house. I find a certain satisfaction in watching these women play cards or sit in their quilting circle. Their presence is proof that hatchets can be buried, if the will to do so exists. Perhaps one day Curtis will realise that fact and he and Angus will be together, as I always believed they were meant to be.

Perhaps. One day. Who knows?

Ann Charlton has lived most of her life in Wollongong and has travelled widely throughout Australia. Her work experience ranges from shop assistant to part owner of a small advertising business. She has won awards and written short stories, plays and children's novels under the name of Ann C Whitehead.